IGNITION

Nicole Stillwater

Ignition

Copyright © 2019 Nicole Stillwater

All rights reserved.

This is a work of fiction. Names, characters, places and incidents are either the product of the author's imagination or are used fictitiously, and any resemblance to actual persons living or dead, business establishments, events or locales is entirely coincidental.

Cover typography and artwork by Miblart
Cover design by Nicole Stillwater

First Printing: October 2019

ISBN 978-1-9992702-0-9

Published by Nicole Stillwater

www.nicolestillwater.com

*Expose yourself to your deepest fear; after that,
fear has no power, and the fear of freedom shrinks
and vanishes. You are free.*

— Jim Morrison

1

Get Your Motor Running

In the darkness she could see a dim, far-off light. A shadow stepped forward, blocking the light, a faceless silhouette. It was her jailer, come to peek in on her. Taunt her. Make her cower.

Gasping, Ashlyn sat bolt upright. That dream again! She shuddered. Then scowling with exasperation, she muttered, "Gawd! What demon is having his way with me?"

As the panic subsided, slowly diffusing out of her pores, she recognized that the darkness now surrounding her was simply the stillness of night. She reached over to her bedside table and fumbled for her phone. 5:33 a.m.

Groan.

Realizing that morning was irritatingly close at hand, she withdrew her hand and stuffed it back under the covers. She pouted a little, too. On her other side, she heard a few grunts and felt the bed shimmy as her boyfriend shifted, still in a deep and satisfying sleep, no doubt. *What I wouldn't give to be able to sleep in "rock" mode.* Stubbornly, she settled deeper under the covers to claim the last twenty-seven minutes of precious sleep, refusing to let wakefulness take her into the day.

~BAM! BAM! My mother told me to skin you alive!~

Both Ashlyn and David woke abruptly to the alarm—David's radio alarm, which was set to the death metal station. Her heart skittered into her throat, certain a masked psychopath stood over her with an ax. She gulped great lungsful of air to dislodge her heart. If she could've reached the damned radio herself, she'd have beat him over the head with it.

This can't be a healthy way to start the day.

She ran her fingers through her bangs, pulling them back from her face to look over at David. The heart-stopping noise didn't appear to faze him in the least. Flopping her head back onto her pillow, she shut her eyes against the world. She felt him sit up, and heard him scratch behind his neck, stand, scratch his crotch, and then shuffle off to the bathroom to shower.

She lingered, lying half asleep and fighting with herself to just wake up. The sleep that happened between "gotta get up soon" and "time to get up for work" was often the sweetest, deepest, most satisfying sleep, and always too short.

She roused herself enough to at least sit up. Then took another minute to get her other eye open, and finally untangle her legs from the comforter. Eyelids still heavy with sleep, she, at last, shuffled obediently into the morning routine: shower, dress, breakfast. Coffee.

As usual, the minutes slipped by too quickly, and panic set in. David suddenly surged into a frenzy of activity, forcing Ashlyn to swing her mug out of his path. In a flurry of wild arms and barks of frustration, David stomped around the apartment in search of his keys and jacket.

"Where's my goddamned jack—? . . . Oh, there it is."

Tornado David ended when he clapped the weathered, oilskin ball cap over his thick, chestnut brown hair, the untamed waves peeking out from underneath.

"Have a good day." He waved a hand over his shoulder as he hurried toward the door, no time for even a peck on the cheek.

Ashlyn raised her mug in a silent salute to his disappearing back, trying to imagine what morning would look like for morning people. *Would it be so frantic?* Then calm returned to the apartment.

Ashlyn didn't need to be out the door quite as early as David. Better to get up, though, than to listen to him bash his way through the morning rituals. She let the quiet embrace her, savoring the moment. *Ahhh, peace.*

Ashlyn strolled back to the bedroom to dress. Standing in front of the closet with a self-satisfied smile, she began flicking through the clothes, idly whiling away these early morning minutes. It only took her five minutes to assemble a smart look for the day, but lost in her fantasy fashion-world, the time trickled by, seeming more like twenty, luxurious, soaking in a hot bath, overflowing with suds, kind of minutes.

Ah! That will do nicely. She smiled to herself, a spark of joy lighting up her sea-green eyes. Finding an old, cobalt blue, cashmere scarf still draped loosely over the shoulders of her winter coat, she snatched it excitedly, like a child at Christmas, and deftly wrapped it around her neck as the final touch. Her golden-brown locks stood out against the dark backdrop of her coat, the scarf enhancing the ensemble, drawing the eye to her face like the mat in a picture frame.

"Ready to greet the day", she said to her reflection in the front hall mirror.

Ashlyn locked the apartment door and headed out to the street. The last couple of days, she had noticed a little bite in the air that greeted her. The summer season might be slinking away, but that meant a whole new parade of fashion delights and fashion faux pas to entertain her as she walked to work.

Accompanied by the *click-clack* of her own heels, the show began. Surreptitiously, she admired the smart-looking suit as he passed. Around the corner, she frowned disapprovingly at the mismatched, hermit-woodsman facial hair paired with the throwback Thursday skinny jeans. *That's just not a good look for anyone!*

Across the street, she heard yet another fashion victim *click-clack-griiinding* her way along the busy sidewalk. *Never compromise on shoes, even if they are a brand name!*

All of humanity bumped and jostled by, most looking harried. *Probably on their way to cubicles or waiting rooms leading to dentists' chairs.* She wrinkled her nose at the thought. Maybe she was being judgy, but she loved her private fashion parade. She couldn't help herself, she was fascinated with the designs and the patterns and the vibe of the people wearing them.

It took twenty-five-minutes to walk from her front door to her office, including a stop at the One-Shot Espresso stand. Here, she joined the other devotees, waiting in line for her half-caf mocha latte.

"Good morning, Marty," she said cheerfully. Her eyes twinkled in anticipation of the playful banter she shared with Marty.

Marty, from Peru, was the latest street barista to operate the One-Shot Espresso stand and everyone's favorite already.

"Good morning, my sweet *orchidea porcelain*," he beamed back. "It is getting cold here, no? Jou come away with me and I will show jou the most a–mazing visions of nature."

He nodded encouragingly, then continued, his eyes bright. "It is coming into *primavera*—spring—in my village. The hills will be lush and green and we will go to hunt for the bea–u–tiful orchids."

He paused, frowning at her and shaking his head slightly, "They are always hiding. So hard to find."

Ashlyn tilted her head. *Did I just get scolded?* Her mouth hung open to retort, but in a blink, he was smiling again.

The moment had passed.

"What—is this flower you keep mentioning?"

He topped her latte with a rosette design, finishing with a flourish. Then he gave her a wide smile, and lovingly handed her his artfully crafted cup of java. "It is a simple white flower, with lines of green. The lines are delicate. But the displays are . . . *maravilloso.*"

She lowered her gaze, feeling the redness rush into her cheeks. Marty was quirky, but harmless. She rather enjoyed his relentless flirting, but he certainly got the better of her today. Turning, still blushing a little, she rejoined the throng of working folks threading their way along the city sidewalks.

Though she openly stared at her unknowing models, she rarely met their eyes and no one ever acknowledged her critical gaze. She walked, cradling her coffee, holding it close like a wee kitten needing warmth and security—elbows *in* lest someone clip her arm and dump the sweet elixir of Magic Awake Juice all over her.

Oooo, now there's a delightful ensemble, flattering button-up shirt, handsome sports coat, and I like the way he wears his pants. She smiled devilishly into her coffee. Daring to take a lusty peek over her shoulder, she watched him smile brightly as he met his friend—Oh, a close friend—and gently taking the man's hand, he leaned over and planted a light kiss on the other's cheek. Mildly crestfallen, Ashlyn resumed her forward march. I should have known, gay men are always dressed so well!

Moving on, she joined the huddle forming at the street corner waiting to cross. While pondering the meaning and significance of avoiding white after Labor Day, something intruded as the Don't Walk signal switched to Walk. Involuntarily, she hesitated, and glanced across the plaza toward the glass doors of her office building.

She cradled her coffee closer, letting the current of pedestrians carry her forward. She searched the faces that streamed passed for a set of eyes looking back at her. A deeply unsettling feeling stirred in her belly as she stepped onto the opposite curb. Someone *was* watching her.

The invader was lost behind a throng of bodies marching past until a break in the flow created a temporary window. It opened up just enough to give her a glimpse beyond the busy foot traffic, where she suddenly locked eyes with a stranger.

Just as abruptly, the stranger disappeared behind another wave of polyester pants, skinny jeans and leggings. *Those are* not *pants*.

As a new window appeared, her attention was jolted back to the intense blue eyes of a grizzled old man sitting on a park bench. He sat squarely in the middle of the bench, unmistakably staring directly at her. Time slowed as the next set of legs and skirts swept past, and she stood frozen, her heart thudding in her ears.

Sound. Movement. Everything became muted, until she was roughly jarred from behind. Recovering her balance, and her latte, she searched numbly for the person who had run into her. He, or she, was gone. The spell was broken. She resumed walking, her neck and shoulders rigid and holding her breath. She stole glances out of the corner of her eye, but dared not look directly over to the park bench. Still, she felt his steely gaze following her all the way to the glass doors.

2

FiberWorx

A typical day for Ashlyn started at 8:30 a.m. in her cubicle, checking for urgent email or meeting notifications. This morning, however, the mouse quivered in Ashlyn's hands, making it difficult to check anything. She kept deleting notifications she'd meant to open.

"Arrgh!" She released the mouse and vigorously shook her hands, hoping to shake out the heebie-jeebies.

Ashlyn O'Monahan had been working in the laboratory at FiberWorx Textiles and Manufacturing for seven years. Now a mid-level research associate, she typically worked in one of the three independent, hermetically sealed laboratory workspaces. Laboratory #3, to be precise. It was dedicated to quality control testing.

Still shaken from her encounter with the stranger in the plaza, Ashlyn was unable to concentrate. She gave up on her admin tasks around nine o'clock. Assuming nothing extraordinary had landed in her inbox, she headed to the lab and donned the—ever-so-sexy—silicon safety goggles, and pristine white lab coat. Coffee in one hand, she pressed against the lab door with the other, pushing until she heard the air lock engage.

FiberWorx specialized in fire retardant fabrics. It was her job to repeat the experiments that were done by Research and Development. She would either confirm their results, and production would continue as planned. Or, if things didn't add up, she would tinker with the chemical formulations, using the prescribed methodology, looking to find some way to improve the product.

She had hoped that by now she would have left Lab #3 to join the team in R&D. That's where the cutting-edge work happened. Experiments were complex, demanding creative problem solving, and inspired thinking. *Challenging* work. This is where she believed she was headed.

Forcing out a cleansing exhale, she dismissed all thoughts of the stranger in the plaza, then spun on the spot to face her workbench, ready to start her trials. She checked her clipboard for the instructions she'd left herself the day before, set about collecting her vials and droppers, and then arranged the equipment to run the day's experiment: another reaction to test the strength and durability of cotton fiber. Or hemp fiber. Or some new man-made fiber. It might be synthetic or natural, or maybe have a slightly different weave, but it was always the same question: *How can I make this fabric burn?*

As her experiments ran, Ashlyn fought distraction to keep a steady tempo, walking through her regular circuit: from the rotovap to the white board, back to the . . .

Wait—where was I? She stood, facing the workbench, holding a tray of vials and wearing a blank expression.

"Mass spec. Right."

Which was behind her, against the back wall. With all the other diagnostic equipment. *Bah.* She rolled her eyes.

After carefully loading the machine, she returned to the lab's computer to reread the instructions for today's trials. The very same instructions from the day before. And the day before that.

Once her reaction had run its course, Ashlyn recorded the results, both on paper and in the database. Analysis of the data would determine whether she had created a miracle solution. Or, more likely, whether she had only proved the existing formulation was done right the first time.

"Aaaaand, that's lunch." She tossed the pencil and clipboard onto the computer desk, and draped her lab coat over the chair before exiting the lab.

Most Friday afternoons, Ashlyn ate at her desk, preparing her updates for the weekly meeting with the other research associates. But the inhabitants of the cube farm in her section were unusually quiet today. Which meant that Ashlyn would have to catch the crowd at the coffee station for a little human contact. She rarely made it to the coffee station gatherings—"Because you're always head down, ass up," was how David had put it. It was David who had clued her into the fact that the coffee station was where she needed to be because that's where she'd hear the rumors or hints dropped about openings in the R&D lab.

Ashlyn was nervously eying the clock as she began her usual afternoon circuit in the lab.

She checked the lab's computer—*Where did I leave off?*

Ashlyn read aloud off the screen, ". . . verification of the bromine number."

OK, set up the electrochemical titration.

Go to the ventilated cabinet—Ashlyn grabbed the container of mercury catalyst.

Gah! She scuttled back to the computer. *Which one am I doing, again?* She marched back to the workbench. *Start the titration.*

She checked her watch.

Tapping her foot, Ashlyn hovered over the workbench. The sequence underway would take two hours and she had been planning her escape from the lab for the three o'clock coffee break.

She never seemed able to time her breaks right. Just as she stepped out of the secured work area, she saw the congregation of lab associates at the coffee station dispersing. Freezing in her tracks, half in, half out, she stood in the doorway, a far-off gaze taking over. The heavy door to the lab, programmed to self-seal after a timed delay, finally shoved her fully out, interrupting her trance. She had missed her opportunity today. Again. And now she was locked out. She stood, with her head resting on the door, embarrassed and a little defeated.

"Ashlyn?"

Kendra.

Oh bother.

"Are you locked out of your lab? Again? That's, like, the third time now?" Kendra paused, "Since . . . since when? You losin' it, girl?"

Ashlyn snapped her head back up and waited for *kindly Kendra, from the R&D lab, to the rescue—Ha!*—to make her way up the hall. She considered the question as Kendra, with a sly smirk, swiped her electronic key to open the lab door. *Yeah, maybe three times, now. Since—*

"—since Janine left," they said in unison. They both smiled.

"There you go," Kendra said sweetly, then added, "Back into your cage!"

"Haha," Ashlyn droned, but smiled sheepishly, "Thank you."

Lab #3 was very quiet compared to the coffee station down the hall, where she could hear lively chatter. And very empty.

In her head, Ashlyn replayed the conversation in the hall, *Are you locked out of your lab?*

My lab? I guess. In all the time she worked together with Janine in Lab #3, they'd always referred to it as "Lab #3." *And it was always Janine who was getting locked out, not me.* Especially near the end, when Janine decided to leave.

Ashlyn donned her white lab coat and picked up the clipboard, clutching it like a treasured teddy.

At least I'll finish my trials on time today.

~

At five o'clock, she surveyed the lab. Not only had she finished the experiments, but she'd managed to clean off her entire workbench and wash all the glass equipment. Ashlyn bit her lip, unable to think of any other reason she needed to stay. Late. On a Friday.

With a sigh, she shut the lights and pulled on the door until she heard the *sssssst* of the air lock.

It had been a perfectly ordinary day. *Aside from the alarming encounter with homeless man in the plaza.* She frowned as she pictured him sitting, still as a statue, on his perch. His disheveled form and tattered old clothes were a stark contrast to the manicured park that adorned the plaza. *But that's not what made him stand out. Something else about him . . .*

She paused at the exit of the FiberWorx building. No sign of the bedraggled stranger. Maybe she'd just imagined it. Still, she walked home quicker than usual that evening, and was greatly relieved to feel the door to the apartment close shut. She dropped her keys into the decorative tin plate on the curio table in the front hall. It made a wretched, hollow and off-key sound, but it signaled that she was home.

Ashlyn had installed the decorative plate on the curio, without consulting David, after losing her keys for the sixth or seventh time.

"The *keys en place*," David had quipped, a play on the French *mise en place*.

"Yes, it might be a bit anal," she had conceded, "but my subconscious needs to hear the clang of the keys hitting the plate."

David hated to be boxed in by "everything in its place," but reluctantly admitted that the key dish had been a smart idea.

The ring of the keys on tin was interrupted by a series of off-color comments and accusations of rampant incompetence streaming down the hallway.

"—the *fuck*! . . . they gotta nitpick . . . ," David, evidently, was still changing out of his work clothes. "*Every. God. Damned. Time . . .*"

The volume rose and fell, but the choice words cut through the drywall unhindered.

". . . those useless *cocksuckers* set *foot* on site!"

His words were punctuated by heavy-duty metal clasps hitting the wall as he viciously slung his filthy work clothes into the closet. Ashlyn pictured the dried-on bits of mud breaking off and finding their way into her nice shoes.

She knew better than to remind him where the vacuum was when he was like this. She made a face as she considered whether or not to mention the creepy man in the park.

"*Fuckers!* Always gotta put everything on *me . . .*"

On second thought, perhaps she would just remain silent.

Ashlyn stood with one boot on and one boot off, lost in her own, silent tirade. *I don't think I spoke to another person all day? Except Kendra.* She grimaced. *Did I leave Lab #3 even once? What the hell is up with that grizzled old man, anyway?*

David eventually did reach a state of calm.

"Are you ready to go?" he called from the bedroom, ten minutes later.

She hadn't yet moved from the front hall. No, she wasn't ready. She didn't want to go out tonight.

"Yeah," she sighed quietly. "Just gotta switch my bag," she chirped back.

David emerged a moment later, dressed in light olive chinos, a tight-fitting, white V-neck T-shirt and navy-blue blazer, complete with square-toed shoes, his go-to "business casual" outfit. She preferred to call it his "pub uniform". He had at least three sets of the uniform combo—it made Ashlyn crazy. Surveying his ensemble, she recalled the last time they had gone shopping together when she had dared him to try something new. He had willingly wandered through the men's clothing store at her behest, and came back proudly displaying his find: a gray, cable-knit sweater. Ashlyn had hung her head, defeated. "You've really reached out, with that pick. Really stretched outside your comfort zone, there, dear," she'd said, wryly. She'd given up after that.

Ashlyn opened her mouth to say something, but swallowed her words, choosing, instead, to pull the first boot back on.

3

Matte vs Glossy

Ashlyn leaned in toward the mirror on Monday morning, examining the dark circles under her eyes.

"You look fine, babe. Much less *Dawn of the Dead* this morning. No nightmares?" David asked, before swatting her ass with a sharp *smack!*

She winced a little and threw him a sour look. He'd carried on past her without waiting for a response, and was already in the bedroom dressing.

"Yeah, I do look better today," she agreed.

She held on to that thought, refusing to allow any dark thoughts to hijack her morning. When David, at last, vanished through the front door, she exhaled all the built-up tension of holding her tongue. In his absence, the *pit-pat* of light rain on the window drifted into her consciousness.

"Yeeesss!" Ashlyn let out a little squeak of delight, clapping her hands excitedly. "It's time to dig out my shiny raincoat hiding in the back of the closet."

The dark coral jacket provided a shock of color in the wet gray, as well as being water repellent. It was exactly the right choice. The rain steadily increased as she made her way up and down the streets, wending her way toward the office. She stayed mostly dry until she reached the One-Shot Espresso lineup, where the wind blew in her face and repeatedly lifted the hood off her head. *At least it's a short line today.*

Ashlyn smiled brightly at Marty when she stepped up to the front of the line. He held up a finger, asking her to wait a moment. Turned slightly away from Ashlyn, he began to mutter words in

Quechua, his native tongue, into his hands. Once finished, he returned his full attention to Ashlyn, smiling as he replaced the string of charms onto a hook tucked under the countertop.

"What are those?" she asked, her eyes wide.

He didn't answer, but immediately began steaming her a large mocha. "Choc-o-late for jou, I think."

But Ashlyn, having waited patiently, didn't let it slide this time.

"Are those bones?" Then she looked at him sideways. "Are you asking a Peruvian god to change this weather? Bring back the sun?"

Marty bowed his head, conceding. "Jes. They are like prayer beads. These," he lifted the string slightly, "are pi-ra-nha jaws. In my village, they represent strength." And with that, he handed her the sweet-smelling chocolate-coffee delight.

"Strength?" Then she nodded. "Ah, yes, to stay strong out here on icky days like today."

"It is not for me," he smiled, then turned his attention to the next brave soul holding his collar against the prevailing wind.

As often happened when she talked to Marty, she walked away, somewhat bemused, from the coffee stand. She blinked up at the rainy sky, but the weather gods had not changed their minds. Shrugging, she continued on with her commute, carrying her One-Shot mocha like a running back carries the football, close to the body, using the other arm to block the rain.

Wind from every direction met at the intersection, forcing Ashlyn to grab the flopping hood with her free hand and hold it down to keep the rain off. She marched awkwardly across the street toward the plaza, no longer enamored by the moody weather and eager to reach the dry indoors.

At the sight of the grizzled old man from yesterday, Ashlyn swallowed hard, feeling suddenly like an orange traffic cone, a brightly lit beacon at one end of the plaza. His hair fell in salt and pepper dreadlocks over those intense blue eyes that fixed on her. Even with the relentless drops of rain trickling over his stone face, he didn't twitch a muscle.

Ashlyn averted her eyes and walked the length of the plaza holding her hood down over her face. She very nearly walked into the glass doors of the FiberWorx building before looking up.

Once inside, she took a hearty gulp of her coffee—all the better to get it into her veins faster. Impulsively, she chanced another look toward the park bench. *That homeless . . . grizzled . . . old . . . man . . . The GOM.* She sneered inwardly at him for making her feel all awkward and self-conscious.

He sat on the same bench as last week, the third one from the street. The same ratty, brown, boiled wool overcoat. The same scrutinizing—or was it patronizing?—stare. He sat, unmoving and aloof, watching her. Studying her. Waiting, it seemed, like he had all the time in the world, but impatient at the same time.

She held his gaze until she could no longer stand the gnawing discomfort. He suddenly leaned forward, as though to rise and come striding toward her, like a bull charging the matador. Alarm rose from the back of her neck, the heat making her ears burn and cheeks flush. She looked away and scuttled toward the elevators, safely beyond the reach of his penetrating stare.

Shaking, Ashlyn shut her eyes and shut the encounter out of her mind as she escaped the lobby into the elevator. *OK . . .* She took another big gulp of her coffee, letting the sweet chocolate coat her tongue. When the elevator opened on her floor, she sucked in a deep breath and blew the air back out. *Forget him, you have work to do.*

~

"Ack!" Ashlyn grunted. Monitors hummed in the background, under the high-pitched whine of the centrifuge and the steady flow of air being vented throughout the enclosed space of the lab, where she worked alone. Looking down at her watch, she realized it was time for a coffee break. Not her time, but if she wanted to "lean in," this would be a good place to start.

Lean in. She had read about the idea in a *Huffington Post* article . . . or was it a *New York Times* article? Or maybe *BuzzFeed? It's so hard to keep track of what I've read and where I dug it up.*

The article referred to Sheryl Sandberg's upcoming book, *Lean In*, based on her TEDTalk encouraging women to say yes to the new project, to go for that promotion, to "sit at the table."

I want to sit at the table.

Ashlyn poked her head out of Lab #3. Bursts of laughter rippled down the hallway from the usual suspects gathered at the coffee station. She hesitated as another thought intruded: *Was it an article in the* San Francisco Chronicle, *maybe? That advocated the virtues of leaning out?* According to the article, men in high-powered positions were finding that the time dedicated to the job was too much. They could, and many had, chosen to leave their desks, and their work altogether, at five o'clock, choosing, instead, to spend their valuable time with non-work pursuits.

I like leaving at 5 o'clock . . .

Oh, just get on with it! She urged her feet forward.

"OK, let's have the board. Who were the nominees for Worst Dressed, Most Embarrassing Moment, Worst Speech, and 'Most Likely to Be High'?" The speaker's voice carried over the general chatter.

Oh, right! The VTV All-American Music and Video Awards. The staff had created a pool for the award show. The office event behind the event, where armchair fans created their own awards pool. Two dollars a square.

Ashlyn checked over her shoulder. Could she leave the experiments running? *Just five minutes.*

Pasting a smile on her face before confidently stepping into the coffee station, Ashlyn repeated the mantra in her head: *Lean in. OK, let's do this. Seat at the table. Relax.*

A mix of suits and lab coats had gathered to hear the results. When Ashlyn entered, the debate raged on.

"I don't know, Joan, the faux human skin stole isn't nearly as bad as Lady Gaga's meat dress!" Matt argued.

"Yeah, she definitely put in a good effort that show," Joan chortled.

"I still vote DNCE with the worst outfits," said Matt.

"No way! Cole rocked that man-skirt." Joan gave Matt a playful shove. "You don't have to be shy, Matt. You can wear one in the lab, no judgment," she teased. "My favorite outfit, by far, was Dencia in the RockyG bodysuit. It was amazing!"

Ashlyn squeezed further into crowded coffee station and immediately picked up one of the papers lying open on the table. It had a photo spread showing highlights of attendees walking the red carpet. The headline read:

**Fashion Dodgers Didn't Disappoint at This
Star-Studded Event**

Ashlyn hadn't actually watched the award show like she normally would have. David had parked in front of the TV on one of his quests last night, and she had busied herself in the bedroom going through old clothes.

"What about Rhianna's dress? I think that's the clear winner for Worst Dressed!" Carlene snickered.

Ashlyn had been looking right at the photo of Rihanna, puzzling over what, exactly, it was that she wore. At Carlene's words, she understood.

"It looks like Saran Wrap," Ashlyn mused out loud.

"Hey, here's last year's champ-*eeen!*" crowed Kendra.

Ashlyn felt the blood rush into her cheeks as all eyes turned toward her. "I didn't—um . . ."

"Exactly!" Carlene enthusiastically agreed. Ignoring Kendra, she walked over to Ashlyn like a lawyer approaching the evidence table. "Precisely my point!"

"Your name's not on here anywhere," Matt said to Ashlyn.

"Slipped my mind," Ashlyn said, leaning in to examine the lottery board. "So, who's winning?" she asked, redirecting.

"I have five squares paid out, so far!" beamed Amy.

"Ghastly!" Kendra exclaimed from across the room. She was referring to the "dress" hanging off Miley Cyrus's boney frame. "What *was* that girl thinking? What is it about the red carpet that draws out the weird clothes, anyway?" She scrunched up her face and tilted her head thoughtfully. "D'ya think they're trying to actually make a statement? If you wanna get a message out to the masses, wouldn't you want to say something that the rest of us can understand?"

It was odd to listen to these criticisms, coming from Kendra. She was a petite woman with a wide frame and an apparent love of polka dots. Big ones. Ashlyn had gently suggested a few wardrobe tweaks to Kendra from time to time. Most of the other people in the office had been quite receptive to Ashlyn's suggestions, she had even garnered something of a reputation as the go-to person for fashion advice.

But not Kendra. Perhaps the advice fell on deaf ears because speaking in **BOLD, ALL CAPS** was not Ashlyn's style. But Kendra owned it, so Ashlyn respectfully admitted defeat, and washed her hands of it. Instead, Ashlyn did her best to compliment Kendra on any item she wore that had a positive effect on her ensemble. Most days she said nothing.

As for the rest of the fashion actors in Ashlyn's private theater, she was hard-pressed to find a coherent picture from any of them. Her mind wandered away from the conversation, instead latching on to a suit jacket where the seam of the shoulder and arm met at an odd angle, creating a craggy shoulder line. *Probably too many trips to the cleaners,* she concluded.

On the opposite side of the scrum, around the lottery board, stood Richard Bowerman, the senior operations manager for the Research and Development Division. He was maybe 35, but, armed with an MBA and an aptitude for spotting talent, Richard had breezed through the middle management positions, and now headed up R&D. He wore his best, custom-tailored suits on Mondays, when all the executive meetings happened. The jacket, expertly cut to fit his scrumptious frame, featured shoulders pads that accented his commanding posture. Crisp, front lapels perfectly outlined the contour of his barrel chest, and the base of the jacket draped perfectly over the curved part of his buttocks. The pants, also stunning, did not hide his runners' legs, but deftly hinted at the muscle and power beneath the dark fabric. Here was a man who would be the master of his own destiny. At least, that's what his clothing expressed. Ashlyn noted that, even standing in a casual manner, he oozed confidence. You could almost smell it.

"Ashlyn?" he said, his look shifting from puzzled to concerned. "Ashlyn." He showed her the face of his mobile. "There's an alarm going off in Lab #3. Shouldn't you go check it out?"

Ashlyn inhaled sharply.

The lively chatter faltered as the tension rose. Ashlyn realized that she had been staring at Richard and now he, and everyone else, was staring back.

"Right. Gotta go. M-minor, I'm sure . . ."

Bumping and jostling bodies out of her way, Ashlyn walk-ran back to her lab, fighting back the tears. *This is not going to get me a seat at the table.*

4

Chain Reaction

The fashion parade slipped past Ashlyn, unseen, as she plodded along her route the next morning, stewing about yesterday's blunder. *Every step forward, I get pushed back two.* She had been lucky, the alarm triggered in Lab #3 was minor. But the damage was done.

Ahead, a black and yellow barricade informed her the sidewalk was closed to pedestrians. She stepped off the curb, rerouting around the barricade. A cynical smile tugged at one side of her mouth. *Every dodge or weave around an obstruction, I redirect, but always end up in the same place? The path always leads to the same destination: FiberWorx.*

She looked beyond the street, beyond the tall buildings downtown, forward onto the horizon where the gray of the sky met the gray of the sea. Somewhere, in that general direction, was Moss Beach, where her mother, Cheryl, had moved the family—herself and her brother Dylan—after the accident. A fiery auto crash in 1992 took the life of Ted, their firefighter dad. That was the end, and the beginning, of everything. She pulled her attention forward, not wanting to picture that time in her life. Instead, she let her mind wander through the detritus of moments and images, skipping from one waypost to another, stitching together the path that led her to FiberWorx.

An orange school bus rolled into view, obstructing her view of the sea, punctuated by the familiar grind and squeal of the bus rattling to a stop. She heard the raucous noise coming from inside the belly of the beast and caught the faraway look cast out the window by one dream teen. *That could easily have been my face junior year.*

In her silent reverie, teenaged Ashlyn daydreamed about making the world a safer place from fire and explosions. It was all she could imagine after her father's death.

Her guidance counselor, Mr. Benson, had steered her toward chemistry. "You'll love the challenge of running the reactions and learning how to use all manner of wacky equipment. Mass spectrometers, rotovaps, HPLC . . . ," he rambled. "I know you like puzzles, too. There are an infinite number of combinations of chemicals that need to be tested, tincture by tincture . . ."

This was the point at which fifteen-year-old Ashlyn's eyes glazed over. Mr. Benson's enthusiasm was not contagious. He smiled ruefully at her, sitting across from him in his drab little office. Ashlyn was a good student with good grades but tended toward introversion.

Mr. Benson changed tactics. "I spent many hours, in many labs, as a chemist. I worked with some great people. Sometimes we worked side by side, but quietly lost in our *own* little world, running our *own* experiments," he raised an eyebrow, watching to see if his words had hit their mark. Then he suddenly burst out laughing. "But we had our fun, too. I can't *tell* you the number of times I set off the fire alarm."

She lifted the corner of her mouth in a weak smile.

"Ashlyn, what do you want to be when you grow up?" The inevitable question.

The school bus engine revved to life again as it pulled away from the curb. Ahead, the vista of the wide sea opened up before her once again.

The question continued to echo in her head as she arrived at the One-Shot Espresso stand. It marked the threshold between her personal world and her work world. Her half-caf mocha latte was a frivolous treat, maybe, but on days like today, this coffee stop was a necessary ritual. She needed a healthy dollop of good vibrations to start her day.

". . . and the lush rainforests. It is the time we go to seek the healing plants that grow near my village." Marty was happily chatting away, tempting her to run away with him.

Genuine or not, Ashlyn adored him. And today, at least, he hadn't mentioned herding any goats. That was part of Marty's magic. He served up remedies for the soul.

Remembering the barricade earlier, Ashlyn decided to walk around to the back of her building, to avoid the GOM. She was still stuck on the inevitable question from the guidance counselor, and didn't notice the distinct lack of pedestrians as she made her way around. The smell hit her first, but not soon enough to slow her stride. As she rounded the corner to the back alley, she nearly stepped into a steaming pile that looked suspiciously like . . .

"Oh, come off it!" barked a woman with weathered skin and unkempt hair squatting a few steps farther ahead.

Ashlyn danced on the spot, unsure where to put her feet next. A FiberWorx delivery van zoomed by and turned into the loading bay farther along. Overwhelmed by the smell and the shock, Ashlyn could only wince apologetically at the homeless woman and followed the path of the van.

Eyes wide, pointing and stammering, Ashlyn wanted to tell the man at the shipping dock about what she'd just witnessed.

"Yeah, I know. I've already put in a request to the city for a steamer cleaner," he said in a casual tone. "You know, you can't get in this way. Company policy."

Ashlyn gaped.

"You work with Kendra, right?"

She nodded. *Same floor, anyway,* she thought, a pleading smiling on her face.

"Yeah, alright. Tell Kendra Reggie says hi, 'K?"

She nodded gratefully. "Thank you, Reggie," she managed to squeak.

~

Kendra was not interested in anything Reggie had to say, but Ashlyn attempted to deliver the message anyway.

"Hmmf," Kendra responded and walked past Ashlyn into the R&D lab.

Like a ray of sun after a shitty start to the day, her friend and colleague Budhil spotted Ashlyn through the open door. She mimed drinking a cup of coffee and pointed at her watch, their signal to meet for a coffee later.

He smiled and nodded just before Kendra returned to shut the lab door. Budhil Patel was the one person Ashlyn had no trouble talking to. Budhil and Ashlyn were both research associates at FiberWorx, except Budhil had his PhD and got to work on the sexy projects.

Budhil texted later, ready to accept Ashlyn's invitation to escape for a "networking meeting." They met at the lobby doors and headed for the coffee house down the block.

"So, Reggie in Shipping and Receiving, he tells me I can't go through that way," Ashlyn said and began relating the events of the morning.

"Why would you go all the way around to the back of the building to come in?"

Ashlyn's breath caught in her throat. She didn't want to make a thing—*the GOM*—a *some*thing that wasn't a thing . . . *Is it a thing?*

"Oh. I wasn't paying attention . . ." *Yeah, that's better.* "I was just caught up in my thoughts. I've been thinking about moving on from Lab #3. Remember, we talked about what I can do to get in front of Richard?"

"Yes, yes, very good," Budhil said encouragingly.

"Well, yesterday I left the lab to do some socializing at the coffee station, and . . ." She began to wring her hands. "I still just felt like an outsider. Apart *from* the conversation, not in it," Ashlyn complained.

Budhil clasped his hands under his chin, his index fingers lightly tapping his lips as he listened.

"I forgot all about the *VTV* Awards pool, so I just listened to everyone else."

"Did you get to hear about my newest initiative?" he asked hopefully.

Ashlyn gave him a sideways glance. "Mmmm—no. They were going over the office pool winners," she admitted.

Budhil said nothing, instead taking a sip of his coffee.

"You're right. If I'd have jumped in and started talking about some of your recent papers, maybe I could have sparked a conversation about what's going on in the R&D lab."

Budhil continued to smile, but remained silent, inviting Ashlyn to speak openly.

"But, then, Kendra was there. She would've derailed that conversation in a heartbeat: 'Pu-*lease*, Ashlyn, I came here for a break from shop talk'." She frowned. "Kendra doesn't appear at all concerned about what she says and to whom." Ashlyn started speaking with her hands. "She just says what's in her head. That kind of talk is not going to serve her well on her performance review."

When Ashlyn finished her tirade, she lifted her own coffee mug to take a sip.

Budhil spoke softly, "Maybe Kendra does not need a performance review to tell her what she should want or who she is."

"But—," Ashlyn stopped. "OK. Right, let it go."

"And you can talk to me. You can ask me 'What is going on in the R&D lab?'"

Ashlyn face-palmed. "Of course."

Budhil's face brightened. He did, however, get worked up about the *experiments*. The chemistry. "What do you know about smart fabrics?" he asked, shuffling to sit forward in his chair.

Ashlyn shook her head and fell silent as Budhil described his current project. He happily chattered away about his latest research. ". . . Imagine! Clothing with electronic capabilities! Forget the mood ring. I would know to stay out of your way when your lab coat is bright red," he teased.

And he easily shared the stumbling blocks that plagued the R&D team. "The impetus to focus on commercially profitable research vs curiosity driven research seems misguided . . ."

Ashlyn listened intently. At these coffee meetings, he sometimes got downright giddy talking shop.

"I like these meetings we have," said Budhil, smiling pleasantly. "We do not talk about the children's clothing, or the always increasing banking fees, or what to bring to the Evanses for dinner on Thursday."

And then his face soured, almost imperceptibly. "Or about how I must stay late on Thursday to include Richard's changes to my progress report."

Richard, as the head of the R&D division, was Budhil's supervisor. On Friday, Richard was scheduled to present the quarterly report to the board of directors. So, he had requested a meeting with Budhil on Thursday evening to ensure the scientist's progress report ". . . accurately reflected the division's advancements in R&D."

The color drained from Ashlyn's face. "Oh, god. I forgot to mention. I did 'make an impression' at the coffee station." She covered her face with her hands and let out a long, pathetic groan. "He showed me the live systems feed on his mobile. There was an alarm going off in Lab #3 while I was busy discussing the office pool winners." Her words were muffled.

"You mean, you made a mistake?" Budhil said calmly.

She removed her hands from her face in time to see him shrug non-commitally.

"Ve all make mistakes. This is the way we learn to make better choices—." Budhil stopped, an ever-widening smile crossing his face, accompanied by a look of inspiration. He stood up abruptly and put his hands together, as if in prayer. *Namaste.* "You have given me an idea. I must go," he said.

And that was how the coffee meeting ended.

"Happy I could be of help!" she called after him as he skipped out the door.

She stayed behind and sipped her lukewarm coffee.

In the fresh silence, her heart sank. She hadn't resolved anything. There was no mistaking the fire in Budhil's eyes when he talked about his experiments. He was exactly where he wanted to be. He knew the answer to the inevitable question.

When she had initially considered the question, she had been looking through the reference books and academic calendars Mr. Benson had given her. Yes, there had been fire, literally: One evening, young Ashlyn had the calendars in her lap, when her mother came and sat down next to her on the couch. Her mom turned on the evening news in time to hear the KRON4 News theme song announcing the start of the newscast:

> "Our top story tonight: An explosion at the
> Alfred P. Murrah Federal Building has rocked
> Oklahoma City . . ."

Her mother placed her hand over her mouth in quiet dismay. Ashlyn stared, horrified at the TV screen.

> "Police and fire personnel have found fragments
> of what appears to be a homemade pipe bomb
> . . ."

The news story brought the anguish of losing her father right back to the surface. Ashlyn's young mind reeled. Tears welled in her eyes.

When the newscast broke for a commercial, she looked down at the course catalog laying open in her lap. Through the watery veil of tears, she read:

> For example, chemistry plays an integral role in enhancing the performance of industrial chemicals, improving everyday medications in pharmaceuticals, and developing new, innovative fabrics such as synthetics and flame-resistant fabric treatments, to name a few. In this course, you will be introduced to the proper and safe use of equipment and chemicals.

"Every day you'll be fighting the good fight, might as well meet it head-on." Her father's motto. She remembered his words as her finger hovered over the course description.

Ashlyn sighed as she placed her, now empty, coffee cup in the bussing tray by the door of the coffee house. That was it. That was the choice that landed her here, working at FiberWorx, a textile manufacturer specializing in fire retardant fabrics.

5

Off the Shelf

Since she and David had moved to a downtown apartment, Ashlyn had enjoyed her walk to work. Every morning for the past four years she had commuted on foot, in peace, in her own good time. She silently acknowledged the fashion forward lady in the flattering silk blouse and classy wool pants. Then tipped an invisible hat to the rich jewel tones worn by the saxophone player serenading commuters with soulful notes. Drinking in the theater of life that shuffled, flitted, sauntered and marched by her had become her favorite part of her day.

The drop in the early morning temperature started to show in the wardrobe parade, as the season transitioned from the golden days of summer to darker and grayer fall days. There was a definite chill in the air this morning. Fellow commuters held their collars against the harsh breeze. Ashlyn too resisted the crisp, biting chill coming off the water. Her wardrobe choice for this lackluster day resembled city camouflage: cheerless grays to match the sky above, and matte blacks to match the pavement below. Dressed this way, in her urban cloak of invisibility, maybe the icy breeze off the water wouldn't penetrate. Maybe she could blend in and elude *his* haughty stare.

Her solitary morning commute, a sacred ritual, was now marred by an unsettled feeling she got every time she reached the plaza. *The GOM* had glowered at her every single morning the previous week. From the corner of her eye, she saw his gaze following her every step. He continued to stare, except lately his expression was one of puzzlement, as if evaluating her. Instead of staring with biting accusation, he wore a look of . . . disappointment, almost defeat. She slowed her pace and let her arms drop with chagrin. *What?!*

Though she hardly stood out from the crowd, he'd found her, and he'd managed to get under her skin. Ashlyn tried a different tack. A polite, sheepish smile earned her a dismissive sneer. *Fail!*

Suit yourself. She opted to self-consciously sip her steaming coffee, then stare at the ground in front of her, avoiding his looks of condemnation altogether.

~

Everybody, it seemed, was out of sorts. Ashlyn had come out of her lab looking for an excuse to go to the coffee station, when she happened on Budhil pacing in the hall. Budhil was visibly flustered, completely out of character for him. He scratched his head, looking perplexed as he poured over the printed memo he held in his hands.

"What do they think? Up there in the tower of ivory? That we can just . . . re-write the laws of physics?" Budhil's Hindi accent was unmistakable when he grew excited or, in this case, agitated.

The memo contained the latest dictum that had come from management. The R&D team was expected to make a "new and improved", all-in-one chemical—a wrinkle-resistant, stain-resistant, fire-resistant, and non-itching formula—for commercial application to garments, regardless of the type of the fabric.

"There is no rhyme or reason to it." He chewed at his thumbnail as he paced. "Did they even *look* at the synopsis I prepared? The economic limitations and practical outcomes are clearly demonstrated!"

Budhil had proposed shifting the focus of the experiments to improvements in the fabric technology, instead of trying to invent new chemicals or improve on existing ones.

"Where did those over-priced, pompous suits get their degrees? In Wonderland?!" chimed in Kendra. Budhil, openly distressed, was attracting a crowd.

"Their growth projections are unattainable." He shook his head. "Their forecasts are not based in reality," he continued, loud enough for everyone to hear, but addressing no one in particular. "There is no holy grail in chemical treatments. You cannot have one chemical formulation do it all. And it will break the piggy bank to try to do it," he finished.

"It's like in nature," said Ashlyn. "If you want to enhance one attribute, it will diminish the performance somewhere else. There's always trade-offs, right?" Ashlyn remembered reading that in one of Budhil's papers she'd downloaded. Then regretted saying it—rather than sounding intelligent, it felt like sucking up.

"They would probably rather see the company go bankrupt than to admit one of us peons in R&D had a good idea!" Kendra continued, all fired up. Even though she was new to Budhil's team, she never seemed concerned about how her outbursts were perceived. Budhil was mad as hell, so she was mad as hell. And she had no qualms about letting everybody know about it.

Ding!

The elevator door opened, interrupting the impromptu meeting in the hallway. Richard stepped out and immediately the heated conversation became quiet mutterings.

He adjusted his suit jacket as he eyed up the crowd. Then he flashed everyone a toothy smile, giving a brief nod of acknowledgment to those in his division, and motioned for Budhil to follow him to his office.

"Budhil, a word?" His manner was abrupt, but he never crossed the line to being an outright asshole, either.

Unseen coils pinned Ashlyn's arms to her sides and squeezed, immobilizing her, in anticipation of a confrontation.

Budhil looked up from the offending paper. "Yes, very good."

His composure and agreeable tone immediately eased the tension in the air. The mob slowly dispersed, bringing the meeting to adjournment. Ashlyn exhaled and reached out to touch Budhil's arm gently before he walked away. "Text me if you want to have a networking meeting later?" she offered.

Budhil, nodded distractedly, seeming not to have heard Ashlyn. He turned to walk down the hall with Richard. Ashlyn couldn't help but notice Richard had a single-mindedness and confidence that was echoed by his wardrobe: sharp, clean lines, expert workmanship, commanding respect. Curiously, Budhil, whose frame was smaller and more narrow than that of Richard's, appeared untouched by the tension in the air. He openly shared his frustration with Richard while maintaining his usual mild-mannered composure as he strode alongside him.

"How's he not waving that paper in Richard's face?" Kendra whispered to Ashlyn, waving an invisible sheet of paper angrily up at an invisible Richard. Ashlyn shook her head.

~

At five o'clock, Ashlyn shut off the lights in the lab with a satisfying *click*. She wasn't in a rush to get home, but then remembered David would be at kickboxing. *The apartment will be empty.*

That made her happy. Happy enough to risk a curious glance at the park bench in the plaza. No sign of the GOM and his menacing stare. Her smile grew wider. She was free and clear to walk through the plaza and waltz into her home without fear.

Somewhere, in the back of her mind, an awareness triggered a silent alarm. But her good feeling groove was unshakable this evening, so she slapped the snooze button on the alarm and stuffed it back into its dark corner.

Still feeling lighthearted and playful when she got home, she hummed to herself as she hung her coat in the front closet.

"What do *I* want for dinner?" she asked out loud in the empty apartment. She didn't know.

She went into the kitchen and opened the fridge to scan the contents for inspiration. Most of the fresh vegetables were wilted, some were swimming in the brown juice of rot. There was a collection of unmarked Styrofoam containers of unknown origin and date, most of them from the food trucks that passed by David's construction site. Who knew how much money he spent on half-eaten giant burritos and curry dishes that ended up in the trash? Alongside the fresh produce they never got around to eating. *I always imagined I would eat better as an adult.*

"I should cook something nice!" she said, suddenly inspired.

But what would David like after his kickboxing class? What if she made something he didn't feel like eating? She didn't want to accidentally give them both food poisoning using the suspect vegetables. And it was too late to run to the store for fresh ingredients *and* have something ready in time.

Deflated, Ashlyn decided she wasn't very hungry. She found the chocolate-flavored IdealShape in the cupboard, nearing the best before date. She mixed herself a smoothie then raised her glass in a mock toast. *Dinner is served.*

Instead of sitting down in front of the TV, though, Ashlyn wandered aimlessly through the apartment. First, she strolled to the clothes closet in the bedroom. Seasons were changing. It would be a good time to sort through her wardrobe, that always gave her a boost. *Not feeling it today.*

Slurping her smoothie through the straw, she gravitated toward the bookshelves back in the living room. She noticed the undissolved grit and began rolling it between her teeth and her tongue as she idly fingered her way through the titles on the fiction shelf. *Read it. Read it. Not in the mood . . .*

She switched to the non-fiction titles, mostly travel guides to places they'd never been but dreamed of going. There were some magazines, like *Fight!* and other mixed martial arts magazines. "His."

High Times. "His."

Vogue, Wallpaper. "Mine."

There were also several special interest and how-to reference books that had been accumulating on their bookshelf, unopened and unread over many Christmases and birthdays gone by. She happened across a pretty, new sketchbook with a brave little schooner battling the stormy sea on the cover. Inside, there was an inspirational quote, and a different one appeared in the corner on every other page of the book.

> A ship in harbor is safe, but that's not what a
> ship is built for.

> Great things never came from comfort zones.

Hmmm. I should pull this out later.

She paused, straightening her back. *Why later?*

Ashlyn looked down into the brown-speckled froth lining the bottom of her glass, unsatisfied and feeling about as empty. And why couldn't she just have made something for dinner, David be damned. If he didn't want to eat what she made, then he could go pound sand.

That's when the deadbolt clicked open. David lumbered in, flushed from the workout, but even-tempered, bordering on pleasant.

"Ah, protein shake. Great idea!" he said, spying her empty glass.

After hanging his coat, he went straight to the kitchen to fix himself a shake. He chatted happily to her, replaying the lessons from the evening's class.

"So, the spinning back kick . . . ," he handed her his cup and hopped off the back of the couch to demonstrate. "You place your heel," his voice, bright with excitement, "and—UNH!"

Ashlyn nodded appreciatively, though his words faded to the background, overshadowed by the dull clunking of his spoon against the sides of the large plastic Big Gulp cup. Ashlyn resisted an eye twitch, looking on as her life partner, a touch of gray at his temples, his youthful Big Gulp days behind him, appeared utterly content with the world.

"Were you going to watch something on the TV?" he asked.

"No." The sound of her own voice surprised her. She'd been anticipating an argument.

"Cool. Kevin and I were talking in class, we think we know how to retrieve the device and finish this level."

He was referring to his gaming buddy and their current quest in Assassin's Creed. "Should be a huge body count! You should come sit with me," he said. It was tempting when he was pleasant like this.

"Uh . . . I'm sure it will be a spectacular spectacle. But I've got some research papers I need to read for work," she replied.

She much preferred to disappear when he was gaming. He had set up a cozy reading corner, just for her, right by the front window, with an iPod dock and a dedicated set of "awesome headphones with bitchin' sound." She didn't really want to read the papers either, but it guaranteed her uninterrupted time in her little refuge.

Three hours later, Ashlyn's eyes were glazing over. It was time to free herself from the reading chair. As she unkinked her legs and folded her favorite plush throw—a Cat in the Hat blanket. *Now who's not letting go of her youth?*—over the arm of the reading chair, she glanced over at David. He was hunched forward, intent on the action bouncing around the screen. It never ceased to amaze her how much time David invested in front of the screen, fixated on his quests.

She opened her mouth to say something, but, she had to admit, she spent hours in front of a computer screen at her desk and in the lab. *They say sitting is the new smoking.*

David clearly wasn't ready for bed, so she waited for a break in the action and then silently laid a hand on his shoulder. With a gentle squeeze, she signaled that she was headed off to bed.

"Goodnight!" he called over his shoulder.

6

Shadows

As she pulled the covers up to her chin, the emptiness within pushed outward. Shadows of disappointment and regret filled the room, swallowing her whole—mind, body and spirit. It spat her out into the dimly lit dungeon. She was cowering in the darkness, again. She sensed someone on the other side of the door, but no words were spoken. Terror-stricken, she waited for the intense blue eyes to peer at her through the iron bars that let in traces of light from the other side.

A moment? An eternity?

She stared, wide-eyed and holding her breath. At last the silence was broken. The presence she sensed, her tormentor, had backed away from the door and begun to walk away. The hollow *click-clacking* of footsteps faded into the distance, nebulous and unhurried.

Ashlyn stood up angrily and approached the door. Grabbing hold of the bars, teeth clenched, she peered through the bars. She had questions for her jailer.

"Hey!" she shouted out.

Drumming up some courage, Ashlyn shouted out again, louder, "Hey! Don't go!"

She watched, helpless, as the indistinct form of her jailer slipped into the shadows out of reach of the light.

7

Laboratory #3

Ashlyn approached the plaza, all her attention focused on her One-Shot latte. When she brought the cup down, she saw him. He sat with his back against the arm of the bench so they faced each other. Holding her breath, she willed herself to show the same composure she witnessed from Budhil the day before.

He wore neither the look of disappointment, nor the usual disdainful and probing looks of previous encounters. This time he was almost smug. He held up a high-end shopping bag, turning the twisted-paper handles to show off the logo: A schooner battling stormy seas. The same brave schooner being buffeted by the same stormy waves as on the sketchbook she'd found on her bookshelf last night.

In my home.

Her stomach flip-flopped.

She couldn't tear her eyes from the logo as she drew closer with every step. When she did finally look away, she caught his piercing gaze. It was electric. Her shoulders stiffened as she inhaled sharply. The intensity lasted only mere seconds, for the fifteen feet of unobstructed sidewalk that stretched between her and his park bench. For those few moments, they were hardwired together and time stopped. She dared not breathe, concentrating on moving forward without her legs buckling. Once past him, the connection broke.

Maybe I should go to Security . . . or do something!

She felt hot under her collar and looked up, surprised to be face to face with the elevator doors. As the doors opened, she was swept forward with the rush to squeeze in.

Agitated, she tapped her fingers on her purse. Her ring hitting the buckle made an off-key clank of metal on plastic, which she found soothing as it kept time with the torrent of thoughts smashing around in her head.

"Sorry." She abruptly stopped the tapping when the person next to her shot her a nasty look.

Ashlyn looked away and pulled out her phone. A text from Budhil: *Coffee house? There are some changes coming to the R&D lab.*

Ashlyn's mind flashed back to the uncomfortable scene in the hallway outside Lab #3: a flustered Budhil being led away to meet with Richard and the powers that worked to curtail his genius.

Ashlyn bit her lip. Her thoughts ricocheted between the horror of her home being invaded and reliving the constricted feeling of yesterday's scene.

Last time there were "changes in the R&D lab," management had reallocated all the junior research associates to Budhil's new program. Ashlyn hadn't been too bothered by it at the time, since she'd found a kindred spirit in her lab partner, Janine.

Together, they had made QA/QC fun. Between sequences, they peered out of the small viewing window to observe the hallway-cum-fashion-runway. "No plaid, today. It seems Matt's new girlfriend has had a breakout month, bravo!" Ashlyn said, adopting the tone of the color commentator.

"Dear god! What is Kendra thinking?" Janine said, shaking her thick auburn ponytail. She stood behind Ashlyn peering over her slightly lower shoulder, tsk-tsking.

Both their faces were now squeezed into the little glass frame. "Do you suppose she's vision impaired, or just out for the attention?"

"Maybe," Ashlyn said, thoughtfully. "She did get selected for the new program in R&D, though."

"Let's give a standing O to Richard's tailor." Janine had moved on, and was observing other passersby.

"Janine, staring at his ass is not going to get you promoted." Ashlyn backed away from the window and returned to setting up the glassware for their next sequence.

They also did a lot of sharing in Lab #3. They talked about music, festivals, travel, their big dreams. And boyfriends.

"I'm sure David didn't mean anything by it."

"If he was my boyfriend, I'd drop him like a hot potato." She spread her long, narrow fingers, miming the expulsion of the objectionable tuber.

"Yeah. I know. But he really *thought* he was saving a damsel in distress. He's just one of those people who can't help but jump in. That was what my dad was like."

"So this was, what, your *third* time dragging him to be stitched up in the ER? Stuck in the waiting room in the wee hours?"

"Second."

"Never mind. Speaking of waiting, or, rather, *not* waiting. I booked my trip! I'm going on safari!"

"Squeeee!!" they gushed together and did a little happy dance.

"Omigosh-omigosh-omigosh! That's fantastic, Janine!"

Ashlyn had been genuinely excited for Janine. She worked diligently on her own, eagerly awaiting updates from Janine. And she never set foot outside of Lab #3, hoping to maintain the status quo until Janine's return from Africa.

Janine returned with a brilliant fire in her eyes.

"A roaring lion kills no game," she told Ashlyn, who blinked back, uncomprehending.

"It means, we *talk* about leaving this lab and doing something really great! But all we do is *talk*," Janine explained.

Then she started to vibrate, before blurting, "I just gave them my notice."

An invisible fist connected with Ashlyn's solar plexus.

"That's . . . bold, Janine," Ashlyn managed, her voice quivering. "Good for you," she added, without conviction.

Ashlyn had envisioned doing great things *in Budhil's R&D lab*. Instead, Janine had come back from her African safari and quit.

"I got you a parting gift, though," Janine said sweetly.

"Me? But you're the one leaving . . . Shouldn't I get you—?"

"No," Janine shook her head. "It was a crime of opportunity. I just *had* to get it for you."

She handed Ashlyn a purse-friendly sketchbook. On the cover, in bold, purple, cursive letters:

Stay Afraid, But Do It Anyway
— Carrie Fisher

"Oooo. It's so pretty. Thank you," Ashlyn said, timidly taking the sketchbook in her hands.

"Well, I figured you were going to run out of surfaces to do your sketches on."

To demonstrate her point, Janine flipped through pages of sketches hidden in the pad of graph paper on Ashlyn's desk, and then opened the MSDS binder to the back where more sketches were hidden.

"You're like an alcoholic hiding her drinks everywhere, thinking I won't find them."

"Awww! Unkind!" Ashlyn exclaimed with mock offense. "They're just doodles. And I'm *not* hiding them."

Janine laughed, shaking her head.

Janine had been gone for months now. But the empty, hollow feeling of having the wind knocked out of her was just as potent. Recalling her lab partner's departure washed over Ashlyn.

Janine has moved on, and I am on my own in Lab #3.

Her mind ground to a halt when the tinny taste of blood hit her tongue.

She eased the pressure on her lip, and her mind resumed the anxious churning. *What changes are coming to the R&D lab?*

Ashlyn stepped off the elevator into the FiberWorx lobby. Coworkers and other staff were to-ing and fro-ing, a couple of them waved hi to Ashlyn. Ashlyn wanted to disappear.

She looked down at her phone and sent a reply to Budhil: *Great idea. But, can we maybe do it this afternoon?*

~

After Janine left, Ashlyn had wasted no time in arranging the workspace in Lab #3 exactly as she liked it. The mobile carts and equipment racks were set up between the workbench and the chemicals storage cabinet so she never crossed back and forth across the lab. There was always, *always* a clear path between the chemicals and the workbench, to the eyewash station and sinks, and to the exit.

Good thing. After the GOM had mingled their two worlds, she spent the morning doing battle with her rattled nerves and trying to get her experiments underway.

Despite being completely preoccupied, she'd had the sense to set a reminder to get out for a coffee break. It was performance review time at FiberWorx. Predictably, the banter at the coffee station centered around the upcoming reviews. If she didn't get out for these coffee conversations, she wasn't likely to get out of Lab #3. Ever.

"Hey, that's a great sweater, Ash," Carlene said as Ashlyn stepped into the coffee station.

"Thanks." Ashlyn smiled. That was the first occasion she'd had to smile all morning.

"Makes you look pale," said Kendra. "Kinda bland for you, isn't it?"

"No one wants to compete with your color palette, Kendra," Carlene intervened.

Ashlyn's hackles had gone up.

But Kendra wasn't taking her or anyone seriously. "Yeah, I do knock it out of the park, don't I?" she laughed easily. No malice. In an instant, she had moved on.

OK, maybe I could take a page out of that book. Ashlyn shrugged off the insult and moved into the semi-circle gathered around the bulletin board.

"'Questions to Consider for Your Performance Review: Where do you see yourself in five years?'" Ashlyn read aloud from the information sheet that the HR department had posted.

"Why can't we ask the questions? 'What do I gotta do to get a beer fridge at my desk?'" Matt joked. "And 'Are you deliberating on the size of said fridge in those *important* meetings?' All they have to do is ask."

"You mean the 'Well, there's two hours I'll never get back' meetings?" Kendra snorted.

"To be honest, this nine-to-five life is sucking the marrow out of me," Carlene moaned.

"Isn't it supposed to be the other way around?" asked Matt, being cheeky, because he was an old movie buff, too, like Carlene.

Ashlyn smiled. "*Dead Poet's Society*. It was my dad's favorite."

Matt touched his finger to the side of his nose, the *You sniffed it out, clever you* signal.

Inside, Ashlyn felt a small tug at her heart. She'd watched the movie with her dad many times. She'd been a bit young for it, but

Ashlyn had been persistent. And it *was* his favorite movie, so, of course he had caved.

Maybe she was feeling a lack of marrow sucking, too. Maybe it was just "the seven-year itch," that point in a relationship, with your partner or your job or your interior decor, at which you just seem to pause, take stock, and think "Hey, where is this going?"

Matt gave her a nudge. "You're staring off into space again," he whispered.

She tuned back into the conversation to hear Kendra saying, "You live, you work, you die, you see some pretty cool stuff along the way." A sentiment Kendra was fond of sharing.

"So, *I* told Richard about my awesome life hack that would work great here," Reggie from Shipping piped up.

Crickets.

"Aaaand what did he think of it?" Ashlyn prompted, a little too loud.

Reggie eyed her accusingly, then recognizing her, continued, "Yeah, I told him all the benefits and stuff, and he says . . . ," Reggie made a face and sneered as he spoke, "'Well, that's an idea'. I know it's an *idea*! What do you *think* of the idea, ya yutz?" He finished with a little derisive snort and looked expectantly around at the faces of his audience.

"That's time, ladies and gentlemen," Kendra announced.

Like clockwork, the coffee break ended precisely after fifteen minutes. Although, it was never announced . . . *That was uncalled for, Kendra.*

At the threshold between the hallway and the sanctuary of Lab #3, Ashlyn exhaled, leaving her anxiety at the doorway. Inside, she donned her safety goggles and set about getting her next trial started.

She'd built up a head of steam, moving the experiment along, and didn't even notice when Richard poked his head into the lab. Richard had a card that could access every office space at FiberWorx, including Lab #3. When Ashlyn turned around, she jumped, surprised to see him. She was even more surprised to see him carelessly handling the beaker with the bright purple rubber ring around the neck. The cover trapping the toxic vapors in the beaker was only loosely attached, which made Ashlyn very nervous.

"THAT!" Ashlyn said, alarmed. "Is bromine water. It's very caustic," she added in a calmer tone.

Richard immediately put down the beaker. His cheeks colored a little. "Ahem. Right. I should know better. I, uh . . . ," he stammered. Then he caught himself, and his manner returned to one of composed authority. "I, ahem, just popped in to ask if you had selected one of the meeting options I had sent you?"

It was Ashlyn's turn to look sheepish. "No. I, uh, haven't checked my email. Since this morning. Since I got in." She was tripping over her own tongue.

She inhaled deeply before calmly replying, "I'll have a look and send a reply as soon as this sequence is finished." She gestured to the tower of glass tubes and pipes behind her.

He looked where she was pointing and saw that the droplets of fluorescent orange liquid in the tubes vanished when they hit the surface of the clear liquid in the receiving flask. The receiving flask had a red rubber ring around its neck.

"What's with the rubber bands around the jars?" he asked.

She spun quickly, nearly knocking over the very beaker she'd asked him to be careful with.

Looking where he was pointing, she exhaled with silent relief. "Oh, I use those to help me keep the chemicals straight," she answered easily.

"I figured management might look unfavorably on the person who accidentally leveled the building with a misplaced eye dropper of sodium," she quipped, then silently winced at her attempt at humor.

Richard only half-smiled. "I haven't seen this in any of the other labs," he continued, his brow now raised, considering her thoughtfully.

"Well, I'm the only one in here, so I needed some way to keep myself safe while keeping ahead of my sequence," she explained without hesitation.

He nodded, satisfied, then turned and headed out the door without so much as a wave or *adios*.

He had all but disappeared into the other world of the office, when he did a strange thing. He paused, just before pulling the door shut, and poked his head back in.

"Can you outline your color-coding protocol and send it to me in a brief email?"

Surprised to have caught his attention, Ashlyn replied timidly, "Uh, sure."

He nodded and was gone. She stared at the closed door in stunned silence. Ashlyn flinched a little, not sure where to go next. Back to the workbench? Or straight to her desk to compose a smart, attention-grabbing email?

Has the tide finally turned?

8

The Silence is Deafening

Ashlyn had her head down, composing a text to Budhil as she walked into work, *Sorry I didn't get back to you yesterday. Can we meet for coff—*

ROOOAAA-ROOAAA-ROOOAAAF!

"Je-zuz!" Ashlyn exclaimed in reply, glaring at the white dog on the other side of the fence. "Goddammit, Cujo! What is your *deal?!"*

Too busy texting, she had mistakenly turned down "King" Street. She didn't actually know the name of the street, she and David called it King Street on account of the horror factor: there was *Christine*, the possessed car in one driveway, next door to the *Pet Cemetery* front garden, and then, across the street where she stood frozen in terror, was the hell-hound they despised, *Cujo*. The dog's name wasn't actually Cujo, that's just what she and David called him. The white bull terrier who patrolled his fifteen feet of fence along the sidewalk, enthusiastically guarding his territory. He was not a nice dog. He scared the shit out of her.

She waited until she arrived at the lineup for the One-Shot Espresso before resuming her text to Budhil—*coffee today? I have some good news, too. =)*

"That's a most unusual hat, Marty. Kind of a Rastafarian-meets-Peruvian herdsman look. I love it!" Ashlyn said, heartened by the cheerful burst of color. Small Peruvian symbols, stitched in every color of the rainbow, danced between rainbow stripes on the border of his hat.

"Jes. I love it, too. It is my favorite color. But, jou . . . jou look pale," he said cocking his head.

"Yeah." She frowned, shaking her head. "There's this dog. We call him Cujo. He's just—a *nasty* dog! I wasn't paying attention, and I went down the wrong street . . ." She paused to laugh. "I *saw* someone ahead cross the street to avoid walking by the hell-hound's fence."

She closed her eyes and pinched the bridge of her nose as she confessed her big mistake: "I didn't cross. And I should have. And he scared the life out of me!"

She opened her eyes to see Marty nodding, like a psychiatrist conducting a clinical assessment.

"I give you dolce latte, today, jes."

Gratefully, she accepted the steaming hot coffee from Marty, and headed across to the plaza. She held the sweet-smelling coffee right under her nose, inhaling the rich aroma, and defiantly avoided the GOM's watchful eyes.

~

And . . . Send.

Tap.

Ashlyn stood up. ready to head to Lab #3. She smiled to herself, pleased with the simple but smartly worded email she'd just sent to Richard.

"Oh hey, Ash." Kendra suddenly appeared at the threshold to Ashlyn's cubicle.

"What do you think of this dress?" She did a pirouette to show off the new garment. It was a simple shirtdress in a rich, indigo fabric, adorned with marble-size white polka dots. The subtly tapered waist perfectly complimented the ample halter, which fit comfortably around her full bosom.

"It's—uh, lovely," Ashlyn stammered, mentally grinding the gears from lab processes to fashion advising. "Actually, it's quite flattering on you." She nodded approvingly, a rarity when assessing Kendra's attire.

"Thanks." Kendra beamed. "I had a little extra on my last paycheck, so I splurged at that vintage and alternative clothing consignment store." Kendra was practically gushing.

"The Eclectic Emporium?"

"Yes, that one. Thanks for the recommendation! I adore it! All the different subculture factions all mishmashed into one store."

It was Ashlyn's favorite store, too. From hippy wear, to grunge wear á la 1990, to the goth and punk styles, and a smattering of BDSM clothing. *Wonder which "faction" she gravitated toward?*

"Glad I could be of help," Ashlyn said coolly and grabbed her latte from her desk. "Duty calls," she said, raising the coffee cup, only too happy to leave the cube farm for Lab #3.

Stomping her way around the lab until she had everything running smoothly helped to relieve the resentment she'd carried with her from the encounter. Then she picked up the One-Shot coffee cup and noticed it was disappointingly light. *Sigh.* Somewhere behind her, she heard a beeping. Her sequence was nearly finished. *Yes!*

Ashlyn texted Budhil: *Ready for coffee in 5?*
Sure

When they met at the glass doors, it was Ashlyn who was at ease and Budhil who appeared distracted. He, nonetheless, held the door for Ashlyn, like the gentleman that he was.

Ashlyn hesitated, taking a quick look down the center pathway through the plaza, toward the cursed park bench. It was empty. "Thank god," she breathed out the words.

"Vell, I don't know about 'Godt', but you are most welcome," smiled Budhil, gesturing to Ashlyn to go through the open glass door.

In their favorite coffee house, they swooped into freshly vacated seats at a table next to the window.

"I can see the light sparking in your eye," Budhil said. "You have some good news to share?"

"Yes!" she replied, scrunching her nose to hold in the excitement. "I just sent Richard an email, as per his request," she said, adding a haughty air to the second phrase.

"Ah, I see." Budhil nodded.

Ashlyn jumped in before he could get another word out. "He's asked me to present my safety innovations—my solution to keeping myself from burning the building down."

"That is a good thing, yes." His eyes darted to the miniature pitcher of cream in danger of being cast off the table by Ashlyn's wildly talking hands.

"I know it's a small thing, but I'm hoping it cancels out getting busted goofing off in the coffee station while alarms are going off in the lab."

"You are right, that will help to leave a good impression," he replied, moving the pitcher to safety.

Ashlyn's good news had less impact than she had expected. Dread seeped into her consciousness. She didn't want to ask Budhil about his news.

"How did your meeting go with Richard last week?" she asked, wincing a little.

"Oh yes, the changes coming to the R&D lab. Well, I may have spoken out of place. It seems my newest initiative must be approved by the FiberWorx board before I may apply for any grants from any outside institutions."

"What institution are you applying to?"

"Vell, I don't believe that the institution in question is the problem." Bending at the elbows, he lifted his narrow fingers to his lips, tapping contemplatively.

"I know, 'confidential nature of ongoing work.' You can't give me any details." Ashlyn folded her arms, picturing Kendra, in her expensive new shirt, looking smug. "But, if they *did* approve the grant application, how would that change the R&D lab?"

"I cannot say if it will change for you, Ashlyn. You are doing good work where you are."

The words rang unpleasantly in her ears.

~

Ashlyn let the door of her apartment close behind her and leaned back against it, shutting her eyes in silent celebration of another day ended. Shutting out the world, if just for a moment.

Her relief was short-lived. Again.

"Gotcha!" A voice came from the living room. David was already home and happily killing zombies.

She could find no refuge these days; work was suffocatingly awkward and unfulfilling, and home was depressingly empty.

"How does stir-fry sound?" she called flatly from the front hall.

"Yeah! Good!" he hollered back.

With some effort, she mustered the energy to propel herself from leaning against the door and half-heartedly drag herself into her home. She busied herself chopping peppers and scraping carrots for the stir-fry dinner she'd proposed. Food preparation, in general, and chopping vegetables in particular, offered Ashlyn a window of time for quiet contemplation.

Mindful of the very sharp knife, she began the ritual purification—ridding herself of the stress of the day—by chopping vigorously. She let the tension and melancholy of the day collect at her fingertips, and then slowly released it into the rhythmic *chop-chop-chop* as the knife sliced through the vegetables.

Her tempo slowed, her mind placid, she pressed Play to resume the podcast that she'd downloaded for her walk home. She had her earbuds in to shut out the game being played in the next room. A theatrical voice filled her ears. The speaker, delivering a TED Talk, spoke passionately about quiet.

> And isn't it interesting that we don't hesitate to
> sign up for that spin class, to attend to the needs
> of the body. And that we have TED talks,
> podcasts, streaming music, and YouTube videos
> to teach us and to provide endless
> entertainment, to feed our minds.
>
> But what about our spirit? . . . Isn't it interesting
> that we're so over-stimulated that we feel
> discomfort when we're at rest? That we are
> uncomfortable in our own presence.
>
> That we don't know what to do when we
> experience silence . . .

Silence.
Ashlyn stilled her knife hand as she let the thought sink in.
It is *in short supply*.
She paused the podcast. Silence surrounded her. She let it soak in for a moment. Then resumed her chopping, allowing the dull *thock-thock-thock* of the blade on the wooden cutting board into the silence.

Her mind began to wander. She didn't resist the free-association thoughts that jumped from one track to another.

That was *a rather flattering dress that Kendra wore today. Quite tasteful, by her usual standards.*

Thock-thock-thock.

Kendra can be abrasive, but she's usually the first to admit no harm, no foul. I shouldn't be directing my resentment at her.

Thock-thock-thock.

Reginald had come trudging toward the coffee station, clipboard in hand. He had the look of a man on a mission, until he spotted Kendra. Or, rather, her dress. He had stood, stock still, unnerved, by the sight of Kendra, then retreated back down the hall from where he'd come.

"I think he has trypophobia," Kendra had sniggered. "A fear of holes."

"Is that a real thing?" Carlene had asked. "Or maybe it was because you shooed him out of the coffee station yesterday."

Poor Reggie. Ashlyn smiled. *Everyone now knows Reggie has a crush on her.*

Thock-thock-thock.

Budhil had a lot on his mind . . .

Thock-thock-thock.

You are doing good work where you are. She recalled Budhil's words. Keep doing a good job and they will want to keep you exactly where you are. *Was that the message?*

It had been rather tense, throughout the office, the last few days. People had been on edge, morale was down.

Or was it?

Maybe everyone else was fine, and only she saw everything in shades of gray because *her* morale was down?

Where is this all leading? Life. Work. The Universe. Everything?

Her brow furrowed. Hadn't she set out on this path, this journey called life with the highest of expectations? With the confidence that she would get there, even though she didn't know where *there* was? Didn't she have the intestinal fortitude to conquer whatever obstacles lay before her?

What a load of shit.

The space in the galley kitchen seemed especially small at that moment.

9

Obliger Rebellion

She looked across the table at David. He was munching away at his stir-fry, fork in one hand, the fingers of his other hand busily swiping over his iPad. She stared at him. Empty. Numb.

"Pass the salt, please," she asked, not really wanting the salt.

Intent on the article on the screen, he reached over for the salt and slid it across the table in her general direction without looking up.

"There was a creepy old man in the park today. I could've sworn he was staring at me," she said, testing the waters.

No response.

"He's been there every day for nearly two weeks," she continued.

Still nothing.

"My pants are on fire," she said dryly, giving up.

"That's interesting," he replied, absently.

I'm getting nowhere with you.

Disappointment, originating in the pit of her stomach, began to flood her senses. A dull hollowness that pushed against her, expanding the space the separated them. It was the exact opposite of the powerful intensity that drew her toward the GOM.

Her heart ached for more . . . something. But she couldn't name it. The thought of the GOM invaded her thoughts. As though suggesting that he might have a "something" to offer. *Well that's absurd!* The idea that he had anything to offer her was terrifying. But the push-pull between the two forces was maddening. Her throat was dry, making it difficult to swallow her mouthful of stir-fry.

David continued to chew at the meal she'd prepared. His expression shifting from a frown to a goofy smirk as he clicked onto a new article . . . a million miles away.

Ashlyn looked past him, remembering a time when the sight of David had her heart swell. *Sigh.* Tonight, her heart felt heavy.

She looked down at her now empty plate and stood, then motioned she would clear the dishes. He nodded, but said nothing. No sooner had she taken the plate, than he slid his tablet off the table and headed in the opposite direction. She went to the kitchen with their empty dishes.

~

That night, he reached for her and scooped her into his arms, drawing her in close.

"Thank you for making dinner," he whispered.

He brushed aside the loose tangle of wavy locks below her ear and began kissing her neck. Torn, not wanting this, but unsure of *what* she wanted, she allowed him his gratification. Afterward, she let him sweep her in, like his teddy bear, like his squeeze toy.

His embrace no longer evoked contentment. She lay there, eyes open, waiting. Could he detect her discomfort? When enough time had passed, she held her breath, probing the silence for the telltale signs that David had slipped off into deep slumber. Careful not to disturb him, she slowly unwrapped herself and rolled away.

Something very important is missing from this relationship.

A simple thing. As delicate as a subtle touch, when present. But when absent, it left a cavernous emptiness like a great cathedral after the celebrants have gone, where only echoes of something wonderful, that has since passed, remains. No, this wasn't love, what she had with David. This was roommates with benefits, at best. At worst, it was comfortable and safe, but dishonest.

David made a little noise, then rolled over so that they had their backs to one other.

Then it dawned on her. *He's happy.* I'm *the one who's unhappy. Waiting for . . . something.* That same something she still couldn't name.

She pursed her lips. *What about what I want? My happiness is important, too. When I have coffee with Budhil, he makes me feel like I matter. Shouldn't sharing a meal with David feel like that?*

The next morning, she spent an inordinate amount of time staring into the open closet in the bedroom. It was her special time and she fully intended to enjoy it, to immerse herself in it. She shoved a set of tops to one side, mentally composing the complete outfit.

"It's colder than a witch's tit outside," David offered on his way through.

"No it's not, you just wanted to say 'tit.'"

Besides, I'm not just looking for the right layers. She was on a personal mission to create. Ashlyn found joy in creating new outfits from old things, dreaming up new and unexplored ensembles that caught the eye and sparked the imagination. She was in search of a fresh new look from a well-worn palette.

Even so engaged, she could still hear David stomping back and forth in the background, getting his things together. She was still in front of the closest, pulling hangers down and then replacing them on the rod, when he breezed by the doorway again.

"Are you gonna finally do something with all your shit?" he asked. He didn't wait for an answer and kept walking toward the front hall.

That was fine by her. All her focus turned inward. Time and space disappeared to the periphery as she indulged her creative self. *The adventure is in the* process.

"Why do you make it so complicated?" David asked.

"AHH!" Ashlyn jumped. David had appeared out of nowhere. "Just pick a sweater and get on with it."

"Am I in your way?" she said, finally looking at him, scowling.

"No." Then he stepped back, smiling, opening his arms. "I came in for a hug."

She looked at him a little suspiciously before accepting his invitation.

"Maybe something a little brighter, like you used to wear," he said, looking past her into the closet. "I'm outta here."

The unexpected show of affection lingered on her where he'd squeezed her gently. Then she returned her attention to her wardrobe. But, instead of scanning the coats and sweaters for inspiration, the memories attached to each item wandered into her backstage dressing room. There was the varsity jacket of David's that Ashlyn liked to wear to the 49ers games. *When was the last time we went to a game together?*

There was the funky-chic trench coat she had last worn to the art gallery in the spring. The show had been curated by Janine, her first in her newly adopted career. *I wonder what corner of the world Janine is exploring these days?*

Then the memories began to tumble over each other, like when you flip through a magazine, images jumping out in flashes, one chased away by another in rapid succession. A carousel of memories, people and places, sounds and smells, emerged from the colors and textures and patterns hanging in the closet. Half a lifetime of moments relived.

Her eye landed on the black, polyester blend sweater underlain by the white, satiny fabric adorned with marble-size black polka dots. Not unlike the polka dots on Kendra's, much more eye-catching. shirtdress the day before.

Maybe David's right, I need a little color.

The old Ashlyn had an outfit for every occasion. The old Ashlyn had a sure-fire strategy to beat back the cold and gray that was forecast in the days ahead. The old Ashlyn had lived by her father's motto: *Meet the day, head-on.*

Her gaze was slowly drawn to the full-length mirror, as though guided by an invisible hand. She stared right through her reflection into memory, seeing, instead, her father's eyes looking expectantly at her.

Meet the day, head-on.

A defiant *Oh yeah?* smile crept onto her reflection. It surprised her a little, then egged her on further. She was going to push back against the sterile shades of white walls and brushed steel appliances and clear glassware in Lab #3. It was time to pull out her brightest reds and flashiest purples. Scarves and hats and overcoats that screamed "Look at me!" seemed to pop out from the recesses of the closet.

The image of forgotten frocks dancing in a cheery chorus line popped into her head. She laughed out loud suddenly, bringing the comical chorus line to life, her legs kicking high into the air. Clad in leggings with a vibrant mosaic, Ashlyn felt a primal impulse to dance. Her hands grabbed the loose-fitting tunic that fell to her mid-thigh and she began swish-swishing like a flapper from the 1920s, rejoicing in the comfort of her own skin in these quiet, early morning minutes . . . before day imposed itself on her, with its expectations and prejudices and rules and limitations.

At last, she stepped out on to the stoop of her brownstone apartment, her face flushed from the exertion of the spontaneous dance party. Her lively red coat was the perfect contrast to the monochrome color palette of the day that greeted her outside.

"I'm ready to meet the day, head-on," she declared.

Another cool and crisp fall morning. She nuzzled her chin deeper into her cozy, bouclé scarf and pulled the collar of the heavy felt peacoat tighter around her face to shut out the cold. She tucked her bangs underneath the white knit ski hat, its playful braided toggles bouncing on her shoulders as she walked—the picture of street chic.

From now on, on these chilly mornings, she would smile at those faces she caught looking her way. *They always smile back. They can't help it.* She hoped her little shock of color made their day.

"Jou look maaavelous," Marty said, doing a fabulous impression of Billy Crystal.

Ashlyn flashed him a coy look over her shoulder, puckering her lips and posing for the imaginary camera. He beamed back at her. She quickly gave up the pretense and threw her head back to let out a self-conscious laugh.

"Oh, my lovely girl. Jou can shine so bright, if only jou would let yourself," Marty chided gently, handing her a grande Americano.

She raised her cuppa java in salute to Marty as she walked away from his stand.

'Cause there's a spark in you,
You just gotta ignite,
the light . . .

Ashlyn hummed to herself, still holding her head high, bordering on smug.

His words echoed in her mind as she merged into the morning foot traffic plodding hither and thither. She decided, firstly, that, contrary to her feminist leanings, she didn't mind being called "girl" or "darling," at least, not coming from Marty.

And secondly, in spite of Marty's mild accusation, she reckoned she, and her bright, shiny self, *had* done her part to inspire cheerfulness on this gray day. She caught more than one glazed look change to one of pleasant surprise in response to her mad splash of color. *Mission accomplished.*

She slowed her steps, though, when she stepped from the street onto the plaza. Her confidence was faltering, her happy groove feeling more like a mask—artificial and contrived. Her conviction would not stand up to his scrutiny.

The color drained from her face, but that didn't diminish the bright red of her coat. The GOM spotted her immediately. His eyes locked on hers, and he had the self-satisfied look of the dealer withholding the merchandise from the addict. In his hands, something flashed, despite the diffuse morning light. She watched him, with guarded curiosity, as the object rotated in his hands, as he fiddled with the thing she couldn't identify.

Is that . . . some kind of medieval key? A cold sweat gripped her entire body. *A dungeon key?*

As she neared him, the object seemed unreal, a trick of the eye. It suddenly lost the solid form of an iron key, as she had first thought, and instead shimmered, like liquid. It was fabric. With one hand, he pulled it through the open fist of the other, like a magician. The object she thought she'd seen was merely a silver-gold image stitched on the midnight blue cloth that played through his fingers.

She watched his performance, wary of some sleight of hand, but acutely conscious of his stare burrowing deep, as though burning a hole right into her core. She took a nervous swallow of her coffee and scalded her throat. Coughing and spluttering, she broke from the trance and pushed her way across the plaza to the glass doors.

10

PINQ

Ashlyn stumbled out of the elevator, red-faced and eyes watering, a kaleidoscope of colorful clothing and barely audible profanity, drawing the attention of the people in casual conversation on the other side of the lobby.

"Than-k . . . you . . . ," Richard's words faltered, then, pulling his eyes away from the spectacle near the elevator, he continued, "for meeting with me, Marguerite."

The smooth baritone of Richard's voice reached Ashlyn's ears, momentarily numbing the tickle in her throat that lingered from the hot coffee. She held her breath. But it wouldn't be suppressed.

"My ple—"

Cough-cough-COUGH!

"'Scuse me," Ashlyn wheezed. She offered an apologetic wave toward the finely dressed, executive types and disappeared down the hall and out of sight.

It took most of the day for Ashlyn to regain some composure. It was all she could do to stay on task. Every twitch and misstep of the morning replayed over and over, and she squirmed in self-doubt for every uncomfortable moment.

How can . . . ?

I started with such a strong, positive attitude . . .

What was that . . . thing in his hands? How can the GOM know just which buttons to push?

Groan. I didn't even see who was standing there watching me get off the elevator like a deranged peacock . . .

"Everything about this day just feels so horribly wrong." The words forced themselves out. "And my throat still hurts."

She considered bailing on the ladies' event she'd agreed to go to that evening, marching over to the computer half a dozen times to send an email to the hostess.

But I said I would go.

~

Her dithering forced her to stay late to finish her trials for the day. No matter. *At least I won't have to deal with David tonight.* She leaned in close to the mirror in the ladies' washroom to remove her daytime makeup and apply a fresh look for an evening of fun with some fun ladies. *You* need *to do this.*

The PINQ ladies—Professionals Into Nosh and Questcapades—was a group comprising busy women stealing a little recreation time, a group dedicated to finding new ways to get out of tired, old habits. Originally called Women's Dinner Club with an Adventure Problem, it had grown into a huge network that promoted personal development, with a healthy dose of frivolity. It was at the scotch tasting event that the group name was pared down to *PINQ*.

Seated around an elegant table with sleek lines and a modern finish, eight ladies were at the ready for the card-making workshop. Ashlyn glanced awkwardly around the dining room table full of eager faces, looking for an opportunity to jump into the conversation. She took a deep breath and opened her mouth to speak . . .

"OK, let's get started," announced the workshop presenter. The high achievers seated at the table began assembling their handmade greeting cards at breakneck speed.

Ashlyn sighed, audibly, and began sifting through the selection of pre-stamped shapes. Much to her relief, the lively conversation on all sides easily masked her discomfort.

It was an eclectic group of women at this PINQ event: two stay-at-home moms, one of whom was the independent sales consultant leading the workshop, two teachers, one accountant, two marketing agents, and a chemist. There wasn't a single artist in the room, at least not professionally. Every woman gathered here wanted to express her artistic side.

Ashlyn had participated in a wide range of fun PINQ activities: dragon boat clinics, sushi making classes, pole fitness classes. But none of the activities had brought her closer to her PINQ sisters. She had been involved long enough to see alliances morph into strong bonds, into a sisterhood. She had purposefully surrounded herself with fun, outgoing and encouraging people, hoping their dynamism would be contagious. The sheer pleasure of like-minded company and their shared camaraderie was enviable, but better still, they all seemed to be drawing strength from each other. This sisterhood, evidently, helped these ladies to leap hurdles and climb mountains and . . . *deal!*

A pair of scissors came clattering toward her.

"I *do* like the cards," Ashlyn blurted, justifying her raison d'être at the table.

"Hahaha, sorry!" came a chuckle across the table. "Those were meant for Marguerite."

The tempo of the card making had reached a frantic pace, as did the happy chatter around the table.

"So, is this a 'gateway' activity? Is this going to get us hooked on a brand new obsession?" asked one of the marketing agents. "I really dig this jack-o'-lantern punch! I'm gonna end up with a closet full of these shape cutters," she confessed gleefully.

"Possibly. But to make the obsession stick, you'll need another glass of wine," said the hostess, smiling as she promptly started to refill the empty glasses.

"Don't forget Ashlyn," said the woman to her left. "It is Ashlyn, right?"

Ashlyn looked over to see an older woman smiling warmly at her. "Yes, that's—me." It sounded more like a question as a vague sense of déjà vu washed over her. "Yes, to another glass of wine, as well."

"You look familiar. Didn't I see you this morning at FiberWorx?" asked the same woman.

Oh god! Ashlyn felt her skin flush as the hostess poured a generous glass of wine.

"Guilty as charged," she answered as lightheartedly as she could manage. "And you must be Marguerite?"

Ashlyn's heart pounded, desperate not to relive the embarrassment of her grand entrance. She picked up the glue stick in front of her and leaned forward in her chair, turning her attention to the greeting cards on the table in front of her.

"All these piles of stickers and ribbons and scraps of craft paper remind me of the crazy collection of swatches and color fans and paint chips I saved from my mom's work when I was a kid," she deflected. "I had boxes and boxes of stuff."

"Yeah, me too. I remember I used to have a box full of shapes I'd cut out, by hand, from magazines and cereal packages when I was little," said the workshop consultant.

"Well, actually, they say that if you look back to what you did when you were ten, it would supposedly be a good predictor of the kind of career you would enjoy as an adult," one of the teachers shared.

"That so?" asked the accountant. She paused, thoughtfully. "Nope. I got nuthin'. I have no recollection of counting beans," she said, waving the glue stick around. "But the money's good," she cackled.

The teasing and banter faded into the background as Ashlyn's heart rate returned to normal. Grateful not to be the center of attention, she retreated into her own thoughts. What was that one, magical activity for her at age ten? That thing that consumed her and would define her future?

Ten-year-old Ashlyn had played designer. She'd had scraps of fabric from clothes, from carpets, from towels, from curtains, whatever her mother had discarded. Her mother, an interior designer, would amass materials in a rainbow of colors and patterns every time she embarked on a new project. Ashlyn liked to daydream about the settings and occasions that required her special expertise, and imagine she was designing the stage for the Christmas concert at school. Or dream up costume ideas for the school play. Or design a fashionable suit that her dad might actually agree to wear.

For her tenth birthday, her father had given her a very professional looking sketchbook, the same kind her mother used. Sketchbook in hand, ten-year-old Ashlyn had whiled away many hours in their bay window, sitting and people watching and sketching. Ashlyn watched, entranced, as the runway of humanity drifted by her front window, curious about what made each person tick. *Who* was the person inside the clothes? She wanted to get into their head.

That sketchbook had been the last birthday gift that she ever received from her father. A blurry picture of the cover of the sketchbook hovered in her mind's eye. The misty image wouldn't come into focus. She couldn't recall ever seeing that sketchbook after the accident. It was probably tucked away in one of those long-forgotten boxes. *Somewhere, along the way, I traded that sketchbook for chemistry textbooks.*

She started picking at the adhesive backing on a card embellishment, when a voice to her left interrupted her thoughts.

"Ashlyn?"

"Huh? What?" she stammered.

"I was saying that FiberWorx just gave us some print copy. Something about 'e-wear'. Is that like 'smart clothing'?" asked Marguerite, bringing Ashlyn back to the present and back to the card making table.

"Um, yeah. I mean, I don't know exactly . . . What?"

"You know, like the T-shirt that monitors your heart rate, or something?"

"Oh, yeah—yeah." Scrambling through the sound bites from the weekly meetings that she had attended, she remembered there was some talk about that.

She placed her palm to her forehead. "Ah, nuts. Yeah. You're right. We had a meeting about that last week. And I was totally not paying attention," she admitted. *That would've been something worth paying attention to. And now Richard has an eyewitness that I'm not staying current on R&D initiatives.*

"Oh, I know what you mean, Ash," piped up one of the stay-at-home moms. "I remember all those *meetings*," she groaned. "When I used to work in an office, I was always frustrated by the amount of time we'd burn getting absolutely nothing done. That was before kids. Now I would kill for two hours of people talking past me and not giving a damn if I was listening or not," she said, laughing.

The frenetic card making resumed as the conversation moved on to "Confessions of Motherhood."

Ashlyn slipped into embarrassed silence, numb with regret. She'd embarrassed herself in front of a potential work contact. And then couldn't speak intelligently about cutting-edge work happening in her own company. Marguerite gave Ashlyn a concerned look, then jumped back into the conversation around the table.

Ashlyn could see the connectedness, the glue that held this group of ladies together, but couldn't *feel* it for herself. A witness, but not a participant. She struggled within herself to reach out, to engage, but could only look in from the outside. Staring blankly into space, she tried to imagine what she would rather be doing at that moment. She didn't know.

11

Rattling the Cage

Tired as she was, Ashlyn had a restless night. She started to dream, first picturing the still frames of the car crash scene plastered on the front page of the newspaper, joined next by her own memories of emergency lights coming at her from every direction. She was back in the pumper truck, hands pressed against the window, screaming "NOOOOO!" but no sound came out. Then the lights disappeared and everything went dark and silent.

The windowpane separating her from the blast had now become a set of iron bars. A faint light coming from nowhere illuminated the bars, just enough that she could see that she was back in the dungeon.

Confused, she let go of the bars and stepped back from the heavy wooden door. She spun around to examine her prison. There was nothing but blackness all around. She stared into the nothingness with no frame of reference. She could see no walls, no ceiling, she wasn't even certain there was a floor. How big was her prison?

More importantly, who was keeping her here?

From the other side of the door, off in the distance, she heard a distinctive *click-clack* of heels echoing, cold and hollow, filling the emptiness. The source could not be seen through the bars. The footfalls were steady, unhurried.

Squinting through the bars, Ashlyn could still see nothing. She grew frustrated and started rattling the bars. "Who are you?!"

No response.

"I *demand* to know why you've locked me in here!" she hollered into the blackness.

The *click-clack*ing halted. Ashlyn listened intently. She was suddenly alone again. The pounding in her heart now the only sound. It skipped a beat and began to race. Trapped.

The air shifted. She held her breath, listening for more clues.

She hadn't felt anything, but realized she had something in her hands. She looked down to see the GOM's scarf, illuminated in the eerie light.

Gasp!

Her eyes flew open. Ashlyn sat up in bed. Covered in sweat, her heart pounding, just like last time. Just like every time. But this had been the first time her daytime fears had crept into her nightmares.

12

Add a Little Spark

Staring blankly into her front hall closet, Ashlyn contemplated another day at the office. After learning from the PINQ ladies about the new initiative at FiberWorx, Ashlyn decided she ought to make a serious effort to hang out at the coffee station and find out what was going on.

She chose a creamy white turtleneck sweater and a smart-looking pencil skirt, the kind the lady lawyers wear. She found a playful, light scarf that showed off her inner geek. It had unusual shapes on it, which were actually pictograms of molecules, like chocolate, and alcohol. *Two of my favorite things—in moderation, of course.*

She was banking on the engineers and scientists she worked with to recognize that the patterns were actually symbols for organic compounds. It might well be that her efforts would be lost on most of her coworkers. Especially the scientists and engineers in the Star Wars T-shirts under the plain, half-zip cotton sweaters, or the short-sleeved, checkered button-up shirts and skinny jeans. But no matter. This time, this journey of creativity gave her immense pleasure. In this space, she answered to no one.

Please, let the scarf *be the catalyst for conversation, not me spilling coffee on my beloved white sweater!*

"OK. Let's do this," she coached her reflection in the mirror. Then, with a confident nod, she headed out the door.

She had started the day yesterday happy and blissfully ignorant. Today, leery of misguided optimism, she pondered her situation. At 33, shouldn't she be patting herself on the back, taking great pleasure in her marvelous life, celebrating her marvelous achievements? Or were her expectations out of touch with reality?

Reality. Hmmm. Her mind flashed to the GOM. A poor, homeless old man. *What does he have to celebrate?*

It had been two weeks since the gnarled old face first appeared in the plaza. *Actually, it wasn't all that gnarled . . . Perhaps it's that grim expression he always wears that makes him look so haggard.*

Maybe he didn't single me out.

Maybe he's scowling at everyone.

Maybe he's just an unfortunate soul, a homeless man with mental health issues?

Maybe he never had it out for me after all?

"Maybe we see that which we choose to see, rather than see things as they are." Marty interrupted Ashlyn's silent monologue.

"Huh?" Ashlyn gaped. Marty was staring at her expectantly. She clutched at the lapels of her coat, pulling them over her neck and chin, feeling exposed, like Marty had used his magic to make her clothes suddenly vanish.

"Many people see from the inside out, and not from the outside in," he continued, pointing at the foamy rosette. "It's a gift."

Ashlyn walked away in a bit of a stupor.

She puzzled over Marty's uncanny knack to get inside her head. *His innocent comments seem less and less innocent.*

Completely consumed by her thoughts, Ashlyn's consciousness spiraled inward, grasping for threads of understanding, like someone rummaging in the unlit corners of the closet. Like she had done as a kid in the bay window. Like she had done on the school bus growing up without her dad to talk to. Like she had last night, drifting in and out of the PINQ conversations happening all around her. Lost in her head, Ashlyn didn't notice she was approaching the third bench on the left. She didn't notice the GOM stand as she drew nearer.

He leaned in close, his piercing blue eyes reaching in to touch her soul.

"You can ignore me," he spoke slowly, watching her like a cat watches a mouse. "But you can't ignore it."

Ashlyn froze, her eyes wide, her breath caught in her throat.

"It's burning you inside. I can *see* it," he hissed. "I *know* how it burns. The F——."

Ashlyn kicked him in the shin and shoved him aside, running for the glass doors without looking back.

IGNITION

13

Texting Sweet Nothings

Burning? Inside? What *could he see?* She shuddered.

He said he *felt something burning?*

Her face puckered. *Eww, I hope he wasn't talking about some itch, some . . .* where *in his nether regions . . . Uuuugh!*

Her whole body shuddered this time.

She flopped down heavily into the chair in her cubicle, holding her head up with her fingers threaded into her hair. She stared, unseeing, at the boot-up screen. She didn't remember turning on her desk light or computer. Had she taken the elevator? Had she walked through the corridors to her desk without encountering a soul? It was eerily quiet in the cube farm. She strained to hear the sound of others. Silence.

Her arms and legs began to tingle, her vision became dark and distorted at the edges, her mouth went dry. *Oh god, where am I?*

"Budhil, line 3. Call for Budhil. Line 3."

The monotone voice of the receptionist broke through Ashlyn's trance, rescuing her from the dark illusion of her nightmare invading her work world. Relief washed over every inch of Ashlyn's body. She put her head down to massage her temples and give thanks as the adrenaline subsided and the feeling returned to her limbs.

Deep breaths. She blew out the last one and looked up at her screen. Before she had even considered what to do next, an email *pinged* into her Inbox.

Subject: R&D Division Meeting

Ms. Monahan,
I'd like to hear more about your innovations.

We'll be discussing strategies for improving
laboratory protocols at the next division
meeting.

I'd like you to present your ideas.
0900. Monday.

See you there.

Richard Bowerman III, MBA, CBAP, PMP
Director, Research and Development,
FiberWorx Inc

Ashlyn chewed on her lip, weighing her options. *Report the GOM? What would I say? Would they want me to discuss the situation at the division meeting?*

No way!

Whoa, whoa—the meeting is Monday. What am I going to do about today?

Oh, Janine, I could really use a friend right now. Her friend and confidante would've been able to talk her back from the ledge, and then have joined her in jumping up and down in a little happy dance, celebrating the invitation to the division meeting. Her heart ached a little.

Maybe I should talk to Budhil, first?

At the risk of putting her trials off target for the month, Ashlyn summoned Budhil for another one of their coffee meetings: *Need to bend your ear*, she texted.

Yes, very good. 9:30?

At 9:35 a.m., Ashlyn and Budhil settled themselves at a quiet table down a dead-end arm of the coffee house. *OK. Here goes.*

"I . . . have a . . . problem," she stammered as she looked across the table to Budhil. "There was a . . . " The words caught in her throat.

Losing her resolve, she inhaled deeply and started over. "I . . . received an email. From Richard. To present my ideas at the next division meeting," she blurted. "I was . . . wondering what I should do to prepare. For the meeting. And if there is any way I can promote the idea that—." The words tumbled out like Alphabet cereal. She recognized the words, but no coherent message appeared in the bowl. "That this would open the door for someone else to take over the QA/QC lab. And then I could be considered for your lab?"

When there were no more words, Ashlyn clamped her mouth shut and frowned uncertainly at Budhil.

Budhil gave her a knowing smile. "I see you are working very diligently. We all see that you are dedicated. These actions serve you well."

Ashlyn let out a small, but audible, sigh of relief. "Honestly, I would much rather just work really hard and let my results speak for themselves. Can't that be enough?"

"I, too, have been frustrated with some of the decisions of the management," he said, nodding in agreement. "But, no, that is not enough. You need to be an advocate for yourself."

Isn't that what I'm doing here? Every time she had enlisted Budhil's help, hoping he would bring her aboard in the R&D lab, he had been evasive. He may not have final say as to who worked in the R&D lab, but every candidate would certainly be vetted by him. Ashlyn lowered her head. "I don't think I know how to do that," she confessed.

He drew his hands together in the namaste greeting—Budhil's way of blending Indian tradition and Western gestures of friendship and comfort. "The Vedic teachings tell us that 'purity of heart is lost when the mind, unsteady and restless, strays away from the spirit.'"

Ashlyn searched Budhil's face for more, for something *concrete*, something she could act on.

"It is very simple. If you know who you are, and what you want," he clarified.

He got a faraway look, then added, "This morning, my wife said to me 'You will never be punished for choosing what is right for you.'" The smile on his face lit up his eyes, and it appeared as though a shadow of doubt had lifted off his own shoulders.

"I know that you are very organized, but I can see that you have been distracted lately," Budhil continued. He paused, looking at her the way he looked at data reports that didn't quite make sense.

"When I need to sort through many competing ideas, and I have an important decision to make, I talk to my wife."

A sudden blare of sirens stampeded through their intimate conversation, and both yanked their heads toward the window in time to see an ambulance race by.

Ashlyn continued to stare at the window, stunned and silent, the image of the ambulance lingering like an imprint in the sand as the sound drifted further away.

"Hell-o-o . . . This is the earth to Ashlyn." Budhil was tapping on the table.

"Uh? Oh." She frowned like she just woke up and didn't know where she was.

"I have just received a text from my wife, asking me if I have 'sorted it out.'" He shook his head in amused disbelief. "It is uncanny how she knows when to ask how my day is going."

"I guess our coffee meeting is done." She flashed Budhil a smile, trying to disguise her confusion.

"Yes. Very good."

After parting ways with Budhil, Ashlyn slunk into Lab #3, twisted in knots about what to do about the GOM. And could she, should she, consult David for his advice? And getting her damned trials started for the day.

She began arranging the vials and flasks for the first experiment. One of the glass stirring rods rolled off the workbench and landed with a very disheartening and distinctly broken, tinkle.

"*Grrr!* That's the last one!" she fumed. She had been referring to the rod, but perhaps it was equally applicable to her last nerve.

She stormed over to the desk where her cell phone lay and typed furiously:

David, I had an incident this morning. I'm kinda freaked out. Can you call me when you can?

Send.

She tossed the phone back onto the desk and stood over it for a few moments, staring at the screen, willing it to show a reply, until it finally went black. It was rare for David to see or hear his phone on the work site. She'd have to wait a bit. But, at the very least, the SOS text had helped calm her nerves enough to allow her to get on with her work.

She made it all the way to the end of the day, staying on top of her sequences, and she didn't smash any more glassware. Remember to celebrate small victories. She did a weak fist pump to the sky.

She was about the shut off the lights in Lab #3 when her phone vibrated in her pocket.

Sorry. Got busy. Figured your Mayday had blown over since you didn't text again. Meeting the guys at the pub in Kevin's building. Want to come?

Kevin's building?

With one hand on the light switch and the other gripping the phone, Ashlyn looked away from the screen. "So, you can text your buddy to plan Friday beers, but not even pause to ask if I'm OK?"

Most of the machines in Lab #3 had been shut down, and the overhead ventilation was barely a whisper. Her words echoed dully off the walls. Tears welled up in her eyes, threatening to spill over.

She didn't report the GOM to Security. She didn't get actionable advice from Budhil. She didn't get any support from her partner. Were her expectations really that unrealistic? How much more could she lower the bar?

Everything would be better if the GOM just went away. And maybe David, too.

14

Important Meetings

Ashlyn, in her robe, was on her way to the kitchen when David poured himself into their apartment.

"You goin' t'bed now?" he said, his words slurring.

"Yep."

"'K, I'll be in shortly," he half smiled, half leered at her.

"I won't hold my breath."

David was too busy untying his shoes to pick up on her dry tone.

She found him asleep on the sofa with the game console in his hand the next morning.

Later, while he was nursing his hangover or making plans for Frisbee golf with his buddies, she busied herself with composing and formatting handouts for the division executives. Her meeting prep kept her occupied enough to successfully avoid talking to David all weekend. Ashlyn was prepared for anything.

~

"0-900. Monday." She reread the email from Richard for the umpteenth time. The important meetings happened on Monday. Yes, indeed, Ashlyn had actually been invited to one of those important meetings. All thoughts of the horrible encounter with the GOM were brushed aside.

Her happy, little, inside voice chirped away as the morning minutes elapsed. *Let's see what's at the back of the closet, shall we? Rediscover some forgotten treasure?* She was a little excited, but growing more and more nervous *really knock 'em dead with—*.

Ashlyn abruptly silenced the voice. She needed to mentally ground herself for the meeting. Today. First thing. *This meeting is too important to indulge in playful coordinates matchmaking.* The happy voice stopped, like the needle knocked of its track on the record, making a jarring, scratching noise.

Not today. I don't have time for this.

The happy voice went silent, but sent a dejected little shiver through her as it retreated into the recesses of her mind. Her stomach did a little flip-flop as the voice disappeared.

No, that won't work. Ashlyn frowned. She yanked a different shirt out of the closet. *Yes, silk . . . and what else?*

Vexed, she chewed at her lip and tapped her foot impatiently, twisting herself in knots to assemble the *perfect* outfit for today's meeting. It had seemed like she was never going to make an impression on the decision makers. She'd almost resigned herself to believing her career path couldn't be anything other than the slow and tedious climb up the corporate ladder on a predetermined schedule, over which she had no say. It was a suffocating prospect.

Which galvanized her, and inspired the final composition: a tan and cream tweed ensemble that channeled the polished look of the power suits and business outfits of the most senior women in her office.

Satisfied with her outfit, Ashlyn put her best business face on. It perfectly matched the ensemble she had created.

Eyes on the prize. She blocked out the silent narratives about passersby as she marched to work, completely ignoring her on-the-street models. She shut out the stories that she read from their clothes, their gait, their expressions.

No silly games today.

There was no skipping the One-Shot Espresso, however. Ashlyn was not really a morning person and could not function without that first cup of coffee. As far as rituals go, this was second only to breathing. As she turned to leave, Marty stopped her.

"Here. This is for jou." He handed her a rather large paper bag.

"What is it?"

"It is from the old gentleman from the park," he answered, nodding and pointing toward the plaza in front of the FiberWorx building.

Ashlyn went rigid. Holding her breath, she scanned the plaza, her eyes darting erratically over the lawn and flower beds, the benches, and the spaces between the bodies that crisscrossed the sidewalk. The iron and wood bench that was normally occupied by the grizzled old man in the faded, brown, boiled wool overcoat was empty. He was not there.

Holding it as far from her as she could, Ashlyn finally looked at the bag in her hands. It was the shopping bag with the schooner logo.

"I don't want it!" She tried to hand it back.

Marty didn't flinch. "He say it was for jou. I give it to jou." He smiled his pleasant smile and turned to the next customer in line.

So, clutching her steaming cup of coffee, and the unwelcome paper bag, Ashlyn shuffled forward, resuming her march to work, in a frazzled daze. She advanced slowly, reluctant to go forward, her Kate Spade leather boots heavy like blocks of cement as she approached the first bench. Then, passing the second bench, her pace and her heart rate accelerated.

Empty.

The third bench was *really* empty.

Stunned, she looked around for anyone who could explain. No one seemed to be aware that something was wrong, that something was missing.

She swallowed hard. *This can't be.*

An unexpected cold sweat crept up the back of her neck. *He's gone.*

It completely unnerved Ashlyn. Unnerved her, not only because the GOM was missing, but more so because she was so *struck* by his absence. Last week, she would have been only too happy to have him disappear after he'd threatened her.

His chilling words echoed in the dark chambers of her mind: You can't ignore it. It's burning you inside.

What does that mean?

The plaza was getting busy as working bodies shuttled themselves to their work places. A light jostle from one side knocked her off balance. She righted herself by grabbing onto the arm of the bench, dropping the paper bag and dumping its contents in the process. She could feel the cold of the steel bar through her thin gloves. The cold touched her soul.

As she stood staring at the empty space, a chill breeze muscled its way across the plaza, creating little eddies of swirling, dried leaves. She brushed away bits of leaves and revealed something made of fine cloth . . .

She gasped. *His scarf!*

It was navy, or midnight blue, or a rich and dark indigo. She had never seen the scarf up close. The mysterious, shape-shifting fabric which he wore underneath the washed-out brown trench coat. The thing he had played with, his slight-of-hand playing tricks on her eyes.

Another eddy skittered across her toes this time, and lifted one end of the lifeless scarf as it passed by. The scarf waved weakly, the tassels lifting and dropping like impatient fingers tapping. The emptiness of his space was mirrored in her heart. She stared at the scarf on the bench, fearful of disturbing any part of his dark and twisted throne. The air felt denser, like gravity was somehow stronger here. The weight of his absence made her legs wobble.

The tassels, like fingers, waved again, exposing another item that had fallen out of the bag. She cocked her head at the sight of the neatly folded yellowed newspaper. This, she hadn't seen before. Her eyes grew wide with surprise. An old issue of the *San Francisco Chronicle*. The date, though faded, could still be read: August 13, 1992. The paper was twenty years old!

Standing next to the bench, utterly confused, her attention bounced from the empty seat to the crowded sidewalk to the glass doors of her office building. The doors swung open and closed, keeping time with a silent clock, as a steady stream of bodies entered and were swallowed by the building.

She couldn't afford to linger here any longer. But she felt compelled to stay. To make a witness statement? Or file a missing persons report? But who for? She didn't know who he was. She didn't even know if he was missing. What information could she offer?

The dull light of the sun reflected off the glass, flashing a warning: time's up.

BONG! BONG!

Oh, shit!

The clock tower in the plaza began to chime the hour. Ashlyn caught her breath and leapt at the scarf. She grabbed it and stuffed it back in the cursed bag, a little surprised by the burning impulse *not* to lose the mysterious items. She hadn't wanted anything to do with the bag when Marty forced it into her hands.

BONG!

Time to go.

She rammed the old newspaper into the bag, too, as the present moment came bearing down on her. Her coffee was long gone, dropped somewhere.

Today's meeting is too important. She burst into a stilted sprint, her strides restricted by the narrow skirt, while fumbling in her purse for her FiberWorx access card.

Exactly how she had *not* pictured it, she swept into the boardroom, bumbling and awkward, her coat half on, half off, her teeth gripping the file folder of documents she might need for the meeting. Luckily, only a few people were seated, their attention locked on their phones or tablets. A couple of senior managers paused their conversation to appraise the brash young woman who had just barged in.

"She's with R&D, right?" asked one. The other nodded, then resumed their quiet discussion.

Grateful for this small reprieve, Ashlyn took a moment to compose herself, wipe the sweat from her upper lip, and settle into one of the comfy faux leather swivel chairs that are standard issue for the corporate boardroom.

Eventually, the seats were filled and Richard entered, closing the door behind him.

"Good morning." His commanding voice had a hint of cheer. "I trust everyone had a rejuvenating weekend." He rubbed his hands together vigorously. "OK, let's get started."

His enthusiasm was not lost on Ashlyn, but as the meeting progressed through the agenda items, her eagerness faded. She scanned the faces of the other meeting attendees in the dimmed light. The sales and marketing folks were rapt, hanging on every word, nodding their approval. Meanwhile, the senior scientists hadn't bothered to take off their lab coats, which didn't disguise, in any way, their attempts to use this meeting time to catch up on email.

The younger staff were less concerned with being discrete, they were staring unabashedly at their phones, tweeting #MondayBlues, #morningmeetingssuck, #killmenow.

Ashlyn began to wonder if there would even be time to introduce her proposal. She had started the meeting sitting stiffly upright and attentive, but now, fighting heavy eyelids, her head bobbed drowsily.

"Are we keeping you up?" whispered Kendra.

Damn! Snap out of it! Double damn! Why is the coffee always gone?

"Thanks," Ashlyn whispered back.

Ashlyn looked over at Kendra's handwritten scribbles.

"Budhil had an appointment, so I'm just taking notes. I don't know why he needs them, they never make any decisions in these meetings."

"Thank you, John. OK . . ." Richard scanned the agenda. "New business. OK, yes, QA/QC. Ashley here," he said, gesturing to Ashlyn, "Ashley is a one-woman show in the QA/QC lab and has devised a simple, yet effective, color-coded strategy for labeling the dangerous chemicals she's working with."

"Ashley, you're up. What have you got for us?"

"Well, um . . ." Ashlyn rolled her chair away from the massive table, undecided on whether to stand or stayed seated. No one else who had presented had stood. They had all used the laptop and projector to present slides of information.

"I, uh, didn't know how many . . . people . . . copies to make. I'll just pass them around." She split the stack in two and sent one in either direction.

"There are . . . Before I start a sequence, I use the thick elastic bands around the beakers and test tubes to label what's in them. Blue is for . . . ," she looked down to the table in front of her and realized she'd handed away her own cheat sheet.

"Well, if you look at the list, there, each color is associated with a chemical. I reserve the red bands as a reminder not to add anything to that vessel without double checking what is already in it . . . ," her words trailed off as the associates began shuffling their papers into folders or binders or whatever they'd brought and collecting their coffee mugs and dirty side plates from the pastries.

"Yeah, I guess it's pretty self-explanatory." No one was paying attention anymore.

"I put my local on the bottom if . . . in case anyone has any questions." She sat down abruptly.

"All right, team. That's it. Thanks for coming, everyone," announced Richard.

That was it. She'd spent most of the weekend preparing for a thirty-second presentation. Not at all what she had hoped for. The people, dismissed, moved en masse to get on with their day. Ashlyn's heart sank.

15

San Francisco Chronicle, 1992

It wasn't until late that evening that Ashlyn gently slid her treasures out from her handbag. David had already gone to bed. She hadn't wanted to share any details of this with him. She wasn't even sure what *this* was. Ever so carefully she extracted the folded newspaper, as though she was playing *Operation*, lest keys come tumbling out, jangling, and alert David to her clandestine activities.

Omigod, lighten up. She laughed at herself. *What is with the cloak-and-dagger act?* She relaxed a little. She hadn't seen the GOM this morning, nor at the end of the day. *Maybe this was a parting gift, his way of saying goodbye?. Good riddance, I say.*

Cautiously, she unfolded the yellowed newspaper and began to read the article. She was surprised how well the paper had weathered twenty years. *And all on the street?.* It was largely intact. Bold letters on top announced:

Hero's Daughter Witnesses Carnage on JFK Drive

She looked at the date again and unrolled the paper a little more. On the front page was a photo of a Maserati engulfed in flames, and alongside it, a photo of a local celebrity: Rory Mannix.

"This is Dad's story," she gasped.

Holding her breath, she opened the whole paper to expose the entire front page. Below the dramatic image of the fiery Maserati were two headshots of local heroes: two firefighters, one sent to hospital in critical condition, and one whose life was lost in the line of duty. Staring up at Ashlyn was the smiling face of her father.

She had been twelve at the time. It all came rushing back. Deeply buried images returned as foggy snapshots from her childhood. The newspaper was from the day after the accident. According to the article, few details could yet be confirmed. The car appeared to belong to Rory Mannix, a rising fashion design star.

> Rory Mannix, having achieved international acclaim, was showing his latest collection at the San Francisco Fashion Expo in the city he now calls home. *Called home.* He had just returned to the US coming off a wildly successful fashion tour hitting Budapest, Tokyo, Prague, and Moscow.
>
> The evening ended dramatically when an explosion lit up the night. Authorities confirmed that the yellow Maserati, belonging to Mannix, exploded. Nobody was expecting it. There had been no fire. There had been no warning.
>
> The horrific event was witnessed by many on the street and one, now fatherless, child, who watched helplessly from the rear of the fire truck on scene.

With tears welling up in her eyes, she forced herself to look at the photo of the helpless child watching from the fire truck. She could barely focus on the remainder of the article.

> One of the firefighters survived the blast, but reportedly remains in critical condition. He was rushed to hospital in the first ambulance, lights blazing. The second ambulance left quietly, lights on, but no sirens.

Shutting her eyes tight, she lifted her face to the ceiling and began drifting back to that night.

16

Pumper #9

It had been another quiet day at the station. Her father had been on the last night of a two-week night shift rotation and Ashlyn had pleaded with him to let her visit at the station. Not having seen his little Jelly Bean for the better part of two weeks, he had agreed. They spent the early part of the evening making super sudsy water to scrub the fire truck clean while they listened in on the emergency services radio.

Then they dined on, as he explained in his most serious voice, "Extra-sticky-gooey pizza, a fireman's staple.". Later, Ashlyn amused herself playing tug of war with the station-house dog, Hawkeye, a shaggy, muskrat-looking stray that the crew had adopted. Ashlyn's dad slipped away while she played, and had a chat with the chief.

"Say, Bill, if we get a low priority call, y'know, like a basic fender bender, d'ya think I can take my little girl for a ride-along?" he asked.

Bill was a big man, but a soft touch. Ashlyn strained to hear what the adults were saying while Hawkeye yanked determinedly on the rope toy in her hands.

"She's a good kid. 'Course she can go for a ride-along," he said at last. "You just make sure she understands that she stays. In. The. Truck."

"Of course! You got it, Chief. Wouldn't have it any other way. She stays in back," Ted agreed. "She's gonna love it!" he said, turning with a happy hop and jogging over to Ashlyn to tell her the good news.

"You rock!" she hollered from across the station. Bill broke into an ear-to-ear grin.

Most excitement for the station happened on Friday and Saturday nights when all stripes and types of working stiffs headed for the pubs and dance clubs to blow off a week's worth of suit-wearing, time-card-punching, crowded-bus-riding frustration.

But it was Thursday night, so things were expected to be a little tamer. Though, even for a Thursday, it was dreadfully quiet. A couple of cats in trees and one false alarm from the Capital One building in the Richmond District. The Haight, right next door, on the other hand, was by far the most exciting neighborhood in the city—there must have been one call every hour. Ted's station did not service The Haight.

Sadly, for Ashlyn, her time at the Richmond station had been anticlimactic on that particular evening. They had washed the truck, worn out Hawkeye, and grown tired of playing table hockey using a quarter and sliding it across the countertop. Boredom slowly gave way to heavy eyelids and a bobbing head. It was getting late and Ashlyn couldn't chase away the yawns.

"Ah well, Jelly Bean, I had a fun night just getting to spend time with you." He tousled her hair affectionately. "I'm sorry we couldn't conjure up some carnage or a minor catastrophe for you tonight."

"Da-ad. You mean the opposite," she fake protested. She had witnessed her dad play the peacekeeper numerous times—like when he gave the flustered store clerk a break when everyone else was grumpy. Or like when, instead of demanding quiet, he listened patiently to the hard-luck story of the neighbors in the noisy apartment above theirs. Ted helped out where he could. In a nutshell, he was an outgoing, likable guy.

And Ashlyn was the apple fallen from Ted's tree.

The radio suddenly crackled to life.

Through the static, the 911 operator announced that there had been an automobile collision at 7th and 10th. *The Haight, again.* The lead firefighter on the Haight-Ashbury District truck came on to respond to the operator.

"We're still at the jackknife on the turnpike. It's a big mess. Looks like we're not going anywhere for another 2-3 hours. Pumper#7 is jacked up for repairs. Can you send someone else for this one?"

"Roger that, #6. We'll go 'round the horn. That's you up, then, Richmond. Single motor vehicle. Impacted barriers on east side of Golden Gate Park, exiting John F. Kennedy Drive, under Fell Street overpass. You got this one?"

She sounds kinda bored. Then she heard a familiar voice.

"This is Pumper #9, Richmond District. Yeah, we got this."

Ted's voice came sputtering through the radio, and Ashlyn's face lit up. She flew out of her seat, grabbed the Trainee firefighter coat and ran up to the red line marking the "safe" spot where she was instructed to stand. She looked up at the fireman standing on the Pumper #9 running board, holding her breath for the OK. He looked down at her with a serious look on his face, then broke into a wide smile. "Yeah, c'mon up, kiddo. This is it!"

Ted came running up beside her and helped her scrambled into the truck, his heavy fireman's jacket half on and hat still in his hand. "Ryan, you drive."

The truck revved to life, the engine roared, the lights were switched on and began their dizzying twirl atop the truck's cab. The sirens blared as the truck barreled out of the station's center bay.

Ryan navigated his way along the city streets without much trouble, but as they neared the city's core, it got tighter. Ryan didn't spare the horn, nor the profanity. "What, are you Billy Graham or some goddamn prophet? Git. Outta. The waaaaay, jackass! . . ." Then, remembering Ashlyn, he tossed an "Uh, sorry" over his shoulder toward Ted and his twelve-year-old daughter.

Ashlyn hadn't heard. Her eyes were wide, taking in everything.

The red lines of the digital clock on the wall in the station had read 10-O-O just when the voice had come over the radio. She knew that was the time that *Dynasty* came on.

Downtown, the ebb and flow of traffic was mystifying. She had assumed everyone was home, kids in bed and parents happily watching TV.

A billboard whizzed by her field of view.

4th Annual San Francisco Fashion Expo
August 13th, 1992
Latest collections from top designers

Ashlyn had recently started reading her mom's fashion and design magazines and knew that San Francisco's fashion scene had not achieved the prestige of a New York, or a London, or a Paris. But this event, according to her mom, was expected to at least put San Francisco on the fashion map.

And, typical for any big event, like after a 49ers game, there was a big traffic snarl afterward. Hundreds of cars slowly inched out of the parking garages and side streets, all jockeying for position to get to the exits one car sooner. The sheer number of vehicles always resulted in clogged roadways.

"This," Ted pointed out at the glaring headlights in every direction, "is why we wait it out in Candlestick Park, Ash. This traffic creates mayhem for emergency personnel."

At last, Pumper #9 nudged and shouldered its way through the jammed-up exit route to the scene of the accident. The mood on the truck immediately changed. This was the job and the men were On.

Ted looked directly at Ashlyn, conveying without a word, *Don't even* think *about messing around*, and then leapt out of the truck.

"I won't move an inch," she replied.

With a quick nod and a wink, he put his hat on his head and bounded out of the truck and hurried over to survey the accident scene.

There seemed to be an awful lot of emergency folks gathered around, though she couldn't be sure. She'd driven by accident scenes before, but had never been to a 911 call. It seemed, too, like an awful lot of people had taken a special interest in this calamity. People lined the border of the park. People crowded around on the far side of the barricaded intersection.

The mob near the barricade shifted and made way for a white panel van, which screeched to a halt, coming as close as the police cruiser would allow. Then another. And a third. They all had satellite dishes on top.

TV trucks? she wondered.

Ashlyn had her face pressed up against the pumper's window, watching everything in view: the car, flipped on its lid, its nose smashed in; the shattered glass on the road; the police and firemen yanking on the driver's side door of the car; and the paramedics hauling the stretcher from the ambulance, in no particular hurry.

She watched the news reporters and cameraman spill out from the white panel vans, craning their necks to see what was going on.

She noticed the crowd growing in number. By all accounts, this seemed like a bad accident, and someone was undoubtedly hurt, but there was no spectacle to be spectated, so why the special interest?

Maybe someone got killed? Ashlyn's heart skipped a beat at the thought.

While the emergency personnel chatted among themselves, pointing and gesturing, she began scanning the faces in the crowd. A lot of them seemed pretty dressed up. They looked like the kind of people that would go to see a ballet or opera, which was very much at odds with the morbid curiosity they displayed looking out over the carnage at the intersection of 7th and 10th.

Mixed in the with sparkly evening gowns were the hooligans, the telltale spray paint still glistening on their hands, and the joggers, and the guys playing pickup on the basketball courts. All these people had abandoned their activities to join the crowd.

Her father and Ryan, weighed down by the Jaws of Life, jogged toward the upside-down car. A sudden, blinding flash of blue-white light turned night into day and erased the world.

Ashlyn squeezed her eyes shut, breaking the surface tension of the fat, wet tears brimming under her eyes. They fell, heavy with heartache, *splat-splat—splat* onto the twenty-year-old newspaper.

17

Recalibrating

Shaken to the core, Ashlyn lingered in her bed in a daze. On the one hand, to her great relief, she might be free of the GOM's menacing stare. But on the other . . . his parting gift had dredged up painful memories. Refusing to open those old wounds any further, she focused, instead on the scarf.

What was the significance of the scarf?

Was there any significance?

Maybe the GOM had just been lucky to find such a luxury item and had had the sense to keep it? Maybe it was meant to buy him a warm bed on a too-cold winter night?

Maybe it was a remnant from his old life. Maybe that was why he was an angry *homeless man.*

These questions raced through her mind as she shuffled out of bed finally. David was already in the bathroom, shaving.

Most mornings it was she who cracked a smile and touched his shoulder lovingly as she brushed by him on her way to the shower. Most mornings, if he noticed at all, she was rewarded with a grunt as an acknowledgment. Preoccupied with questions about the peculiar artifacts, Ashlyn was, quite frankly, not interested in going out of her way to pay David any attention this morning.

Yet, this morning, he did notice. She caught his eye in the mirror and he stopped shaving, all his attention on her. Without so much as a word, she walked past him and disrobed with her back to him. She could feel his eyes looking her over. As she stepped into the shower, she hesitated and cast a curious glance at both their reflections. He cocked his head slightly, seeming to admire her, as though seeing her for the first time after a long separation. Then he winked and went back to his grooming.

As the woman he'd been sharing a bed with for nearly a decade, shouldn't that look of familiarity mixed with desire stir some kind of reciprocal response in her? She searched inside, appealing to her gut for some kind of reaction. Nothing. She disappeared behind the shower curtain, her thoughts once more on to the GOM's curious artifacts.

~

On her walk to the office, she was conscious of the mismatched patterns worn by the uninspired: horizontal stripes inflating a wider figure, and vertical stripes stretching on forever on the lanky, basketball-player frame; the polka dots on the plump lady with the cherub-face, her petite frame made shorter by the starkly contrasting white top cut off at the bottom by the long black skirt. Ashlyn's habit of observing her sidewalk models was so well ingrained, she couldn't help but notice them, but she had no appetite for the parade today.

She did, however, hold her breath as she stepped into the plaza. The bench was still empty. *His* bench. She considered the empty space for a long while. Standing like a statue she waited, willing the empty space to tell her, absolutely, it was all over.

Whatever his motivation, Ashlyn had a sinking feeling that the unrelenting specter of the GOM was driving her to re-examine the circumstances of her father's death twenty years ago.

I just can't go there.

Ashlyn considered the matter closed.

In her lab, she struggled to focus on the, literally, hundreds of steps in the reactions she carried out on a daily basis. She watched, as if in a stupor, the droplets of FD&C blue #1 food dye seep into her test swatches and wick through the threads, spreading into indeterminate ink blots. The blue of the dye was deep and rich, much like the GOM's scarf.

Later, she found herself staring absently at the bottle of indigo carmine indicator solution. She was seeing indigo everywhere. It was maddening.

At last, Ashlyn gave in and indulged in a little sleuthing. An hour of sporadic Googling provided some relief. She determined that the scarf had once been a gorgeous, hand-woven, Jamawar wool scarf of Kashmiri design. Then an alarm went off.

Ashlyn! Dummy! Every eyedropper of catalyst needs to be added in at just the right time. Pay attention.

Shaking her head, she shut her personal laptop and picked up the lab manual for the formula she was *supposed* to be testing. She needed to follow the sequence of reagents and catalysts as prescribed, no step could be interrupted or fast-tracked. Any misstep in the sequence could spoil the experiment.

"Ugh." She grimaced. She needed to restock the reagent—the one that comes in a large plastic bag inside in a box, but the valve on the bag never lines up with the hole in the top of the box. Ashlyn heaved it carelessly onto the workbench, dropping the box on its side to align the valve and the hole. It landed with a dull thud, sending the plastic valve shooting off across the lab. When the valve came to rest, her ears picked up the disconcerting *glug-glug-glug-splatter* of five liters of reagent pouring out the open spout and splashing onto the floor.

"Shit!" She quickly righted the box to stop the flow. Luckily, she had already labeled the receiving flasks using her color-coded elastic bands. "Phew! No red. Safe from disfiguring burns or permanent brain damage from toxic fumes," she muttered as she wheeled the bucket and mop out of the broom closet.

Her mind elsewhere, none of her experiments ran smoothly. In the afternoon, she pulled a Sharpie out of the autoclave. Not wanting to spend more time cleaning than working, Ashlyn tossed the suspect pen into the trash next to the desk. The tip exploded on impact, spraying indelible ink around the rim of the aluminum bin.

"Thank god I'm not working on anything potentially lethal today," she said, admiring the interesting splatter pattern now decorating the inside of the trash bin.

After a fruitless day in the lab, Ashlyn was ever so grateful when the clock stuck five. Gripping the bar on the glass door, ready to leave the building, Ashlyn took a moment to scan the plaza. The bench remained pleasingly empty. Overhead, a mix of sun and cloud held the wind and the rain in suspension, in limbo. Like the weather, Ashlyn chose to hold back. She would put her curiosity about the

GOM's odd parting gifts on hold. For now. She decided to go to her Tuesday yoga class after all.

Though she got paid for a forty-hour work week, there had been too many sixty-hour weeks lately, and it was draining her. One hour and thirty minutes of yoga was her remedy. That's how long it took to replace five, six, or sometimes seven days of pent-up frustration, anxiety, and restlessness with "Ommmm."

The popular yoga studio at the fitness center in her neighborhood was always full, with a wait list. But she had landed a spot in the class since Budhil's cousin, Sanjay, was the instructor. Ashlyn had to leave her office especially early if she wanted to get into the yoga studio to claim her space near the back corner. She preferred the back where mirrors to the sides allowed her to check her form in the Eagle Pose, but dreaded being front and center. And she also had a better vantage point to study the latest styles in yoga fashion worn by the real devotees.

Her day in the lab may have been a bust, but scoring her favorite spot in the studio helped make up for it. After setting up her mat, her bolster, and blankets, she grabbed a pair of foam blocks and a strap, and refilled her water bottle.

As she crisscrossed the studio, she cast her eyes over the steady influx of students. On her right, a leggy woman in black capris stood up. Her cropped pants added even more length to her shapely legs, and imparted a look of grace to her figure, like that of a ballerina.

Sidling along the front of the room, a petite figure with a pixie hair cut bounced by Ashlyn's mat to claim the last spot on the far side of the studio. She was definitely too busty for her top *But good on ya, sista, you own it!* Ashlyn silently cheered.

Up front and center, in his usual spot, was the uninhibited man in the snug-fitting, Onzie square-cut shorts. Ashlyn regarded his minimalist apparel out of curiosity. *He is remarkably fit and his form is truly stunning, but really, those shorts leave nothing to the imagination . . .* She shook her head. *You're staring, look away!*

She shifted her eyes to her own reflection in the mirror up front. Her attire, and her presence, was on the modest side, understated.

"Namaste."

Hands held in prayer over his heart-center, yogi Sanjay softly greeted his class, bowing gently in a sweeping motion to address the four corners of the studio. "Velcome."

"Namaste," came the chorus from the students.

"I hope we are all feeling rested and present. Your thoughts of your day behind you, tucked away into your lockers." He smiled. "You have fed the engine that fuels your legs that carry you through your day, your hands that open the doors to the places you vish to go. You have answered the calls of those who are depending on you. You are here, now, to feed your soul. Here, we will recharge the spirit. It is this connection that allows the mind and body to function as Godt intended."

Ommmm.

18

Who is Rory Mannix?

David looked surprised, and delighted, to find Ashlyn already at home on Wednesday evening. He walked up to her with a bit of a bounce in his step and swept her hair back to press his lips to her neck in a series of sensual kisses. She stiffened. He didn't seem to notice. He continued to kiss gently along her neck and whispered into her ear, "Hey. I was thinking . . ."

"No, you weren't," she interrupted, being cheeky, though maybe a little insensitive— she knew he hated when she teased him that way.

"Haaa-aa, funny girl." He stood up now, a little dejected, but undeterred. "I was thinking, let's skip the hassle of cooking and just go out for dinner."

"Umm, I—"

He cut her off excitedly. "There's a game on tonight. The 49ers are playing Green Bay!"

Making a face, Ashlyn twisted from her lounging position on the sofa, and sat up to face David. She was all decked out in her comfiest of comfy clothes. Not only did she have on her favorite ragg wool socks, bunched up over zigzag leggings, but also a snug-fitting old concert T-shirt that was no longer fit to be seen in public. She showcased her comfy clothes ensemble to David, and made no move to change.

"I'm not really hungry. And you know I don't really get excited about the games until the playoffs. You know I'd come if it was a playoff game."

"Are you sure?" he asked, his tone hinting that he would make it worth her while. "I pictured dinner out with m'lady, then hanging with some good friends, and then some romantic time . . ." he raised his eyebrows à la Tom Selleck. It was more comical than suggestive, and not in the least tempting.

Translation: Dinner at the pub, watchin' the game with the guys, barely aware that I'm even there, and ending his *perfect evening with a roll in the sack.*

"You go ahead. I'll bet the guys are probably already down there, anyway." She was banking on him choosing an evening out with the guys.

He'll be expecting to get two out of the three things he listed. If I'm lucky, he'll be happy with a free pass with the guys and I'm off the hook by the time he stumbles in later. She forced more sunshine into her smile.

David quickly changed out of his dusty work clothes, swooped by her on the couch, and dropped another kiss on her cheek on his way out.

"See ya," he waved over his shoulder.

What would she have done if he'd thought to plant a shocker of a kiss on her? Would his kiss still leave her breathless? As David slipped out the door, she waited to feel that pang of longing, that moment of apprehension that letting him go without her was a mistake. She felt no panic. No sudden aching for him as he strode out of reach, out of sight, out the door. No, she would not be waiting anxiously for him to come home to ravish her.

Click.

The door lock slipped into place. She was alone.

"Fiiiinally," she drawled, daring to speak out loud.

Feeling much braver tonight, Ashlyn was prepared this time when she pulled the newspaper out from the drawer. Over top her concert T-shirt, she wore an oversize cable-knit cardigan sweater with excessively long sleeves and wide, generous pockets. She loved to burrow down into the folds of the soft wool on chilly, damp nights. She had chosen the leggings because she knew they wouldn't get caught under her ass like the flappy legs on flannel pajama pants. She was free to shimmy and stretch to reach for her glass of wine or the hummus and pita chips that she would call dinner. To complete the ensemble, she had accessorized with a large bouclé shawl-cum-light-blanket. Settled at last, she tucked her legs under her backside, ready to dive into this mystery.

OK, enough noodling around. The table is set. Dig in.

She unfolded the newspaper again, to gaze upon the man whose car was a ball of flame on the cover of the twenty-year-old newspaper. His name was Rory Mannix.

She had never forgotten that name, but her family had made an unspoken accord when they moved to Moss Beach. "Let's only take with us the happy memories," her mother had said as they waved goodbye to San Francisco.

But now, after so many years, so many layers of cobwebs and dust, that name . . . She felt a slight tremor from the dark corner where that name had been filed. She set the newspaper aside and, business-like, typed his name in the search box of her web browser. Then, pulling out a journal from her purse, she started making notes. From Wikipedia:

- Rory Mannix
- fashion designer, born September 16, 1962
- worked in New Jersey tailor shop . . .
- no formal training – rose from obscurity to stardom in the fashion industry

She jotted down more details found in another article in the *New Yorker*:

- Margeurite Coeurbel, Rory Mannix's new publicist (1988)
- A savvy and insightful agent in the fashion industry, Mme Coeurbel has her work cut out for her
- "new trails blazed by young upstart from Jersey may actually be burning bridges in his wake . . ."

He sounds like a real piece of work. Further down the results page, she found his one and only magazine interview in a 1989 issue of *Cosmo*:

Cosmo: How did you get here?

RM: Where do I begin? I was born at a very early age . . .

Cosmo: [Laughs]. Maybe not that far back. But, no, where did you get your start?

RM: I guess it all started when I was an apprentice in a tailor shop. It was in a rough neighborhood in Jersey, but Vincenzo—I called him Enzo—would've done well anywhere. His work was impeccable. Clients came from all over New York State. He was a master of his craft.

Cosmo: So, you spent a lot of years working with an Italian tailor? Your strong Irish roots didn't clash with Enzo's?

RM: I stayed in the *back* of the shop. And was happy to. [Laughs]

Cosmo: That must have helped you become knowledgeable about the art of suit making. But how does that translate into forging a whole new path in fashion?

RM: Enzo was my mentor for the tailoring—the cutting and stitching. But he also had a way with his clients. When he talked with the customers, they relaxed around him. They liked to unload their troubles at work, complain about their wives at home, you know.

Cosmo: Kind of the man's equivalent of a gossip session at the hair salon?

RM: Yeah, exactly like that. [Laughs]

Gossip session at the hair salon? Ashlyn rolled her eyes indignantly. *No, wait, that still happens.*

Companies were downsizing, interest rates were skyrocketing. Mostly we saw working folks in the shop. But there were also some Wall Street types. What did they all have in common? A sense of being disenchanted with the modern, neon and plastic version of the American Dream. I heard it day after day. It was like an epidemic. Like the Hong Kong flu.

Cosmo: The Hong Kong flu inspired you to break away from tailored suits in the New Jersey shop?

RM: Ah, yes, I digress. Rich. Poor. I could see that all people feel the same need to express themselves, to be seen *and* heard. I became acutely aware that people express themselves through fashion. As teens and until the day we die. It's been that way for thousands of years. That's when I really started to listen to their stories.

Cosmo: So, this is the lens through which you came to view the customers. What did you see?

RM: Every client who returned to that little shop was a blank canvas. Each man was looking to tell his story.

Cosmo: Lending credence to the phrase "The clothes that make the man . . . or woman."

You go, Cosmo. She leered a little at the text in front of her, and took a healthy swig of wine for good measure.

RM: I know clothing. That's my medium. Man. Woman. Whoever is the wearer. But in the shop, they were able to speak freely, let go the pretense of their workday self. I began imagining what they would look like in a different setting. I used my medium to give them an outlet for the other facets of their personalities.

Cosmo: You set out trying to give Wall Street a personality? That's ambitious!

RM: Maybe. [Laughs]. I just saw it as, we aren't meant to be locked up in a factory or an office for sixteen hours a day. My designs began as rough explorations into redefining the boundary between the working man—person—and their true identity. I began creating clothing to contrast the suffocating mantra of "live to work."

Cosmo: Don't mince words, Rory. Tell us how you *really* feel! Although we at Cosmo, and your fans, couldn't agree with you more, all work and no play makes for a dull boy or girl. So, designing the look for after hours, creating bitchin' threads? Not a lot of interest in expressing that persona along the Eastern seaboard, I imagine?

RM: That, you are correct! The uptight, business-centric, workaholics that came into Enzo's shop had no time for my designs. It was a visitor from the West Coast who noticed my work. I was wearing some of my original pieces and he was totally blown away. I knew, in that instant, I needed to bring my work out West.

Cosmo: Did you experience culture shock when you landed in San Francisco?

RM: No, not really. The biggest revelation was that I needed solitude to come to know the universal truths. I was alone, at first. I lived like a monk. But that's when the ideas came. The unobstructed access to viewing the human condition. I had tasted divine enlightenment.

Divine enlightenment? She bristled. *Mom was right, these celebrities are all self-centered, egotistical . . .*

That was probably the pivotal moment that set me on my path.

Cosmo: Sounds like quite the trip. Back here on Earth, though, I would say you're no longer on the path, Rory. You're on the leading edge, and forging the path. Can you give us a sneak peek of what we can expect to see next?

RM: The artist never knows where his muse will take him. Solving the mystery of the human condition is what drives me. Bringing joy and excitement, pleasure and fun, and beauty to people's lives, that's my mission. But I haven't discovered the universal key, yet. The unifying theory that connects the mind to the body and to the spirit.

Ashlyn raised an eyebrow. Sanjay was always talking about unifying the mind, body, and spirit. It hurt her brain to think of Sanjay and Rory Mannix in the same context.

Cosmo: From the streets of New Jersey to the path of enlightenment. That's quite a leap! Thanks for talking with us today, Rory.

The interview had occurred three years before the deadly car crash that ended his short career. *He had everything to live for . . . and then it was all gone. Just like that.*
She drained the last of the wine in her glass.

19

Will That Make You Happy?

She had meant to Google "Rory Mannix" and "Vincenzo's Tailoring" and "1960s New Jersey" and "Wall Street fashion", and . . . but after refilling her glass, she couldn't resist the temptation to follow some of the many links taking her off course. She absently burned an hour? two? losing herself in a fun trip through all things fashion: the advice columns, the gossip, and the endless how-to lists and relationship quizzes.

Including a classic quiz explaining "How to Tell When Love Has Gone Stale, Distinguishing Stud from Dud." And a link to "Top 10 Ways to Ditch a Dud."

"Why are you wasting your time on that tripe?" David said, who had suddenly appeared over her shoulder. It was late. She hadn't noticed the time. She hadn't noticed him come home. Hadn't even noticed the familiar sound of him fumbling with his keys in the lock. Only now did she notice the aroma of four hours at the pub.

Ashlyn hastily minimized the browser window to hide what she'd been reading, and wheeled around, horrified that he might have seen those last two headlines on her screen.

"Oh, dunno, I was . . . just . . . uh," she stammered, "looking something up . . . and got sidetracked."

She hazarded a glance up at him, shrugging innocently. "Can't look away from the shiny stuff today. Bit of a magpie, I guess," she said, making light of what she'd been reading.

David worked in construction. He had little interest in following the latest fashion trends. He had his Carhartts for work, and his Levis for play. Or the chinos-T-shirt-blazer combo, for something a little dressier. He had on his skinny chinos with the navy blazer tonight.

The look on his face told her he didn't care what she'd been reading. He'd come home from a fun night out and was clearly pleased that she was still awake. He lumbered toward her in a playful, stalking motion, as the predator would approach his prey, alert and ready to pounce.

Caught off guard, Ashlyn did not play along. She hadn't planned on still being up when he returned home, specifically to avoid this situation.

How was she going to placate him? *Give him the "Oh babe, I've got a headache tonight"?*

No, he's not going to buy that. I've been home, relaxing.

Should I try to distract him?

Accuse him of being too drunk and tell him that he should just go to bed?

Her mind reeled, grasping for an escape hatch. She looked down at her laptop, recalling the last thing she'd read. Unfortunately for Ashlyn, who had opened the link to the "Top 10 Ways to Ditch a Dud," #4 advised: Tell him straight out that he's a terrible lover.

What if I go for the jugular . . .

"Oh babe," she said, sighing with a hint of ennui. "Are we going to have to do that thing, where you do that low growl, like a hungry panther? And I pretend I'm cornered and then you toss me on my front, on the bed, and drag me to the edge of the bed?"

He stopped. His shoulders sank and he glowered down at her.

"What's your problem, man? You've been untouchable for a couple weeks. You needed some space. I get it. I gave you some space tonight. You think you could give me somethin' *I* need?" he asked accusingly.

Oh shit. "Uhh, David, I uh . . ."

"You, uh, *what?*" he said, the anger rising in his voice. "You getting to be a star performer at the office now?" he jeered. "Too good for the roughneck, lowlife roofer? You told me you *liked* the growling!"

She had, once. She had, at some time before, felt a thrill at his touch. She had sunk so willingly into his tight embrace, his arms were so strong, sincere, secure. There had been sweet tenderness, too, and she had felt treasured.

She looked up at him, hoping to see some remnant of that tenderness. He stared back, his jaw set. They were at an impasse. A stalemate. Straight-faced, she closed her laptop and set it aside, stacking her journal and pen on top in a show of giving him her undivided attention. His expression softened a little.

"You're right. I haven't made space for us tonight." She scooped up the bouclé shawl and patted the sofa cushion, inviting him to sit with her.

"Where did you end up going tonight?" she asked.

He pursed his lips, eyeing the seat cushion, her olive branch.

He let out a sigh, then sat heavily next to her, combing his fingers through his wavy hair.

"Well, it started out shitty—good thing you weren't there." He gave her a crooked smile. "That same pecker-head bouncer from last week was there—"

"You tried to go to Booker's? Haven't you been kicked out of there enough?"

He glared at her.

"Sorry. I just . . . well. Never mind, where *did* you go?" She tried to show David the tenderness she missed coming from him.

"OK. Yeah, I had to text the guys to come out and meet me. They were happy to leave, that bitch waitress was there too."

Is everybody going to be a piece of shit in this story, Ashlyn wondered, but said nothing.

"Oh, yeah." He perked up, smiling at her with a twinkle in his eye. That devil-may-care twinkle that had first captured her attention in college. He had been the bad boy that all girls loved to love.

"Remember when we were in Boston, and it had just snowed? We loaded that sled with stones and dragged it all over the quad?"

"And you and your friends made giant penises and other . . . rude pictures," she added. "But there's no snow here."

"Yeah!" His smile was so wide, the endearing crinkles appeared at the corners of his eyes. "Well." He was chuckling to himself, making it difficult to get the words out. "We went to the back of Booker's and found a huge bag of shredded paper. Caleb pulled out his knife and slit the bag open. He thought it was garbage, and was just going to leave the trash everywhere . . ."

Ashlyn stiffened, resisting the urge to shake her head with disapproval.

"I said 'Nah, man, I've got a better idea.' There was tons of paper. We made a huge dick, then——," he wheezed, he was laughing so hard, "and then Caleb starts pissing on our masterpiece. 'Gotta make sure it sticks, fer posterity, y'know?' he says."

"Yep, that sounds like something Caleb would do."

When she had been in college, it had been invigorating to break the rules. David's college-age pranks had been a refreshing contrast to the heavy workload of studying and exams and tutorials and time in the labs.

Except it got old. And he didn't. Over thirty, and refusing to let go of being eighteen. For as long as she had known him, David's personal time was largely allocated to having a good time. He made friends easily and had cultivated a huge network of friends. But few people made it into his inner space, his private self. He was fiercely protective of his close friendships, so long as they kept to the code

. . .

"Caleb reminds me of—what was his name? Back in Boston?"

"Don't mention that asshat," he seethed.

David lived by some unknowable code by which those friendship bonds were fragile and, when broken, almost impossible to repair. Ashlyn had been with him nearly ten years and had yet to crack through to the inner sanctum of this deeply wounded boy in a man's body. Now, comfortably in their thirties, many of their high school and college friends had begun to move on, except for the drifters—the ones refusing to grow up.

Everyone should hold on to his or her inner child, but there's a distinct line between child-like and child-ish.

It was becoming painfully evident which one described David. As she waited for David to open up to her, she began to see him in a new light. He was holding out on her. Some part of him was off-limits. And it was inhibiting their relationship.

"We had a lot of fun in Boston. I learned a lot on that co-op at Boston Chemical," Ashlyn said, hoping to resurrect some happy memories.

"Yeah. That was fun." He got up and went into the kitchen.

When he returned, he was carrying a glass of water, for himself.

But, he was smiling again. *Phew.*

"The people and culture are so much more refined back in Boston," he said thoughtfully.

When he took a big gulp of his water, Ashlyn could feel a dry tickle in her throat, but the anticipation of getting past that wall of his held her fast in her seat.

He suddenly looked sad. "I wish you would've taken that job offer in Houston instead of here. The people are friendlier, more neighborly back in Dallas."

When he had met Ashlyn in Boston, he pined for Dallas, where he grew up. When he later joined Ashlyn in San Francisco, after she landed a job at FiberWorx, he pined for Boston. Always looking back. He hadn't changed.

She had. She used to stand up for herself. In the past, she would have called him out for not thinking to get her a glass of water, too. Maybe she'd allowed herself to change too much, given up fighting for things that were important to her. Given up fighting altogether.

"David, what do you want?" she asked, point blank.

"I don't want anything, now" he said coolly.

"No, I don't mean sex. I mean, what do you want out of this relationship? Out of this life?" She hadn't meant to turn this into a no holds barred heart-to-heart, but somehow that's where it was headed, and she couldn't stop herself.

"I thought we were going to start putting away money to travel the world? I thought you wanted to go back to school to do some IT training. So you could work anywhere in the world."

"Jee-zuz, woman! What are you yammering on about now?" His brown eyes were sunken and dark, the deep creases at the corners telling of the years spent outside on construction sites. He was aging like everyone else, despite his refusal to go gracefully. He always got defensive when she asked these questions, like he resented the world, like it had stripped away his youth before he was done with it.

Tonight, she had him cornered. So many times she'd wanted to have this conversation, but never dared to force it. A doorway had opened, just a crack, and now she found herself in the middle of new territory. His face twitched as he wrestled with the questions. She waited patiently for the answers, resisting the urge to intervene as he struggled to respond.

"What will make you happy?" she asked, gently, but unrelenting. "What do you want out of life?" She was forcing him to look down the barrel of adulthood.

He moved away from her and flopped into the leather recliner next to the sofa, seeming to contemplate, to seriously consider, her questions. A flicker of acknowledgment played across his face.

Does he see it? Finally? An acknowledgment that time marches on, and it will leave him behind, without apology?

After several minutes of reflection, with the questions hanging silent, heavy, in the air, he replied flatly, "I don't know."

~

It was quiet in the apartment the next morning. David was at the table shoveling cereal into his mouth, reading something on his iPad. He ignored her as she walked by.

David left for work at the usual time.

She felt . . . pity. And sadness. But not remorse for cornering him last night. Nor for demanding an emotional response from him. She wasn't sure where they were headed now, but she was adamant that she was not going to continue as they were. She glumly flicked her way through the hangers in the front hall closet and selected an unassuming gray wrap to throw over the shoulders of her navy peacoat, then headed off to work.

No silly inner monologue entertained her on her morning commute. She listened, instead, to the *splitch-splitch* sound her Blundstones made on the wet sidewalk.

He "doesn't know". He doesn't know what will make him happy? Does he even know if he's capable of being happy? What do you say to that?

The emotions swam in a tangle inside her head. *How many years had been good years? Does he deserve my understanding? My pity?*

How could his dreams come true if he didn't have any?

Ashlyn needed to look forward. Her mind, body, and spirit were all out of whack and she could feel something—something powerful—propelling her forward. And it seemed David was unwilling to go that direction, refusing to let go of the past.

Lost in her dreary thoughts, she'd completely missed the One-Shot. When she did finally snap back to the present, she was standing next to the GOM's park bench. His absence felt . . . incomplete.

Small pools of icy rainwater collected in amorphic shapes, like in a lava lamp, on the bench seat. Mesmerized, she watched the pools merge and begin spilling over the edge, as though pushed by some unseen force.

20

Unraveling the Mystery

David had hardly been home since their confrontation, but had finally accepted a text from her late Friday night. Ashlyn found him asleep on the sofa Saturday morning. She took the blanket from her reading chair and gently placed it over him. He didn't stir. Maybe her barrage of questions had sunk in. Maybe he needed extra time to process it.

With a sigh, she scribbled a note for him and then placed it on the table in front of him, pinning it down with a bottle of ibuprofen.

I hope your head doesn't hurt too much. Going to the coffee shop to chillax. Maybe we can talk later about making life fun again? I'll make chicken-fried steak.

Chicken-fried steak was *not* her favorite. But it was for a good cause.

And, it being the weekend—*finally*—she intended to enjoy a lazy morning by herself. She loved to spend time in the coffee houses—the coffee shop, the coffee bar, the café. Immersed in humanity, but patently separate from it.

Sanctuary.

She headed for her favorite coffee shop down the street from her apartment, but not early enough to get one of the big, cushy leather seats. *Nuts.*

The popular café hummed with life. She could choose to people watch, or she could lose herself in a novel, or a magazine, or she could gaze out the window lost in a daydream. That's what she came for, not the cushy leather seats. She chose the last sunlit table near the entrance.

It would be a busy spot, but today Ashlyn was intent on unraveling the mystery of the grizzled old man. *OK, tiny, wobbly-legged café table, hope you're up to the challenge.* She pulled out all her mystery-busting tools. The buzz of the busy café surrounded her with a soothing white noise.

"Pumpkin spice soy latte for Ashlyn!" announced the barista.

She trotted up to collect her prize, grinning at the hostess, absurdly delighted by her coffee treat, then spun on her toes and darted back to her window-side seat. The early morning light broke over the peak of the adjacent building, beaming warm sunshine right on her face. She closed her eyes and let the energy of the sun wash over her. She paused to sink into the comfort of her sanctuary, a practice her mother had insisted on during her yoga phase.

Ashlyn could hear her mom's voice. "Stop. Savor the moment."

She took a sip of her pumpkin spice soy latte, relishing the sweetness and warmth.

"Ahhhh," she sighed.

Ok. Coffee, check. Laptop, check. Phone on vibrate, check. Internet password entered and working, check. She flicked through the apps on her phone to find the to-do list she'd compiled to keep her focused, having learned her lesson from getting hijacked by mindless surfing last time.

Thanks to the GOM's twenty-year-old newspaper, and a clear head, she began to recall the details of the fashion personality who blew up her entire world when he blew himself up. In her journal she wrote:

> - The car in the accident belonged to Rory Mannix.
> - Rory Mannix was a fashion designer.
> - He was the headliner for the 4th Annual San Francisco Fashion Expo the night of the accident.

She'd always known these little details, deep down; the memories were buried, not forgotten. In the days and weeks after the accident, she'd learned to hate fashion. Anything to do with the fashion industry evoked resistance, like the repelling force between two magnets of the same polarity, pushing Ashlyn in another direction.

Just reading the name Rory Mannix made Ashlyn quake. *The accident feels so remote, but the pain . . .* An involuntary rush of emotion stole her breath away. *God, I miss you, Dad!* She wiped a rogue tear that threatened to spill over.

Ashlyn had mended the old wounds years ago, but the stitches began to fray as she cautiously peered into this story from her past, dredging up the tender emotions. Pursing her lips, she set aside the newspaper as the old resentment pushed the pain aside. *It doesn't matter, he's gone.*

Her father was gone. But she suspected that the GOM, and whatever fresh hell he intended to stir up, was not. If she could know the GOM's secrets, maybe that would drive off the creepy aura that clung to his park bench. *Maybe that would rid me of all my nightmares.*

In the familiar comfort of the coffee house, Ashlyn suspended her personal moratorium on all things related to the fashion industry. And here, in her sanctuary, abuzz with conversation, the queasiness she had felt staring across the plaza at the surly face of the GOM was overshadowed by her curiosity about this old newspaper that he had been carrying around.

A twenty-year-old newspaper with the story of my father's death . . .

Who was Rory Mannix to the grizzled old man?

The first articles that popped up in her search results told her that Rory Mannix was young, wild, and reckless outside of his shows. Several articles described scandalous behavior all over the globe. The earliest instance had occurred in Budapest.

Where, exactly, is Budapest? That's where she would start.

Hungary was one of the countries laid to waste during World War I and later ensconced behind the Iron Curtain under Communist rule following World War II. In the 1970s and 1980s, some of the more progressive cities were testing the waters with Western culture: big and small names on the music scene, like Depeche Mode and Rough Trade, held concerts in Budapest in 1985; Western brands, like Nike and Levis, began to show up on store shelves.

A few optimistic entrepreneurs had tried to establish a world-class fashion event, the likes of which had been limited to New York, Paris, and London. The initiative was launched in 1990 with the vision of becoming an historic venture into the fashion industry. Local organizers promoted top designers side by side with their own up-and-comers, and included a lottery for a few unknown names from the international scene.

Like clipping articles from a newspaper or magazine, Ashlyn highlighted fragments of interviews and editorials and copied them, amassing exposés and commentaries to help her piece together the story of Rory Mannix. She was hoping to find the dots that connected the GOM to the accident that killed her father. Her tattered emotions were hoping not to find them.

After an hour of searching, copying, and pasting, she sat back in her chair. She swallowed the last, now disappointingly cold, sip of pumpkin spice soy latte and reviewed her jumble of notes.

"Much to our disgrace, we offered Rory Mannix
one of the international spots for our inaugural
Budapest Fashion Week," lamented Estoban
Sjolak, the event's organizer. "He was an
abomination!"
— Les Hessman, *News of the World*

When asked, other designers from the show had
this to say: "He is a nobody."

"His pieces, at this respectable event, in the
beautiful city of Budapest, *my* Budapest, were
not so good. He couldn't measure up to
Hungarian talent," said one local designer.

"He wanted all the attention, like a spoiled
child!" said another.

But the fashion design enthusiasts said
otherwise. They loved his pieces.

— Cherry Lang, *Rolling Stone*

Authorities indicated Mannix had arrived
without incident. Somehow, he had managed to
acquire the necessary papers to enter
Communist Hungary. But he refused to abide by
their restrictions and curfews. And that's when
he got into trouble.
— Wesley Domas, *The Economist*

Spurned by the critics, Rory Mannix made a
spectacle of himself last night. He stumbled out
onto the runway with two of the models.
Clinging to the two ladies, he addressed the
crowd with false gratitude and sloppy gestures,
before dropping his drawers. From the front
row, where I sat, he appeared to be
simultaneously laughing and seething with rage.
He also reeked of whiskey.

The security guards reacted quickly, preventing
him from urinating off the runway. Mannix
avoided being tackled on the stage, but sources
tell me he was very shortly escorted out, and
dropped like a bag of refuse by the dumpster out
back.
—Cori Bradshaw, *Venus in Fashion Magazine*

The state-approved media sources provided a series of photos
including men with bleeding and swollen eyes, a lineup of strong-
backed men handcuffed and facing a gray cinderblock wall, and
women being shoved into the back of a police cruiser—the
"official" story, which accused Rory Mannix of inciting the locals to
rise up against the authorities.

This was the story cited for his expulsion from Budapest.
Guess that was embarrassing for the Hungarians. Ashlyn made a face at her
screen. At least, that's how she always felt when the police instructed
her to "take him home." Any one of the images could have been

David with a split lip or bloodied knuckles after having pummeled some other guy's face at the pub.

Behind her, someone dropped a mug. The sound of it smashing on the floor intruded into her consciousness, calling her back through the portal, out from the dark alley in the photograph, and back into the brightly lit coffee house. The sound hung in the air, causing a momentary lull in the buzz of conversation as everyone looked around. Then the steamer went back to steaming, and the clink of metal spoons in oversize coffee mugs went on clinking, and the hum of the coffee house resumed.

She continued to stare, chuckling to herself as she watched the apologetic patrons trying to out-polite each other: "Oh, I'm sorry!", "No, my fault. I wasn't looking where I was going.","You're OK? You didn't get any hot coffee on you?", "No, no, fine. You?"

People are so civil in the cafés. The manners showdown at the OK Corral Café. She giggled.

Then she sighed. *This is probably why I prefer the coffee house by myself to the pubs with David.*

"I got it, guys." The barista stepped between the two gentlemen to clear away the broken shards of coffee mug and mop up the grande half-caf-mocha with almond milk.

The high from her Internet sleuthing was cut short. Beyond the crouched barista, the GOM appeared.

The color drained from Ashlyn's face. From between the dueling gentlemen, his solemn expression appeared, his piercing blue eyes were fixed on her. She swallowed hard. Unable to look away, she stared back, wide-eyed, her breath caught in her throat. She had never expected to see him anywhere else besides the park bench.

She sat, twisted round and transfixed in her seat, unable to move, or breathe.

21

The Lines Have Blurred

The barista then stood up, breaking Ashlyn's line of sight. The soothing hum of the café was torn away, replaced by clattering spoons and the hair-raising rasp of metal legs being dragged across the tile floor. The jarring noise of the café flooded in, overwhelming her senses.

A light breeze chilled the back of her neck as the door, now behind her, opened and closed. Another tinkle of the bell above the café door finally broke the spell and she remembered to breathe. The polite gentlemen had moved on and Ashlyn could see clearly that *he* was gone.

Rattled, she slowly uncoiled herself and returned her attention to her laptop. Her fragile veil of contentment stolen from her, Ashlyn shivered. With shaking hands, she shut her laptop and went to collect her things. Someone had lazily dropped their newspaper on her teeny-tiny café table on their way out the door. It took a moment for her to register what this foreign object was.

The unfamiliar paper lay folded, with half of the black bold-type letters of the headline disappearing over the curve of the paper. But two of the words were enough to grab her attention: Fashion Mystery.

She snatched the paper up.

"Fashion Mystery Reopened?" she read aloud. Her eyes darted to the top corner. *This is from Tuesday?*

Below the headline, the byline announced:

> Rory Mannix, infamous 1980s fashion designer
> long believed dead, rushed to UCSF Medical

Center, where he died only hours later. Tracey
Curic investigates.

Seeing the image of the GOM before her felt like a slap in the
face.

Except it wasn't a grizzled old man featured in the photo.
Instead, a young man, maybe in his late twenties, appeared in the
black and white stock photo. Unlike the people in the candid shots
from Budapest, there was no mistaking that penetrating stare
captured in the studio portrait. Even without color, she could see
the intense look in those eyes.

Frantically, she skimmed the words in the article.

> . . . elderly man . . . rushed to hospital . . .
> shortly after 9:30am, Friday morning . . .

I saw him Friday morning.

> The street vendor who found him, collapsed
> near a park bench, directed paramedics to UCSF
> Medical Center, where the patient had a private
> room . . .

And the ambulance . . . at coffee with Budhil.

Ashlyn gripped the paper tighter, trying to hold her shaking
hands steady, reading on:

> A few hours later, he died . . . had been fighting
> a losing battle against liver disease.

> Hospital staff refused to release the identity . . .

> A source inside the Center, wishing to remain
> anonymous, claimed the patient was Rory
> Mannix.

The café air was suffocating. She couldn't process what she
had read, which was in direct contradiction with what she had just
witnessed. Her fractured reality clashed like cymbals inside her head.

Completely shaken up, Ashlyn fumbled the paper. It fell to the floor with a *thwack*, the electric stare still locked onto her from the tile at her feet. She ran out the door a hot mess, her bright red winter coat fluttering behind like a medieval royal cloak.

Striding at a furious pace, she was oblivious to her surroundings, trying to outrun her fear. Some minutes later—ten? twenty?—she found herself at her favorite park trail. It was wooded and peaceful. No cars, just dog walkers and cyclists.

"That was him!" she gasped, at last stopping to catch her breath.

But how could he be in the café if he's dead? Her mind reeled.

As she walked, she tried to stitch together the disparate images of Rory Mannix, fashion icon, and visions of an old and haggard Rory Mannix, now deceased, a.k.a, *the GOM.*

She had been happily connecting far-off, impersonal dots in the café, enjoying the satisfaction of teasing out clues to a puzzle that linked a menacing, scarf-wielding homeless man in the plaza, a twenty-year-old newspaper, and her father's death.

Knowing his secrets would leave him nothing to hold over me, right? Ashlyn had believed that was all that was needed to banish him, that he would simply disappear from her life.

Now, with the knowledge that the GOM was dead, it seemed he would still have the last laugh. His icy gaze, slicing coldly through the busy coffee house, had told her that. Recalling the vision of him in the café sent another cascade of terrifying thoughts through her, like glass shattering overhead, sharp-edged and cutting deep.

Was he alive when he was taunting me on the park bench?

Or was he already dead and haunting me?

The fashion designer that everyone believed was dead, whom she'd been posthumously stalking online, was, in fact, not dead? Until just days ago?

And the GOM, who had been haunting her, alive and in-person, was now dead? *But, maybe not?*

Her thoughts, a confused jumble, mixed with murky details from her past. And she had a growing sense she was being followed.

She detected shifting movement behind her, just beyond her peripheral vision. Spinning, she looked back to see, very clearly, the wooden Dogs on Leash signpost that she had just walked past but hadn't noticed. It was solid. Not moving.

She slowly turned forward again to resume her walk, pensive, agitated. She shook her arms and brushed off her sleeves, a cleansing action her mom had taught her "to rid yourself of unpleasant and unhelpful thoughts."

It didn't help. Resuming a rhythmic tempo in her gait along the trail, Ashlyn puzzled over the fact that the GOM was dead. *How can he be dead?*

And if he's really dead, then Rory Mannix is really dead this time?

And, if he's really dead, why is he haunting me?

But I don't even believe in ghosts! So, what did I see?

Her attention was pulled away from the stormy churning of ideas inside her head, and turned outward, first noticing the dull sound of her heels on the pavement. *Clack. Clack. Clack.*

Then, again, out of the corner of her eye, an object on the very edge of her vision seemed to shimmer. Frowning, Ashlyn stopped walking, and turned boldly to face whoever or whatever was poking at her subconscious.

Nothing. Not even the slightest breeze. Even the flag atop the flagpole marking a monument in the park sagged limply against the pole.

She started walking again.

The young man pictured on the front page of the daily that was casually left on her table had lived. And her father had not. She didn't know what to feel. She had locked away those feelings a long time ago. Twenty years ago, in fact.

So, why, if he lived, did he disappear? Why did he walk away from all that he had achieved?

And why was old man Rory tormenting me? Like he wasn't satisfied with yanking my father out of my life forever?

Her pace slowed as she thought about her father. It made her sad. She searched her feelings, but there was nothing left of the denial and the bargaining and the wishing him back into her life, just the sadness.

So why had the GOM made her so uncomfortable? Her now knowing the details of Rory's life—the drinking, the raging, the lashing out . . .

Surely, that would silence his taunting?

Her knowing that he had walked away from the accident, knowing that his overindulgence in the free-flowing champagne and coke at the after-party was his shame to wear.

Surely, knowing all of that would take away the sting of his accusations?

"Dead or alive, now I know exactly who sat on that park bench, Rory Mannix," she said triumphantly to the stray waft of air that gently lifted her scarf from her chest.

She searched her heart for the confidence behind the sudden outburst. It wasn't there. The thoughtful chambers of her mind were silent. Listening.

She pictured his eyes with brows knit together in angry condemnation. *They did seem to hint at a vengeful spirit.* In life, he could only menace her from his bench during her waking hours. Now, his spirit, unbound from the flesh, could haunt her anytime, anywhere. Her blood ran cold.

But he *took something from* me*! I should be the one seeking vengeance.* She felt her own brows draw together, mimicking his disdainful scowl.

She stopped walking suddenly and closed her eyes. Holding her breath, she reached into her coat pocket. She was carrying the scarf around with her. "Is it the scarf?" she gasped, looking around for someone to answer.

Is his spirit attached to this scarf?

"Is that why you gave it to me?" she demanded of unseen ears in the park. "So you could continue to . . . to burn me from the inside out?"

She stared at the scarf. It remained balled up and limp in her fist. Then she rolled her eyes, chiding herself. *This isn't like some ridiculous episode of Supernatural. I'm not going to burn this scarf!*

Despite the reassurances of her rational self, she delicately tucked the scarf back in her pocket, thinking she would find someplace else to keep it, somewhere she would feel a little less vulnerable, and maybe examine it closer there.

22

Persistence is the Vehicle to Success

When she returned to the apartment, the note, and bottle of pills, were gone. The blanket she'd covered David with was neatly folded and placed over the arm of the reading chair. Ashlyn stared. Her mind, like the little spinning beach ball was processing. *He never tidies. What does that mean?*

For the rest of the weekend, Ashlyn kept herself busy in the security of the apartment. But walked on eggshells, waiting for a response from David. She didn't have another duel in her, so she kept out of his way, avoiding further confrontation.

"Coffee?" he asked Sunday morning.

Ashlyn jumped. "What about it?"

He frowned slightly, then held up the near-empty carafe. "Want some?"

"Oh. Yes. Please." Each word rolled out awkwardly.

For his part, he was pleasant, but kept his distance.

Her Monday commute was also a somber experience. She walked with her head down, fearing some other manifestation of the GOM would appear out of thin air. She barely breathed for the entire length of the plaza and didn't fully relax until she was safely inside Lab #3.

In the brightly lit, tightly sealed space of the lab, Ashlyn let out a great sigh of relief, then immediately began scanning the room for somewhere to stash the GOM's cursed artifacts. On the far side of the lab, past the workbench, sat the company desktop computer, where all the data were entered. The computer table abutted a wheeled partition panel that had once separated two desks, hers and Janine's, the intention being to give the illusion of a private workspace. Janine's desk was gone, but the wheeled partition wall remained.

She eyed the partition wall, noting that, in addition to the whiteboard facing her on one side, it also had a tackable, burlap fabric on the other. As the panel was currently arranged, the burlap panel and whatever she pinned to it were hidden from view.

Perfect.

She inserted a line of pins into the burlap side of the panel and carefully draped the GOM's scarf over them. With great satisfaction, she washed her hands of it, and walked to the "work" side of the desk.

~

At five o'clock, Ashlyn hung her lab coat on its hook. She couldn't wait to get away from the lab, which was starting to feel less like a stepping stone to bigger and better opportunities, and more like solitary confinement. But she'd had enough of tiptoeing around David at home all weekend. Somewhere between the elevators and the glass doors, she would need to decide where to go.

The City College of San Francisco Library is close by . . .

This she knew, having been sent by the company on occasion to use the library for project-related research. The buildings were starting to look a little dated, but it was always brightly lit, and busy.

She found a table in the center of the library and immediately spread her things out all over the surface. *OK, Rory.* She glared at her screen. *You're not scaring me off today.* You *are going to reveal your secrets to* me.

At the library, with the security of other people around, but no interruptions, she could try to piece together the life and times of Rory Mannix. She spent all day, every day, sifting through data. *Surely there's a clue in here that tells me where he went* after *the accident.* Researching the secret life of a fashion icon would be a welcome distraction from feeling taken for granted at FiberWorx, and from dealing with David's being standoffish.

The last thing she'd written in her notes from the coffee house:

- *Kicked out of Budapest*

She typed "Rory Mannix" and began the hunt. The search term generated 862,000 results. She skimmed the pieces chronicling Rory's unexpected rise from obscurity: from Budapest to Tokyo, to Sydney, to London, to Moscow, and, finally, to San Francisco.

"Ashlyn?"

Ashlyn looked around in surprise. "Lin! Omigosh!"

Lin blanched a little and looked around nervously.

"Whoops, sorry," Ashlyn said, lowering her voice.

"It's OK, I surprised you." Lin's concern warmed to a smile.

Ashlyn stood to give her longtime, rarely-seen-these-days friend from high school.

"You must be working on something pretty intense. I'm volunteering here, can I help?"

Ashlyn gawped, completely at a loss. *Help?* After failing to confide in David or Budhil, she'd resigned herself to walking this path alone.

"I've been thinking about you," Lin said when no words came out of Ashlyn's busily working mouth. "I read in the news about the fashion designer who died recently? The guy everyone thought died twenty years ago?"

Ashlyn inhaled sharply.

Lin put a reassuring hand on Ashlyn's shoulder. "That was the accident that . . . That was how your dad died."

Ashlyn nodded slowly. "Yeah."

Ashlyn put her hand over Lin's, relief washing over her. *The accident. The death of my father. And a fashion celebrity . . . none of this is a secret. Help? Yes, I could use some help!* Her eyes grew wide with excitement.

"That's quite the story, hey?" Her voice cracked a little.

"Yeah," agreed Lin. "He *wasn't* dead, but then he comes back after being gone for decades, and then dies for real."

Ashlyn tried to slide her fingers into the little pockets in her jeans, then hooked her fingers in the belt loops instead, but that wasn't comfortable either. Her mind was working as furiously as her hands to figure out what to do. "That's kinda . . . ," she inhaled nervously, "what I'm here for. To see if I can find out what happened to him after the accident."

"By 'him,' you mean Rory Mannix?"

Nearly a month had passed since all the horrible memories had begun resurfacing. In all that time, she had never uttered his name.

"Yeah . . . Rory Mannix."

"Oooo. Intrigue." Lin's deep brown eyes sparkled as she took the seat next to Ashlyn's. "I'd like to help," she said. With perfectly manicured fingernails, she delicately tucked her dark brown hair behind her ears, ready for the juicy details.

To Ashlyn's surprise, she felt a thrill to finally have someone to share her mystery with. "So far, I've only been able to dredge up some of the back story."

"I'm on it." Lin rubbed her hands together and headed toward the Staff Only door.

On her own, Ashlyn spent an hour following link after link to newspaper clippings, fashion magazine articles, risqué images with click-bait headings. Seems Rory was the original rebel rock star—hotel rooms destroyed, posh family names dragged through the mud . . .

Whoa, Budapest was only the first of many transgressions.

In Japan, for example, where he was invited to show his work at the Tokyo Fashion Week in 1991. In spite of Budapest. Ashlyn clicked the link to a newspaper article from a Japanese paper.

Ashlyn couldn't read the kanji characters, so looked instead at the images and the translated captions.

American tourist apprehended by Tokyo Police.

The accompanying photo showed a small-framed Japanese woman in a long black trench coat, blocking her face from the camera's lens. Meanwhile, Rory Mannix was led away in handcuffs.

Another caption:

Collection of S&M paraphernalia seized in American man's hotel room.

Laid out in a tidy, orderly fashion was the inventory of sex toys seized from the American's hotel room.

"My, my," Lin said slyly from over Ashlyn's shoulder. "I thought we were researching the mysterious life of one Rory Mannix?"

"Yeah, I know, right? This one's great!" Ashlyn replied. "Here, read this."

Another photo, also with an interesting caption.

Yokozuna Fujiama Taishō, a.k.a. "The Crusher," celebrates anniversary of twenty-fifth Grand Sumo tournament win.

In the photo above the caption, a very regal looking Fujiama Taishō posed in his long-retired *keshō-mawashi,* at a prestigious event celebrating his distinguished career. With him, his family, including a dour-looking young Geisha, labeled as his daughter.

"Soooo, this demure-looking girl," Lin pointed at the Geisha, "is the same as the trench coat wearing woman busted with Rory Mannix?"

"Yep."

"And he and the young Japanese debutante got caught together in the wee hours," Lin said, relishing the scandal of it.

"Everyone knows the bad boys are fun, right?" They laughed together.

"'The unwitting American didn't know he had seduced the daughter of a revered Sumo champion'," Lin read over Ashlyn's shoulder.

"I bet he knew all along, but didn't care, cheeky bastard!" Ashlyn scoffed.

"I didn't find anything that racy. It's almost an entirely different narrative," Lin said as she sat down with her tablet in hand.

"In 1990, Budapest was still a communist country, with tightly controlled media. These are photographs from uncensored accounts leaked out from under the noses of the authorities."

Dark and grainy photos with partial translations of the captions and headlines rolled across Lin's screen.

"Backstage passes to a 'verboten' city?" Ashlyn asked.

"And free of any chaperon . . . Looks like Rory went on a private tour." Lin's tablet displayed a steady stream of candid images.

"The info I had on Budapest said he ended the night as a sloppy heap of disgrace outside the cultural center," Ashlyn said, pulling out her notebook. "They left him to sleep it off."

"Evidently, Mr. Mannix picked himself up from the pavement, and went for a stroll," Lin said, pulling up a photograph showing Rory elbow to elbow with the local twenty-something crowd. All had raised glasses, celebrating the camaraderie of—Ashlyn squinted at the caption:

Hungarian: Az élat boldogsága
English: The happiness of life

Another image, underexposed and blurred, claimed to show Rory Mannix engrossed in hushed conversation, lurking in a dark and secretive alcove.

"I can't really check the authenticity of the photographs, but the images do suggest another version of Rory Mannix. These all show a congenial, every man's, good-time guy," Lin commented.

Ashlyn felt like she was traveling through space and time to watch, unseen, as Rory's story unfolded. She lingered there, studying the details and artifacts captured in the photos.

After a few moments of intense scrutiny, Ashlyn finally commented in agreement, "These completely contradict the official story." She nodded her head thoughtfully as she spoke.

"I wasn't able find details of *where* any of this happened. It could have been one? some? maybe all? of the trendy bars that were established in the old ruins left after the war."

From Budapest, to Tokyo and Sydney, to London, and to Moscow. In every location, his collections, his masterful work, was overshadowed by his reckless behavior. All behavior that occurred before the accident.

"This is great. But . . ."

"I know what you're thinking," Lin interrupted, "We still don't have any clues as to where he was after . . ."

"After 1992. The accident happened in 1992," Ashlyn finished for her. "Someone must have seen him in the past twenty years, right?"

"Exactly! People are still spotting Elvis half a century later, for crying out loud!"

Ashlyn tapped her pencil on the table, pondering the question. *He had to be* somewhere *for twenty years before showing up as a grizzled old man . . . sitting on a park bench . . . in downtown San Francisco!*

"Maybe we're asking the wrong questions? We want to know what happened *after* he was mistakenly pronounced dead! But I have some duties that I have to take care of." Lin stood up. "I'll follow that line of questioning and come find you later, OK?"

"Thanks!" replied Ashlyn.

Yes, you can dig as deep as you like on the details of the accident. Ashlyn already knew the ultimate fate of Rory Mannix after the accident: He used the car crash to disappear.

I have another question: Why disappear?

23

A Ship in Harbor

Lin returned about an hour later.

"I haven't had a chance to preview any of these, but my shift is almost over, so let's have a look, shall we?"

"'Hero's Daughter Witnesses Carnage on JFK Drive'," Lin read the headline aloud, and Ashlyn's whole body stiffened.

"Yeah, I think you know what happened there, sorry." Lin skimmed ahead to the next flagged article. "OK, this one's from the Valley Echo: 'The remains of the driver were charred beyond recognition. Even dental records were inconclusive, leaving forensic dentists scratching their heads.'"

Ashlyn was busy jotting down rapid-fire bullet notes as Lin read the articles out loud.

"This one, from the San Fran Daily Star, says: 'Initial reports stated that the remains of only one body were found at the scene, though eyewitnesses claimed that there had been a passenger in the car at the time of the accident.'"

Ashlyn's hand suddenly faltered. "A passenger?"

She stared down the alleyway between the bookshelves across from her. At no point in time did she expect this twisted tango between her and the GOM to include a third person.

In her journal, she traced a dark circle around one of the bullets.

    - Passenger?

"What about . . ." Lin scrolled past a few more articles she'd flagged. "'A week after the accident, the San Francisco Fashion Expo organizers reported a missing person following the event.'"

Ashlyn leaned over the tablet, her eyes darted over the text. "Doesn't say who?"

"No. I found a few more reports and articles. But they come from . . . ," Lin made a face, ". . . questionable sources. I don't think they'll be very helpful."

Not helpful if you're looking for facts. But what if you're chasing a ghost?

"But they *are* fun to read," Ashlyn said, not wanting to miss any clues.

"OK." Lin continued reading out loud, skimming and emphasizing here and there: "'Mannix label has become synonymous with innovation . . .', 'Those close to him hinted Mannix had the Rosetta Stone for divining the intentions of the rich and powerful . . .', 'Do Versace, Armani, and Prada . . . have ties to the Mafia?'".

Lin and Ashlyn rolled their eyes at each other.

Then Lin interrupted herself to snicker. "Oh, this'll be good. DevoNews has the best conspiracy theories. 'Did these fashion icons have a hand in making Rory Mannix and his magical label disappear? Or perhaps Mr. Mannix's bad behavior in Budapest, Japan, the UK, and now Moscow, has captured the attention of the Kremlin . . .'."

"Seriously? That's not at all cliché," said Ashlyn.

"'He's likely behind the Iron Curtain, kidnapped to divulge the secret of his label . . . to unlock his success . . . bring Russia glory on the fashion stage.'

"That's about it. The headlines about Rory Mannix's unconfirmed death petered out, and they moved onto a new scandal involving Madonna's new book, Sex," Lin said placing the tablet in her lap.

"Nothing in the results gave the cause of the explosion?"

"Not these results. But I only know a few of the search engine hacks. The librarians here are the real wizards."

Bzzzzt-bzzzt.

Ashlyn's phone vibrated. She pulled it out reluctantly.

"It's David."

For a fraction of a second, Lin's smile twisted into a wince, but she said nothing. Then, with a tiny shake of her head, she resumed discussing the quest. "I don't think I'll have time this evening, but I can get a search on the explosion started for you, if you like?"

"Yeah, that'd be great! Thank you."

When Lin disappeared from sight, Ashlyn read the text. *Where are you? You fucked up my favorite sweater! It's not supposed to go in the dryer!! I'm pissed.*

"Shit," she muttered. She never heard "Thank you" for always doing his laundry, but she sure heard about it when she didn't get it right.

"W h a t – d o – y o u – w a n t – m e – t o – d o – a b o u t – i t . . . ," she started to type. Then deleted it.

Before she could think of a response, her phone buzzed again. An email this time. The subject line read *Where are your weeklies?* It was from Richard, who was looking for the weekly summary she was supposed to provide on her trial results.

Ashlyn cringed. *Dammit!* In her rush to get away from the office, Ashlyn had forgotten to send the update to Richard.

She didn't want to deal with either of them. Ashlyn shut her eyes, shut them both out, cutting off their petulant demands.

Ugh. She slouched lower in her chair. Turned out the library was a refuge, but no fortress, against intrusions. She didn't have the strength to deal with any of it. She chose to ignore the outside world, stuffing her phone into her backpack and continuing on with her mystery.

Why disappear?
Who was the passenger?
Where has Rory Mannix been for twenty years?
And why come back to San Francisco now . . .

". . . weeks before dying . . . for real this time," She whispered, as much a statement as a question.

When she looked back at her laptop, her screen was blank, and then a completely new set of results appeared. Ashlyn cocked her head, perplexed. *What did I click on?*

Ashlyn wheeled down the page. Eye-catching articles of clothing streamed by with captions that claimed they were feature pieces from various Rory Mannix collections.

"But these are all dated post-1992," she said breathlessly.

Well, now this is interesting . . . Ashlyn continued to scroll through the images.

Or, rather, the *images* of images. She realized that she wasn't viewing the actual documents and complete files. Ashlyn checked the URL. The domain belonged to the Academy of Art University, to which she didn't have access. Ashlyn looked around for Lin. *How am I seeing this?*

Several references with the phrase "the Mannix Label" in bold type tap danced across her screen. Like the mesmerizing *Riverdance,* the tapping began slowly, growing persistently to a heart-swelling thunder . . . Had she struck gold? She dialed the wheel further down the results, realizing she didn't care *how* she was able to view the private school's library catalog.

She leaned in to admire a purple crushed-velvet gypsy top. Then zoomed in as much as the image would allow. Staring at the photo, she became lost in the intricate details of the pattern, the Gothic-themed, bobbin-lace motifs in black lace, and the deep indigo thread embroidered down the long, slender sleeves, evoking a vampy look.

That's what the 90s looked like. Ashlyn nodded approvingly at the screen. *But the patterns . . . remind me of Lin's photos from Budapest . . . ?*

Time stopped and her mind was transported to Budapest. Ashlyn studied the piece draped over the model's skeletal frame. *The intention of the piece . . . it's not simply a reproduction of some icon or emblem of Hungarian culture. It's a . . . reinterpretation of their traditional costumes, of the nomads and explorers.*

"Amazing," she exhaled, not realizing she had been holding her breath.

Ashlyn examined several more pieces from unknown collections purporting to be the work of Rory Mannix.

A smart pant suit in subtle pastels, every bit as feminine as the timeless jacket and skirt combo, with strong, clean lines on the legs and lapels that conveyed strength and confidence, paired with the tapered waist to acknowledge the female form.

An eye-catching crimson, floor-length dress in satin, with delicate folds along the plunging neckline, the chiffon ensuring a flattering look, the exposed skin not overdone. Opulence expressed quietly, with clean and simple lines using elegant fabrics.

His pieces demonstrated a real departure from the working man/recreational man dichotomy of his earliest designs, and entered a new realm exploring the deeper questions of human desire.

"This is like a chronology of the evolution of his talent," Ashlyn said aloud, completely forgetting where she was. "These pieces hint at the raw form of core cultural beliefs . . . but expressed in the modern age." She chewed on her thumbnail as she dissected the designs, feeling like she was on the cusp of . . . *Discovering "the secret of his label."*

Ashlyn shivered as a sensation of knowing, of some bizarre connection between the subconscious and the cosmic, washed over her. His clothing spoke to her. With her finger hovering near the screen, she traced the lines along the waist of the crimson dress. The way the fabric was gathered gave the impression of a wide sash . . . *like a Japanese kimono.*

Ashlyn sat back in her chair, her mind grasping for the meaning of the sensation. *Primal, and untameable. It seems like some sort of hidden language?* But without words.

The voice—no, the awareness, *that speaks this language . . . where did it come from?* The one that clearly understood Rory's designs?

No answer came.

Unable to define the experience in words, Ashlyn reached a draw in a tug of war with an unseen opponent. Ashlyn sat back in her chair and let go. She was suddenly aware of being by herself in the library. Completely, anonymously, whereabouts unknown alone. No urgent requests competing for her attention in this moment. No nagging chore staring her in the face.

Tucked partway into her backpack, buried underneath some actual research papers, her sketchbook peeked out. The one that had been purchased and promptly added to the shelf of unrealized intentions to collect dust. The one with the schooner logo.

Ashlyn vibrated nervously. . . No. With excited anticipation, as she pulled it out of hiding.

She contemplated the intrepid schooner battling the stormy seas, fighting to survive. Then, easing her way in, read a few of the inspirational quotes that were printed on every other page.

> "There's the whole Buddhist thing about the essence of a bowl being its emptiness—that's why it's useful. Its emptiness allows it to hold something."

– Frank Chimero

Huh? Ashlyn tilted her head like a confused puppy. She tried another page.

"You don't think your way to creative work.
You work your way to creative thinking."
–George Nelson

OK, that one I get.

At first, she stared unenthusiastically at the crisp, white page in front of her before choosing a soft charcoal pencil from the "Artist's Collection," another rediscovered gift from David. Placing her pencil lightly on the paper, she began to sketch, her mind as blank as the page before her. Her pencil strokes were cautious, timid. *Boy am I rusty!*

After twenty minutes, she finished a sketch of the bookshelves, including the library cart across from her and the potted plant at the end of the row to her left. *Not bad.*

Encouraged by her first attempt, she boldly started another drawing, scrutinizing the wardrobes of other library patrons for ideas.

A flourish of color on the woman tutoring the teen. Let's bring out her eyes.

Let's put a button-up shirt under the hoodie for the teen hiding behind his thick glasses and Transformers *T-shirt.*

Ashlyn grimaced at these sketches. *Somewhat underwhelming.*

OK, how about a classy navy scarf for the hipster grad student at the checkout . . .

Just.

Like.

The GOM's scarf. Her shoulders slumped, her momentum deflated.

Frowning at the pieces she'd just sketched, she crumpled the papers in a silent tantrum. *This isn't bold. This isn't groundbreaking.*

She slammed the sketchbook shut, annoyed with herself.

Frustrated, she glared at a series of self-help books all lined up in a tidy row on the library cart. She read the titles on the spines. The letters seemed like hundreds of little daggers jabbing out at her, their messages boring under her skin: *The Happiness Project, Awaken the Giant Within, The Power to Shape Your Destiny . . .*

Ashlyn rolled her eyes. She wasn't in the mood for personal introspection at the moment. *Probably a good time to go home.*

The library would close soon, anyway. As she moved to gather up her things, a strap from a passing backpack snagged her journal of mystery data and tracking notes, sending it to the floor where it made a flat *thud.*

"Yep, time to call it quits," she muttered as she bent to retrieve the journal. On the other side of her table, a pair of colorful tribal-looking boots caught her attention. *Tibetan, maybe?*

The boots paused directly across from where she sat. *Oooo, those look amazing . . . and toasty, too.*

They remained motionless for what seemed like an age, then abruptly turned and strode, unhurried, toward the library's exit. She cracked her skull on the underside of the table as she went to pop her head back up.

Arrrgh! Her eyes watered while her hands reached up to rub the tender spot. Slowly, carefully, she pulled her head out from under the table for the second time. The entire contents of her backpack were strewn across her table.

WTF? Quickly, she rifled through the debris. Nothing was missing.

She looked around for the owner of the tribal-patterned footwear, but there wasn't a soul in the aisle where she sat. In front of her, lay her sketchbook. The one she'd planned to fill with inspired creations, but which currently held only a paltry three pages of doodles. The one she had just slammed shut, utterly defeated.

The book sat open to a fresh page, where ghostly letters screamed:

You will die in that cage!

24

Serenity Now

Her hands shaking, Ashlyn reached for the book and slammed it shut a second time.

"The library will be closing in ten minutes . . ." It was Lin, placing a gentle hand on Ashlyn's shoulder.

Ashlyn let out a helpless whimper.

"Omigod. Are you OK? You look white as a sheet!"

The look on Lin's face did nothing to ease the terror of being threatened by, what appeared to be, a very corporeal pair of boots.

"Did you . . . see . . . I just saw . . . someone. They were wearing—," Ashlyn stammered.

"You're the last one in here, Ashlyn." Lin shook her head slowly. "I didn't see anyone else."

A tall, lanky guy in an orange, puffy jacket poked his head in through the front doors, obviously looking for someone.

"There's my ride." Lin waved at the orange puffy jacket wearer. "Do you want us to take you home?"

Ashlyn looked up at Lin, who frowned back, "Never mind, we *are* taking you home. C'mon."

"I'd love a ride," she said, and finally exhaled. Ashlyn gathered her things, feeling as though she was moving through water.

At the car, after shutting Ashlyn's door for her, Lin plunked herself in the front seat and leaned over to greet her boyfriend, Jeff, with a kiss before saying anything else.

"How was your day?" Jeff asked as soon as Lin was buckled in.

"Baah, my workshop in Boston keeps getting rescheduled." Lin rubbed her eyes. "The company wants . . ."

Ashlyn stared numbly into the dark window fronts of the shops as they passed, catching only snippets of Lin's day as she related it to Jeff.

"But, I got to catch up a little with Ashlyn," Lin said a few minutes later. "And help her with an interesting quest . . . ," she added with an air of mystery

Then she turned in her seat, suddenly sidetracked. "Did you have any trouble with the Wi-Fi today, Ash?"

Ashlyn turned to face Lin, a blank expression on her face. She had struggled to follow the conversation in the car, her attention thrashing randomly between the revelations of her findings and the message scrawled in her sketchbook.

"Huh?"

"I was just telling Jeff that we had some wonky stuff happen with the library computers. Did you notice anything?"

"Um. I dunno." Ashlyn's mind was stuck on the sketchbook.

As they pulled up to Ashlyn's apartment building, she gathered her wits enough to string together some complete sentences. "Thanks for the ride, Jeff. You've been a great help, Lin. Thanks."

"It was fun, Ashlyn. We should get together."

"Yeah," Ashlyn said, finally landing back in the present. "Yeah, I'd like that."

She gave a final wave as they pulled away and dashed up the stairs into the building.

In the safety of her apartment, she allowed her mind to rest, silencing all thought. The apartment was dark, only the hum of the refrigerator intruded. *David's still at kickboxing, right.*

Ashlyn flicked on the lights and bolted the door behind her, then absently dropped her keys into the decorative tin plate, which made a wretched, hollow and off-key sound. But it signaled that she was home. She nervously eyed her backpack. It lay in front of her, cutting her off from the rest of the apartment. She twitched nervously, indecision taking hold.

"Baaahhh!" She lunged at the pack and yanked out the sketchbook, dropping the pack on her foot. She ignored the pain, as she furiously flicked through the pages. The message, scrawled in her sketchbook by some unseen hand, wasn't there. Her legs nearly gave out as the tension instantly evaporated.

"Owww," she moaned, a delayed acknowledgment of the bag full of heavy books crushing her foot. She momentarily stopped rubbing her foot when she noticed an eerie glow remained on the offending page. It was like a spotlight on the inspirational quote in the corner of that page. The quote was:

"The only thing keeping you from getting what you want is the story you keep telling yourself about why you can't have it." — Tony Robbins.

What story am I telling myself? She was tired, way beyond reasoning her way to any kind of understanding. She left her book, her bag, everything in the hall where they lay and went to bed.

~

The next morning, she glanced suspiciously at her sketchbook peeking out from her backpack on the floor. She shivered, then glared at the book. *Mental note: I need a new sketchbook.*

And my foot still hurts.

She'd had no epiphany during her restless sleep, nor had she been able to divine the intent of the graffiti artist in the library. Leaving her sketchbook behind, she grabbed her yoga mat instead, deciding it would be best to fully immerse herself in meditative poses at yoga class after work. Her chakra tank was running low.

Ashlyn spent the entire morning in the quiet solitude of Lab #3, finishing the second test of the formulation she had started last week (and messed up repeatedly). She was about to start a long and tedious titration when a mob of lab coats came clattering out of a door down the hall. She got to her little glass window in time to see Matt scurry over to the eyewash station across from her door.

As soon as the seal on her door released, she could hear his yowling, which told her the water wasn't giving any relief.

Over the wailing and excited voices, Budhil tried to get their attention, to bring calm to the team. Ashlyn looked to Budhil for an explanation.

"It is chili oil. He has splashed it in his eyes," he said, exasperated. "If he vould just calm down, I have some milk right here."

"We're testing different food stains against the stain-resistant fabric treatments," Carlene explained. "And Matt, here," she rolled her eyes as she pointed at him, "used his finger to wipe away a drop of the chili oil from the rim of a test tube."

"I forgot! And then I scratched an itchy spot. Near my eye," he whimpered.

It took three lab associates to restrain Matt's arms and administer a glass of milk to the inflamed eye. Meanwhile, Budhil stood in front of him, patiently reassuring him, "No, there will not be permanent damage to your eye."

After about five minutes more of fussing and carrying on, Budhil shook his head, ready to move on. "OK, Matt. Please sit out here for a few more minutes and rest your eyes."

Turning to the team, he said, "The rest of you, ve vill need to clean up the mess and reattach the electrodes."

Kendra threw her head back with a heavy sigh. "Awww man. It took us six *hours* to get all those leads to line up."

"I've got time, I'm between reactions. I can keep an eye on him," Ashlyn volunteered. "Oh. Sorry." She looked over at Matt sympathetically. "No pun intended."

"No worries," he replied.

She led him down to the coffee station, where he slumped down in a chair and held the cold compress over his burning eye. "I knew it was just chili oil, but it kept getting more and more intense! I hope Budhil doesn't boot me from the team."

"That's not up to Budhil," interrupted Richard, who appeared from around the corner. "Unless you know of any electrical engineers who are less clumsy, your position on the team is secure." He smiled, clapping Matt firmly on the shoulder. "Then again, if we had more safety-conscious associates, like Ashlyn, here. . ."

He winked at her, then pulled his phone out of his pocket and excused himself.

Ashlyn froze, dumbstruck. When Richard was out of sight, she mouthed the words, "What the hell?"

"You mean the veiled 'watch your back' comments? You know that he's really just a smarmy salesman, right? It's all about PR. And reminding everyone that he's in charge," Matt said.

"Does he wink at you, too?" Ashlyn frowned.

"Oh." He looked truly dismayed, "I missed that. Not cool."

"How's your eye?" she asked, happy to feel like she had *someone* in her corner.

"Meh. It's fine. I might just hang out here." He reclined in the chair, and added with a touch of sass, "Kendra wasn't kidding, those sensors are a pain in the ass to attach!"

~

Late again, dammit. She would've been on time for class, except for Richard's 4:58 p.m. email asking, again—*double damn!*—for her weekly reports.

Sighing heavily to herself, she stood in the doorway of the yoga studio, weighing her options. One of two spots remained: front and left, or front and right, of the instructor. *Lovely.*

Taking the shortest path, she tiptoed her way through the minefield of bodies doing the warm-up stretch, and rolled out her mat just as Sanjay greeted the class.

"Velcome. Now, please, join me . . ."

With that, he stood and the class followed suit. He took a deep breath, and swept his arms wide and high above his head. "Open your heart-center. Take a deep breath to fill your lungs."

Ashlyn, along with the other students, obeyed. She immersed herself in the choreography of each pose: aligning her outstretched arm over her knee in Horizon; squaring her hips and feeling the energy of the earth surge through her as she stood, motionless, in Warrior II; fixing her gaze on one spot on the parquet floor to keep her balance in Eagle Pose.

Yoga is wonderful. She smiled inwardly.

Her mind and body were consumed with the task of achieving the perfect balance, the perfect form, a perfect stillness in her mind, body, and soul.

"Open your heart-center and feel your spirit flow," Sanjay guided the class.

Ashlyn pictured her breath as a white, silk ribbon, dancing and spiraling, carefree in her inner space. *Ommmmm.*

"Now," Sanjay's voice was soft but commanding, "sit deeper into the pose."

The ribbon continued to dance. In Ashlyn's mind's eye, it settled on the shoulders of the petite woman with the pixie haircut. Paired with a vibrant blue top, the white silk accented the ample bosom, neither muting nor amplifying her features. *Hmmm, stunning. I should sketch that.*

"Pull the elbows away from the chest," Sanjay instructed, "and lift your entwined arms up to the sky."

Free to imagine, to explore, a part of Ashlyn began to sing inside.

"Keep your chin up. Hold your balance by looking straight ahead through the diamond-shaped vindow vhere your wrists meet."

Ashlyn inhaled deeply, filling her lungs as directed, and sat deeper into the pose as she exhaled. Drawing her arms up to the sky, her eyes searched for an anchor, somewhere to set her gaze to keep her balance. She found a chip in the glass surface of the mirror, right along the seam joining the two mirrors in front of her.

Fee-in. Cree-tim.

Unfamiliar words, whispered so close to her ear. She looked to her left and to her right. Nobody had moved from their pose. She hadn't even felt the breath of the words being whispered. It came from . . . *Inside my head?*

Then, a diabolical scream.

Everyone remained exactly where they appeared in the mirror. Ashlyn watched the color drain from her own face. The scream was audible only to her. The sound, her inner peace being shattered. Her inner sanctuary, violated. And every ounce of serenity she had managed to accrue during the last forty-five minutes, vanished.

The GOM's grim face glowered at her from the back of the room. His specter stood motionless, appearing solid, as real as any other person in the studio.

Ashlyn crumpled to the floor, helpless to break her fall, very nearly knocking over her neighbors like dominoes. Mortified, she looked up at the faces, now all focused on her.

"Sorry," she whispered, breathless. She scrambled to collect her mat, her water bottle, her towel, and the last shreds of dignity that might be lying around.

Averting her eyes from the class and from the mirrors, she shuffled out of the studio and into the frosty change room. She sat on the bench, trying to hold it together, trying to compose herself, gulping in air, her breaths more like hiccups. Her hands and feet went numb in the cold. Panic began to creep into her heart-center. Very near tears, she hurried to dress and to leave that place.

25

Where's the Love?

Ashlyn had kept her head down, avoiding eye contact with anyone on her walk to work. Or in the elevator. Or in the FiberWorx lobby. She grabbed a coffee from the office coffee machine and headed straight to Lab #3, avoiding everyone.

She'd almost made it into the secure space of Lab #3 when Richard intercepted.

"Ashlyn. Glad I caught you. How would you feel about sharing your lab with another associate?" he asked. "We're understaffed in personnel with adequate knowledge of FiberWorx safety protocols. I'd like you to pass on your expertise."

"I—"

"Great. It won't happen right away. In the meantime," he pulled out his phone and began thumbing the screen, "I've got a new set of trials for you to get started on. The list and the new deadline are in the email. That. I'm. Sending . . . Now."

He finally looked up from his device. "Just give me a shout if you have any questions." He gave her an "atta-girl" smile and continued on down the hall. The weak smile she'd offered in response disappeared as soon as his back was turned, and she concentrated instead on juggling the coffee, her bag, her coat, the paper files she'd grabbed from her desk, and her key card.

Inside the lab, her first sip of coffee woke her from her stupor. "This coffee has no love in it," she said flatly.

She put the coffee down to retrieve the email from Richard. It was like being dowsed with a bucket of cold water. No comments on any of the results he'd been haranguing her for. He'd simply moved up the next quarter's targets, which nearly doubled her workload. She still hadn't completed the previous set of trials! He would know that if he'd read her weekly report. *Surely he reads everything, even if he doesn't comment, right?*

Ashlyn shook her head in disbelief and muddled her way through setting up the next experiment. She worked continuously through the day, diligently tackling the backlog of trials to close the gap. *I don't want a new lab partner, I want a replacement, so I can move forward.*

Ashlyn wondered if, in the spirit of moving forward, she should confide in David about the GOM. *Would he believe me?*

But when she neared their apartment building at the end of the day, something held her back. She stared up at the dark window of their apartment, knowing David would not yet be home. The very idea of putting words to her visions gave her an uncomfortable chill. *Apparition? Vengeful spirit? Ghost?*

She could hear David's words in response: *Delusion? Hallucination? I think you're working too hard.*

~

Ashlyn spent the rest of that week isolated in her lab. Outside of work, she resorted to timing her exits and entries around David's. With each passing day, she kept more to herself, fearful the GOM could appear anywhere, anytime. Her nightmares were intruding into her waking hours.

At the week's end, Ashlyn could bear no more. She needed to confide in someone. Confide everything. David. The GOM. Being trapped in Lab #3. She needed to go home, to Moss Beach.

She raced to her apartment, frantic to get her things together before David came home. She flung a few essentials into her overnight bag and hustled off to find her car keys. She fished wildly around inside the curio table drawers, searching but coming up empty.

"Arrrgh!" She slammed the drawer shut. "What the hell are all these keys *for* anyway?"

Hands on her hips, she fumed, trying to recall the last time she'd had her car keys. That's when she remembered the GOM's newspaper and her journal full of disjointed threads of the story of

Rory Mannix. She grabbed the newspaper, her journal, and her laptop and zipped them into her overnight bag.

With a renewed sense of urgency to get away, she stomped back to the curio and yanked the drawer open, sending the contents sloshing forward. There they were. The keys she'd been hunting for. *Right there, plain as day.*

Ashlyn perked up as she heaved her bag into the car. The promise of distance, to gain some perspective, gave her hope. *A trip home will help me sort this all out.*

It was about an hour's drive to her mother's place in Moss Beach. If she left now, she would be there in time for a hot toddy. When she was settled behind the wheel, with the key in the ignition, Ashlyn dialed her mother.

"Hi Mom," Ashlyn said, with as much cheer as she could muster.

"Oh, my goodness, Ashlyn, sweetie, what a nice surprise," her mom replied.

Ashlyn hesitated. *What surprise? I call often . . . enough, don't I?*

Ashlyn usually called on Sunday evenings. Usually, but not always, or maybe just a couple of times a month, or maybe just sometimes.

"Huh? Oh, yeah, I guess it's Friday evening. Usually find us in the pub on Friday evening, riiiight," Ashlyn mused. "But not tonight!" she said brightly.

"So, does that mean you have other plans for tonight?" her mom prodded.

"Well, I hope to . . ." Ashlyn said, faltering a little, realizing that she had never even considered that her mom might have plans.

"It's always a good time for you to visit, Ashlyn," her mom cheerfully interrupted.

"You're the best, Mom." Ashlyn sighed with relief. She hadn't been aware of how tense she was up until that moment. She knew she wanted to be out the door and well on her way before David got home. Any delay would mean having to explain herself to him.

She never used to have to explain herself to David, or to anyone, for that matter. Once upon a time, she had been nobody's girl, confident and self-directed.

Where has that girl gone?

Over time, she had learned to fight a little less, back down a little more . . .

To what end? To keep the peace?

By placating him, am I getting the David I want to be with? Or am I just getting walked all over?

This thought made her angry. She was bottling up her own desires and letting her own personality erode away in a failed attempt to make *him* happy. She wanted that confident, former self to come back!

It had been a hard-fought battle to reclaim her *joie de vivre* after witnessing her dad's traumatic death. Ashlyn had always been Daddy's girl.

Without her father, her personal cheerleader, her mischief-making coach, and her sage adviser, Ashlyn was lost.

26

She's Come Undone

It was dark when Ashlyn left the apartment. She zipped through the electrified streets in her plucky little compact, a lime green Chevy Spark, heading south. It was exquisitely darker when she left the dense city streets, heading for the complete blackness that stretched for thirty miles between the furthest suburbs of San Francisco and the distant exurb of Moss Beach.

Ashlyn stopped religiously at her favorite pullout that overlooked the open ocean. Here, she found a little piece of heaven on earth. "You need to fill the well, and fill it often," her mother would advise her and her brother. "It's very easy to run it dry."

Stopping there always felt like reclaiming a piece of her soul. The hypnotic rhythm of the solemn and relentless crashing of the waves on the rocky outcrops, and the familiar smell of the sea air, recharged her deflated heart.

But Ashlyn wasn't going to stop tonight. She couldn't. She could barely drum up the courage to look in her rearview mirror out of fear she would be greeted by the dark stare of the GOM. She had no idea what had enraged him, what had prompted the cruel message he had scrawled in her notebook in . . . *what? Special ghost ink?*

And what was that word he whispered in my ear?

Her blood ran cold, and her knuckles went white as she gripped the steering wheel tighter. She pictured his grizzled old hands reaching for her throat from the back seat. Her well was definitely run dry.

"Damn you!" she growled inside the empty car.

Immediately she shoved the image from her mind. Ashlyn could not cope with another vision. She accelerated, anxious to be home.

It had taken her an hour and a half to get to Moss Beach. A sudden squall brought big, fat rain drops that pelted so hard and so fast that her windshield wipers couldn't keep up. When she finally pulled into the graveled driveway, her mother was eagerly waiting, standing under the porch light, on the phone.

". . . oh, here she is. She's here now," her mom informed the person on the other end of the line.

"It's David," she called out to Ashlyn. "He's worried."

"What? Why?" she shouted back. "I left him a note."

And she hadn't expected him to even be home yet. He was rarely reliable for much, yet remarkably reliable for going out on a Friday after work.

Completely worn out from the white-knuckle drive through the torrential downpour, and having worked herself into a lather expecting to see ghosts around every corner, Ashlyn fell into her mother's waiting arms and gave her a heartfelt and grateful hug. Ashlyn held on tight, resisting the urge to crumble, holding on to the tension, squeezing it, forcing it inward.

Cheryl waited until Ashlyn broke free before saying softly, "I told him you'll call when you're settled in." She opened the front door and led Ashlyn in. "I'm sure a text will suffice."

Inside, Ashlyn could smell that her mother had been baking. *Mmmmm, banana bread.*

"Are there chocolate chips in it?" Ashlyn shouted toward the kitchen with mock accusation.

"Why, yes, I believe the chocolate chips add a *je ne c'est quoi* that brings out the rum in the hot toddy, don't you agree?" replied Cheryl, playing along.

Her mother's presence was comforting, but Ashlyn was not ready to open up entirely. She still couldn't bring herself to speak the words. To say the words, out loud, would make the nightmares seem more real, wouldn't they? She didn't want to give voice to the claustrophobic dreams of being locked in a dungeon, nor acknowledge the apparitions of a, now dead, grizzled old man who haunted her waking life.

She also couldn't face the downward spiral that was her relationship with David. That only left work to talk about. *Ugh.*

Sitting down at the table in the brightly lit kitchen, Ashlyn cupped the warm glass tumbler of rum-laced tea and drank in the aroma of fresh-baked banana bread.

"It really is a nice surprise to see you, honey," her mom said, breaking the silence.

"Oh, sorry, Mom, I was just . . . I'm a little rattled . . . still vibrating from the drive here. It was bucketing down!" Ashlyn replied.

"It sure was!" her mom agreed. "Let's go sit by the fire. It'll warm you up and calm you down," she said, leading Ashlyn out of the kitchen.

"I didn't check the road conditions before I left. And there wasn't a drop of rain in the city," Ashlyn began, then paused. Her mom was no dummy. She didn't need a weather report. She would most certainly know that something was up.

Ding-ding! A little bicycle bell sound tinkled from the phone on the breakfast counter. Cheryl casually went back to the phone and slid the ringer to silent without glancing at the screen.

Ashlyn looked at her mom's hand on the phone and then noticed a set of candles bunched on a tray and pushed off to the corner of the counter. Liquid wax still pooled in the middle. She looked over at the fresh banana bread cooling on the counter next to a tidy collection of baking dishes, all cleaned and drying on the rack.

"Oh shit, Mom!" Ashlyn said, pulling the neck of her sweater up trying to hide her face in it. "I've ruined your evening plans!"

Her mom smiled. "It's fine. I've already rescheduled with Antonio. But give me some credit, too. You wouldn't just rush out, last minute, on a whim. What's up?"

"Who's Antonio?" Ashlyn asked without thinking.

"Nuh-uh," her mom wagged her finger. "You first," she said, pulling her legs up to tuck them underneath the afghan. Her mom leaned back against one end of the couch, sitting so she faced Ashlyn.

Ashlyn slumped on her end of the couch, considering her mom's prompt, an invitation to spill her guts. That's what she'd come here to do, after all. But doubt crept forward into her consciousness: how much did she dare to confess? She squirmed to get comfortable, pulling her sleeves over her hands and sitting on them.

Where do I begin?

Finally, pulling her knees up to her chin and turning to face her mother, Ashlyn buried her face in her sleeve-clad hands and let the floodgates open.

"Ah, Mom, it's all turning to shit!" she wailed.

"David is a . . ."

"I can't . . ."

"I don't *feel* anything anymore. It's just . . . crumbling apart. Into roommates." Ashlyn looked up angrily. "And he's a shitty roommate."

Her mom handed her a tissue. "Honey, I'm so sorry. Matters of the heart, well . . ." She paused, looking at Ashlyn's sullen face. "Here." She handed Ashlyn the whole box.

After a moment, Ashlyn continued, speaking as much as she was thinking out loud. "And I think he's actually *happy*," she sobbed. "He doesn't see anything *wrong* with our relationship. He just needs someone to hang out with when he's not out drinking or gaming. I want more than that."

"As you should. I remember—," her mom began.

"And at work . . . well, I might as well be invisible," Ashlyn interrupted. She knew her mom was going to compare David to her dad. She didn't want to hear it.

"I can't seem to break the secret . . . promotion . . . code," she said, so mad she could barely get the words out. "Doesn't my work speak for itself? Do I *literally* need to sleep with someone to get anywhere? To be taken seriously?"

"And then . . ." She stopped there. The pain, like it was fresh and new, like in the coffee shop, boiled to the surface as she attempted to form the words "newspaper from 1992." She resisted bringing up the memories of the night her dad died. Neither of them needed to relive that pain.

Without the newspaper for context, she certainly couldn't mention anything about being stalked by a dead homeless man. *Can you even say that and expect people to take you seriously?*

No more words would come. Ashlyn reached for the hot toddy on the table. It was still warm.

Her mom stretched a hand across the cushions to rub Ashlyn's knees in a supportive-mom kinda way. "Sweetheart, I . . ." She paused.

Ashlyn's eyes were red, but she was no longer shaking with months—possibly years?—of bottled up emotions and pent-up frustration.

"You're exhausted, my dear. Why don't you go snuggle in under that hand-tied fleece blanket you always loved so much? I pulled it out for you." Her mom stood up from the couch, the crackle of the wood fire filling the silence.

"Tomorrow you can look through your collection of old stuff in the closet. That might take your mind off things for a while," she said, reaching for Ashlyn's empty glass.

As she headed for the kitchen, she added, "Maybe you could take your treasures back with you, too." She smiled pointedly, helping to lighten the mood.

"That's sounds like an absolutely fantabulous idea." Ashlyn stood up, too, wiping the last of the tears from her face. "Good night, Mom."

27

Monsters In the Closet

The next morning, Ashlyn woke up feeling refreshed. For the first time in a long time . . . *How long?* Since Janine had veered onto her own path, unmarked, with no road signs. *And without signaling.* A little laugh escaped Ashlyn, part headshake, part respect, as she rolled out of bed.

Speaking of signaling, Ashlyn hadn't texted David yet. *What are the chances that he'll see my ignoring his phone call to Mom the* same *as when he ignored my Mayday text?* She fired off a quick text: *Sorry, got caught up chatting with Mom. See you tomorrow.* She left her phone on the bedside table and headed downstairs.

She found her mother sitting at the breakfast table, nestled in a little nook off the kitchen, clasping her favorite mug: a Mother's Day gift from eons ago. On it were two goofy faces with crossed eyes and smiles missing some teeth, and in hand-printed letters the words *Special brew, Courtesy of Thing 1 and Thing 2*. A photograph capturing a happy time in all their lives.

Shuffling into the kitchen, Ashlyn interrupted her mother's reverie. "Good morning, Mom," she said cheerily.

Smiling, her mother nodded over to the counter, indicating *You know where to find the mugs.*

Ashlyn poured herself a cuppa, sat down next to her mom, and joined in staring out the window. It was foggy. It was always foggy here. The fog cast a mystical, but peaceful shroud over the streets and houses that zigzagged their way down to the ocean. On a clear day, the view from the kitchen nook offered slices of the sea below. The sea lay somewhere beyond, hidden behind a veil of mist, on this quiet Saturday morning.

Maybe it'll clear off later.

Clunk.

Her mom put her mug down heavily on the table, clearing her throat before breaking the golden silence. "How did you sleep, my dear?"

"Best. Sleep. Ever," said Ashlyn, adding a wide, Cheshire Cat grin.

"I'm so glad to hear it!" her mom said, sitting up and turning to face Ashlyn.

Ashlyn registered her mom's invitation to open up, but the visions and the nightmares were just too near, still too real and untamed. She needed more distance, a better understanding of the monsters she faced.

Yes, I really should let my mother in.

Ashlyn knew that sometimes . . . often, the moment we give voice to a thing, an idea, it becomes less menacing, less of a mystery. Speaking the words, we can hold them out, away from us and examine them. And silence the maelstrom of conflicting ideas firing all the synapses in our heads at once.

But I can't.

Not yet.

Ashlyn chewed on her lip, considering her options. The shoulds and should nots of opening up tumbled in circles like a pair of running shoes in the dryer, bashing each other and clunking against the sides of the drum, making a deafening racket, making a decision impossible.

"I spoke with your brother the other day," Her mom's voice was gentle and sweet, but her eyes were intent on Ashlyn's face. "He wants to know what we're planning for Christmas. Will—," her voice grew even softer, "will David be joining us?"

Ashlyn smiled wryly. "David won't decide what he wants to do until the last minute, you know that."

Her mom bobbed her head in a "Yeah-kinda-figured-that" motion.

"Well, Dylan and his family want to book flights from Chicago soon. He's looking forward to seeing you. *I'm* looking forward to family time with you."

Ashlyn stared off into space, a montage of fond Christmas memories playing in her private theater—the ones that had left a lasting impression of contentment, of happiness. Her heart grew heavy as she realized, in many of these memories, David was absent.

Her mom sighed and folded her hands in her lap, changing the subject. "You remember your collection of swatches and patches and patterns and old sketchbooks . . . oh my?" she asked, referring to Ashlyn's many boxes of old treasures.

That broke the torrent of thoughts cycling in Ashlyn's head. "Yes! I was hoping you still had my stuff!" Her face lit up again. "Is it all in the office closet?"

"Of course."

Ashlyn jumped up from the table and gave her mom a grateful squeeze, then grabbed her mug before disappearing into the office, at the front of the house.

As a kid, Ashlyn had loved to sit in the very grown-up-looking office chair. Her mom allowed her to sit there as long as she promised not to mess with the up and down. Otherwise, she could swivel 'til she puked (not on the carpet, of course).

Ashlyn didn't need to adjust the seat height now, but she gave the chair a gentle spin, just for old times' sake.

From the recesses of the closet, Ashlyn dragged out a series of boxes containing many of her childhood mega-projects: outfits and ensembles for epic fashion shows for all seven Linie dolls; furniture upholstery and window treatment plans for the Linie mansion. Her mom had finally drawn the line when Ashlyn started bringing in her brother's Lego to build the Linie mansion. Ashlyn smiled cheekily to herself, recalling how incensed Dylan was that she had taken his Lego. *For the Linie mansion, no less.* Happy memories. But all these things had happened before the accident.

When they moved to Moss Beach, Ashlyn lost her bay window, but her mom had offered an 8-foot-square area of the office, plus the space under the drafting table, exclusively for Ashlyn and her projects.

Kneeling in front of the closet, Ashlyn looked at her miniature design space. She shoved the mega-project boxes up against the wall, recreating the kid-size studio and hoping to recall happy memories. No memories came back to her. There were no images of a laughing child, chattering happily to herself. No makeshift runway for her Linie models to strut across. No wide, excited eyes staring up at her mother, eager to announce the details of the fashion show. Ashlyn had made no such happy memories to recall. Her love for her projects had died with her father. She slumped back onto her legs.

With a sigh, she brushed away the bangs that continued to droop limply over her eyes as she stared into the closet.

Aha! There's the box! My sketchbook from Dad should be in there.

She shuffled the large cardboard box out into the light. For a fleeting moment, she thought she might be disappointed when she opened the box, that the anticipation had grown too big, and all for naught. Maybe there were no answers here.

Slowly, she unfolded the box lid and reached in. She pulled out a series of shoe boxes, each stacked neatly inside the larger box, each containing the detritus of Ashlyn's childhood. A small plastic box lay at the bottom. Her most prized possession. She snapped open the little blue lid and smiled to herself. *Right where I left it.*

Her best sketches were in that book. Her masterpieces. The gypsy-style skirt with lots of plump ruffles, the stone-washed overalls with a crop top, and more, filled the pages of the well-loved sketchbook. Even the cover was adorned with doodles and kooky symbols.

"Gothic, Celtic, zodiac, alchemy," she recited as she ran her fingers over the doodles.

"Seven Planetary Metals…" At this one, she laughed. "Guess it's no surprise I went into chemistry."

"What's this?" she said, pulling out a loose sheet.

On it, a solitary doodle she didn't recognize, carefully rendered in the center of the page. Angular lines, mimicking the coarse letters of ancient runes, formed a peculiar symbol. The crisp, straight lines of the symbol, emphasized by contrasting shades of light and dark graphite, gave it a mystical air. And even though the drawing was done in pencil, there were no smudges. It very nearly floated off the page.

Treasure in hand, she swung her legs around to sit cross-legged, her attention focused on the drawing. Something familiar, yet primal, stirred in her gut, filling her with a light thrill. A sense of harmony, of coming home, washed over her. She got butterflies. The good ones. The ones that tell you you're on the right track. She was about to put the container on the floor next to the shoe boxes, when a newspaper clipping, which had been stuck to the bottom of the container, unstuck and fluttered to the floor.

Ashlyn picked up the folded clipping. Holding it close in the dim light of the closet, she saw the bold letters of the headline:

Super Star Designer Goes Super Nova

It was her dad's story, again, different paper. The same two headshots of the firefighter heroes stared up at her from her shaking hand. The spark of exhilaration in her gut was doused, like someone had thrown a bucket of ice water over her. She closed her eyes, not wanting to remember any more. She curled into a ball, and wept.

When the tears wouldn't come anymore, she picked up the clipping again.

> Initial reports stated that the remains of only one body were found at the scene, though eyewitnesses claimed that there had been a passenger in the car at the time of the accident.

The article that Lin had read excerpts from in the library. Ashlyn hadn't actually viewed it with her own eyes. She blinked hard, forcing the tears out to see more clearly.

> When asked, investigators stated they had collected the remains of one body, recovered from inside the car, but could offer no further details . . . waiting on the coroner's report . . .
> — Jonathan Walker, *San Francisco Daily Star.*

Her heart aching, she flipped over the clipping from the night of August 13th, 1992. On the folded underside, the photo of her sullen little face, framed by the window of the pumper truck. Reflections of the flames danced on the sides of the fire truck. Tears threatened again as she read the caption under her picture:

Hero's daughter a witness to the spectacular explosion.

Holding it close she noticed, perhaps for the first time?, that this was not the same photo as the one in the GOM's newspaper. This one was zoomed out, taking in the whole scene. So many people had been gathered around the crash. Police, fire, ambulance, of course, but also a huge number of curious onlookers.

She wiped at her eyes, trying to dry out the watery film. Her eyes red and sore from crying, she couldn't trust what she was now looking at. There was a face, almost hidden in the trees, almost, that bordered the park.

That night in the pumper truck came back to her, as real and vivid as though it were yesterday.

From her perch inside the truck, she watched the people gathering around the crash. Her eyes moved slowly over the crowd, seeing the people point and shake their heads. She followed the string of faces moving away from the scene, toward the park.

At the end, there was a man . . . near the trees . . . on the fringe of the scene of the accident. The man wasn't wearing jogging pants or a sweatband like other bystanders who had emerged from the park, he was dressed in all black: a slim-fitting black turtleneck, black leather coat, black jeans. He caught her looking at him, so Ashlyn quickly looked away.

A bright flash suddenly lit up the sky. For a moment, the world was washed out by a brilliant light with a strange symbol made of a silver, liquid flame, burning in the center of her vision. *It's so bright.* Ashlyn had to look away. She looked back to the man in the trees.

He saw it, too.

The man tossed his head to get the thick swath of dark hair out of his eyes. For a brief moment, his intense blue eyes locked on Ashlyn's, then he slid backward into the trees, disappearing into the shadows.

Ashlyn remembered that moment, captured in the photo, when she had been in the truck, staring out. The young man in the trees seemed as though he was taking one last look on the scene before slipping out of existence, swallowed by the staggered trunks of the cypress trees.

They had both witnessed it. The ephemeral symbol that appeared in the newspaper photograph, reflected on the side of the fire truck. She had drawn that symbol, the last sketch she ever drew before locking it away in her box of memories.

Ashlyn's mouth went dry and her hand started to tremble. The newspaper clipping made a fluttering noise that echoed the sickly panic rattling through her entire being. She had known those eyes all along.

What else had she locked away that night? What other terror was lurking beneath the surface? Her stomach squeezed itself into a tight knot and the room started to spin.

28

What's at Stake

"The journey . . ."

A voice, in the nothingness that surrounded her. The words, spoken barely above a whisper, echoed off the blackness.

". . . cannot be shared."

A voice. Inside her private dungeon. She'd never heard words spoken here before. She couldn't identify the voice, but it sounded familiar.

A wall took shape off to one side of the heavy door. It was a featureless, cinder block wall.

"The destination is a profound secret."

Hard-edged lines, like slashes, appeared. Graffiti-like letters written by an invisible hand.

"The fate of the soul is on the line."

The slashes began to burn through the blocks of cold stone, slowly coming together, taking the form of the symbol—the one from her drawing all those years ago. As the last lines appeared, the first scratches were deep gouges, glowing white hot as molten lava and dripping onto the ground. The air was getting thin in the searing heat.

Like the heat from the inferno that had engulfed her father.

She raised her arm defensively, the light was too bright, too intense. She turned her head, averting her eyes. She didn't want to see.

29

Opportunities Are Seized

Her weekend escape home to Moss Beach had been fruitful, but hardly an "escape." Along with the other doleful faces of people reluctant to face a new work week, Ashlyn stared, glassy-eyed, as she waited silently in the One-Shot Espresso line. Fresh nightmares, darker and deeper, raising more questions than answers, had consumed her thoughts all the way home. And all along her morning commute.

". . . The journey, ees a process." Marty was speaking to her.

She wasn't paying attention.

". . . To know is a profound secret," he continued.

"Huh? Secret process? Marty, your coffee is divine, I wouldn't dream of going anywhere else," Ashlyn replied absently.

He gave her a funny look as she waved and turned toward the FiberWorx office.

~

It had taken some effort, like deliberately setting a reminder to *ping* on her phone when it was time to check in at the coffee station, but the habit was starting to take hold. She answered the *ping* today, and was rewarded with a lively conversation already underway.

"Have you seen this, Ashlyn?" Carlene asked, almost yelling at her.

"Uhhh, seen what?" She recoiled slightly at the finger pointing at her.

"Management posted a new position. They're looking to hire."

Ashlyn blinked, unsure what crime had occurred. "And that's bad because . . . ?"

Seeing that Ashlyn was clearly out of the loop as well, Carlene's accusing tone switched to outrage, inviting Ashlyn to join her in feeling offended. "They've posted the job ad on the FiberWorx *public* website and a few job-hunting websites like HireIndeed.com. But it's *not* posted under New Jobs on the Intraweb or bulletin boards outside the coffee stations, *like it's supposed to be.*"

Ashlyn felt the blood drain from her face. Why did she have a shrinking feeling all of a sudden? "Let's see the ad. Do you have a copy?"

"Yes. I printed it out," said Carlene.

"And *I* made copies and pinned it on all the bulletin boards on every floor!" Kendra announced, fired up with self-righteous indignation. She raised a hand that held a beefy looking stapler, then smiled devilishly. "I used those extra long staples so it'll be a pain in the ass to pull 'em off."

Ashlyn took the sheet from Carlene and read the job description. As she read, her expression darkened. The volume in the coffee station lulled.

"Does—," Ashlyn's voice cracked. *Ahem.* "Does anyone know if this position is for QA/QC or R&D?"

The other research associates looked at each other. Kendra rubbed her own arm, as if uncomfortable. "R&D. Richard was asking if any of us could recite safety protocols 'chapter and verse, like Ashlyn.'"

"This position, Ashlyn," Carlene pointed at the prerequisites, "is beneath you. You've got over five years of experience."

Ashlyn's shoulders dropped, weighed down with the realization she'd been overlooked, again. And worse, she was certain Richard had as much as told her she would be training the person who would ultimately take the position she'd been vying for. She wore the sting of it on her face, making no effort to mask it. What they didn't know, couldn't know, was how deep the wound cut.

Combing over the words on the sheet, she could've sworn the job description came directly out of her most recent Performance Review and Personal One-Year Development Plan. With the exception of community volunteering and having a professional stamp, like the engineers did, she had everything they wanted.

Why does it feel like I'm doing everything right and I'm still getting the shaft?

"Thanks." She handed the sheet back to Carlene, offering a weak attempt at a smile before returning to her lab.

She walked stiffly, holding everything in, until she could shut the door to her lab—she might as well accept it, *her* lab—and waited to hear the sound of the air lock sealing shut. She glanced out the small, one-foot square glass portal in her door, then rolled out of view. landing with her back pressed against the adjacent wall. Alone in her silent lab, what had become her one remaining refuge outside her apartment, tears began to well up. She'd had one letdown after another lately. Surely, she was due for a victory, somewhere in this life!

Through watery eyes, she looked all around her, at sterile surfaces, blank walls, empty vials and jars, empty room.

Ashlyn wiped her eyes as she shuffled toward the lab's computer, then slumped into the chair, her mind numb. Hesitantly, she pulled open the small desk drawer, where the pads of paper and pens were kept. She pulled out the copy of her performance review form, the one that HR uses to streamline the review process, and reread her comments and proposed goals for the coming year.

Yep. Almost verbatim.

She shoved the paper away and turned on the screen.

Bzzzt.

A text from Budhil: *Coffee meeting?*

She ignored it.

The next set of sequences in the trials she was validating flickered at her from the screen. She half-heartedly tapped the Down arrow to see how many more lines of instructions lay ahead. *How far to the end?* She had as much to go as she had done.

Going nowhere fast. She tapped her way back up to where she needed to start.

She didn't feel like starting. She pushed away from the desk and walked around the divider to the back side. The GOM's scarf snaked across the line of pins, his twenty-year-old newspaper lay on the table. A few colorful strings crisscrossed the divider, held in place by metal push pins, connecting random scraps of information and some images she'd printed out. All pieces of the Rory Mannix mystery, hidden and silent. None of the items had any answers for her.

She picked up the scarf. Nothing happened. Nothing, it seemed, would touch her in here. Even the emotional upheaval she'd felt in the coffee station appeared to be on the other side of the sealed door.

Cautiously, she began playing with it, pulling it through her hands as she had watched him do, the way he had taunted her.

It was soft, but the threads were strong, and there were no snags or imperfections. *How old is this thing?*

Oh, it has a tag.

She hadn't noticed it before, hadn't thought to look—hadn't dared to look that close.

Thin, silvery-white stitches set against the midnight blue tag shimmered at her fingertips. When she pulled the tag taut, she saw that the stitches formed the stylized initials *R* and *M*. The subtle contrast of light and dark threads distinguished the letters, projected them outward against the recessed backdrop. Together they formed a unique symbol.

Her symbol. The one she'd meticulously rendered in pencil, and carefully stowed in her treasure box. Twenty years ago.

Rory's logo, his version of the symbol, was fused to the head of an old-fashioned key. The straight lines of the letters gave an edgy feel to the logo, and also bound them together, rigid and unyielding. The unified symbol played with the eye, like a painting in reverse, with the foreground squeezed to a point and the detail expanding outward in the background.

Ashlyn stared in stunned silence at the symbol.

Then she tentatively glanced at the two faces on the twenty-year-old newspaper pinned to the wall.

I need some answers.

Both remained silent.

I'm just wasting time here. What I need, is to get back to work.

Ignoring the eyes of young Rory Mannix, Ashlyn looked to her father's image for comfort.

You just gotta face it head-on.

She squeezed her eyes shut and opened them again, willing herself to take back the reins and bring her life back under control.

She replaced the scarf on the pins and went back to the lab computer. Taking a deep breath, she opened the company's public webpage to look at the job posting again.

The job description indicated a candidate's resume should include ". . . demonstrated contributions to the profession and the community at large." *Maybe it's time I volunteer for one of the steering committees with the San Francisco Association of Commercial Chemists.*

And what else?

She'd seen an ad looking for volunteers in the community gardens across the street from the City College library. *Gardening? What the hell, why not?* She straightened her back and wiped away the salty residue under her eyes. For now, that would get her moving forward.

On her way out at the end of the day, Ashlyn stopped at the little food court on the second floor of her office building. She grabbed a stale ham and cheese sandwich, which, when she was desperate enough, would be enough to sustain her.

She texted David: *Have a meeting. You'll have to make your own plans for dinner.*

30

The Devil Is in the Details

Focused on her mission to be the master of her destiny, Ashlyn strode out of the office building at 5:15 and headed straight for the library. She plucked one of the phone number tabs off the poster requesting extra hands to help with the community garden and began to dial.

"Voicemail." *Sigh.*

Fine. She was determined to make something happen so she left a message and typed in a reminder to follow up. Before she locked her phone, she noted that there was nothing from David.

Good.

Suddenly feeling very hungry, Ashlyn pulled the emergency rations from her purse. She stood for a moment, staring at the bulletin board while munching away, scanning the For Sale and Roommate Wanted ads, then moving over to the Upcoming Events board. Starting in January, Smoking Cessation, Highland Dancing for Beginners, Weavers' Guild AGM. *There's a veritable cornucopia of things to try out!* She smiled.

The promise of new beginnings helped sweep away some of the sadness and disappointment of the day. The happy thought, however, was quickly replaced with disgust as she realized the sandwich she'd bit into was sucking all the moisture out of her mouth.

"Awww-ack!" It was beyond edible. She dumped the offending sandwich in the nearest trash can and gagged a little.

"Onward."

Leaving the sandwich and disgust behind, she pushed firmly on the glass door and walked confidently into the library. She hadn't expected to have this time for herself at the library. She was elated. She made her way to her table, determined to continue with her mystery.

OK. I know who he is. And who he was. *But what happened in the meantime?*

Ashlyn flipped through the notes in her mystery journal. During her last visit to the library she had jotted down a series of call numbers for the images of Rory that appeared to be from a special collection or limited access database. Of special interest were the images that claimed to be Rory's creations post-1992.

A quick tour of the City College library told her she wouldn't be able to find hard copies in this library. But she was dying to get her hands on them.

"Hi, is Lin here today? She's one of your volunteers."

"No, I'm afraid not. Can I help you with something?"

Ashlyn hesitated, uncertain of the legitimacy of her request. Would she get in trouble? Would Lin?

"I have these call numbers and microfiche catalog references that I dug up from . . . your database." She hoped it was in their database. "Can you help me find these articles?" she asked, offering the sheet to the librarian.

"Hmmm, yes. Some of these might take some time, they're from Special Collections . . ." The woman skimmed over Ashlyn's list. "And this series is part of our interlibrary loan program. But everything's being digitized, so we can all share." she looked up and gave a comedic smile. "Isn't that nice?"

Then she wrinkled her nose to give Ashlyn the bad news. "So it's anybody's guess where they're at in the process."

Ashlyn breathed a sigh of relief.

The librarian pushed the thin-wired glasses back onto the bridge of her nose. "When do you need these?"

Well, yesterday, of course . . . but that wouldn't be reasonable . . .

"Whenever you get to them." Ashlyn shrugged.

Then, admiring the DKNY artwork on the librarian's glasses, Ashlyn blurted, "I love those glasses. The embellishments on the arms are so elegant."

"Flattery will get you everywhere." The librarian smiled.

"Oh, no, I—." Ashlyn blushed. "I really do like them."

"How about I get your email and I'll send you what I find as soon as I find it?" She winked at Ashlyn.

Ashlyn tried to shake the red from her cheeks. "That would be great, thank you," she said before nodding and withdrawing back to her table.

After tapping her pencil impatiently on the table for a minute, unable to think of what she could do to move her mystery along, Ashlyn flipped open her mystery journal to one of the back pages and began to doodle.

"I don't *hide* my drawings like a . . . some kind of draw-a-holic," she grumbled, recalling Janine's accusation . . . *Before she gave me . . .* Ashlyn remembered the purse-size sketchbook with the curly, purple lettering. Eagerly, she pulled it out, almost giddy. She admired the clean, smooth surface, hoping some inspiration would draw her pencil to the page and suddenly magic would happen.

Tap. Tap. Tap.

I got nothin'.

Ashlyn was staring off into space when the cheeky librarian walked by and winked. It gave Ashlyn a little jolt, and the surge pushed her attention back to the sketchbook. She played around with the elegant details she had seen on the woman's eyeglasses. The swirls and curlycues made her all happy inside.

Yeah, here we go. I feel good! She started to imagine the fabrics that would be amenable to such delicate details. The fine threads that could produce the effect. The life-setting or occasions that would call for . . .

Voila! My . . .

Wedding dress?

. . . WTF??!!

"*That's* certainly not happening any time soon!" She scowled and sat back, more disheartened than before. A bitter wave of frustration washed over her. She sat up and tore the page out of the sketchbook and tossed it in the trash.

Her heart lurched when she felt a gentle touch on her shoulder. It was the librarian. "I'm sorry, miss. We're closing in five minutes."

~

The next evening, Ashlyn arrived home early, surprising David.

"How come you're not at yoga?" he asked before shoveling a gargantuan mound of chili into his mouth.

"I got there too late," she lied.

"Want some chili?" He pointed with his spoon toward the pot on the stove.

She wasn't really hungry, but he sounded amiable. *His version of an olive branch?*

She helped herself to a small bowl, and sat at the end of the table nearest him. David's attention had returned to his iPad, though. She stared at him expectantly for a moment, but he was lost in his newsfeed.

She looked around for something to keep her busy. *If I sit here long enough, he's sure to notice I'm still here . . . maybe even decide to talk to me?* At least, that was normally how their conversations began.

The only thing within reach, tucked under, between, and around the house plants, was the collection of journals and periodicals and printed materials she'd been carting back and forth to work every day. She had every intention of, eventually, reading through everything before finally putting them away. She plucked the schooner book from the top of one stack. *Pages and pages of inspirational quotes I have yet to read . . . Good enough.* She shrugged.

Both sat in silence, save for the occasional snap of a tortilla chip. Ashlyn finished her smaller bowl first. She took one last look at David, refusing to break the silence. But, wanting to fix what was broken compelled her to do it anyway.

"All done," she said, louder than she meant to. "Thank you," she finished, lowering the volume.

No response.

Fine.

Ashlyn closed her schooner book and took her dishes to the sink.

"Oh, hey," David's cheery voice erupted. "That's the sketchbook I got you. I bought that in Houston."

"Yeah . . . yeah," Ashlyn stammered. His sudden acknowledgment of her presence caught her off guard.

"You know, I was thinking." He gave her a sharp look. "Yes, I was."

Ashlyn bit her tongue.

"I was thinking, maybe it's time to shake things up."

Ashlyn's heart did a little, quiet leap.

"What if we just pack up and move back to Dallas? The people are friendlier there. My old friends are there. I can find work anywhere and not have to work with half-wits anymore."

Ashlyn turned her gaze to the stippled ceiling. *That* would *solve several problems, wouldn't it? I could leave behind Lab #3. There are tons of chemical plants in . . . Houston. I wonder if Houston is on the table?*

And Houston is by the sea. I like living by the sea.

And maybe, maybe, *the GOM will stay here, in San Francisco? Maybe that's what he wanted all along, for me just to get the hell out of here!*

"Earth to Ash-lyn." David waved his meaty hand in front of her spacey eyes.

"I—uh. I think the idea has merit."

He smiled, a big, hearty smile. A smile of the warmth and depth she had been missing for some time.

31

Day of the Dead

Wednesday morning, Tornado David spun through the apartment, as usual, but he stopped at the door and paused. He tiptoed back to the kitchen in his dirty work boots to plant a light kiss on Ashlyn's cheek.

"Sorry about the boots. I'll get it later."

Ashlyn tried not to twitch as another clod of dried mud hit the linoleum floor.

Wednesday evening, however, David was at kickboxing and Ashlyn stayed late at the lab. And the dried mud stayed exactly where it had been left.

That night, they climbed into bed at different times, laying intertwined, but disconnected. Ashlyn and David were back on speaking terms, but, really, nothing else had changed. They still lead, essentially, separate lives, but shared the same apartment.

Thursday, there was no kiss goodbye in the morning, but David picked up her mail that evening. He left her pile in the usual spot in the dark apartment before heading off to the pub.

No note?

I guess that's OK, I'm just getting home now, anyway. She'd worked late, again.

Ashlyn curled up in her reading chair by the window, clutching the schooner sketchbook that had given her a glimmer of hope. But instead of opening it up, she chewed on her pencil and stared out the window, worrying that the small gains of Tuesday evening were already lost.

The sound of keys in the lock broke into her thoughts.

"The Day of the Dead Festival is tomorrow," David announced before the door had even shut.

"Yes. It. Is," she replied, her words stunted as her mind jumped ahead.

The headline *Relationship Saved by Street Festival* popped into Ashlyn's head.

During the festival, a mock funeral procession, attended by thousands of devoted celebrants, would parade along the city streets. Ashlyn adored every part of the event: streets adorned with ancestral altars, colorful and extravagant interactive art, entertainers, food vendors and artisans, all scattered along the procession route.

Revelers, masked and unmasked, would follow alongside, honoring death, some grieving, and others celebrating life. The curious—this is the group Ashlyn and David fell into—came to soak up the energy, to join the masquerade.

"Have you talked to anyone yet? Made any plans?" he asked casually.

Ashlyn's mind started grinding, her mouth twitched and eyebrows furrowed as she tried to grapple with the likely proposition: the usual plan. In festivals past, David's rowdiest friends and their latest girlfriends would meet near Mission Square and branch out from there in search of the loudest live bands and licensed sidewalk cafés.

"I, uh . . . no. No, I haven't made any plans."

So it was decided, they would attend the street festival together, with his squad, like last year. Like always.

~

A gathering of the usual suspects convened near the park where the funeral procession terminated. Ashlyn snapped her fingers, avoiding eye contact while she recited everyone's names— *aaaand . . . Jen! I think she's been with Steve since last year. Good for him.*

Four more familiar faces arrived in time for the motley crew to join the tail end of the procession, which had set out hours earlier. The human millipede swelled as it approached the main stage in the park, coming to a halt at a garish altar set up next to the stage where the participants bid farewell to their loved ones.

The ceremony ended with a volley of fireworks.

"YEAAAHHH!" crowed David as the first live performance kicked off.

David, Kevin, and Steve thrashed and played air guitar for the first set. Thankfully, the group remained on the fringe, poised to seek out other stages located along the parade route, particularly those venues that offered pop-up beer gardens.

That's what the Day of the Dead street festival was to David, just a big beer garden. He and his buddies had checked the lineup published on the *Seek and Destroy Music* web forum and had already agreed on which bands they wanted see. Before leaving the apartment, David had outlined to her which venues and which bands would be playing where and when.

A fine example of a results-oriented effort. Ashlyn was none too excited about the bands he'd listed. *Too bad none of you choose to apply this level of dedication to getting the jobs you say you want.*

"Alright, gents." Jason shook his head until his eyes were no longer covered by his long, stringy bangs. "Who's thirsty?" He pulled a small bottle from his jacket and took a generous gulp before passing it along.

David accepted the bottle and began heading up the street. Ashlyn waved the proffered bottle on to the next person, but encouraged the others to get their feet moving.

"This street festival is like a fashion expo," Ashlyn gushed. "The diversity. The creativity. It's so inspiring."

No one replied. The festival meant different things to different people, maybe they weren't seeing what she was seeing. For Ashlyn, the festival provided a fusion of culture and style, like a smorgasbord of expressions of individuality. It was like her morning walk to work, but on steroids.

Rachel—*Is with? . . . Jason!*—offered the near-empty bottle to Ashlyn.

"Maybe next one, thanks, Rachel," Ashlyn said, declining.

Rachel drained the last of the amber liquid and grimaced. Ashlyn grimaced with her, in solidarity.

The group continued their forward march to the midway beer garden where the road widened and *Rude Awakenings* were scheduled to play. This was the first of many stops planned for the evening.

Ashlyn played with the unopened package of earplugs she'd stowed in her pocket for this very occasion. In the meantime, she continued to ogle the festivalgoers. At the Day of the Dead Festival, people were blissfully happy, and it was *fascinating*.

There was a mom wearing her baby on her back and pushing the double stroller with the toddler and preschooler strapped in. She had ghoulish makeup and wore a fascinator, like Princess Kate. The kids had their faces painted, too: a sparkly unicorn and Olaf the snowman.

There was a business executive—*clean-shaven, Patek Philippe* watch . . . Yep, *definitely an* exec—dressed down in his favorite band hoodie. He carried his kinder-kid on his shoulders, while mom frolicked alongside in her designer leggings. The delightfully morbid skulls, wreathed in red roses, almost came to life as she danced.

There was a cadre of pirates waving tinfoil cutlasses and sabers at the more reserved festivalgoers hanging on the sidelines. And some broody teens in the alleys glowering derisively at the crowd, resisting "the Establishment's" call to conformity.

All these people here, the energy, the vibe . . . A perfect outlet to push back against the isolation and alienation that can intrude into everyday life. She rotated as she walked, as looking in every direction, entranced, drinking it in, feeling herself being drawn into it. David grabbed her elbow and drew her into a chair next to his. They had arrived.

Eli and Kevin returned to their street-side table, each carrying a tray of red Solo cups. David plucked his beer and Ashlyn's Vodka Red Bull from Kevin's tray.

"M'lady," he said with a crooked smile.

Here, in this perfectly incongruous space, everyday people could revel in freedom from convention, from expectation. Even she, admittedly, should just take that crooked smile at face-value.

"Thank you, kind sir," she replied.

Ashlyn recalled the Rory Mannix interview. *In Cosmo, he talked about the mystery of the human condition. This is it.* The collective energy, igniting a strong connection, binding together the mind, body, and spirit of willing souls. It took her breath away.

But it was fleeting, impermanent. She tried to name it, to describe how it felt, being steeped in it . . .

Feee-in . . .

Creee-tim . . .

Words, whispered into her consciousness.

A curse? A mantra? Strange words, and secretly whispered for a second time.

From where?

There was too much of a din on the street to hear anyone speak, to even attempt to have a conversation. But she'd heard the words, clear as a bell.

She turned swiftly to find the speaker. There was a wave of happy souls, a surreal world of masks and movement, prancing along the street. Was she the only one to hear it? All those around her were oblivious to the intrusion into the core of Ashlyn's being.

Ashlyn dismissed the trembling sensation. *My mind, playing tricks in this wonderful chaos.*

She closed her eyes and allowed herself to be swept back into the cacophony of lively chatter and music and drumming. She gave herself completely to the celebration of life surrounding her. Ashlyn could actually *see* the energy, the aura of this mass of humanity; it gyrated and swooned before her, as bold and lithe as the northern lights dancing across the sky. Never had she completely let go, and really immersed herself in the experience of the street festival.

The energy penetrated deep, and the ripples slipped easily past her wary mind and guarded heart-center. She was witnessing the naked expression of the human spirit in all its splendor. Its raw beauty. People unabashedly baring their souls, exposing their richest joys and the scars of their deepest sadness.

"Ash!" David yelled. He had been kind not to holler directly into her ear. "This set is over. Where do you want to go next?"

Over? I didn't even know it had started. Where had her mind been? For how long? The spell may have broken, but she wasn't upset at the interruption. No. She had been shown a doorway into a secret world and the discovery was exhilarating.

David was in his element. And he smelled of cheap beer. *Which means he'll be pawing me all the way home if we pull the plug now.*

"Maybe we can stop for one or two more bands on the way back?" she replied, deferring to the other girlfriends, who were singing the refrain from the last song and taking selfies.

David lit up. "Dead Wraith will be playing the Afterlife stage at midnight. Then we'll have time for another beer, and then head back to the car."

A death metal band, she sighed. *How did I manage to find a guy so desperately eager to push me away? And yet, here I am, still clinging on.*

Ashlyn chatted with the other girlfriends as they dawdled behind their partners en route to the *Afterlife* stage. Inside the corral of the street-side beer garden, Ashlyn ordered another Vodka Red Bull. She only half listened to the shouted conversations on all sides of the table. David and his besties were discussing their favorite lick from the Chopper Zombie set. Jen and Rachel swiped through the selfies they'd posted on Instagram throughout the night. One couple, flush from the excitement of the evening, excused themselves.

"Yeah, get a room, huh?" David said, loud enough to earn a quick scowl from Eli and his new girlfriend.

As they disappeared into the crowd, Ashlyn resumed playing with the red plastic cup that held her drink, barely touched. She absently etched stripes in the condensation with each quarter turn.

I can't remember the last time I felt . . . content *like this.*

Falling, melting into the essence of humanity had been a wonderful, powerful experience. And now, though it had passed, it left a trace of . . . *happiness.* A different presence, inside, emerged quietly. It spoke no words, it was just an urge, an invitation to her to come back, to this place, to happiness, again.

Her mind slipped away from the festival, grasping for the joy she had felt moments ago, but thoughts of her journal of mystery clues intruded instead. They swam around, pulling from her subconscious. *His inspiration came when he witnessed human nature, raw and unfiltered. His best designs followed after he escaped from the lights, from the center of attention. Anonymity.*

"To come to know the 'universal truths,'" Rory Mannix needed solitude, 'like a monk.'" *His own words from that interview.*

Not long after that interview, his popularity had begun to spiral beyond his control. She frowned. *It began to control him. His celebrity made it impossible for him to step back. A kind of self-made prison.*

The air became still and she became aware of a presence, a halting of motion behind her. The festival was still going strong and people in pairs and groups lumbered by, laughing, singing, some moaning, regretting the drunk food they'd hungrily devoured an hour ago.

But always the shadows and reflections dancing across her red cup were moving. Save one reflection. It stood motionless. It was close. It seemed to be blocking the heat from the heat lamp next to their table. No, not blocking. It breathed a chill into the space that the heater couldn't penetrate. The little hairs on the back of her neck prickled.

Petrified, she gripped the cup and pulled it in toward her, slowly. She cast an eye over the faces sitting at her table, still lit up with merriment, enjoying lively conversation. She sucked in her breath. *They can't see him.*

Trembling, a scream threatened to escape her throat. She lifted the drink to her lips, hoping that she would not see anything. But also, some part of her wanted to catch a clear glimpse of his reflection, so she would know that he was real, that she wasn't losing her mind.

No image of the scowling, grizzled old man materialized. When she replaced the cup on the wobbly table, the motionless shadow had vanished. She swiveled in her seat, expecting to see the back of a faded brown overcoat shuffling away into the crowd.

There was no one standing there. No ethereal figure darting into the merry revelers passing by.

32

I Am Watching

Eventually, the dwindling group, back down to six, extracted themselves from the chairs under the heat lamps. The crowd had thinned, but the streets were still alive with jubilant celebrants in somber masks. Ashlyn clung to David's arm, her legs threatening to buckle as they threaded their way back to where they had started. She cast her gaze to the pavement as revelers approached from the opposite direction. She didn't want to see any more skulls from the afterlife.

David stopped talking, briefly, to place his free hand over hers.

"Come over here and say that to my *face!* Pussy!" Angry shouts punctuated the cheerful air.

An ugly scene, unfolding on one of the side streets, grabbed the attention of everyone in earshot. A small crowd gathered around as a couple of college guys, unmistakable in their varsity jackets, puffed out their chests and postured like a couple of male sea lions defending their territory.

Jen rolled her eyes. The situation was escalating. She and Ashlyn kept their guys moving forward, hoping to avoid the scene altogether.

"Distract them and they won't be tempted to go be heroes and break up the fight," Jen whispered.

"Yeah, I could do without another trip to the ER," Ashlyn whispered back. One more ride-along to the emergency room and Janine's last count would be right: number three.

More shouts and the sound of shuffling feet. When the metal patio chairs hit the ground with an echoing clang, David refused to move farther away. The fight was on.

Whomp!

"Ummff!" A punch to the gut.

The crunch of leather bending and folding preceded a dull *crack*.

"Whoa," David said, craning over shoulders to follow the action. "Elbow to the face. Good move. Dropped him to the ground."

"I can*not* understand the need for men to express their maleness by beating the tar out of each other," said Rachel, shaking her head.

Revelers and meanderers closer to the scene began to push outward, into the growing crowd of onlookers.

BANG!

A shot rang out, cutting like a knife through the waning festival noises. Screams drowned out the drums and maracas as people nearby scattered.

"I feel sick," whimpered Jen. "Innocent people . . . getting shot."

David yanked his arm free the next instant, taking the lead and not hesitating to tackle the situation, whatever it was, head-on.

"Jason! No!" begged Rachel, holding on to his sleeve. It was no use, he easily shook her off and slipped out of her grasp. He did a hop-skip to launch himself forward, but looked back and shrugged, as if to say "I can't *not* go."

"Don't worry, Babe. We'll just see if we can help," he called back to reassure her.

Jen, too, clutched at her man's arm, but to no avail. "Steve! C'mon! What're you gonna do? Really?" she pleaded.

David and his buddies broke from their leashes and pushed into the crowd, toward the fracas. Helpless to stop them, the women stood dumbfounded. And afraid.

In these rare, fleeting moments, David reminded Ashlyn of her dad. They were both adrenaline junkies, both eager to get involved, but their motivations differed. The latter, eager to help, the former, eager to disturb shit. That's where their common traits started and ended.

Ashlyn heard sirens approaching from somewhere behind her, but her attention was set on what was unfolding in front of her. She watched intently as David pushed against the surge of bodies trying to get *out*. He was going *in*. She felt her stomach muscles tense. More sirens and lights appeared up the street.

"Get back!"

"Get *back*!"

Uniformed officers and firefighters swarmed the street corner and cleared a path for the ambulance.

"Why in the hell do they have to get involved every time there's a fight?" growled Rachel. "I have half a mind to just leave him to it, go home, and lock him out!"

Jen shook her head. "I don't know. Steve didn't even look like he wanted to go, but it's like he's gotta 'keep to the code,' or some stupid thing."

The police were swift in sorting through the curious onlookers, who were ushered on their way, and any witnesses who cared to give a statement. The tension in the air had almost dissipated when raised voices erupted again. Heads turned toward the voices in time to see officers roughly leading David and Jason out of the center of the commotion.

"Fine! I'm gone!" snarled David, straightening his collar.

"Just trying help out, man," Jason said indignantly.

Steve was close behind, but unescorted. "One shot fired. Missed everyone, near as we can tell," he said calmly.

Ashlyn sucked in her breath, unsure whether she should scream at David for being so reckless or run up to embrace him with relief. The gears in her mind jammed, she could do neither. Instead, she clamped her mouth shut and glared at him, standing rigidly on the spot where he'd left her.

"What?" David's swagger dulled as he approached Ashlyn.

Jen flung her arms around Steve's neck. "Are you ready to go?" he asked her softly.

"Yes, please," Jen replied.

The pair waved toward Jason, who was getting an earful from Rachel, then turned to Ashlyn and David. "See ya," Steve said.

Ashlyn shivered as a chilly breeze, coming off the bay, nosed up the streets. Turning up the collar of her jacket against the cool wind, she watched Rachel tear a strip off Jason. "So, were you helpful? Helpful guys always get shooed away, dragged off by the scruff by the cops?"

Jason didn't fight back. "Yeah, that was maybe not a smart choice."

He placed his hands on her shoulders and leaned forward to press his forehead against hers. Ashlyn couldn't hear what he was saying, but Rachel stopped frowning. After a moment of quiet words, she bounced to her tiptoes to wrap her arms around Jason's neck and squeeze him tight. Jason put his arm over Rachel's shoulders and led her away. He turned briefly back toward David and give him a wink.

"See, look, all is forgiven." David smiled at Ashlyn.

"They're newlyweds. It'll pass," Ashlyn said frostily.

The distinct sound of the air brakes of another fire engine arriving wheezed behind her. She had grown up with that sound. It gave her a sense of comfort, made her feel secure. She looked in the direction of the sound and saw that the fire truck blocked the street, mostly likely to limit any further disturbances spilling out from the street festival.

Her jaw dropped. *The GOM.*

The ghostly image stared at her from the window of the back seat of the pumper truck that had just pulled up. Exactly where she had been sitting when she'd watched her father get swallowed by blinding flash of light.

Time slowed. She was in a silent vacuum, where seconds passed by as minutes. It enveloped her as she stitched together the truth. The loose threads from her own life, that had begun unraveling on that night twenty years ago, spooled out before her, reaching back to that moment in time when she had witnessed her father's death.

The explosion.

The shock wave and the blast of heat that rocked the pumper truck. The debris slicing through the air and raining on the roof of the truck, pelting the window with terrifying cracks and delivering sickening wallops against the side.

That moment, etched in her memory, when the debris hung in the air and 12-year-old Ashlyn looked back toward the trees. That moment, when the mysterious figure slipped into the shadows, neither of them aware that the tragedy would bind them together.

There was more to that moment than she'd uncovered in her treasure trove in Moss Beach. The newspaper photo had demystified the enigma of the old man on the bench., she'd known those eyes forever. *He* was something to *her.*

But, she had wrongly assumed that she was nothing to him. More than twenty years later, the specter of the GOM, staring out the window of the fire truck, told her that he had seen *her,* too, that night.

He knew exactly who I was.

Twelve-year-old Ashlyn had no way of knowing that she would be the only person to witness the narrow escape of Rory Mannix. The only witness to refute his death.

33

Down the Rabbit Hole

Ashlyn was a wreck the next morning. The encounter had chilled her to the core. In the beginning, the GOM had just been a mean-spirited, random old man that she'd made the unfortunate mistake of making eye contact with. *The meeting was just a coincidence . . .*

Even after fitting the pieces together in Moss Beach, she had convinced herself that the GOM—*old Rory Mannix, rather*—was a deranged homeless man who had simply chosen someone vaguely familiar to target. She had happily deluded herself into believing that the story in the twenty-year-old newspaper was about Rory Mannix and her father, that *her* story was somehow separate. And that that chapter in her life was long ago buried.

It wasn't random at all.

A deathly cold ran up her spine. *How on earth did he find me, over twenty years later?*

She paced quietly around the apartment while David moaned on the couch. She could hardly hear him over the disjointed and unhelpful thoughts that clashed in her mind., .

Occasionally, the ghostly whisper *fe-in cre-tim* replayed, interrupting the torrent of thoughts. She wrung her hands, fretting, and forgetting why she had walked into the kitchen. She went back to the hall. Still pacing, up and down the hall, she suddenly caught a glimpse of her father.

Gasp!

It was her own reflection, of course. But it was enough to silence the incessant chattering in her head. She stared blankly at herself, lingering in front of the mirror, motionless. Waiting.

Get a hold of yourself.
Silence.
No jumble of thoughts crowding in for attention. In the quiet, the cold tension that had taken hold finally lifted. She gazed expectantly into her own eyes, letting the feeling of relief take over.

Something behind her in the mirror distracted her. She cocked her head to one side, her attention drawn to the warm glow cast from the window. It lit up the books stacked on top of the bookshelf, particularly those not yet sorted into their places on the shelf. Including the new sketchbook.

"I think . . . I'll go down . . . to my favorite café," Ashlyn said in broken, unsure fragments, "For some quiet reading . . . and . . . and get out of your hair."

Ashlyn smiled pleasantly at David, who still lay prone on the couch, as she scooped the sketchbook off the shelf.

She was lying, of course. She had no intention of going back to the café. It pained her to think that she couldn't muster the courage to go back there and wrap herself in the familiar smells and sounds of her favorite café. One day she would go back, but for now, it gave her the heebie-jeebies.

"Mmmf," he replied. David was nursing a hangover.

"Oy!" Half sitting up, he called to her, wincing. He reached pathetically toward the kitchen, where the painkillers were kept.

"Can you bring me some party smarties and a Gatorade before you go?" he asked sweetly from the couch. "Pleeeeease."

Without question or complaint, she obliged, too preoccupied with last night's visitation to worry about David. She gently placed the glass of Gatorade and two ibuprofen tablets on the table in front of him. Then grabbed her backpack, loaded with laptop, notebook and the GOM's newspaper. She added the new sketchbook and closed her pack before slinging it over her shoulder.

"Whoa," he said, suddenly taking an interest in her activities. "You got yer old chemistry texts in there?" he sniggered.

"Um, yeah. A textbook or two. Can't put anything past you!" she joked. "Budhil is working on some pretty cutting-edge stuff."

"Budhil? You mean Buddy?"

Sighing, she dismissed his disrespectful comment and threaded her arms through the sleeves of her white cashmere wool coat and put on a cute red crocheted winter hat embellished with snowflakes. As she pulled on her favorite black Hunter rubber boots, she decided she'd be better off keeping the peace and finally responded, "Yeah, Buddy."

She walked partway back to the living room. "I thought I should bone up on my fundamentals. It would be really great if I could get on the team working in Budhil's lab."

A foreign thought struck her suddenly: *Would it?* She'd pushed so hard, for so long, for a position in the R&D lab, and never questioned it. Never considered anything other than advancing into the R&D lab.

It *would* be really exciting to work on completely new ideas, doing groundbreaking work in her industry. And it *would* be really nice to be able to work next to Budhil. He was brilliant and easy to talk to.

Who wouldn't want to spend time with that kind of person?

She looked over at David again, unshaven, disheveled, and about to make some kind of derogatory remark about someone she respected.

"Buddy gonna give you a raise if you get outta that prison of a QC lab?"

I'll be damned, he has been listening to me.

But here we go again with the "You're not getting paid enough" digs.

She wanted to snap back with a cutting remark about his shrinking paychecks, but she resisted. "I guess we'll see what the Christmas bonuses look like this year."

At that she waved a mittened hand and quickly slipped out the door. Outside, she felt a blast of cold wind sting her face. That woke her up.

"Take yourself out on a date." This was the advice from the *The Artist's Way*, one of the many reference books she had recently cracked open after years of collecting dust on the bookshelf. *Sage advice, I think. I'm not backing down from a fight, I'm taking myself out on a date.*

After considering myriad places and spaces, she decided that she would brave the library again. She couldn't think of any other place where she was likely to find the meaning of *fein cretim*. *With any luck, Lin will be there to help.*

And the way the . . . hex? or mantra? or maybe it's a sacred site? is buzzing around my head, I'm not likely to get any peace until I find its meaning.

She looked up to their street-side window, picturing the moaning, groaning, half-man, half-zombie in tighty-whities she'd left inside.

Yes, library it is.

~

A long row of worktables, nestled end-to-end, ran down the center of the library, holding the building together like a spinal column. Stretching outward from the spinal column were the aisles of floor to ceiling shelves that held the library books. The shelves sat perpendicular to the spine, like rows and rows of ribs extending out from the heart-center. Here, at the heart-center, was "her" table.

Once settled, Ashlyn set to work on unearthing the meaning of *fein cretim* and how it related to the GOM. A basic search revealed that *fein* and *cretim* were old. They were the building blocks for Latin and Gothic and Celtic words, and even predated Sanskrit and Hittite,

"…and helped to shape many other languages emerging out of the Neolithic," she read from her screen.

Well, that doesn't tell me much. She frowned.

She scanned the list of results and read the brief excerpts displayed beneath. An abundance of websites offering astrological explanations gave her pause. Knowing her curiosity and penchant for paralysis by analysis, she reluctantly proceeded down the list of results, wary of going too deep down this rabbit hole.

Ashlyn wove her fingers together and stretched her arms as far up as they could reach to loosen the joints. She could feel the words in suspended animation in her consciousness, waiting to be revealed. *Fein cretim,* she was sure, held the answers.

Would the words explain Rory's disappearance off the face of the earth? Would they lead her directly to the connection between Rory Mannix and her father? *No, not Dad. It's me he's targeting. Remember, I need to ask the* right *questions.*

Ashlyn approached the question in the same way she ran her sequences in the lab, one variable at a time. This method, she knew, would produce a straightforward output: True, or False.

Nope. Instead, she found a dizzying set of vague concepts and circular logic. At the end of an hour, she had a copied and pasted a collection of barely comprehensible quotes about the metaphysical and journeys to self-actualization.

> "The journey that binds the earth to the sea and
> to the air, the harmony of body, mind and spirit,
> and brings one to know love, wisdom and
> truth."

> "The *fein cretim* stands for not simply inspiration,
> but for inspiration of truth. Without it one
> cannot proclaim truth."

> "*Fein cretim* is part of the cycle of initiations.
> Associations with the phoenix, fire and ignis . . ."

> "The point of light at the opening, and the
> journey leading to the path representing
> unbounded awareness, where perception is no
> longer within boundaries . . ."

> "the struggle for awareness"

> "the union of mind, body, and spirit"

> "a harmony of opposites in the universe"

But the concrete information, the logical conclusion emerging from rigorous testing and critical observation that Ashlyn sought, was absent.

How did I get from cutting-edge fashion to needing a . . . she squinted at the screen, sounding out the word *phil-ol-o-gist?*

She tried Google Scholar. Those results provided numerous academic papers, but without understanding what she was looking at, it was all just a jumble of hypotheses and suppositions.

> **Fein:** from two ancient words, "fe" and "en,"
> the first meaning "iron," in reference to the
> heart, and the second meaning "spirit". . .

None of the entries under *fein* occurred with the second word, *cretim.* She searched it separately.

> **Cretim**: "flowing spirit," or, more literally, an
> ancient Celtic word for "oneself."

This . . . cryptic phrase . . . doesn't appear anywhere.

Is it some hokey-pokey incantation? Do I recite it three times before walking over hot coals?

"This makes even less sense when considering the debaucherous life of one unhinged, albeit brilliant, fashion designer," she muttered.

It didn't help that Ashlyn had a boundless curiosity, about everything. Always wanting to know *more*, to achieve a *deeper* understanding. Even in her day-to-day work in the lab, she never felt like she knew enough. *Who tests the test methods?* It was enough to make anyone's head spin.

Glancing over her spreadsheet full of notes, Ashlyn realized that she had amassed several scraps of ideas that may or may not be a trail of breadcrumbs in her mystery. "Gah! I wish Lin was volunteering today."

So far, she had uncovered details of Rory Mannix's life *before* the accident: his dazzling ascent to fashion stardom; his great works on display at increasingly prestigious fashion events around the world; and his reputation tarnished by outrageous acts of defiance. Based on the evidence, Rory Mannix completely despised the fashion community who adored him.

There's nothing transcendental about this man.

She tapped her pen on the table with agitation. The same pattern of visionary brilliance followed by self-sabotage, repeated over four years as he showed his work around the globe. After Tokyo, he'd been to Sydney, then Prague, Istanbul, Milan, Dublin, Nepal, and finally to Moscow just before what would be his final show, in San Francisco.

Not ready to concede defeat, though, Ashlyn took a trip around the library that matched Rory's travels around the globe, exploring the ancient traditions of the cultures Rory had encountered on his rise to stardom.

"Thank you," she whispered to the library volunteer as she took another armload of stacked books and placed it on her table. The volunteer nodded and wheeled the empty cart away. Ashlyn turned to look at her improvised workstation. Magazines and journals and hardcover textbooks were stacked precariously in a jumble of colors and sizes and thicknesses. Hands on her hips, she sighed, slightly amused. *Look. You made a fort.*

Undeterred by the volume of reference materials, she didn't want to go home, and had nowhere else to be, she set out on a new path to discover the hidden life of Rory Mannix.

34

Stay Afraid

"Another rabbit hole," Ashlyn declared, shoving the last reference book to the side.

There was no unifying theory she could divine from all that she had read. *I'm just going in circles! Have I missed something?*

Rory was in Japan. "The Kanji 'Mind Sword Body,' or 'Spirit, Sword, and Body as One,'" she read her note out loud. No light bulb appeared over her head.

Dead end.

Rory in Hungary pictured with "taltos for performing cleansing rituals . . ."

Not helpful.

Rory in Nepal. "The Buddhist Auspicious Drawing." Ashlyn stared at the image, holding her breath, waiting for the explanation to reveal itself.

Just another dead end.

Istanbul . . . Dead end.

Dublin . . . Dead end.

Dead end. Dead end. Dead end.

Arrrrrgggh.

All these symbols and traditions talk about bringing together *the mind, body, and spirit. By all accounts, Rory Mannix was* broken *when he returned to San Francisco!*

Giving up on her towers of reference materials, she scrolled back to the top of the results on her computer screen.

"What's this?"

She hit the Back arrow. Her mouse hovered over an underlined phrase: "spiritual pain."

I don't remember clicking that.
She clicked it again to see where the link had taken her.

"You're only given a little spark of madness. You
mustn't lose it."
— Robin Williams

"People are like stained-glass windows. They
sparkle and shine when the sun is out, but when
the darkness sets in, their true beauty is revealed
only if there is a light from within."
— Elisabeth Kübler-Ross

"What happens when you can't reconcile the
thing you're after for the price you pay?"
— Phillip Seymour Hoffman

She wrinkled her nose, processing the deep thoughts in print
on her screen. *With all due respect, wise sages, I don't see how this helps me.*

Ashlyn sat back, rubbing her eyes, growing impatient with the
discontinuity of the information she'd dredged up, feeling like a dog
chasing its own tail.

Changing tack, Ashlyn opened her inbox, fingers crossed that
the librarian had had better luck. On first glance, the results
appeared to be more of the same kinds of things she'd already seen.
All were dated well after the accident, and most were images with
bland captions of everyday events from around the world:

Subject: Nutrura Café, Damascus

The first message contained a photo of a completely
unfamiliar-looking café in some far flung corner of the world.
Bulleted notes below the photo were also unhelpful.

- A well-known place of gathering.
- Built of mud and stone over 250 years ago.
- One of the oldest cafés in Damascus,
boasting a long-standing tradition of oral
storytelling that goes back centuries.

Another message containing another photo. This one of a pair
of bedraggled-looking Muscovites hunched over a small table facing
off over vodka shots. It was accompanied by a brief note.

Subject: White Nights-Black Days Bar, Minsk,
Belarus

- Travel blogs rave that fads come and go,
  but the nightlife in Minsk has a language all
  its own

Ummm . . . Ashlyn pursed her lips, completely at a loss as to how these photos were supposed to help her on her quest. There was no definitive connection to Rory Mannix. Ashlyn's hope started to wane.

Subject: Romkocsma, Budapest, Hungary

Budapest . . . I already know what happened in Budapest. Ashlyn didn't bother to open the email. *Next.*

Subject: Testing of laser capabilities of vapors of
complex organic compounds using pulses of
heat pumped through a plasma substrate.

What's this doing in here? Ah nuts, I've mixed up my work and personal email.
She snatched her notebook, that was now partially buried, out from under the middle tower of reference material. "None of this is making sense," she muttered, exasperated.
She was rewarded with a cascade of books and journals and magazines tumbling into her lap and onto the floor. Rolling her eyes at her clumsiness, she reached down to clean up her mess. When she sat back up, her body went rigid and her throat closed, choking off a gasp of terror.
In the now empty gap where the tower had been, *he* sat directly across from her. He held his hands near his face, his fingertips pressed together. His eyes peered over his fingertips, his gaze intense and unrelenting, boring into her.
Ashlyn sprang back from the table, toppling the other two towers, her chair, and herself, sending books, bags, arms, and chair all up in to the air. And all came crashing down in a heap beside her worktable.
From under the pile of debris on the floor, Ashlyn, head swimming, looked over to the opposite side of the table. He was still there. She watched as he stood, unhurried, and began to walk away.

She couldn't tell if he had stepped out of sight, or if his legs had just vanished into thin air. Then everything went black.

She was out for less than a minute, but the calamity had brought over all the staff and a few others in the library who now stood over her. She gazed up to see a circle of faces looking down on her with great concern.

"Are you OK?"

Ashlyn rubbed her head, then her shoulders, checking for bumps or gaping wounds. Then she pulled one pant leg up, exposing a throbbing lump that had started to swell.

"That's going to leave a mark! I think that's the worst of it, though," she said.

With help from the standers-by, she got to her feet and brushed herself off. "I think maybe that's enough research for today."

The library volunteer who had brought her many of the books that were now on the floor stooped to pick them up. "Do you want me to keep any of these on the cart for you?"

"No!" she blurted, then softer, "Um, no, thank you. I—I've got enough for now. In fact, I think I'm done."

Ashlyn packed up her laptop and gathered her things from the floor. She sat down again, her hands trembling. That was the closest encounter yet. Just thinking about it made her blood run cold.

She really was done here. Done for the night, and done with the whole damned mystery.

~

"Hey, you're ba—," David started to say.

A dark cloud of tension overshadowed her face. He didn't say another word.

At bedtime, he followed her into the bedroom, a hopeful look on his face.

"Feeling better?" she asked coolly over her shoulder.

"Yeah, f—." He paused as she stooped to put socks on. "Fine."

She could hear the disappointment in his voice. He hated when she wore socks to bed. She knew it would turn him off.

"G'night," she said and turned her back to him and immediately turned off her bedside lamp. *If nothing else, this foul mood is keeping him at arm's length.*

She tossed and turned. *I don't know what's worse! The tangled mess of nonsense I've been wasting my time trying to decipher? Or visitations by an angry, restless spirit who's dead set against me getting to the bottom of this mystery? Does it all go away if we move to Houston?*

She gently rolled over to stare up into the darkness and listen for the heavy rhythm of David's breathing. When her eyes adjusted, Ashlyn stole a glance at him. In the cracks of light sneaking through the blinds, she could make out his features. Thick dark brows, misshapen nose from a fistfight ages ago, freckles on the round of his cheeks from all his time spent baking under the sun.

What am I doing here? What am I still *doing here?*

Ashlyn laid awake for what felt like hours. Her mind churning over and over. How had all the choices she'd made up until this point amounted so much *wrong* in her life?

And how do I fix it?

The more her mind bore down on the question, the more elusive the answer seemed. Somehow, in the throes of mental teeth-gnashing and self-pity, she drifted off.

She was standing in the middle of the bedroom, wide awake. *No, wait, the room is all wrong, the bureau is missing, the closet . . .*

She turned to leave the bedroom. On the other side of the bedroom door, it was dark. And dank. Her heartbeat became a galloping horse in her ears. She wanted to retreat, to go back to her bedroom, back to bed, and pull the covers over her head, but there was no way out.

Darkness greeted her on the other side of the bedroom doorway now, too.

She drew shorter, sharper breaths, starting to hyperventilate. The bedroom door was nowhere. The furniture, gone. She rotated, slowly, until a sallow glow emerged from the barred window of the dungeon door that materialized where her bed had been.

"That was a funny trick you pulled in the library today," she sneered, indignation replacing the fear. Really, why haven't you gone? Shouldn't you move on, already?!" she shouted through the bars.

"*Feeee-in. Creeee-tim.*"

That voice . . .

Do I know that voice?

The featureless concrete block wall reappeared, illuminated by the same pale light that framed the door. A flash of brilliant light lit up the space, then dimmed as a thin line slowly appeared, accompanied by sparks. An unseen welder etched a single line into the wall, and then another, and another. Each crisp shape burned through the concrete in slow, but intense, fiery red-orange. Three distinct symbols.

Ashlyn watched, hypnotized by each line and arc meticulously cut into the cinder block. It wasn't until the last stem of the *M* was completed that she realized she was encircled by a wall of fire.

"Ashlyn!"

Her eyes burst open. A different light, with a weak gray glow. It came from the bedroom window.

"Jeez. You look like you've seen a ghost," said David.

Ashlyn stared up at him, wild-eyed and confused.

He looked at her, his amusement shifting to concern. "You were thrashing around. I thought maybe I should wake you up before . . . y'know, you knocked the lamp onto your head, or somethin'. You OK?"

"I—uh."

She shivered, unable to move and quite unsure where she was. "Yeah," she managed after a few moments. "Thanks."

She sat up and brushed her bangs out of her eyes. They were damp. Her face felt hot. Like she'd been standing in front of a fire.

35

Grasping on to the Wheel

"Do you want some cream for your coffee?" David asked.

He stood by the table, the coffee pot in one hand and a carton of cream in the other, wearing only a pair of tattered boxer shorts with Kiss M Bass printed on the backside.

Ashlyn was trying her best to give him the silent treatment, but he persisted, lifting the coffee pot and then the cream, indicating she should make a choice. *We could be here all day . . .*

She held up her mug. "Yes, please."

When he'd finished serving her, he flopped into the chair to her right, splashing a little hot coffee out of his mug. He jumped up quickly, narrowly avoiding hot coffee in the crotch.

Ashlyn snorted, despite her best efforts to keep a straight face.

"I can still make you smile. That's a good sign," he said, grabbing the dish cloth and wiping his seat. He tossed the soggy rag into the sink, landing on the dishes that he'd yet to wash.

"I *will* do those," he said quickly.

Then he got himself settled and leaned over the table, chin in his hand. "Hi, how are you? Haven't seen you 'round here much? You live here?"

After taking a moment to stare into her coffee, she let the wall of anger drop. "*Touché.* I guess I've been less available lately, even before your 'heroic' act at the festival."

"Yes, well. About that. Jason and Steve both aren't allowed out to play with me, for a while, they tell me."

"Ha! Good for all'a ya," Ashlyn laughed.

"I appreciate that you don't try to put a short leash on me," he said, placing his hand on hers.

"You are free to fuck up in any way you choose, just don't expect me to bail you out of jail."

"Fair enough."

He took a sip of his coffee, looking at her expectantly. Ashlyn said nothing.

"So . . . ," he swirled his coffee while choosing his words, "How about let's start making some plans to do different things? Maybe get out with other friends?"

"OK."

This time David waited out the silence.

"You know," she relented, "I just ran into Lin. I'll see if they have plans for this weekend."

"Yeah. We haven't seen them in ages!" David lit up. "Maybe a hike . . . or, Jeff is a hard-core climber, isn't he? We could go bouldering or . . ."

"Slow down, cowboy. I think we need to build up to something epic like that." She was smiling, but shaking her head. "Bu-ut, if you want to get out of the city, maybe we could do a wine tour in Napa Valley? Or even something much simpler, like dinner and a movie. Or—"

"Yeah, you're right. Probably hurt myself if I tried mountain climbing hot off the couch." He rubbed the stubble on his chin as he spoke. "And then I wouldn't be able to work, and you'd be back to putting in extra-extra time at the lab so we can pay the rent . . ."

She winked and mimed "bang on target," firing her finger at him like a gun.

"So, what happened after that big meeting you spent a whole Sunday getting ready for?"

Ashlyn's shoulders slumped, "Ugh. Not much. I made a quick presentation and haven't heard anything more about it." She frowned, to herself mostly. "I even asked Richard if there was more I could do. If they would consider letting me do the safety audit in the R&D lab—anything to get a foot in the door."

Cradling her coffee mug in both hands, she felt like, for the first time in a long time, she had his undivided attention. That they could share the experience of the mundane parts of a relationship without jeopardizing it. *It's all part of the deal.*

"What did he say about the audit?"

"Well, he didn't 'say' anything, I only suggested it in one of my regular email updates I send to him." She made a face. "Too passive?"

David nodded.

She sighed. "Meanwhile, when I'm stuck in the lab babysitting the—a machine, I've been cramming as much information from technical papers into my head as I can stand."

"My god, I don't know how you can stand to be stuck in that lab. All day. By yourself." He looked devastated on her behalf. David was a very social animal.

"Yeah, well, I had been making regular appearances in the coffee station, until Richard doubled my workload."

"But no increase in pay?" Now David was frowning.

"No. But I have applied for a couple of jobs in the R&D lab in the last month, with, yes, higher pay. But—"

"What about Dallas? Did you apply for anything in Dallas?" David jumped in eagerly.

"Mmm, nooo, but," she winced, knowing she hadn't given any further thought to Houston or Dallas, "I did join a local community group."

David looked at her like a confused puppy.

"To help beef up my CV. It's the community garden project near the City College library."

David grimaced. "Gardening? Really?"

"I know." She laughed and shrugged her shoulders. "I thought it would be fun to do something completely new *and* have something to show for it. You like food, don't you?"

"Yeah, I like food. Wanna go out for brunch?" David stood up and drained the last of his coffee. "I'll go get dressed."

"Good idea."

Alone in the kitchen, Ashlyn stared out the small frosted window that allowed light in but that you couldn't see out. *Hmmm.* The hours she had previously spent with David or at yoga or PINQ events, she had filled by throwing herself into her self-guided study, and volunteering, and more professional meetings . . . *How am I going to make more room for David and me?*

I guess that's about to change, since I'm no longer chasing a ghost.

~

Monday morning, Ashlyn swapped her bouclé cardigan for her lab coat and grabbed her One-Shot cup. She hadn't even taken a sip, though, so when she lifted the plastic lid, a still perfectly formed fern leaf, etched in the coffee foam, greeted her.

Marty, you make every day special.

Feeling especially buoyant, Ashlyn nodded approvingly at her workbench. Things had been set in motion. She had plans with David to look forward to. She had managed to eliminate a potentially career-ending distraction: her quest. Ashlyn could now put all of her energy into her goal to get out of the QA lab.

All that remained was to keep all the balls in the air: the self-guided study in e-textiles, the volunteer work with her professional groups, and, of course, the long days in the lab, making sure she met her deadlines.

She buzzed around her quiet lab, collecting swatches and chemicals and vials and flasks, and returning every few minutes to check the work plan for the day's trials and take another sip of her coffee. Morning crept forward. It was going to be a slow day.

Ashlyn turned away from the whirling centrifuge and grabbed her phone from the desk. It was time to check in at the coffee station. Then she looked at her spreadsheet showing the list of trials and the target dates for completion. There were far fewer check marks than there should have been.

She tapped her legs with flat hands as she scanned the workbench. She didn't dare walk out just now, the pressure of looming deadlines prevented her from leaving Lab #3.

"Hmmm, I have a few minutes . . ."

She grabbed a pad of lined papers and sat down to indulge in some stress-relieving doodling. Though, the stark walls of the lab, adorned only with product advertisements and health and safety posters, lacked for anything inspirational worth sketching. The schooner sketchbook, with the nice paper, was just on the other side of the divider . . .

"And that's where it will stay," she said firmly, glancing up at the whiteboard side of the divider where she couldn't help but see the list of all the trials she had yet to complete.

Sigh.

She sank into her chair and spun her drawing pencil on her thumb, continuing to scan the lab. Her eyes fell on the labels on the jars of chemicals on the top shelf of the storage cabinet *picric acid, elemental sodium, hydrogen peroxide—laboratory grade . . . all potentially explosive . . .*

The image of the GOM and his cruel eyes flashed into her mind's eye.

"No! I'm done with that," she said, waving her hands defensively.

You free for coffee today? She paused, considering what more to say in her message to Budhil. *Hmmm, no pretext, just a friendly coffee invitation, I think.*

Send.

Lin, it's Ashlyn. I hope this is still your cell =) Are you and Jeff free this weekend?

Send.

Her screensaver was cycling through the elements of the periodic table. Each element was featured with a bit of history or a parody or diagram of its atomic structure.

"Hmmf. Fitting," she grumbled at the screen.

Wa: 121 – WasteTimeian:
A highly reactive molecule, readily combines
with **Me122.**

Me: 122 – MeetingOverdose:
A radioactive molecule with a long half-life,
spawning many daughter isotopes with
increasingly long half-lives (generally two times
the length of the meeting agenda).

"I appear to have discovered a large deposit of wastetimeian," she said flatly to the empty lab.

Bzzzt. A text.

I'm gone all this week. Training gig in Seattle. Back next Tuesday. How about dinner and a movie on Thursday?

Done. I'll let David know.

Lin and Jeff have plans for the weekend. Decided on dinner and a movie NEXT Thursday. Does that work for you? We can do our own adventure this weekend =)

Send.

Beep. Beep. Beep.

The centrifuge finished spinning, pulling her back to the lab and the work ahead. She dutifully spent the morning running chromatography columns and stacking samples of fabrics to be tested. She focused on the experiments, ignoring her phone and placing satisfying check marks by the trials as she completed them.

"Two down . . ." She used a thick green dry erase marker to make the check. ". . . sixteen to go."

In the afternoon, she headed to the regularly scheduled research associates' meeting with a slight bounce in her step.

"Here you go, Lisa," Ashlyn said, handing her a pair of thin binders. "The symposium notes you loaned me."

"A little light reading over the weekend?" asked Kendra as she rolled her eyes. "You really need to learn how to have a little fun!"

"Ack! Don't mind her, she never reads anything past the abstract. I just picked up a few more documents that Budhil wants his team to look over. You wanna borrow those?"

"Sure," Ashlyn replied, looking like a deer in headlights. *More?*

"He said these experiments were pretty scant on real innovation, but gave him loads of ideas for new projects. Maybe in the new year?"

"New projects in the new year . . . That sounds very promising." She beamed at Lisa.

Indeed, Ashlyn had set things in motion. *No more yoga, date night with David instead, yay! No more digging into the past, just working on getting into Budhil's R&D lab. Steady on course.*

36

Chaos is a Ladder

For the rest of the week, Ashlyn ran a tight ship, breaking up her days into regimented compartments to maximize her productivity. In the mornings, she diligently set about running her experiments and providing regular updates to Richard. As the week progressed, the crossed-out trials on the list slowly overtook the number of trials yet to be completed. *Yessss!*

In the afternoons, she made regular appearances in the coffee station.

On Tuesday, she asked for suggestions on where she and David should go for dinner.

"Try that Greek place where they let you smash the dishes!" Kendra suggested.

"You know, that's a great idea. I think David would totally go for that!"

"Why do you sound surprised that I had a good idea?" Kendra scowled.

Wednesday, Ashlyn asked what professional organizations everyone belonged to.

She got a few enthusiastic responses, and followed up with, "And how much do you pay in annual dues? Does FiberWorx cover that?"

Which elicited some mumbles and head shaking.

"Haha. Way to clear the room, Ash," Kendra chortled.

OK, salary and compensation are not *coffee station topics. Noted.* Ashlyn's head lowered as she exited the coffee station.

"I have an appointment with Joan in HR next week," she began during the coffee gathering on Thursday. "Soooo, what, exactly, do I say to her?"

"You let *her* know what *your* career goals are. She's not a mind reader!"

"You ask her what the *criteria* are for the job you're after. Keep emotion out of it."

"You need to read in your industry. Voraciously."

"You need to promote yourself relentlessly to management. She can't do anything for you."

And on it went.

In between time, Ashlyn threw herself into her volunteer work. Seated at her office desk in the cube farm, she spent her spare minutes either reviewing meeting minutes or scrolling through the slew of email that had been sent around to the committee members. Please Review the Action Items. Update on Action Items. Action Items Needing a Champion.

Shaking her head, Ashlyn reviewed the orphaned tasks and chose one.

Re: Action Items Needing a Champion

I will review the documents on fertilizers.

To clarify, the Grow-Opp Co-op is looking for: locally sourced, non-GMO, organic options for the rutabagas, correct?

Ashlyn O' Monahan,
Research Associate, FiberWorx Inc

Ashlyn cringed as she hit Reply All.
I don't know if I'll make it to spring.
How badly do I really want to "feel the joy of touching the earth with my bare hands"?

~

The following week, as she walked to work she reviewed her progress in patching up her relationship and focusing her efforts on meeting the criteria in the job description for the R&D lab.

The nice dinner out with David was . . . nice.

"We have to come here again," he'd gushed after the plate-smashing part of dinner.

And their weekend adventure to Napa Valley was really nice. "I could do this again," she'd said, giggling, before toppling over into the shrubbery.

See, Kendra. I do know how to have fun.

And all the conference presentations and symposium transcripts she'd absorbed. *Reading 'voraciously' in my industry.* It made her head hurt to think of grappling her way through one more paper.

Her heels *click-clacking* on the sidewalk sounded hollow to her ears.

Sigh. Maybe Joan can help me set out a clear path.

Ashlyn had to wait until Thursday before she found herself seated across from Joan.

"Soon, I think," Joan said as she scanned her "O'Monahan, A." file. "You've got great experience in the QA/QC lab . . . I see you've got some recent—very recent—volunteering experience."

She looked up from the file and smiled brightly. "You're nearly there. I don't see the American Chemical Society on here under professional affiliations."

Ashlyn smiled back flatly. "Yes. I've submitted some applications for membership, but just waiting on paperwork. So they tell me."

"OK. So, it looks like you're right on track, then. I look forward to seeing your application for the new R&D position."

I already sent that, didn't I?

Joan blinked expectantly at Ashlyn. It took Ashlyn a moment to realize that she had been dismissed.

"Uh. Thank you . . . ," her eyes glossy, she stood, "for seeing me today." She left the HR office, closing the door softly.

What had happened to her completed application? *Maybe I didn't send it?*

Lab #3 was down two floors. Every step closer felt like walking through cement.

Ashlyn checked her phone. "Budhil, where are you?" There had been no reply to her email from last week. He had been exceptionally evasive lately. She decided to go find him. She *needed* to find him.

She found him. Quite unexpectedly, as they each rounded the corner from opposite directions and very nearly collided. Instead of brushing her off with a flustered wave of his hand, this time he stopped.

He looked her over, then said, "You look terrible."

His expression softened from a look of deep concentration to one of concern, like that of a father for a daughter. "You're vorking too hard, I think," he concluded. "You need to get out and play."

That was all. His expression hardened again and he continued on his way.

Ashlyn, too stunned to say anything, slowly walked back to her lab, not sure where else to go.

Once again, she found herself alone in Lab #3.

37

Fight Night

With a heavy heart, Ashlyn looked out the glass doors of the FiberWorx building at the gray twilight. Her eyes followed the trail of a raindrop running down the glass as the futility of *trying* took hold of her. Trying to achieve better. Trying to understand her shortfalls and overcome them, all in an effort to make the cut for the R&D lab.

There's always just one more hurdle.

As for actual work, this week had produced mixed results. She'd cruised through half a dozen trials on Monday and Tuesday, then had one interruption after another on Wednesday. *Who knew there would be so much gardening work to discuss in November?*

"How is it Thursday already?" she said out loud, forgetting where she was.

"I know, right?" answered a random stranger. He smiled at her as he unsnapped his umbrella and pushed on the glass door, admitting a waft of damp evening air.

If not my results, then can I rely on my work ethic to speak for itself? She winced at the thought.

With a sigh, she wrapped herself in the forest-green lambswool-blend coat, and wound the tangerine pashmina scarf around her neck before stepping outside. The chill still bit right through. She squeezed her shoulders up, lifting her collar up to her chin to block out the cold, like a turtle tucking itself into the safety of its shell, and headed home.

Once inside the warm and dry of the front hall of the apartment, Ashlyn took her time unwrapping herself from all the layers that separated her from the relentless drizzle and cool damp of November. She allowed herself a moment to embrace gratitude for her safe haven. Then gave her wet coat a shake, and fluffed out the oversize collar of her cream-colored, mohair turtleneck sweater.

The relief and comfort of arriving home was short-lived. As she kicked off her boots, David poked his head around the corner.

"Don't put your coat away! We gotta go!" he said excitedly.

"Huh? Go where?" she looked up, confused.

He stared at her incredulously. "The big event! Floyd Mayweather and Manny Pacquiao." His eyes grew wide with excitement and he began shadowboxing in front of her.

Silence.

"We're meeting everybody at the pub, remember? It was your idea to get together with Jeff and Lin," he offered, trying to prod her memory.

"Ack! I totally forgot about tonight!"

Ashlyn felt a momentary crush of guilt, as though being pummeled by a load of bricks. The wave of guilt was swiftly shoved aside by a flash of anger. "The plan was for dinner and a movie." She eyed him suspiciously.

"Oh. Didn't I mention it? Oh. Oh, well. Whatever. I texted Jeff to see if they wanted to meet us at the Crazy Horse instead of the restaurant you suggested. And I invited Kevin and Diane, too."

Ashlyn paused and regarded him coolly. "I see."

"It's going to be *awwwwe-some!*" he said in a sing-songy voice. "And I think it would be good for you to get out . . . Get out and play, y'know?"

Ashlyn stiffened. *First Budhil, and now David.*

Seeing Ashlyn's expression, David changed tactics. "To spend more time with each other, I mean," he pressed.

It *had* been her idea to meet tonight. And she was looking forward to hanging out with Lin. And now Diane, that would be nice, too. *But Fight Night?* She'd been fighting for recognition at work and fighting at home with David. And fighting for some semblance of peace and order in her thoughts.

I've had just about enough of fighting.

She caved. "OK."

David lit up. Under the front hall light she could see he was dressed pretty sharp, for him. He wore a handsome combo: a navy Aloha dress-shirt made of fine cotton, under the body-hugging, camel-colored merino wool sweater she had given him, and a new pair of dark wash Rag & Bone jeans. *Hmmf. He looks good.*

David slid his charcoal gray wool-blend peacoat with the high collar over his shoulders, and was ready to head out the door before she'd even rezipped her shiny black boots.

Oh yeah. The Crazy Horse is a little more upscale. Even after nearly ten years together, he still managed to surprise her. *Maybe tonight, he might choose to follow the rules.*

Cautiously optimistic, she grabbed her shoulder bag. Maybe tonight, because he had elected to blend in rather than stand out. *Maybe I can look forward to an enjoyable evening out.*

Too many times, she'd held her breath, watching a "nice evening out" degrade as the peacocks began to posture. Too many times, she'd had to step back from the fray, as the fists flew up and swung wildly. Her gut clenched just imagining another disastrous scene unfolding. *That's the kind of thinking that will give a person colon cancer . . . Stop.*

Maybe tonight, she wouldn't have to be vigilant. Maybe tonight, she could just relax. *That would be a nice change of pace.*

Kevin and Diane were already at the pub. They'd scored a huge table with an unobstructed view of the big screen that would be showing the fight. *More good news. Front row seats should keep David happy tonight.*

"Hey, you're blocking the door, man," growled a voice from behind them.

Ashlyn eyelids fluttered shut. The familiar sinking feeling gripped her throat and her stomach, her shoulders slumped with dread. But David was smiling. She swiveled to see Jeff and Lin. She smiled, too, relieved. *Nope. Can't let down my guard, even for a minute.*

"Hey, man." David grabbed Jeff in a manly hug, then added a series of firm back slaps. "Haven't seen you in ages!"

"Yeah—." Jeff stepped back after the enthusiastic greeting, but then added, "Good to see you, too, dude."

They all shuffled en masse to the table and settled in to watch the fight. The ladies all huddled at one end of the table to catch up.

"I have a new job," Diane announced proudly.

"Again?" It was out before Ashlyn could stop herself. "Sorry, I mean, is it another accounts assistant position, or something new?"

Lin nudged her, a knowing smirk on her face. Diane had jumped ship three times in as many months. She was her own little soap opera.

"Yeah. This time it's with a small firm." She bit her lip, holding back her excitement. "It has more of a family feel to it. And way more opportunities for advancement."

Ashlyn and Lin just nodded and smiled as Diane regaled them with her tales of conquest and betrayal in the file room.

Diane's diatribe was interrupted by a text. "I gotta call my sitter," she said, and excused herself.

She sailed off to where there was less noise, her leopard print shawl trailing in her wake like a party streamer. Lin and Ashlyn watched her disappear, somewhat mesmerized, half expecting something to blow up before she reached the front door.

"SMH," said Lin and smiled, thankful for the reprieve. Ashlyn inhaled deeply, as if to say something, but then suspecting neither of them wanted to give any more air time to Diane's dramas, refrained.

"Oh, hey! I almost forgot. I got some . . . trippy information for your mystery."

Lin untangled herself from the long cross-shoulder purse strap and extracted a tidy, but plump, wad of folded papers.

Ashlyn recoiled slightly.

"I know, who prints stuff out anymore?" Lin said as she started to unfold the papers. "I guess I just need to see things in print sometimes. But most of this is chemistry stuff that I couldn't wrap my head around."

Ashlyn took a sip from the heavy glass stein in front of her. The beer was no longer cold and frothy.

Lin continued on, speaking without reservation, eager to share what she knew. "I tried to dig deeper into the investigations into the cause of the accident. Seems they never figured out what made the car explode."

"Explosions? My goodness, what have I missed?" asked Diane as she reclaimed her seat.

"We're trying to solve the mystery surrounding the unconfirmed death of Rory Mannix," Lin answered.

"Ooooo, the fashion designer who died recently? The guy everyone thought died twenty years ago?" Diane swooned, clearly relishing the intrigue.

Ashlyn tried watching the fight on the big screen, hoping they would just run out of things to say about it and change the subject.

"Yeah. He wasn't dead, but then he comes back after being gone for decades, and then dies." Her eyes sparkled as she recalled the details. "Before anyone can find out where he's *been* all this time!" she added.

Ashlyn went rigid. She took another sip of warm beer. "Plahh," she said, making a face.

Both Diane and Lin stopped speaking and looked at Ashlyn.

"My beer's warm."

Lin gave her a questioning look. "This is your mystery. You haven't said much so far . . ."

Ashlyn squirmed under the pair of expectant stares, then lifted the heavy mug to her lips but couldn't bring herself to drink the warm, amber liquid it held.

"Well, I . . . I saw him," the words came slowly. "Before he died," she added.

She swallowed hard and continued. "I walked by him every day and didn't even know it was him!"

Ashlyn was rewarded with a rush of relief. She had internalized this whole quest, set on single-handedly unmasking Rory Mannix's story.

"There was a grizzled old man who started hanging out in the plaza by my office," Ashlyn told the pair, using the same "rumor has it" tone Diane had been using earlier.

"Oooo, that's creepy. I don't like old people," said Diane.

Lin laughed, shaking her head. "The 'grizzled old man' was the fashion designer that everybody had thought died twenty years ago."

Diane became very animated, she loved celebrity gossip. "Right. Rory Mannix. Yeah. He made some *great* stuff. But he was a real piece of work! They say he had no patience for, um . . . well, he was just really insensitive."

"Didn't suffer fools gladly?" Lin asked.

"Yeah, kinda. He wasn't vindictive, just, everybody was a doormat. And he was definitely impulsive."

Diane reeled off of the "facts" as she knew them. "There were a ton of crazy rumors. Like it was a Mafia hit. And he went into witness protection. Because they planted a bomb in his car. Coz the

Italian designers were fed up with the young punk crashing their scene!" She drew in a great breath when she'd finished.

Ashlyn and Lin shared a knowing glance. They were never quite sure where Diane got her information, nor how reliable it was. She was prone to embellishing.

"But what about the passenger?" Lin asked.

"What passenger?" Diane looked at Lin suspiciously.

"I found a bunch of police reports—which is weird, because we don't normally have access to that kind of thing . . . But, anyway, yeah. There are a lot of 'unknowns,' including whether or not there was a passenger. And his or her identity."

"My friend, she owns the Eclectic Emporium, she's got all the inside stories on the fashion industry. She never said anything about a passenger. So, anyway . . ."

Ashlyn was grateful to have the attention redirected. She only half listened as Diane recited the stories from Budapest and Tokyo and Moscow. She wasn't going to go digging up any more history, so none of these details mattered. Ashlyn leaned back in her chair and made herself comfortable.

Diane paused her storytelling to throw back the rest of her gin and tonic.

"He had a really slick logo, too, didn't he?" asked Lin.

"It wasn't so much a logo as a riddle," Diane corrected.

"My friend at the Eclectic Emporium, she told me that the *R* and the *M'* are based on ancient symbols that have been found all over the globe. Including every city where Rory Mannix showed his work."

Ashlyn sat up, suddenly quite interested in what information Diane had to share.

38

Cujo

The "Main Event" was everything David had promised: fast and furious punches, Pacquiao's aggressive, all-attacking style, Mayweather on the ropes—all the excitement and intensity that fans come out to see . . . completely lost on Ashlyn. As they left the pub, Ashlyn stuffed her hands in her pockets, breathing in the cool night air.

It's not raining.

Walking slowly, she reflected on the evening. Being at the pub, spending time with friends, she'd been surprised by how freeing it felt to have friends she could confide in. That they hardly batted an eyelash about her encounter with the GOM, and that allowed her to drop her guard. Her mind at ease for an entire evening. *It* was *good to get out and play.*

"I can't remember the last time I was feeling this light at the end of the day," she said aloud.

"See, I told you it would be fun," said David, crediting himself.

"I had fun," she admitted.

David cheerfully gave her the play-by-play of the fight highlights. Lost in her own thoughts again, Ashlyn walked silently alongside him, allowing the peace of empty thoughts to play across the stage in her mind. It was hypnotic, like the snow effect that used to come on the TV when the station had ended its broadcast for the night. She lazily rolled the new puzzle piece over and back in her mind as they made their way home. *A riddle?*

Away from the vibrant business district and neon glow of storefront signs, their path became a patchwork of glaring sidewalks, wet from the rain earlier, reflecting the bright light from the street lamps. The stark contrast between the darkness of the night and the circles of light under the street lamps cast an unnatural glow over their faces as they passed under the light.

"Hey, remember that fight we saw the night of the festival?"

She got an instant chill.

"Yeah," he said, punching the air like Pacquiao had done. "We stopped that little tango from getting outta hand," he continued, nodding as a pat on the back to himself for his heroic act.

"Hey, let's go up 'King Street'," David said.

OK, OK. I'm not paying enough attention to you. You now have my attention.

She looked directly at him, her expression firm. "No."

"C'mon," he egged her on. "It'll be fun! It'll be extra spooky at night." He looked like a demon possessed in the eerie light cast by the street lamps.

Her hesitation had been enough to encourage him to guide her, unwillingly, up the street. Objects and shadows in this light played with the mind.

"What was that?" She thought she detected movement.

Hyperaware now, she expected to see the specter of the GOM around every corner. Something leapt at her. Barking and snarling, white fangs and white fur flashing between the slats in the fence.

David doubled over, laughing. "Wow, Cujo got you good this time!"

Ashlyn jumped out of her skin, too frightened to even manage a scream. She stood, frozen, shutting her eyes until the thudding of her heart in her ears settled to a dull throb. David was still chuckling when she finally stopped shaking and opened her eyes.

"Shut up, Cujo!" David said, kicking at the fence. He'd got his laugh and now the fun was over, time to move on. The dog, incensed, launched into a fresh round of ferocious snarling and barking.

"Ah, fuck you, Cujo," David said as he began walking, taking Ashlyn by her arm and leading her away.

The front porch light of Cujo's house came on. "Hey man, what'd you say to my dog?" The light escaping the doorway on the porch illuminated the silhouette of a large-framed man standing with his thick shoulders squared, like a WWE wrestler posturing, about to march down to the ring. "Cookie, come here," he instructed.

"Cookie? Hahaha, you gotta be kidding me!" David spouted.

A familiar dread replaced the terror inside Ashlyn. Alarm bells were going off. Her brain scrambled. *How can I diffuse this situation?*

"You can tell . . . *Cookie* that we're just passing by," she said, trying to sound pleasant, unconcerned. "We'll be past her stretch of fence in two shakes."

She tugged at David, encouraging him to move on. She was offering a categorically non-violent option for the behemoth standing in the doorway, desperately hoping that he would accept it, and that they could continue on without incident.

"That's right, I'll take care 'a my bitch, an' you take care 'a yours," sneered the man.

Ashlyn swallowed hard. *Oh god, it's on.*

Thankfully David was lucid enough to realize jumping *into* the man's yard to confront him would end badly. He stood at the gate, where the fence was low enough for neighbors on either side to have a lovely conversation on a spring-timey day, but high enough that a hysterical bull terrier was safely confined within the yard.

The ornery man in the doorway lumbered down his front steps and marched along his walkway to the gate. David was fired up. He was clearly vibrating on adrenaline, and too charged up to notice the baseball bat that the man had discreetly brought with him.

"David!" screamed Ashlyn, "He's got a ba—"

Too late.

Cookie's owner swung the bat and connected with David's right arm, which he'd raised defensively over his face. David yelped, but didn't hesitate and swung with his left. His hook only grazed the bat wielder's chin, but it was enough to set the man's jaw off kilter. David followed with another jab, but missed. His knuckles ground right into the edge of the wooden slats. The impact jammed his fingers, and he lost a few layers of skin to boot.

Cookie's snarls were now downright hostile, spurred on by her owner's aggression. With lightning quickness, she launched herself at the gate to snap at David's fingers and managed to slice deep into his flesh.

David stepped back, glaring with pure malice, his nostrils flared, like a bull about to charge. Ashlyn, beside herself with genuine terror, grabbed David by his right arm. He winced in surprise, but it was enough to break him out of his blind rage.

"He fucking broke my arm!" He turned back to the gate. "Y' fuckwit, you broke my fucking arm!" he growled.

Ashlyn looked down at David's left hand. There was a long gash with blood seeping out. The wet of the blood shone in the lamplight.

"If this gets infected, you better believe I'm calling animal control. They'll be back to put that bitch down," David threatened.

The hulk of a man cracked up with vicious laughter. "C'mon Cookie. Fun's over. You scared that girly man away. Who's a good girl?" He scratched Cookie behind the ear, and led the proud dog back into the house.

David let Ashlyn assist him on their way. As his breathing returned to normal, he began to fidget and fuss.

"My right arm is killing me," he moaned.

"Serves you goddamned right!" It took everything Ashlyn had not to scream the words. "What. The. Hell. Is . . . " she swatted at his good arm with every word, "*wrong* with you?"

When she was done, she clamped her mouth firmly shut and steered him toward the nearest hospital. It wasn't until they reached the well-lit Emergency entry of the hospital that they could really appreciate the misshapen form of his right arm. It hung from his elbow at a nauseatingly odd angle.

~

It was two hours before a nurse admitted him. The couple sat silently and watched other emergencies come and go. Finally, David was sent to X-ray.

"I'll wait out here," Ashlyn seethed through clenched teeth.

The waiting gnawed away at Ashlyn's anger until it finally gave way to full-body exhaustion. Memories of hospital visits from the past forced their way in. First in erratic, disjointed flashes, then slowing to long, lingering memories as the film reel brought up memories of Ryan, the pumper truck driver on the night of the accident in 1992. She tried not to remember. Tried not to see these hallways from twenty years ago, as she walked alongside her mother, who had come to check on Ryan.

Her mom never said what she hoped to see each day they visited Ryan in the hospital. Was he Ted's good friend? Or the man who survived the blast? Both Ryan and Ted had been lifted off their feet when the Maserati exploded. Would it bring comfort if Ryan lived? Or would it be better if he died, too? Then her mom wouldn't be tormented by *Why did it have to be Ted?*

Enough. Ashlyn sat up straighter and rubbed her cheeks roughly, refusing to relive those memories. But her present reality wasn't any rosier. *How do I keep finding my way back here?*

About an hour later, a nurse approached Ashlyn. "The doctor will be with your husband shortly. He'd like you to come in. The doctor, that is. He needs a responsible adult present to hear the post-treatment instructions."

"He's not my husband," Ashlyn said flatly. "And what if I was an irresponsible adult? And who gets dragged in if our roles were reversed?" she added curtly.

"Amen, sista," replied the nurse.

Ashlyn had learned that ER nurses have a sense of humor, too, this not being her first trip to an emergency room at this late hour. She'd sat in one uncomfortable chair after another waiting for David to be stitched up on at least two? three? previous occasions. She didn't want to count.

Each time, the doctors and nurses had given Ashlyn a cursory examination before turning their attention to David. David might be a dick, but he wasn't abusive. For that, she was thankful. He had a mean streak, but, for better or for worse, he most often chose to take it out on himself in one form or another.

The doctor had a close look at the wound inflicted by the dog and ordered testing for rabies.

"Yeah! That'll teach that ass-fuck," David muttered.

David smelled of alcohol. The doctor shot a quick, questioning look up at Ashlyn. She shook her head slightly and shut her eyes, signaling that it was not a matter worth pursuing. David wasn't falling down drunk, nor being belligerent, so the doctor resumed his assessment.

"Well, I suspect the test will come back negative. But we'll run it, it's hospital policy. As for your arm, I'm sure you don't need me to tell you. It's broken." He slid the X-rays into place on the light frame and stroked his chin as he studied the slides.

"It's a compound fracture. And the bone's out of alignment. I think the easiest thing to do is force it back into place and put a cast on it. Now, we have some wonderful drugs here to help you with the pain." He looked down at David over the top of his glasses. David seemed sober enough now. The doctor instructed the nurse to prepare 60cc of buprenorphine.

Ashlyn raised an eyebrow. Pharmaceutical chemistry was not her strong suit, but she knew that the drug they were about to administer was a strong opioid.

"Morphine will not be enough to numb the pain," the doctor explained. "The pain of adjusting the bones to realign them will be overwhelming. And the dose of morphine that would be necessary would likely kill him. So, we use buprenorphine. He'll feel some of the pain, but the buprenorphine will make him forget it."

"OK. Let's do this!" David said, getting fired up again.

"We need you to relax, son," said the doctor. "We'll administer the buprenorphine and give you a few minutes to let it take effect. Then we'll get you to lie down and . . . would you mind removing your leather belt? You may want to have that to bite down on."

Turning to Ashlyn, he said, "OK. He'll need constant supervision for about eight hours after he's discharged. Here's a prescription for two to three days' painkillers." He handed her a small square of paper with illegible scribbles that, presumably, the pharmacist would be able to decipher.

"He'll be in a cast for at least six weeks. I recommend nothing more than desk work . . . What does he do?

"Construction."

"Oh." The doctor frowned. "Even light-duty lifting is out if he wants the bones to heal."

Ashlyn smiled ruefully.

"You'll have to go back to the waiting room now, while we set the bones."

Ashlyn gathered their coats and her purse and headed for the waiting lounge. The wall clock showed 3:04 in uncaring red numerals.

Great.

39

Baby, Don't Do Me Like That

Shy of shuffle-walking with her arms out in front and moaning, *The Walking Dead* version of Ashlyn headed straight for her lab with barely a hello to anyone.

Finally, she sat. Fatigue, from the long night in the emergency ward, combined with the weight of depressing thoughts, dragged Ashlyn down into a deep funk. *I might not have the strength to stand. Ever again.*

Gloom saturated her entire being. "Uuuuuuggggh," she sighed, like a child who was just told to clean her room before she would be allowed to watch any TV.

Ashlyn took a moment to lazily scan the workbench and, seeing that the sequence was comfortably underway, sat back in the chair and began to spin. She let out another pathetic whimper of protest. "Ohhh, I don't want to adult today."

Her eyes were tired. Her mind was tired. Even her computer was tired. She switched it on and stared impassively at the pulsing, gyrating periodic table screensaver as the computer chugged through its boot-up routine. Above the screen, the whiteboard showing her glacially slow progress on the trials taunted her.

She played nervously with her fingers, resisting the urge to wheel her chair around to the opposite side of the whiteboard, where a collection of colorful strings crisscrossed the divider, held in place by push pins. Colored pins also held all the random scraps of information and pieces of the Rory Mannix mystery that she had acquired. She'd hoped it would eventually all fit together in a tidy storyboard that would explain everything, just like on *Criminal Minds*.

That was before being confronted by the ghostly GOM in the library.

"Nope," She said firmly. "Not going there."

Finally, she had the momentum to get up from her chair and get to work.

Hours later, she looked out her little square reinforced glass window to see people happily filing out the door.

"It's Friday!" Matt mouthed from the other side of the glass, framing his face with a big "thumbs up." He'd been really nice since she'd played nurse for him . . . *Was that last week?* She had no idea. He mocked disgust when she returned his cheery grin with a pout, pointing with her thumb backward into her lab.

C'mon, he motioned to her.

When she shook her head, he started walking toward her door. Her eyes widened with panic. *He shouldn't come in!* So she went out to meet him.

"What are you so busy with?" he said, smiling brightly. "It's Friday! Come join us for a beer."

She pretended to entertain the idea, then declined. "I was dragging my butt around all morning. I've still got my reaction running and all my glassware to clean. It'll be at least another hour."

Laughing, Matt persisted. "I'm pretty sure we'll still be there in an hour!" Then lowering his voice, "Budhil's experiments aren't going well, so we're all looking to blow off a little steam." He smiled encouragingly. "You should come."

"Thanks for the invitation, Matt," she replied, genuinely sad that she would miss out. "We'll see," she said as she stepped back into Lab #3.

Before she shut the door, she noticed Richard standing down the hallway that had just emptied of work-weary employees. He was talking with the FiberWorx CEO, whose back was to Ashlyn. Richard's dominant frame towered over the diminutive figure of the CEO. Richard could clearly see Ashlyn, clad in her company-issued white lab coat, as she waved goodbye to her colleagues, who were off to start their weekend.

Look at me, dutifully going back to my lab after punch-out time. On a Friday evening, no less.

So far, her efforts to "build her network" and "be a self-promoter" hadn't gotten her any closer to Budhil's team. There had been a time when she would happily put in extra hours. When she'd started, she had been dedicated to the work, to FiberWorx, to keeping people safe from fire, and bodily harm, and death. That had seemed all-important, once upon a time.

But right now, making a show of staying late just felt like sucking up. *Damned if I do, damned if I don't.*

Hssss. The air lock sucked the door closed, tight, shutting out the world.

~

The hallway was dark when she stepped out of Lab #3 and pulled the door shut behind her.

What are we doing for supper? A text from David.

Leftovers? Delivery? she texted back.

She wasn't really hungry when she had left the office, but by the time she'd reached the apartment, she could distinctly hear her stomach growling from beneath the thick cable-knit sweater and heavy wool coat over top of that. She knew David hadn't picked up the mail from the letterbox, so stopped there first, counting on inspiration from some flyer or other for pizza or donair or Korean BBQ.

Ashlyn had her head down as she came into the apartment, busy sorting through the stack of mail they'd neglected to collect for over a week. She absently dropped her keys into the tin plate, the comforting rattle and clank signaling she was safe at home.

Having shuffled the envelopes into "his" and "hers" stacks, she reached out her hand to the figure standing in the doorway to their galley kitchen. She was about to offer David his stack of mail, when she heard David's voice hailing her from the living room down the hall.

"Anything for me?"

She looked up to see David, far down at the end of the hall, standing by the sofa. Her heart leapt into her throat, her entire body seized up. She wanted to scream, but could only manage a weak whimper.

The shadow in the kitchen doorway was not David.

She didn't want to look, but she couldn't *not* look.

Shaking, she turned to face the figure in the doorway. There was no one there. Her hand shot forward, reaching around the door frame, fumbling for the light switch. She peered nervously into the kitchen. The now brightly lit kitchen was empty.

"What, are you deaf? Do. You have. Anything. For me?" David repeated.

Ashlyn exhaled slowly, her arms going limp as the tension released from every muscle. David placed the game console in the hand suspended by the sling, then snatched his envelopes from her with the free hand. Apparently, his injury excused him from having any manners.

"What the hell? Why are you wrecking my stuff?" he growled. "And why are they wet?" With a look of disgust, he stormed back to the living room and flopped on the sofa to resume his game.

She looked down at her stack of envelopes, which she still held in her other hand. Hers had been crumpled, too, when she'd been seized with terror.

She continued to tremble silently, fighting back tears. *He is completely oblivious.*

And disappointment. *Nothing we discussed made any lasting impression on him. Nothing has changed.*

And anger. *I'm upset, and he couldn't care less.*

As the color returned to her face, she replayed the sequence of events, starting from the moment she had stepped into their apartment. Then it occurred to her. *I haven't confided any of this to David. And I don't think I can . . .* She bit her lip, not sure where to turn. Tired and feeling defeated, her mind roiled, a jumble of emotions and irrational thoughts tripped over each other, playing table tennis with every thought.

He didn't bother to greet me when I came home.

Not until he saw I had his mail.

But I didn't exactly run up to him for a warm "happy to be home hug," either. Or even ask how his arm felt today.

She hadn't had a chance to before he'd gotten curt with her.

But it didn't bother me that he didn't greet me. Not like it used to.

Ashlyn was still standing in the hallway, holding the crumpled envelopes as she digested the situation. Flickers of understanding were threatening to break through. Momentary flashes of clarity were finally taking hold and leading the way to some of the answers that had been eluding her.

Ashlyn had grown indifferent to his impatience. His behavior didn't have the same effect on her anymore. *And nor does my behavior affect him.*

I can't make *him be happy.*

She had tried to be pleasant. And she had tried to be assertive. She had tried being more attentive and engaged with his interests. She had tried being submissive and agreeable to whatever he wanted. He was never happy. Not truly.

It finally dawned on her. *He is responsible for his own happiness.*

She couldn't fulfill his needs. And she was draining her well in trying. Her well—the place she drew from to please, to cajole, to comfort, to support, and to encourage—that space had nearly run dry. *And it hasn't made a damn bit of difference to his happiness.*

She had to admit to herself, it was time to say goodbye.

40

Mix, Decant, and Filter

Ashlyn didn't sleep well. She'd enjoyed a brief reprieve from the nightmares since the library visitation, but they came flooding back with a vengeance. Every time she shut her eyes, the gauzy image of the dark silhouette in her kitchen doorway appeared, more vivid, and the accompanying fear, more intense, than anything before.

She blinked up at the dark ceiling, waiting for the first hints of dawn's gray light. Her wakeful thoughts weren't any more cheery, weighed down by the dread of facing the inevitable: *What am I going to do about David?*

He'd already broken a couple of dishes trying to prepare a meal one-handed, and then cut his foot on one of the broken shards. *What a mess.* She rolled her eyes in the darkness.

At last, faint lines appeared, framing the slats of the blinds. Ashlyn carefully peeled the plump comforter off and slipped out of bed. Staring into the open doors of the closet, she rubbed her eyes, feeling the pupils adjusting to the poor light. David moaned in his sleep behind her, his casted arm resting on her pillow.

Saturday. Tuesday. It's not going to matter for the next six weeks or more.

She put her hands on her hips, searching her brain for someplace she could escape to. No library. No coffee shop. *I could go on our Saturday adventure without him!* She glared at his prone form under the comforter.

Sigh. The FiberWorx office was always an option. It was never devoid of humans, but on a weekend, Ashlyn was reasonably confident she could get a lot done because there would be fewer interruptions. Her timeline was eroding faster than her list of trials. Much faster.

Armed with a large thermos of coffee, Ashlyn headed to the lab.

~

While the current sequence was mixing and decanting and filtering along, she tackled the glassware cleaning—she hadn't lied to Matt, it had piled up. She had no intention of leaving the lab for the next few hours, so she buzzed back and forth between tasks, starting a new reaction and moving swiftly on to a few calibration tests.

With a satisfied smile, she declared, "Check," and drew a line through another trial.

"Now, maybe some of Budhil's research papers on e-textiles . . . " She rummaged in her backpack that she'd stuffed under the computer desk.

Her hand landed on a wad of folded paper. Frowning to herself, she pulled it out.

"*Ohhh*. These are Lin's printouts . . . ," she dropped the papers on the desk, "about the explosion."

She sat back in her swivel chair and laced her fingers over her stomach, eyes locked on the untidy stack. The overhead vents shut off, allowing the sounds of the machines running in the background to take over. The centrifuge, approaching its peak spin rate, began emitting a high-pitched ring that carried an hysterical note to it, evoking the image of a needle-sharp, Spartan metal spear, slowly, steadily drilling into her inner ear. Frozen in her chair, she waited it out.

It stopped. All the machines had finished processing her samples.

The high-pitched wail ceased. The imagined spear disappeared.

All was silent.

I'm not going to outrun this nightmare. Maybe it never ends until I stop running and I start listening?

Ashlyn unfolded Lin's printouts. She'd highlighted sections of newspaper articles and added some of her own notes:

> – August 21ˢᵗ, 1992, a week after the
>   accident:
>
> Investigators confirmed that the colossal
> explosion was the result of a bomb . . .
>
> Though only speculation at this time, insiders
> suggest a Mafia connection. It seems Rory's
> rocket booster ride to superstardom in the
> fashion industry may have ruffled more than a
> few feather boas . . . .
> —US *Globe News, Special Report*

> – Above source is questionable, but this may
>   be where Diane got her info? Interesting
>   note: at that time, most major papers
>   were following the siege at Ruby Ridge (3
>   people killed in a shootout with nutbar
>   landowners vs USMS + FBI), near Naples,
>   Idaho.

"What kind of bomb? What evidence did the investigators find?"

Before she could read further, a buzzer went off in her lab. She would have to be content with a breadcrumb to pick up later. For now, the gas was lit, the reaction was in progress, and if she didn't pay attention, she might have her own colossal disaster.

Between reactions, she considered reviewing some of the current research papers on e-textiles on SciFinder . . .

But her curiosity was gnawing at her and she couldn't resist the call to return to the puzzle. *How had the car blown up in the first place?*

Ashlyn eagerly skimmed more excerpts from Lin's findings.

> When asked for his reaction to the devastating
> news, famous designer Bosco de Venta
> responded: 'This is very unexpected. This does
> not happen in the world of fashion. But then,

who has ever heard of an Irish designer? *Absurd.*
Leave them to their singing and tap dancing.
Their fighting and bombing the Church. That is
their domain. *Design* is the domain of the
Italians. It is part of our DNA.'
— *Weekly World News*

"Not likely." Ashlyn frowned. "Ammonium-nitrate and fuel oil of the IRA variety . . . that's far too destructive. The explosion was more localized, more like an implosion," she mused.

She sat back in her chair, her mind tingling. As though some invisible hand guided her chin, she found herself staring at the jars of chemicals on the top shelf of the storage cabinet. *Last week . . .* her brow was knit tight as she tried to force the memory out. *What was it about these chemicals . . . all very dangerous chemicals . . . under the right conditions.*

Her face lit up. "Under the right conditions," she repeated.

Though Hollywood would have us believe it's perfectly normal for a regular car to be vaporized in a dramatic explosion, it is, in fact, really hard to do. *How many hours did I spend in that chemistry lab at college? With those nut bars who* wanted *to see things blow up!*

Most experiments went pop, *but nothing ever went* BOOM!

It was disheartening to think her lab was her only sanctuary, but this mystery was the most interesting thing going on in Lab #3. She walked around to the back of the divider, to view the storyboard with fresh eyes. The puzzle had taken on a life of its own, the divider now completely covered in breadcrumbs, as it were, hidden on the back, out of sight.

"Still looks like a lot of nonsense," she said, hands on her hips.

A tangle of colored strings crisscrossed the board. The juicy details, yet to be deciphered and added to the collage, were contained in two piles of printouts and random scraps of information labeled Pre-1992 and Post-1992. She'd also received a batch of emails from the library, which she'd sorted into a folder labeled The Accident, but she hadn't yet read through many of them.

Ping. A reminder: "Check your Flagged for Follow-Up email," she read.

Ashlyn rolled her eyes. She had left herself a note to follow up on her follow-up notes. "No wonder I'm getting nowhere fast."

Reluctantly, Ashlyn sat down at the lab computer and opened her inbox. She selected all the flagged email with research papers related to Budhil's work in the R&D lab.

"The Properties and Applications of Ignisium, Ig134," she read in a monotone, like her Chem 210 professor often did.

> When superheated, the resulting complex organic chain has the potential to release highly volatile vapors. The vapors must be captured and contained to avoid interference with laser-focusing properties . . ."

"That sounds really . . . *dangerous!*"

> . . . only a small amount of the Ig134 is required, which can be rendered inert when dissolved in a plasma substrate.

"Is this *really* one of Budhil's projects?"

She looked at the top of the reference. "Vladimir Polchenkov . . . Russia?"

> . . . all sources of ignition were controlled and only pulses of heat were pumped through the substrate. This method proved to be safe and generated positive results. However, experimentation with this complex organic compound must be conducted with extreme caution, as previous experiments have resulted in lethal, explosive chain reactions.

She scrolled down past the abstract, but only the abstract was translated, none of the research was included

"Argggh! Have I mixed up my email folders?" she groaned. *SCREEEECH-SCREECH-SCREECH!*

An alarm sounded from the workbench. Something, some part of her sequence, had gone off the rails.

Ashlyn jumped from her seat. "Shit!"

In her rush to respond to the alarm, she smashed her thighs on the computer table. "Shit! Shit!"

The computer monitor wobbled, and the table, rebounding off the divider, pushed Ashlyn back into her seat.

"Shouldn't you attend to that?" asked Richard.

"Fu—." *Gulp.*

"Huh? I—yeah. I just about knocked over the screen . . . I'm on it."

She nervously glanced at the papers that fluttered off the table behind the divider as she strode hastily to the screaming machine.

"Air bubbles," Ashlyn explained in the blissful quiet. "They can obscure the detector flow cell. This machine is particularly noisy when that happens."

"Is it Russian?" he asked as he turned his attention from her computer screen to her.

Ashlyn went white.

"The machine?" he continued.

She remained mute.

"Looks like you've pulled up the troubleshooting guide already." He smiled. "That's why we're so happy with the work you're doing in here." He winked at her and slipped back out of the lab as quietly as he had entered.

It took her forty-five minutes to reset the sequence. It took nearly as long for her heart to stop pounding. When she finally finished, she was fuming, cursing herself for getting sidetracked.

Plink.

A new email.

Resisting the urge to walk back over to the laptop at the sound of her email alert, Ashlyn pulled her goggles down to her chin and squinted at the screen on the desk. It was a new email from the library. She pushed the safety goggles back into place and peered intently at the demarcations on the graduated cylinder. Carefully, she added the indicator to the solution: *1 . . . 2 . . . 3 . . . drops of beryl blue.* She then added the catalyst and marched back to the beginning and double-checked each step, ignoring the email alerts.

Satisfied that *this time* the reaction was going to run to completion, she strode over to the monitors and gauges and recorded each readout. Next, she compared her handwritten notes against the gauges. She wasn't going to give management any excuse to deny her a position in Budhil's lab!

Barely fifteen minutes into the new sequence, she was already struggling to concentrate as the *plink, plink, plink* of new email arriving in her inbox was driving her to distraction. She couldn't remember how many microfiche and Special Collections requests she had made at the library, but they were coming in fast and furious now.

It wasn't until she had crossed two more sets of trials off her list that she relaxed a little.

"Check. Check."

She glared at her laptop. "You come last."

She surveyed her workbench and checked the time. "Damn." She'd put in a full day already. It was time to clean up and get out. "Alright," she said, as if giving in to a child. "You next." She went around to the back of the divider and picked up the papers that had scattered.

One of Lin's notes lay on top.

- This kept appearing in my results:
  (looks like Greek sigma, but different).
  Don't know what this is, either (can't even
  say it): Ignisium?

Ashlyn stiffened as she returned to the lab computer. Before waking the computer, the gyrating periodic table screen saver stopped spinning and a cube tumbled forward like the roll of a die.

She lurched forward and poked her finger at the screen. "Ig134." She clicked on the icon.

Ig: 134 – Ignisium:
Derived from the Latin for "fire." Diatomic,
non-metal element. Highly reactive. Found only
in the Omsk region in Russia, where, according
to folklore, large meteorite fragments crashed
into the region thousands of years ago.

The virtual die flipped to show the related pictographic symbol. It was the one Lin had scribbled.

41

Trusted News Outlets

Ashlyn had tiptoed her way around the apartment and out the door for work on Monday morning. For his part, David had been mostly pleasant since he'd snapped at her on Friday. *Why wouldn't he be—no work for six weeks, pain killers, gaming all day . . .*

Hey, Babe! I've mastered Level 21! I'm slaying Steve and Jason. Booyah! The third text today.

Ashlyn looked at her list of trials still waiting to be run. Saturday she'd made progress, but today had started poorly and didn't show signs of improvement, so she kept herself locked inside Lab #3. David's texts were her only contact with the outside world.

That, and her storyboard. Though escaping to the past was significantly more fulfilling. She examined one of the fiche photos that she'd received from the library. It featured a "centuries-old café in Damascus", according to the notes from the librarian. The photo itself was labeled "Inside the Nutura Café." Ashlyn studied the fascinating floor to ceiling tapestries. Below the photo, a short description.

> Ancestral tapestries of the nomadic Bedouin
> tribes. The designs, and the symbols used, are
> particular to each tribe and recount their
> histories, going back centuries.

"Very cool," she said, then looked up at the storyboard, trying to figure out where/when Damascus was relevant.

She shrugged, then placed the photo back on the pile, and swallowed the last of the morning's One-Shot latte.

"Eww." It was cold and mostly sugar.

Back on the whiteboard side of the divider, she drew a fat green line through the next trial on her slowly shrinking list. "At least I got another one of these done!"

"Late nights, weekends . . . It never ends." She leaned on her desk, shaking her head. "This lab was meant to have two people in it. Maybe that's what I should've asked Joan in HR about."

Ashlyn stood up and set her jaw. "I am going to leave the office at the same time as everyone else, today!" she declared.

But where should she go? David was still "convalescing" at home. She searched her thoughts. And her heart. David's texts sounded happy. But she still didn't want to be where he was.

Something else called to her. A far-off voice vied for her attention.

"Yes!" Ashlyn suddenly knew the exact place she needed to go: Union Square, the entryway to the Fashion District. She loved the fashion boutiques and home decor stores. She loved the snooty stores that carried name brands next to the quirky shops with kitschy, handmade folk art and one-of-a-kind items.

Smiling to herself, she quickly fired off a text to Lin and Diane: *Early Black Friday shopping, anyone? I'm headed to Union Square.*

Almost immediately, from Diane: *Let's meet at the Eclectic Emporium!!!*

Perfect.

~

Ashlyn pulled the dull gray trench coat off the hook in her cubicle and kicked off her stylish Kate Spade boots, swapping them for her weathered Blundstones. Despite her lackluster shell, Ashlyn was positively beaming as she hit the Fashion District.

Lin's response buzzed in her pocket as she rounded the last corner: *I'm in. See you there in an hour.*

Yesss! I got time, then. Ashlyn was eager to poke her nose in all the shop windows. She looked admiringly at the long, flowing Jacquard knit skirt from Paris in one window. Next door in the Sweater Market window, she admired an authentic Shetland wool sweater that was snuggly fitted over a plastic torso.

She had crossed the street to wend her way back toward the Eclectic Emporium, when something captured her attention, luring her face right up to the store's window. There was something desperately handsome about the moleskin jacket on display in Union-Made Men's Clothing. Glassy-eyed, Ashlyn cocked her head, trying to picture the kind of man that would wear the jacket.

I may have to buy that . . . the instant I find someone who can pull it off.

Stepping back, she considered the piece with a critical eye. *It wouldn't work for David.*

A flash of resentment, but then a realization. *Dressing David is not my problem.*

That was freeing.

Buoyed by the thought, she wandered in. From the "Photographer Slim" jacket, her gaze flitted over the racks and shelves and settled on the chamois shirts in the center of the store.

"For the outdoorsman in your life," the sign read.

The shirt reminded her of her father.

"These chammies for making the trucks all shiny feel just like your shirt, Daddy," she remembered saying during one of her regular visits to the fire hall. She might have been five or six, but she remembered thinking it was odd that his clothes felt like the cleaning rags.

She allowed herself to fall back into the memory. "That's coz they're made of the same cloth," Ted had replied.

Then he'd grabbed a teal-green scrap of velour fabric from the rag box. "This, I believe, was once a fancy leisure suit. You think maybe I should wear clothes like this, instead?" he asked, looking very serious.

Wee Ashlyn made a face. "You can't wear tha-at!"

At that, he cracked a big smile. "Your mom would *love* that!" he said and let out a deep, belly laugh.

His laughter didn't convince her that his judgment could be trusted, and she continued to eye him suspiciously. That only spurred him on to a bigger fit of laughter.

"But what she really wants," her dad said cheekily, "is for me to give up the Birkenstocks with socks."

SMH. Grown-up Ashlyn smiled. *I kinda agree with Mom on that one.*

"Can I help you?" came a voice from behind her.

A sales assistant had come over and interrupted her reverie. Snapping back to the present, Ashlyn realized she'd had her hands all over the mannequin, gently stroking the chamois shirt on the hanger while her mind was lost in the memory.

"Oh. I—. No, I'm just flipping through my . . . mental Christmas list," she stammered. Then, letting go of the sleeve, she added, "Someone I knew loved these shirts. But he's not on my list this year."

Feeling awkward now, she had a quick scan of the rest of the store, and ogled the enchanting "Photographer Slim" jacket one last time, before exiting.

She resumed her leisurely stroll down the street, wandering in and out of a few more stores, biding her time and building up the anticipation for the Eclectic Emporium. She loved to roam through every aisle and *flick! flick! flick!* her way along the hangers.

As she descended the last couple of steps into the basement-level store, she was greeted by a couple of gleeful squeals.

"I'll be over here with all the designer labels, of course," Diane said.

Ashlyn followed Diane toward the designer labels. "I can't afford most of these clothes, even with their 'previously loved' price tag, but a girl can dream, no?" she said.

"I'm headed over there," Lin pointed to a selection of clothing for more moderate tastes.

Not much available in the range of "average" frames, Ashlyn thought as she skimmed along the array of tops on one of the racks.

She stopped suddenly. Her brain was a few hangers behind where her furiously-flicking fingers were. She went back a couple of hangers to take a closer look at an intriguing bouclé top.

"This is adorable," she whispered.

She held up a simple off-white shawl with bold crimson vines and wispy curling tendrils that appeared to germinate, like living vines, out of the shaggy fringe along the bottom.

"You could wear that," Diane said approvingly.

Ashlyn reached for the tag at the back. The label was one she'd never known before meeting the GOM, but immediately recognized now. The top she held in her hands looked so modern, so contemporary. *But this has to be twenty years old . . . doesn't it?*

"You looked confused," Diane said, laughing.

"I didn't realize this was the consignment rack," Ashlyn replied slowly.

"It's not."

Red-faced, Ashlyn replaced the shawl and began flipping wildly through the clothes she'd already perused. There it was again. She had whizzed by his label at least half a dozen times without even registering it.

Seven pieces. Eight. Nine. . . eleven . . . fourteen. Wow.

She pulled another top from the rack and held it up high so she could examine the whole piece. She had seen this pattern earlier that day. *The designs on the tapestries. The Bedouin tribal symbols.*

Ashlyn's mind reeled. *Rory Mannix has not been wandering this earth for centuries, surely.* She shook her head. *Of course not.*

But. Her mind worked, trying to fit the pieces together. *But he* could *have been in Damascus* after *1992.*

She lifted the soft, silky shirt made of sheer gossamer up in front of her again. It was black, with very clean lines down the shoulders opening into wide, tapered sleeves. Both the sleeves and the waist of the shirt terminated with a border reminiscent of the patterns on the tribal tapestries. The pattern wasn't just a trim stitched to the base, but part of the weave of the fabric that began to emerge at the waist and at the elbows, but only became fully apparent at the edges of the garment.

"*Exquisite,*" she whispered.

"I know, isn't it?"

Ashlyn whirled around to see Diane and the storekeeper, who was dressed all in black and had piercings in her eyebrow, nose, lip and tongue. Ashlyn regarded the Gothic-attired, middle-aged woman, a stark contrast to her own rather vanilla appearance.

Then she noticed the Mannix logo, plainly visible on the invisible pockets of the woman's black lace and red leather waistcoat. An appreciation of the depth of Rory's brilliance began to dawn on her. *His clothes* speak *for the wearer. His creations are the essence of storytelling.*

"I'm the owner of the Eclectic Emporium," the woman informed Ashlyn. "Diane said you had questions?"

Ashlyn's mouth went up and down, but no words came out.

"You may or may not be familiar with the designer," the owner jumped in, pointing at the shimmery black top Ashlyn was still holding. "That label has been around for over twenty years.

After the designer died in 1992, his estate sold the rights to the label to a holding company.”

“So, these pieces are not Rory Mannix’s work?” Ashlyn finally found her voice.

“Oh, you *have* heard of him. Fabulous!” The store’s owner beamed. “No. Not Rory’s, of course, he died, as I said. Then the company, created from his estate, began to award grants to new talent all over the globe. You may have noticed the very different pieces with the same label in different sections of the store.”

“Yeah, I did notice. Quite an eclectic mix of styles and patterns,” Ashlyn replied.

The proprietress turned her head, bemused. “Y-ess,” she said, motioning to the store’s name emblazoned in neon lighting above the cash register.

“It *is* the Eclectic Emporium, after all.” Diane gave Ashlyn a playful shove.

Ashlyn smiled sheepishly. “I just mean that the pieces from this one label are so diverse. I—I didn’t know that the label was being used today. That explains a lot, actually.”

Or does it? I’m more confused now than ever! He was not dead, but I saw his label nowhere? Now that he is dead, I see his label on everything.

He’s dead, but his label lives?

Has he been designing clothing all this time? Or are these pieces by other people who received the grants? Others he’s influenced?

“You don’t look convinced,” said the store owner. Then she tossed her head back in the universal “Aha. I see!” gesture. “Oh, you must be getting *mis*-informed by social media!” she chided. “That story? About Rory Mannix. Under witness protection? Pa-lease! ,” she said, shaking her head. “The man died twenty years ago.”

“I *told* her you knew everything there was to know about fashion,” Diane said.

“Whoever that guy was—the one in the papers, that died of liver disease—he was *not* Rory Mannix. DevoNews totally discredited those sources,” she scoffed.

It had never occurred to Ashlyn that she would find any answers in a clothing store in 2012. But, then, she hadn’t been searching for him in any of the places she might actually have seen his work, like a clothing store.

"What about the secret message in his label?" Diane prompted the store owner.

"Right, yes. That's the best part of the Rory Mannix legacy. 'Rory Mannix' was not his given name," the woman continued. "He never did divulge it. But that's not important. The initials *R* and *M* are actually based on the ancient symbols that form the *fein cretim*."

"Excuse me?" asked Ashlyn, feeling the floor drop from under her feet. Pieces of her puzzle slipped easily into place. And all she'd had to do was ask.

"The symbol. On his logo. It's an invitation to greatness."

The woman got a far-off look. "I never cared what his real name was. He was sooooome handsome." She bit her lip. "I went to all of his early shows. *Before* he got big." Her upper lip curled in a lusty snarl, and her attention drifted off to some long-forgotten memory. "Man, he got big . . ."

Ashlyn became uncomfortable.

"I was at his last show. And the after-party," she said, nodding absently. "That's when he told me about the *fein cretim*."

Ashlyn's blood ran hot, but she didn't breathe a word, hoping there was more.

"I offered to get him a whiskey." She looked kind of sad. "He said 'Vlad's mixed something even better for me.' Then he just gave me a wink and left the party."

42

More Than Skin Deep

"It looks good," Ashlyn said, admiring herself in the full-length mirror.

I don't have a full-length mirror!

The Ashlyn in the mirror wore the off-white top she'd seen in the Eclectic Emporium. The Rory Mannix top. Like he knew she would find it. Like it was made for her. The embroidered motif that emerged out of the tangle of threads hinted at an untamed wilderness, the seeds of new growth hidden underneath. The bold vines, free of the jungle, stretched skyward, the tendrils reaching blindly for something solid to grasp on to, something to anchor the body of the vine. The vine, however, bore no blossom, no fruit. The pattern, it seemed, was incomplete, the grand design not fully expressed.

Like he knows my innermost secrets.

The top began to glow, the dull off-white morphed into a pearly sheen, slowly growing in intensity, like someone playing with the dimmer switch, the garment becoming ever brighter, until it was blinding white. The coarse vines, like plump arteries, near the base of the shirt, began to pulse, pushing upward. The finer, constricted capillaries pushed against the thin lines at the leading edge of the pattern, like bony fingers straining upward toward her throat.

Her heart rate quickened, keeping pace to match the pulse of the red threads. She pulled her chin up, stretching away from the advancing tendrils. Panic set in and Ashlyn staggered backward from the mirror, clutching at her throat.

Terror-stricken, Ashlyn sat up, desperately snatching at the cloth around her throat, and instinctively reached over to swat at the bedside lamp. She was in her bed. Alone. The headlights of a passing car swept across her window, the light penetrating between the slats in the blinds.

Bedroom. Not dungeon. She exhaled with great relief.

At last her fingers relaxed, releasing the cotton nightshirt she'd been gripping since sitting up. Ashlyn looked down at the neckline to see fine streaks of fresh blood seeping into the white fabric of her nightshirt. She found little folds of skin under her nails, too.

43

Journey Through the Flames

David was asleep on the couch. Again. She hadn't missed him coming into bed. Especially now, with the cast. His constant shifting and adjusting stole any sleep she managed to get between nightmares. His cast, however, was not impeding his ability to slay zombies.

Ashlyn packed him a small picnic and set the cooler next to the sofa.

He looks more comfortable there anyway.

She brought him the painkillers the doctor had prescribed and lightly placed a blanket on him. Whatever form their future took, it would be far better with a healed and functional David than a cranky, injured, inhibited David.

Ashlyn quietly shut the door and locked it, heading off to work. Her mind was set on the spin cycle. She could give and give of herself, and he would consume it in his relentless search for the fountain of youth, or the secret to living carefree with no obligations to anyone or anything, or whatever it was that would ultimately make him happy.

And it's not my place *to make him happy.*

The answer, the solution to the disharmony in her life, lay somewhere in an unknowable future. *A future that doesn't include David.* The deep *thump* of the heels on her favorite Kate Spade boots hitting the cold San Francisco sidewalk filled the silence that followed that last thought.

"My sweet *orchidea porcelain*," cooed Marty. "Jou do not need to fear, nor despair."

Ashlyn blinked in stunned silence back at Marty, the confusion overwhelming her senses. *Fear? Despair? I stewed in chaotic thoughts for twenty minutes walking here, and he puts it all together in two seconds?*

"Marty, you are truly remarkable," she said after a moment, a hint of accusation in her voice.

"Your aura is unbalanced," he said, shaking his head with a knowing smile. "I sing the *icaros* for jou. A Quechuan healing song."

He handed her a pumpkin spice latte.

It's simple. My aura is unbalanced . . . Hmmf.

She stepped away from the coffee stand, warmed by Marty's reassuring smile. Despite her skepticism, the weight on her shoulders began lifting, little by little.

She became aware of everything outside her, looking out from within. She became aware, once again, of commuters commuting. Of alternating waves of vehicles and pedestrians crisscrossing the intersection. Of the delightful fashion smorgasbord that traipsed into her field of view. *I guess Marty's right, life goes on.*

The white pedestrian sign appeared. Walk. It struck her as a command. She stood, resolutely, at the corner. Then, the flashing Don't Walk command. *Not a command . . . A warning, to keep moving forward.*

Ashlyn pressed forward, crossing to the other side.

Rory Mannix, I know who you are. She stared ahead, locking her gaze on his bench. *I will meet your dark stare. Wherever you decide to intrude.*

Head held high, she walked slowly by his park bench, daring him to taunt her. Ready to meet him head-on. But he wasn't there. He would not meet her there.

He won't give me the satisfaction.

~

Ping!

Ashlyn closed the file on another completed sequence and immediately turned her attention to the new email she'd just received.

"Another police file?" She stared, suspicious. "I hope Lin's not going to get in trouble on my account."

Taking a nervous glance at her workbench where her reaction was nearing its finish, she dared to open the new attachments from the library.

Case File 110981: Maserati involved in Single Vehicle Crash and Fatality.

Witness Interview: 008

Witness stated having conversation with victim between 2030-2200h.

Victim described as "depressed."

Witness stated: "Rory said he felt torn apart. Said 'I just can't live like this.'"

Asked if victim demonstrated any unusual behavior, witness stated: "I offered to get him another whiskey. He said 'Nah, Vlad hooked me up with something better.' I didn't know who Vlad was. And I thought it was weird that he wanted a vodka instead of whiskey."

Another file. It contained a detailed forensic report:

Case File 110981: Maserati involved in Single Vehicle Crash and Fatality.
Forensic Report:

Accelerant used? YES. Fibers of carpet flooring behind passenger seat found saturated.

Type of Accelerant? UNKNOWN.

Items #33, #34, #35A and #35B: these parts likely used as timing device. Further analysis required.

Items #66, #67: glass fragments, likely from a bottle, embossed with "NRTB 03EP." Appear

to be a match for Pyat Ozer or Five Lakes
Vodka.

Items #108, #109: braking system parts.
Evidence of tampering present.

On their own, these details didn't make much sense, but cobbled together with fragments from her own memory, a picture began to take shape in Ashlyn's mind. She went back to the ignisium research paper.

"Vladimir Polchenkov," she confirmed. "One of the researchers experimenting with '. . . a highly reactive', 'unknown' chemical substance. Is this . . . 'Vlad'? And the Pyat Ozer bottle?" she looked back at the case file notes, "Vodka? Or a semi-stable plasma substrate?"

She placed one hand over her mouth, shaking her head in disbelief, then sat back. "That is ab-so-*lutely* a recipe for disaster! *Why* would anyone take such a risk?"

She knew why.

Rory was terrified of losing control of his art and becoming a slave to others' expectations—to the industry. His disappearance was undeniably related to the accident, but the accident . . .

"Based on these police files, it was a misfire."

An escape plan, foiled. Rory Mannix had refused to relinquish control of his life and so conspired with a Russian scientist to escape, forever. *Could he have? Would he really consider it? A final act of defiance: End it all?*

~

The snarling and barking of the white dog echoed in her ears that night. She felt as cold and damp as the wet pavement had been on Fight Night, when the beast had lunged at her and David. The savage growl seemed to be coming at her from every direction in the blackness of her dream world. She couldn't see the dog, but she could feel her muscles tense with each series of barks. The sound would jab at her from above, then quickly fade, as though the dog was far off in the distance. Then the menacing bark would re-emerge, fresh and fierce, from another direction entirely. And fade again, just as quickly.

Every fiber of her body vibrated with terror. She retreated into herself, trying to make herself as small as she could, hoping to make it harder for the noise to find her. There was nothing to hold on to and nowhere to go.

It doesn't matter which direction I choose, there is something dark and terrifying I must face.

Or stay right here. Trapped.

The barking dog retreated into the blackness.

The only sound, her stunted breathing, uneven and shallow. The emptiness swallowed each exhalation.

As her breaths came more evenly, her eyes adjusted to the blackness that surrounded her. It began to shimmer, like ink. Then a light, from nowhere, illuminated milky images on a liquid surface. Muted sounds erupted all around, like she had cotton in her ears.

Before her eyes, two firefighters jogged toward the yellow car, holding the Jaws of Life. Inside the car, only the fair hair of the motionless driver of the Maserati was visible.

"Cars don't just explode," her dad said with a "you already know *that*" look.

But no one knew that, behind the seat, was a Russian vodka bottle containing a highly reactive, relatively unknown chemical substance. Except for the car's owner.

A garbage truck, marked by yellow stripes where the two vehicles had impacted, had veered left and slammed into a memorial statue bearing the Everlasting Flame. Passersby and witnesses came rushing over to assist the driver of the truck. Meanwhile, true to its name, the Everlasting Flame remained lit as its wire basket toppled off the top of the monument.

Ashlyn watched the tumbling basket bouncing and rolling away. When the basket finally came to rest, the flames innocently licked at the pavement.

Only two sets of eyes had seen the wire basket tumble from the monument. One set in the fire truck, the other hidden on the edge of the trees.

Unseen by anyone, the glass bottle in the yellow car had been smashed. The pieces of a puzzle the police investigators never solved. What the police reports had only itemized: "An unknown substance. A saturated floor rug behind the passenger seat. Shards of a glass bottle . . .”

"Ignisium dissolved in plasma,” Ashlyn whispered. "You wouldn't see a trail of flames racing along the liquid that spilled out . . . ” Her thoughts danced between memory and her dream world.

"It was pooled on the floor . . . Waiting for enough heat energy to reach ignition temperature.” Her eyes grew wide. "Rory must have been ejected when the vehicles collided . . .”

Stepping back into her memories, young Ashlyn's eyes locked on Rory hidden in the trees. Time slowed to a trickle.

The flash of world-obliterating light. No one was expecting the car to explode suddenly, with two firefighters caught too close to the blast. No one was expecting a soul to be rent in two.

Illuminated, in the center of the brilliant light, Rory's logo, Ashlyn's symbol sketched in pencil, hung suspended over the scene. Then blackness.

The choice had never been Rory's to make. There would be no final exit. He was not to interfere with what the fates had decreed. It was his destiny to continue to bring his visionary creations into the world. And three souls were sacrificed to keep order in the universe: the unfortunate soul who took the wheel of the Maserati, instead of Rory, the heroic firefighter's, and hers.

44

Not With A Bang, But a Whimper

"Ashlyn, what are you still doing here?"

Ashlyn looked toward the door, where only Richard's torso could be seen.

"It's Thanksgiving tomorrow. Go home. Spend time with your family." He gave her one of his winning smiles. "See you next week." And then the torso disappeared.

Ashlyn did head straight home after work. With each step, she felt as though she was pushing through water up to her waist, dreading a long weekend at home. David would be expecting that they could pull together a full bells-and-whistles turkey feast at the last minute. She knew he would be bitterly disappointed that the stores would be closed tomorrow when *he* was ready to make preparations. That he would blame her for not going out now to get a turkey and stuffing and pumpkin pie. But she didn't care.

I'm exhausted. If he wanted a turkey, he had all day to get groceries. Maybe he can't swing a hammer, but he could get someone to put a turkey in a bag for him.

She was going to go home, empty-handed, and he was going to have to suck it up.

Ah, who am I kidding? I'm going to drag my ass in, tired, and he will be all offended. Then he'll blow it off and do as he pleases.

If anyone was going to feel uneasy, it was going to be her. If she wanted to be in the living room reading a book in the window nook, it wouldn't bother him in the least. He would turn on the TV and play his game or watch the sports highlights. If the noise or the flashing lights bothered her, she could move elsewhere. No, he wouldn't go play on the computer at the desk in the kitchen, or watch highlights on his iPad.

But tonight, she was completely out of "Give a shit!" and if he put one toe across the line, she would let him have it. She stepped into the front hall and stood, silent. Her hand hesitated, about to drop her keys into the tin plate, but then placed them in her purse instead.

I. Am. Home.

She let a big sigh of relief escape her lips.

Relax, Ashlyn. Breathe.

It took less than thirty seconds before David intruded into her peace.

"I know that sound," came a detached voice from the living room.

How can you . . . possibly hear anything? She couldn't even hear her own footsteps over the death metal and gun blasts from the loud speakers on the TV.

And it puzzled her, too, that he wore the headphones during the day, so as not to disturb the neighbors, of course. Who were mostly gone. At their jobs. But during the evening, particularly Friday evenings, the headphones came off. "The city bylaws say I can make noise until 11 p.m.," he'd informed her on numerous occasions.

"Yeeee-hah. Take that!" He was back to his game, not waiting for her response.

She lingered at the front closet. She needed to steel herself for the time it would take to get through the civilities of coming home:

"How was your day?"

"Meh."

"What do you want for dinner?"

"Let's just order pizza?"

"Great idea. Let me change into comfy clothes."

"K."

"K."

But she didn't want to have to slink by him. She didn't want to have to nod hello to whomever was on the screen in the little picture-in-picture box, hunting warlocks with David. She didn't want to have to hide in their bedroom, just to be alone with her thoughts.

She stood in the front hall another moment longer, teetering on the edge.

Her sadness finally overwhelmed her, pushing back against her instinct to bottle it up. When she put her face in her hands, her shoulders immediately folded in, her legs wobbled, and finally, her legs gave out and she crumpled to the floor next to the curio table. There, she wept quietly to herself.

An errant sniffle escaped. She could almost see it undulate down the hall, a single note traveling as a wave from her lips directly to his uncovered ear. David peered curiously around the corner.

"You OK? Ddo you want me to pause the game?" he asked.

"No," she replied, barely above a whisper.

She could hear him shuffle in his seat, struggling to figure out what to do.

No, no, no. You're going to decide to have a conscience now? *For the love of god, just keep playing your game.*

David's conscience was never any match for the impulse to do exactly what he wanted to do, which should have been to continue playing the game. She was counting on it.

"Hang on, Pete. Oh, hey! We killed the Elemental. Nice one! Hey, I gotta take a quick break. I'll go to the Hebrides Inn. Meet you back here in fifteen?"

No, no, NO! Just keep playing your goddamn game! I don't want to do this right now!

She wiped at her eyes and tried to pull herself together. She was not interested in having him suddenly appear the white knight, come to rescue her from her sadness. Too little, too late. *Damn you!*

She stood up quickly, and briskly finished shaking the cloak of weariness from her shoulders. Plastering a fake smile on her face, chin up, she turned to enter her home, putting the burden of her happiness squarely on her own shoulders, and denying him his chance to be a hero.

"So, should we just order pizza, then?" she asked, pulling her sweater down over her hips, straightening the folds and making herself appear comfortable and at ease. *No problem here. Nope. As you were.*

"What? Huh? You were just crying over there. I *saw* you huddled in a—a *pile* by the front table. You were crying your eyes out." He seemed genuinely concerned.

"What gives?" His expression soured. He looked perturbed, like he knew that she was holding out on him.

And she knew that would piss him off. She could see that he had put his friend on hold to attend to her needs. *Yes, I see you've made a special effort, on my behalf, taking time out of your busy, on disability leave, schedule.*

She had also noticed it was a convenient time for him to break from the game. He wasn't prepared to have a meaningful conversation. He was prepared to give her a "there, there" and a supportive hug. To hold her long and tight, just enough to meet his boyfriendly duties, and then he would be able to resume his game and wait for the pizza, that she would order, to be delivered to him at the couch.

"Another bitch of a day at the office?" he said, nodding his head knowingly. He was quick to sympathize with anyone suffering under the boot of unfair working conditions.

"Yeah. The *usj*, you know. Long day, boring. I'm fine," she said in a neutral tone. "It's fine. You can go back to the game. Don't let me interrupt you," she added, hoping not to set off his bullshit detector.

Then she tried to dodge his embrace, but she knew that was a mistake as soon as she had made her move.

"What the fuck?" He stood up straight, throwing his arms out in indignation, game controller still in his good hand. "I'm just trying to help. What's your problem?"

"I didn't say I had a problem," she said flatly, still in motion, heading to the kitchen as though she had a purpose and didn't want to be interrupted. "So, pizza?" she tried again.

"Fuck. Whatever." He dropped his arms and started to turn to head back to the TV and his game. She waited for the sound of the TV. But he must have changed his mind.

Silence.

She had blown him off. And he had been cooped up at home for a few days now. It wouldn't take much to set him off. She braced herself.

"No. Not whatever, actually. What's up with you? I haven't hardly *seen* you the last few months. Then I get injured. Yeah, I can take care of myself, but a little sympathy would be nice!" he snarled.

"Are you seeing someone?" he said suddenly, like the thought had just occurred to him. He looked at her suspiciously, "Are you fucking around on me?!" he accused.

Stunned, she stammered a little. She was not expecting that question. "N—, no." She frowned. "No, I'm not cheating on you," she stated firmly.

Frantically, she searched through the mental images and conversations of the past month. She was pretty sure he hadn't been listening when she mentioned the GOM on her morning commute. And how disturbing it had been to have a strange man stare at her every morning. She was pretty sure he hadn't been listening when she told her girlfriends about the story of the GOM's death in the paper, about having seen the celebrity fashion designer days before he died. And he hadn't probed after waking her up as she thrashed wildly in her sleep. He'd gotten a good laugh out of it instead.

Turning to face him, she told him what she had been doing. "I've been working late in the lab because I can't finish my reactions before the end of the day. I don't get my reactions finished because I'm sneaking out of the coffee station to network, where I find out from coworkers that the job I really want is being posted for an open competition. I don't even *know* my coworkers because they do all their socializing when I'm locked away in that lab by myself . . ."

"Right." His expression softened a little.

This is good, this is safe. We can console each other about how much work sucks.

She wasn't prepared to talk to him about the GOM, and how his story had evolved into the Rory Mannix mystery. A mystery she was now desperate to solve. Nor could she share her nightmares. Those subjects were off-limits. Comfortable on this common ground, she let the momentum carry her forward on this track.

"Yeah, stuck in the lab. And now you're laid up, so I certainly can't afford to be choosy at work. I gotta keep taking what they're giving."

"Wait, you spend all day—alone—in the lab, and then you go off to be alone in the library? Studying to get a promotion . . . so you can spend *more* time in that miserable place?"

"It probably doesn't help my case any to be showing up late and dead tired after babysitting you in the emergency room until four in the morning!"

As she rattled on, she could feel the last of the delicate threads that held together their tattered relationship unraveling.

"You would rather spend all that time alone than come home?"

"Well, maybe if —."

"I thought we were going to make time to do more fun stuff together?"

She looked at the cast on his arm. Broken, like the proverbial straw on the camel's back.

The futility of their relationship was hard to miss. She was done.

Her focus was on all things that had nothing to do with him. *Her* career, where *she* was going. Not making time to spend with *him*, to care for him, and, most notably, *not* having sex with him.

"It's like I don't even know who you are any more," he said at last. Then, more softly, "It's like we aren't even together anymore."

She could tell that he had begun to see what she already knew, that what had been their relationship had deteriorated well past "still seeing each other." They were more or less roommates, with privileges, and even that was debatable.

She looked him directly in the eye, her gaze unwavering, and in a matter-of-fact tone agreed, "No. It's like we aren't."

45

Move On

David's expression darkened. "Guess I'll be looking for a new place."

He stayed up late playing his game and fuming. As Ashlyn headed off to bed, she looked over at him. She didn't love him anymore, but she knew he had a rough time ahead.

In the morning, she found David muttering to himself and furiously texting. He alternated between strong, self-assuredness: "Yeah, Jeff's solid. That'll work," and barking rage when his phone bleeped back with the wrong answer: *No can do, bro.*

"Fuck 'im!" He dropped his hand and looked skyward, frowning.

Then his face lit up. "Pete! He's got no old lady right now."

Nodding in support of his own statements, David began madly texting again. Ashlyn knew better than to say anything when he was like this, so she gave him a wide berth. She slipped out the front door quietly, and headed over to Lin's to watch the Macy's Thanksgiving Day Parade.

When she returned at the end of the day, David had calmed down. He conceded that he couldn't afford the rent for their apartment on his own, so he volunteered to move out, thoughtful soul that he was.

"So, to make things easier on *you*, I arranged to stay with a friend until I find my own place." He had eventually found a sympathetic ear and a couch to surf on for a couple of weeks.

"I'll be back for my things when I find my own place," he said, all business.

He walked passed her, dropped his duffel bag by the door, and then scanned the apartment: the walls, the curio table, the front closet.

"O. . .K. That's. Good," Ashlyn managed. It seemed to be happening so fast, but it really was what she wanted. *Wasn't it?*

She looked deep into his eyes, one last time. This was real. This would be final.

Am I making a mistake?

Was she recklessly throwing something away, or was there really nothing left of their relationship to salvage? They hadn't even considered couples counseling. What if? What about . . . ? Maybe . . .

Maybe nothing.

Is this how it's supposed to feel?

How can something you want *make you feel so awful?*

What was I expecting?

Then the silence between them grew uncomfortable. They were no longer lovers. Probably not even friends any more. Just strangers.

Mercifully, David's cell beeped at him.

"That's Kevin. My ride's here. I got a bag of my clothes packed and a few essentials. D'ya mind grabbing my box of stuff from the bedroom?" he said, waving his cast arm. He picked up his duffel bag in his other hand.

When she returned with the box, Kevin stood behind David in the open doorway. David pushed the door all the way open so Ashlyn could hand the box straight to Kevin, who smiled awkwardly. "Hi Ash."

"Hi Kev. Thanks." She looked between the two men. She wanted to say more, but there were no words.

Kevin gave her a silent nod of understanding, then turned to leave.

"Goodbye," said David. It almost sounded like a question.

Ashlyn wasn't sure she believed it herself. *Is this really happening?*

"Goodbye," she replied, barely above a whisper, the words catching in her throat.

She watched the door close behind him and waited for the *click.*

Ashlyn stood there, motionless, waiting to *feel*. *Something*. She felt numb. She stood until her legs wouldn't hold her anymore, the weight of the moment settling on her like a wet blanket. Weakly, she backed up two steps to lean against the arm of the couch behind her, but couldn't yet sit.

She waited. To feel . . . alright. She felt nothing. She wished to feel sad or angry or hurt. The absence of any emotion left a void of unfathomable emptiness, like opening the pantry when you're starving, only to find bare shelves, coated in dust.

She stared at the door, waiting for the finality of it to set in, for a sense that it was *actually over* to take hold. All the while, images of all that had been—good, bad, and otherwise—played through her mind.

It could have been two hours. Maybe more. Ashlyn stared, numb, awash in silent upheaval. Finally, she jolted back to life. Finally, she felt something: *Move on.*

46

Take it Head-On

"Jou look terrible," said Marty, *tsk-tsking* as he steamed her latte.

"Huh?" Ashlyn stopped rummaging around in her vacuous purse to look up at Marty, a little wounded. *Well, that was unexpected. I've had some rough mornings, but he's always been so kind to not mention it.*

"Jou're not sleeping well?" He wore a look of genuine concern on his face.

And a new winter hat. This one had flaps for the ears and braided ropes that hung from the flaps. The ropes with knots tied on the ends looked like a Chinese rattle-drum when he whipped his head this way and that. He reminded Ashlyn of Jack Russell terriers, every motion they made seemed accentuated by a hop or a bounce.

"I—No. No, I haven't been sleeping well. I've been working late and, just, other stuff. You know." She hadn't expected anything but their usual, flirtatious banter.

"Jes, jes. I see jou walking each day. But jou don't *see* anymore, jour head down, always. It's no good," he said, shaking his head.

She didn't disagree. And she certainly didn't have the wherewithal to debate it with Marty, or anyone, for that matter. She just hoped to get through her day.

"That's a fabulous serape," she said, gesturing to the heavy cotton cape-like wrap he had draped over his shoulders.

The intricate geometric patterns that danced on the ivory-colored wrap were mesmerizing. *Quechuan maybe? From the village he's always talking about?*

He looked down at it, cocked his head—that Jack Russell-ness showing through again—slid it off his shoulders. He walked out from behind his wee coffee counter, holding it out for her like an offering. "It is for jou." Then more firmly, "Jou have this."

Her eyes widened in dismay. "No. NO! I couldn't." She shook her head vigorously.

"It is a cloak painted in the traditional art of the *Shipibo* people. *My* people." He gently, but insistently, held up the cloak for her. "I send for another," he said with a shrug.

"The weave uses the 'Flamestitch' pattern. This design is called 'Communion with the Infinite.' Jou take this." He smiled and patiently stood his ground as the lineup of customers looked on, fidgeting. They were clearly agitated by the delay, but no one wanted to get banned from Marty's coffee stand.

Seeing that *she* would be the target of their disdain, which was growing with every second, she surrendered.

"OK. OK, *but!* I will only *borrow* it. I'll bring it back when I'm back to my old self." She gave him a sideways look, narrowing her eyes. "Deal?"

His face lit up. "Jes! Jou will take this until jou are once again whole. When jou hear my song, bring it back, jes."

She had no sooner taken the weighty wrap than he was right back behind his counter, ready to serve the next customer.

"Jou will feel good when jou hear my song," he threw over his shoulder as he set about hand-crafting the next little miracle in an insulated cup.

It was soft. *Soooo soft.*

It hung in an untidy heap in the crook of her elbow, threatening to slide out of her grip and onto the slushy, mucky sidewalk as she crossed the street. When she got one half tucked safely out of harm's way, the other half nose-dived over her elbow.

Shit! She snagged it on something.

She froze, not wanting to damage her gift. She bent low and backed up a step, hoping to give the cloak some slack and uncatch it from whatever had snagged it. *Please, god, don't let there be a hole or a rip!*

Ashlyn teased the braided tassel out from the spot where it was wedged and inspected the cloak where it had been caught. *No damage.* Relieved, she threw her head back, exasperated with herself.

Her heart skipped a beat. She was right beside *his* bench.

But, he wasn't there, of course. She relaxed and rubbed her eyes, feeling the weariness of too many sleepless nights piled up against each other. Standing here, next to the GOM's bench, she had to admit, to acknowledge how it made her anxious to pass in front of his bench. Ever since he disappeared, she had held her breath as she walked by. Every time. *But why?*

Ashlyn stared at the empty bench seat. A plastic bag rattled between the slats before taking flight with a gust of wind.

It's just a bench.

The fear of it suddenly seemed absurd.

Maybe . . . that other voice dared.

Maybe I just need to stand up in that dungeon . . .

And invite my jailer in?

She broke into a cold sweat just thinking about it.

Her rational mind, however, paused to consider the prospect.

"Ain't no good fighting for how you think things should be, *instead of seeing things how they* are. *You're sure to lose. Might as well just take it head-on."* Her daddy's favorite saying rose to the surface of her thoughts again.

Squeezing her eyes shut, she resolved to stay with it the next time the dungeon nightmare stole into her dreamland. She resolved to hold on and let it play out.

Bong! Bong! Bo—

"Arrrrgh!!" she growled. An innocent passerby jumped back, surprised by her outburst, and shot her a dirty look.

Nine o'clock already. She knew Budhil would be going over the work plans with his team at this very moment. She was *never* going to be on the roster if she couldn't get her ass in her chair for nine-fucking-a.m.!

~

The morning's sequences ran smoothly enough.

"Monday, after a long weekend, and no extra hours, feels no different than any other Monday," she said, feeling utterly disenchanted. She had meetings and a conference call in the afternoon, and yet the pressure to complete the tasks ahead remained constant. Unchanging. Like her actions made no impact.

She was seated at her office desk in the cube farm, with her chin resting in her hand, listening in on the Grow-Opp Co-Op conference call.

"Let's review the action items not completed," said the committee chair.

And bang your head on your desk while we rehash the arguments for decisions already made

Then she heard some voices coming down the hall. She pushed Mute on her desk phone and turned toward them. The people were speaking in hushed, but excited, tones. When they rounded the corner, they found Ashlyn staring in their direction. She pulled the headphones off her head, and placed one foam piece to her ear. "What's up?" she asked.

The group went silent at first, then seeing the floor was vacant except for Ashlyn, rushed over to share the news.

"Did you hear?" Kendra could hardly contain herself.

Still half listening to the conference call, Ashlyn shook her head. "Hear what?" she asked innocently.

Kendra lit up. She loved to be the one with the scoop. "Budhil's leaving! He got headhunted from a competitor."

"Yeah, but he turned them down," Matt continued.

"Yeah, his wife gave him an earful, I guess," chirruped Lisa. "She's had it with the long hours and absentee husband, he told me."

Ashlyn hadn't heard any of this. Come to think of it, she hadn't actually *seen* Budhil in weeks. She was crushed that he hadn't shared any of this with her. She had been squirreled away in her lab, busy studying his papers, trying to get on his lab team, so focused that she had completely neglected their actual friendship. And now he was leaving.

"Well, where's he going?" she finally asked, hoping to sound professionally distant.

"He's going to UC Berkeley," Kendra announced.

"That will be a bit of a pay cut, won't it?" asked Ashlyn.

"Yuuuge! But it gives him the opportunity to do the experiments he wants to do. That's all he ever talks about, since I've been in there," said Matt, shrugging his shoulders.

"Ashlyn? Thoughts?" came the voice in the foam piece she still held up to one ear. Her eyes widened, realizing she was still participating-ish in the conference call.

"Uh, yeah, sorry. Can you repeat that?" she said into her mouthpiece. Her coworkers stood up in unison. Lisa mouthed the words "See you tomorrow," and the three of them scurried off.

Ashlyn managed to fumble her way through the rest of the conference call, reciting back to the volunteer group her list of action items she would have completed for the next meeting.

But what's the point, now?

She had been putting in the extra effort to be able to steer *her* career in the direction of *her* choosing. And now her best chance for making that come together was walking out the door.

Weakened, again, the rug pulled out from under her, she reached for Marty's serape, believing for a minute that it was the enchanted cloak he had promised. Hoping that putting it on would magically make things make sense in her world.

She looked closely at the stitches on the cloak. The oranges and reds and yellows gave the impression of lively, flickering flames.

Communion with the Infinite. Ashlyn shut her eyes and pulled the wrap around her. Like a bright light, the image lingered against her closed eyelids. The stitches did form a pattern. Her symbol. Rory's label. The *fein cretim.*

Her head began to spin.

This was getting to be too much. She wasn't steering anymore. She wasn't sure she had ever been at the wheel. Maybe nobody was, and she was just careening out of control, undoubtedly headed for a collision.

47

The Heart of the Matter

The next morning, she had her head down, her mind bearing down on the endless series of problems with no solutions. Distressing fragments of questions swam in her mind, not the least of which was getting a straight answer on whether or not the rumor about Budhil was true. As she rounded the corner, she nearly bowled Budhil right over.

"I've been looking for you!" they both said simultaneously.

"Coffee?" he suggested.

"Sure." Caught off guard, the word tumbled clumsily out of her mouth. She turned on the spot and went to grab her coat. The two met at the front entrance and headed out the door.

"You know, vee don't have to give up our coffee talks," he began softly, seeing Ashlyn's eyes grow watery.

He didn't waste any words on what had led up to the decision. The decision was made. Instead he continued to show her the bright side.

"The university is not far from here, and I know you vill be very interested to hear about the things vee vill be working on."

She sighed heavily. A sigh of acceptance. They both relaxed, enjoying the familiar comfort of their coffee meetings.

"I know, I've been MIA a bit myself, lately, but I'm really going to miss seeing you in the office," she said.

Coffees in hand, they found a quiet table down a narrow corridor, away from the din of the lively voices talking over the espresso machine and the clanging of dishes in the kitchen.

"I had to make a choice," he explained. "I chose to unburden myself of living under the scrutiny of the business directors. Of the shareholders. I am giving up a respectable paycheck, yes. And a comfortable living, which my wife is not quite ready to talk about yet." He smiled impishly.

Boiled down, the choice was obvious: less husband and more paycheck *or* more husband and less paycheck.

"But I had faith that my path vould lead me where I need to go. Hinduism teaches that 'The Faith is composed of the heart's intention. Light comes through faith.' This is the choice that my heart wanted." He shrugged.

It's that simple, huh? Her finger tapped lightly on her coffee mug as she contemplated his statement. She wanted to believe his words, but resisted.

"The joy I feel when I am unraveling the mysteries of the universe, at the atomic level," he paused to smile, "my wife vill see that pays dividends to our happiness that no paycheck could ever match."

That was the heart of the matter.

"These things, they all vork together, mind, body, and spirit. If one is sick, they all vill suffer."

He leaned over to pull out his wallet. "Vould you like another coffee?" he asked.

The wallet, brown leather and rather plain, was folded in half and just slightly larger than half a dollar bill. It was unremarkable, except for the beefy stitches, brown to match the brown of the leather, which stood out prominently, binding the two halves. When Budhil opened his wallet, the stitches revealed a familiar image: the Mannix logo.

She hadn't seen the spooky apparition of Rory, the grizzled old man version, in over a week, but she was seeing real, tangible items—jeans, scarves, wallets, blouses— emblazoned with his logo everywhere now. It was like the whole world was in on the joke, except her. Even Budhil, with his designer wallet, most likely a gift from his wife, seemed to be privy to some global conspiracy centered around that damned symbol.

~

"So, the Eclectic Emporium woman says the logo has been used to promote young designers all over the world. Providing 'An opportunity to continue telling the story . . .'," she quoted from "The Official Rory Mannix" website. Not much of a clue.

After learning about his estate and the legacy of his logo, Ashlyn re-examined several of the photos and news clippings and cross-referenced the locations mentioned with major fashion events or fashion-related industry news or fashion-related *anything* from the After 1992 clues.

Ashlyn placed the GOM's newspaper in the center of the table and moved the Before 1992 printouts to the left, and set the After 1992 printouts on the right.

"Meaningless," she grumbled, and dropped her PINQ paperweight—a hideous treasure from a glassblowing workshop— on the stack of unhelpful library attachments on the right.

Beep. Beep. Beep.

The mass spec had finished separating the columns, so Ashlyn moved on to the next series of tests. She reluctantly left the table of mystery. *More like table of misery.*

Distractedly, she began a titration. *OK, Budhil may be going, but there are still positions to be filled. Pay attention or you're going to have to start all over and you'll never get out of this goddamned lab!*

Ashlyn stood behind a maze of triangle-shaped flasks and glass vials and piping that resembled a confusing decision tree. A small window, perfectly framed by the clamp stand and the Erlenmeyer flask, focused her attention on a corner of the mystery table. It took her a moment to figure out what she was staring at: a lower case *a* the size of her fist. A peculiarity of glass paperweights, regardless of how well formed they are, is that they behave like a magnifying glass.

The paperweight she'd made with the PINQ ladies mostly resembled a paperweight. It was roundish with an interesting burst of color. In truth, it was hideous, but it was heavy so it served its intended purpose. It sat atop the pile of After 1992 email attachments from the library.

As soon as she had reset the timer, Ashlyn jogged over to inspect the giant *a*. Like a five-year-old with a new toy, she slid the glass ball over other letters, finding simple joy in watching the shapes expand and shrink. Then she moved from the caption to the photo above, enlarging a hand, and the buttons on the chest, and . . .

The grizzled old man!

She released the paperweight, jumping back in surprise.

"Omigosh! *This* is what I've been missing." She shuddered with excitement and bent over the black and white photo to examine it closer, her eye an inch above the glass, like a gemologist studying a precious stone. The innocuous email attachment did, indeed, provide precious information. The slightly out-of-focus image showed the GOM sharing a drink with a comrade.

Not one item from the "after" collection had featured the handsome young man with the intense blue eyes.

Of course, they wouldn't! Ashlyn slapped her forehead. She'd been searching for 1992 Rory Mannix, the young fashion design superstar.

She stood upright again. Her eyes skittered across the storyboard, not really looking at any of it, her mind churning over the revelation: *The accident gave him the opportunity to continue to create. But the pursuit of his craft demanded he deny his very own existence.*

In all the clues she had been sent, his true identity had remained ambiguous.

She took a second look through the "after" articles, photographs, captions, and any annotations she had added.

Club Praha, 1995

- *A popular jazz club in Prague.*

"Correction. Rory *incognito* at Club Praha." He wasn't old yet in the image, but Ashlyn now easily recognized him—how he composed himself, how he immersed himself fully into whatever experience, wherever he was.

Nutrura Café, Damascus, 1999

- *One of the oldest cafés in the Middle East.*
- *Well-known place where storytellers gather.*

"The GOM sharing a Turkish coffee with . . . ," she squinted to read the name in the caption, "Ahmed Faheed, a well-known local storyteller."

Yes, that must be him. The GOM wasn't looking directly at the camera, but leaning in to hear the storyteller's tale.

White Nights-Black Days Bar Minsk, Belarus, 2007

- *A pair of scruffy looking Muscovites*

"'Retired chief of science at the Moscow Institute of Research shares a drink with an old comrade'," Ashlyn read the first line of the article that came with the photo. "That comrade appears to be none other than Grizzled Old Rory."

His unmistakable glower was absent from every one of the photos.

To the young protégés featured in the articles, Rory Mannix didn't exist. But the brilliant fashion designer had insinuated himself into the fabric of leading-edge design work, openly practicing his art, but woven into the background. She now understood where he had been for the past twenty years: '. . . bringing joy and excitement, pleasure and fun, and, yes, beauty to people's lives."' His words from the Cosmo interview.

~

Her hands tightly gripped the bars, unable to let go. She pressed her face up against the heavy wooden door again, her eyes searching the edge of the light on the other side of the bars. Blackness in all directions.

For months now, she had stared into the nothingness. Still, she could make out no shapes, no smells, no sounds. No hint as to who was holding her hostage here, and for what purpose. Like so many of these visits to this dark space, she heard the distinctive *click-clack* of heels echoing through the emptiness. Coming closer, but offering no clues. Her jailer was always beyond the light that reached outside her cell.

Ashlyn, frustrated, started rattling the bars, but only half-heartedly this time. The *click-clack* sound stopped abruptly. She was suddenly alone. Again. She turned away from the wooden door and slumped down to the floor, submitting to her prison.

In the dim light, though, she could see that, once again, she held the GOM's scarf in her hand. Rory Mannix' scarf, that is. This time, however, it offered her a strange comfort. That, somehow, she was no longer alone inside these dark walls.

48

Passion Leads to Pain

Her days began to bleed into each other again, as she shuffled back and forth exclusively between the office and her apartment. Her apartment was always quiet now. A few of David's things had disappeared through the week, but nothing that she would miss. The echoing of sound in the empty spaces reminded her that she was on her own now. But the hurting from their breakup was nothing more than a dull throb.

At the end of the week, she dropped her keys in the tin plate, listening for it's familiar greeting: "You're home."

In a trance-like state, Ashlyn walked through the hall, absorbing the silence. "Funny. I'm alone, but I don't feel lonely."

But is it weird that I'm talking to myself?

Rather than answer the question, Ashlyn found her *Cat in the Hat* blanket and her sketchbook, the one with the Carrie Fisher quote. She sat down in the front window and started to doodle.

~

"Ugh."

Ashlyn found herself back in Lab #3. On a Saturday. She sipped her coffee from home, waiting for the fog of morning to lift and the pistons to fire.

Once the first sequence was underway, she went back to the stockpile of email she had accumulated from the very *helpful* librarian. *Sorry I doubted you.*

After about an hour, she sat back, rubbing her eyes. Her sleep-deprived and over-caffeinated mind struggled to latch on to any clue, any kind of wayfinding sign, to tie all the pieces together. *I know why you left. I know where you went. I know you came back for me. But why?*

Ashlyn had to stop there and get back to the workbench. The buzzer had gone off, giving her a five-minute warning that the reagent should be nearly consumed and it would be time to add the catalyst. This was her third attempt to replicate this experiment, she had to pay attention. She reluctantly walked away from her storyboard.

Later in the afternoon, while she waited for the results from the EDC combustion models, Ashlyn printed off the remaining breadcrumbs sent from the librarian's email address: a page from the City of San Francisco archives; articles from obscure newspapers; photos, some with captions; and a few redacted pages from very odd sources.

On the storyboard side of the divider, she held them up, one at a time, to the tangle of Post-its, strings and photos, and story clippings she had already pinned to the back of the room divider. These latest pieces had no obvious connection to any of the search terms she had left with the librarian.

With her hand on her chin, she quickly scribbled fragments of notes in her journal from the new articles.

- The self is required to balance the self.
- Look within, in silence, for the enemy of your progress.
- The process of becoming whole—the perfectly balanced harmony of mind, body, and spirit—is a profound secret.

"Why does that sound familiar?" Ashlyn asked of the empty lab.

"Mind, body, spirit . . ."

"Mind, body, spirit . . . " She tapped her desk with the eraser end of the pencil, absently repeating the phrase like a mantra.

"Budhil talks about nurturing one's mind, body, spirit . . . ." *But none of these quotes sound like anything he's ever shared.*

"Wait. 'The process is a profound secret'," she mumbled. Ashlyn had thought Marty was talking about the secrets of his magical coffee.

"Fight Night!" She sat up suddenly. "At Fight Night, Diane said that the Mannix logo was some kind of riddle . . ."

"Maybe I'm asking the wrong question again. This latest set of emails are related to . . . a spiritual journey?" Her eyes widened in complete bafflement. "Where to look for the clues that will unlock the secret of the logo?"

Hands on her hips, Ashlyn stared, doe-eyed, at the busy collage. "Moscow does not strike me as a spiritual center," she said sarcastically.

Compelled by curiosity, she reached for the GOM's scarf. She hadn't had the courage to touch it since the library visitation. But today, in the fluorescent glow of the lab, in the safety and assured privacy of her asylum, she would be brave.

Maybe he can't reach me in here.

Maybe a chemistry lab is his Kryptonite after his run-in with ignisium. She smiled, smug with the knowledge that she finally had *one* advantage.

Ashlyn spread the scarf out over the tabletop so she could see all of the markings, inspect every detail. *Show me your secrets, Rory. I know you put meaning into every element of your creations.*

Biting her lip, she pictured Grizzled Old Rory seated on his park bench. Trying to recall the day he had been taunting her and playing with the scarf. With a slight tremor, alternating between excitement and fear, she grasped the scarf firmly in both hands and wrapped the elegant fabric around her neck the way she had seen him wear it. She paused, half expecting the cloth to begin slithering tighter around her neck. Her body went rigid and her heart beat rapidly as she held her breath. But nothing happened.

Giving her head a shake, she strode over to the other side of her desk and opened the camera app on her laptop.

"There it is," she breathed.

Rory's logo, plain as day, was staring her in the face. Draped over each of her shoulders, the R and the M . . . And a funny, lightning bolt shape connecting the two letters, rested over her heart.

A third symbol. The one Lin drew in her notes!

With the third symbol in place, the *fein cretim* was clearly visible. Three pieces united to create a whole.

"Hard at work, still?"

Ashlyn nearly jumped out of her skin. She had not heard the soft *beep* of Richard's card disarming the door, nor the *sssst* of the door seal being released.

"Oh hi!" she said. Her face flushed, unable to hide her shock.

Quickly, she unraveled herself from the scarf and threw it unceremoniously onto the desk, and shut the camera off with what she hoped was excellent slight-of-hand. Rummaging anxiously in her head for an appropriate response, Ashlyn grabbed the manila folder from the Out basket on her desk and walked over to the door, where half of Richard stood as he had only poked his head in.

"I have your results, already," he said, rejecting the folder she offered. "That's why I popped in. Good work, Ash." Richard smiled. "If you can wrap up the last two formulation verifications today, we'll be able to get a jump on the brand new formulations." His look suddenly shifted from one of congratulations to one of expectation, as in *You* will *wrap them up today.*

Her heart stopped. "What do you mean?" she asked with all the calm she could marshal.

"I thought we agreed that when there were two sets of verified data, we would shelf the old products and move on. We can't burn budget and resources getting through the backlog of testing. I need *current* data for the newest formulations," he lectured.

Her stomach tightened and her mouth went dry. "I . . . We . . . um. But I haven't achieved two positive confirmations, yet." She shook her head, confused.

"What do you mean? 'Course you have. Don't you review your own data?" he asked pointedly. "The log files that I received in my inbox show everything is on track. You should have only two formulations left to test."

"Yes, of course, I do—I do look.".

I did look! That's not what I saw. She swallowed hard. *Someone is messing with my data.*

Richard frowned and stepped all the way into the lab. "So, what does this say, then?" he asked, showing her his printouts of her data sets. Six products had been tested and the results met the criteria.

"You know, I'm not trying to cut corners, here," he said, his tone as much assuring her as asking her if she was accusing him of something. "We'll resume these other tests once we've got some data for our newest products."

"I—yes, those data sets are complete," she agreed as she ran her finger down the columns of numbers on the page. "And they meet the requirements . . ."

Those are not the same as the data sets in this folder! Why don't they agree?

Pursing her lips and squaring her shoulders, Ashlyn confessed, "I don't know how I missed that, Richard."

She looked up at him helplessly, at a loss for an explanation. "But you're right, I can finish the last two tests today. I'll get started and let you know as soon as it's complete," she said in her most professional-sounding voice.

She pasted a confident smile on her face and waited for Richard to leave, not even breathing until the heavy lab door slipped into place.

Something's got to give. I can't keep pushing and reaching and trying harder, and not get a hold of something. *I'm due for a victory, aren't I?* She felt the tears burn, trying to force their way out. *What's happening with my data?*

Same thing that happened with my R&D application?

Crestfallen, another distressing question floated into Ashlyn's awareness. *What if I'm not cut out to work in Budhil's lab?*

She had felt like this once before, lost, with no direction and no guiding light to illuminate the path forward. That night, when her father had been engulfed in a blinding flash of light and blistering sound, right before her eyes, she had lost her way. The horror of that moment was indelibly etched on her soul, like a fine drill marking slate tile: Failure means death. And the impression cut deep.

"Right," she declared. "I am not leaving this lab until my data sheets match Richard's."

The path she had chosen—a career that promised a regular paycheck, a predictable succession of promotions, and a comfortable retirement—required her to meet Richard's unrealistic deadline.

"And . . . I will print off my application and hand-deliver it to HR."

Yes, that's what needs to be done. To avoid the risk and heartache of failure, she chose to embrace the illusion of safety.

She hastily put the scarf back on the pins. "You can stay right there," she said to the scarf. "Passion leads to pain. You as much as said so when you decided to blow yourself up!"

49

Holiday Spirit

That Friday, many of the FiberWorx staff were gathered in the large boardroom near the front of the office. Lab #3 looked out into the front office lobby. Cheerful sounds of celebration for Budhil's last day wafted across the hall.

Standing quietly outside Lab #3, Ashlyn saw Budhil being ushered into the boardroom. She ignored the summons over the intercom and slipped back into the lab. It seemed she and the receptionist were the only two people not hoisting a mug of eggnog and toasting a beloved, sure-to-be-missed colleague. The receptionist was a temp, so probably wasn't too put out. Ashlyn couldn't hear any more of it when her lab door sealed shut.

Maybe she was sulking a little bit.

Ding. A text from Budhil. *Please come to the party. I need some good company =)*

I got no holiday spirit right now, she replied. *My mind and body aren't doing much better =(*

You can get some spirit in here. Someone has spiked the eggnog ;)

Was she really going to sulk, alone, in her lab? She could choose to be miserable about something that was completely beyond her control, or she could choose to enjoy the day, however it unfolded.

Alright, she texted back.

I'll need a very big! mug, she added.

She took off her lab coat and paused at the lab door, planting a big, fat smile on her face; she would try acting how she wanted to feel.

When she entered the boardroom, some caroling had already broken out in the corner by the bowl of eggnog. Budhil looked grateful to have the excuse to walk away from the singers to deliver a mug of eggnog, as requested.

"What are you so busy with that you cannot come to say goodbye?" Budhil asked.

"You said we could still meet for coffee." She looked hurt.

"Of course." He smiled warmly. "I only meant that you are still vorking too hard. Even the vise yogi must leave his cave from time to time."

"I suppose . . . ," she reluctantly agreed.

In hushed tones, she told Budhil about all the self-guided studying she'd been doing. And the volunteering. And the funky data sets. And having to resubmit her FiberWorx job application.

"When do you find time to be with David while you are so busy at work?"

As if on cue, the CEO detected the party had reached critical mass. It was time to say some thank yous and words of encouragement, and start winding the party down. With a gesture, he quickly tamed the rowdy carolers and drew attention to himself for some important announcements.

Ashlyn could see Budhil cringe. "Don't worry, this will all be over in thirty minutes," she whispered to him. Members from his R&D team drifted over wearing big, knowing smiles on their faces.

". . . and, finally, a thank you to Budhil Patel for his many years of service. We here at FiberWorx are sad to see you go, but we wish you well in all your future endeavors . . ."

Polite applause.

Budhil was gracious, as always, and humbly accepted the unwanted attention and the plaque commemorating his eighteen years at FiberWorx.

As predicted, the other company announcements were over in less than thirty minutes. Ashlyn was about to raise a glass and toast her good friend when Richard approached the small R&D crowd.

"Congratulations, Budhil." He extended his beefy hand and gave Budhil's slender hand a vigorous shake. Before Budhil even had a chance to acknowledge Richard, he'd turned to address Ashlyn.

"And Ashlyn," Richard looked at her sternly, "I'm still expecting some paperwork from you."

"It's printing as we speak," Ashlyn blurted, stiffening at his harsh tone. "I've had some . . . weird issues with my computer, so I decided to just print everything off," she added hastily.

"What kind of troubles?" Matt asked.

Richard put up his hand, dismissing Matt's question. "Fine. That's fine. Enjoy the rest of the party, folks." He turned and headed toward the door.

Matt frowned behind Richard's back.

Budhil nudged Ashlyn. "Go," he said. "Now."

Ashlyn scuttled off to catch Richard.

"Hi!" she said, a little out of breath. "I also had trouble with the application form for the new position in Budhil's—er, the R&D lab. I had to print that off, too. I left it with Joan."

Richard looked at her, or past her?

"OK," he said and nodded in her general direction, before continuing on his way.

With his back turned, she could see him holding his phone up to his ear as he continued in long, strong strides down the hall.

She went straight back to Lab #3.

A substantial amount of paper had been produced by the modeling computer, but, at last, she had her hands on the final set of results that Richard had requested.

"A few days late, yes, but . . . ," she tamped the pile of printed pages into a neat stack, "he's still here and I can hand them to him personally."

She stuffed them in a manila folder, with a satisfied flourish, and dashed off to find Richard's office.

~

Hallelujah! Finally, she had a complete set of results. Finally, she could start her year-end reports.

Ping.

A notification from the library.

"Oh, shit. I should probably let her know I'm done my research," Ashlyn said. She had solved the mystery of the Rory Mannix disappearance. She didn't have time for any more of it.

Hi Ashlyn,

> We've missed seeing your sunny face and bright
> colors at the library. =)
>
> I'm sorry I wasn't able to provide you with more
> of the research materials you had requested. It
> seems many of the files you had requested do
> not exist in City College's archives. I hope the
> few pieces we did locate were of some use.

Ashlyn blinked in confusion. *Wasn't able to provide materials? What is she talking about?* Ashlyn walked to the back of the divider, where stacks of printed email attachments—newspaper articles, still frames from surveillance footage, journal entries, police files, and so on—sat on her worktable. There was over half a ream of pages.

"I've killed a few trees printing all the research materials she's sent," Ashlyn said guiltily.

Then she took a closer look at the email addresses in her inbox. The address attached to the email she had just read was legitimately from the library. *But these others . . .*

This is not *the library email address. It's like a spam email . . . but not.*

She looked apprehensively around the empty lab. "Rory?" she asked timidly.

The lights didn't flicker.

She spoke more boldly now. "Un-believable! He's been feeding me all these scraps of information? *Why* go to all the trouble? Why not just send me an email?"

She inhaled sharply. *The weird computer issues!*

"*You* were messing with my data sets!" She stewed in outrage for a long, silent moment.

"Nobody likes to be toyed with, you selfish prick!"

She tapped her foot in irritation, then let her eyes drop back down to the next paragraph in the *authentic* library email:

> On an entirely different note, and I hope you
> don't feel this is inappropriate, but I found your
> discarded drawing of a wedding dress in the
> trash. I was wondering what you intended to do
> with it, if anything.
>
> If I may be so bold, I ABSOLUTELY LOVE
> IT!

Would it be possible to have that dress made?
For me? My girlfriend and I are planning to get
married next summer! =)

Best regards,
Emily

"She likes my wedding dress design?"
Ashlyn stood in stunned silence, overwhelmed by two extreme
emotional tidal waves. On the one hand, wanting vengeance on her
saboteur. On the other, experiencing an unexpected boost; her spirit
soared feeling absolution. . . gratification. . . validation. All the things
she'd been craving.

~

Darkness all around, and glistening black pavement underfoot.
Ashlyn drifted off to sleep recalling the night she and David had
been walking home, after Fight Night, when the beast had lunged at
her from the other side of the fence. The snarling and barking of the
white dog filled her ears again.

A heightened awareness rippled through her entire body. Rigid
with terror, she burrowed her head into her chest and hugged herself
close, retreating deeper into herself, chilled to the core.

The next moment, she became uncomfortably warm in her
defensive embrace, the air growing thinner. She could shrink no
smaller, retreat no further. The stale air descended on her like a lead
blanket, taking her breath away. But she held on tight, refusing to
budge from this space. She had vowed to let the dreams play out.

The barking stopped.

Silence.

GHUUUUUUH!

Gulping for air, Ashlyn burst free from her cocoon, bracing
her arms against the wall and floor that she couldn't see but held her
fast in the black space. Her chest heaved as her lungs expanded. The
dog was gone. She knew it to be true. She almost wept for joy.

How could she feel joy when she was still trapped in her nightmare?

It was, however, unmistakably, joy. And it ignited something
deep inside her. She stood slowly, expecting her muscles to protest,
using the wall for support. Her hair clung to her face in wet clumps.

The damp may have come from the mist in the night air that she imagined, or it may have been the perspiration borne in terror of a faceless, ferocious dog.

She shook the chill off.

The chill, it just stopped.

Warm, cold. Day, night. These ceased to exist.

Amazed, Ashlyn looked down at her dream-self, a hazy, evanescent shape whose clothes no longer clung to her shivering body. No damp, no chill, nor fire nor heat could touch her. The air was . . . *irrelevant.*

Her eyes adjusted to the new darkness and she became aware of a light some distance away. It was a foggy circle of light, uniform in intensity with no visible source. How long had she been held taut, frozen in terror? Time was . . . *irrelevant.*

She took one timid step toward the light.

Still silence.

Her footfall made no sound. She couldn't feel what she stood on, or if she was standing on anything at all. The light in the distance came rushing forward and swallowed her, then spat her out into her darkest moment: the night of the accident.

50

Let it Play Out

Her ears were flooded with the sound of sirens. With the thrum of curious onlookers talking to each other in the background. Then the staccato shouts of the police, fire, and EMTs trying to get a handle on the situation. She stood there, on the edge of the scene, on the edge of fear, rewatching each moment of her story unfold in excruciating detail.

Including the moment Rory Mannix was at a crossroads, the moment of his decision to disappear into mystery.

That night, a sign only the two of them witnessed: the symbol of the *fein cretim*. It flashed, bright as the Christmas Star must have been to the Three Wise Men. Not the stylized monogram that Rory had created for his fashion label, but the ancient symbol. The vision, now a mark etched on each spirit, Rory's and Ashlyn's.

The shared anointment would bind one to the other, each one's fate becoming entangled with the other's.

Time, movement, sound . . . reality, melted away.

Witnessing this long-forgotten memory left Ashlyn trembling.

Living that moment had terrified her and scarred her deeply.

She closed her dreaming eyes in quiet acceptance, allowing the horror of that night to crash through her barriers. She surrendered to it, opening herself to the emotional roller coaster and letting it run its course. It seemed inevitable that, through experiencing the tragedy and the forceful emotions that it triggered, she could get to the other side.

At that moment, the nothingness below her feet vanished and she became weightless. From empty blackness, images began to appear, small and distant, like postage stamps. One image at a time drifted closer, growing larger and brighter, but remaining out of focus. She reached out a curious hand to grasp an image and examine it. It disappeared as smoke at her touch.

There were too many images now, coming at her too fast. She couldn't see clearly what they showed nor decipher their meaning. She shut her eyes to her spinning dream world, overcome by the whirling carousel of images. Her legs buckled sending her crumpling to the floor, unable to withstand the onslaught of blurry images.

When the dizziness abated, she opened her eyes again. The room was still. She was still. The fuzzy circle of light in the distance reappeared, but closer now, and sharper, and brighter. The scene had returned to her prison cell. It was small comfort, but at least she knew where she was.

51

A Fork in the Road

Ashlyn swapped her merino wool cardigan for her lab coat, switched on the lab computer, and strode over to the side of the divider. Evidently, the mystery wasn't over yet. She folded her arms and rested her forehead on them.

"What do you want with me, Rory?" she asked.

You walked away from the accident. The accident you set in motion. To escape. Why come back?

Flashes of moments from the most potent dream yet, fired off in her head.

"I tried to go back there, back to the accident, Rory. I tried to let it play out, I did. But I don't know what you're looking for."

Yes, they had shared a moment, twenty years ago. A fateful moment. A moment when he had snatched his life back, and hers had been reduced to ashes. He had already tasted success when his path was altered. She hadn't even set foot on her path, really.

I was only twelve. You had everything you wanted. Why mess with my life?

A fun-house-looking face watched silently from the top of the stack of After 1992 pages. Ashlyn turned her head and squinted at the photo. Warily, she slid the paperweight over the center of the face. Her mouth fell open, she couldn't believe what she was seeing.

"Marty?" she exploded. His impish grin beamed at her from underneath the paperweight. He was arm in arm with the GOM, with Old Rory.

"Marty!" she fumed. "*That's* how Rory found me!"

She tapped the end of her mutilated pencil nub, agitated, hoping to snuff out the bite of betrayal. *I've been making friendly with the enemy. And he's been sharing all the details with my saboteur!*

"Wait. Wait. Wait!" She paced in a small circle in the back corner of her lab.

"How can you think that?" she scolded. "Marty was the one person in your life who made you feel happy in the last two months!"

"But he also sold you out," she argued back. "He *must've* been the one to set the G— Rory on to me."

Her eyes narrowed. She grabbed the photo of Marty with Old Rory, stomped over to get her cardigan, and headed into the hallway. She found a window that looked down onto the plaza. Marty was packing up.

Where do the street vendors go at the end of their day? She had no idea.

Though Marty had played only a minor role in torturing her, she still couldn't help feeling a little resentful at having been deceived. She'd have to hurry to confront him.

On second thought—

She dashed back into Lab #3 to retrieve the serape Marty had loaned her.

Aaaand. . . Almost out the door, she skidded back in for Rory's Jamawar scarf, too. *I want answers!*

Loaded with the clothes and the printout, she clumped awkwardly down the stairwell in chunky-heeled Nelli booties, muttering a fuming diatribe about the injustice of it all. By the time she'd marched down into the mostly deserted plaza, she was fit to be tied, and made no effort to disguise how she felt.

Marty smiled pleasantly, as always, as she approached. That same smile that had beamed up at her from underneath the paperweight.

"Marty, how *could* you?" she accused.

"Choc-o-late?" he offered. "I reserve one more cup for jou, before I put away everything." Not waiting for a reply, he began steaming her a large mocha. "Choc-o-late will sweeten up your day," he said brightly.

It was no use. His big heart was impossible resist. "Why, Marty? Why come here? Why all—this?" She motioned to the coffee stand. "Why couldn't you just tell me about this?" She held up the photo.

Marty took the paper from her. Shaking his head with some disbelief, he said, "I don't know how he does this." Then, addressing the sky, Marty spoke in Quechua.

"I told him, even in death, he is truly gifted," Marty explained.

"How does he do 'this' what?" Ashlyn asked, confused.

Marty just smiled. "I like this picture. He is happy in that moment."

Ashlyn frowned a little, sensing Marty was going to talk in riddles, like he so often did. "OK, so that *is* you, then? And an old and wizened Rory Mannix, right?" she persisted.

Marty nodded.

"Moving on, then. Where was that photo taken?"

"That is my village." He smiled proudly. "My fadda is the village elder. He is what jou call a medicine man. Shaman. Señor Rory come to speak with my fadda. My fadda send me here to help Señor Rory restore his connection with the sacred realms. That is why I wear the 'Communion with the Infinite'." He pointed to his serape slung over her arm.

"I will return to my village when I can read the illnesses of the human spirit. When I can perform the healing work as my fadda does. Here," he gestured to his coffee stand, "I am but a humble student among the people. I am the witness to their joys, their struggles, and I come to know their energies and the maladies of the spirit. And I will learn the ways of healing of the Shipibo people."

"You came here to study people? But it was Rory that sent you to San Francisco, wasn't it? What did he tell you to do?" she asked.

"Jes, my fadda say he, Señor Rory, was sent to help me with my quest. And I him. I come to this place to learn what I must know." He paused, thoughtfully considering Ashlyn. "I saw the disharmony in jou right away. I knew it was jou that Señor Rory must seek out to set him on his right path again."

"But how on earth—"

"My serape sings to me," he interrupted. "It tells me when to listen."

"I haven't heard your serape sing." Ashlyn frowned, remembering that he had promised her she would find happiness when she heard music.

"So why have jou brought it here? Jou are not done with it," he said shaking his head, gently admonishing her in a fatherly way, even though he could easily have been younger than her, who knew?

"And what about that?" he said, pointing to the fancy scarf.

"Oh yeah, what about this scarf?" she said, holding it out to him, wishing he would just give her a straightforward answer. "It's a . . . a puzzle, I think. It's beautiful, but . . . I feel like . . . it seems like it's trying to tell me something," she stammered.

"Jes. That is for jou," he nodded.

"*Why* is it for me?" she asked, exasperated.

"I dunno. All he say is 'I made this for someone. Can you help me find who it is for?'" Marty shrugged.

"So how do you know it's for me, then?" she asked, dizzy from this roundabout interrogation. "Never mind. *What* is it for? Why do I need it?"

His expression became soft, his eyes twinkling with mild amusement. "Jes. Jou are so close, my sweet *orchidea porcelain*. It is not my place to tell you. It is a 'profound secret,' as I told jou. And the journey cannot be shared." His expression became very serious as he pointed at Ashlyn. "It is for *jou* to discover."

With that, he thrust the steaming mocha into her empty hand and turned to finish packing up his coffee stand. "I will go now to the park with the playground. There is many more coffees and smiles to give out yet this morning," he said and winked.

~

Ashlyn paced thoughtfully, walking in *his* shoes, as it were, except she was in Lab #3, a place she had never felt his presence.

She scanned the Before 1992 images: Rory's playboy lifestyle, photos of him clutching a bottle of Jameson's, the defiant glint in his eyes in every single image.

Had he come back to gloat? *No. By all accounts, he was one arrogant SOB, but no.*

She paced some more, chewing on her thumbnail, glancing occasionally at the crazy, tangled strings and photos pinned to her storyboard.

Ashlyn stepped back from her storyboard to take in the whole picture. "His gift, translating our intentions into clothing designs. Witnessing the 'evolution of the human condition,' that was his muse. And with his stardom . . . that voice was drowned out." She paused there momentarily.

Then she began pacing as the postulating resumed. "His life of anonymity allowed him to reclaim that gift, to reclaim the joy that his success, and excess, had stolen away."

She pinned the photo of Marty and Old Rory on her map, on top of Peru. "Then he met Marty on some spiritual quest."

Her pacing became more pensive. "He met Marty. No, the shaman, his father. Who told Rory he needed guidance to 'set him on his right path again.'"

"What was the wrong path?"

"The path leads to . . . me? He came back to find me? Not as Rory Mannix, but as a grizzled old man. Old Rory. Because . . . because I have something he wants? Something of his?"

She looked at the crisscrossing lines of yarn on the storyboard and just shook her head.

"Somehow, we're tied together."

Sigh.

"OK. When terrorizing me didn't work, he messed with my data sets, almost derailing my career plans. Diane said he wasn't vindictive," she wrung her hands as she pondered, "just impulsive and demanding."

"He's trying to tell me . . . what he wants. The scarf. That's for me. Does it hold the answer?"

She whipped her head around to look over at Marty's serape, hoping it would sing. The Flamestitch pattern, again tricking her eyes, gave the impression of motion, but didn't utter a sound. Ashlyn cocked her ear to listen for a telltale "Hallelujah!" as she approached it.

Nada.

She swung it over her shoulders, giving herself a little hug, bracing for the possibility that it might actually start speaking to her. *I hear nothing.* She was disappointed, but not really surprised.

Her phone buzzed from somewhere on the desk. Feeling the irresistible tug, the dopamine trigger, Ashlyn obliged and picked up her phone. *Coffee time.*

Then she paused. Holding her phone up, she stared at the screen, mesmerized. A vague sense of some undeniable truth, willing itself to be discovered, tickled at her subconscious. She held the phone until the screen went black, and her face stared blankly back at her from the reflective surface.

"He was trying to *show* me," she whispered.

She was on the edge of a breakthrough, and she knew it, but she delayed.

Why? Am I afraid that it will be a letdown? That I've built this mystery up into some sort of transformative event that it couldn't possibly live up to?

"Because I don't want it to eat up any more of my time until I get out of Lab #3."

Ashlyn left Lab #3 and sauntered through the hallway, heading for the coffee station. On the way, she walked by Kendra, hardly glancing at her coworker, too lost in thought to notice anyone. Kendra, who was wearing her most outrageous outfit yet: a brown turtleneck with a layered yellow skirt, where the layers of fabric gave the effect of flower petals. She looked like a giant sunflower, complete with smiling, cherubic face and rosy cheeks.

"Ash . . . What time—," Kendra paused. "What are you wearing?" She made a face. "Never mind. What time is your interview?"

"Interview?" Ashlyn stopped in her tracks.

"For the new assistant position . . . in the . . . ," Kendra's words slowed, "R&D lab?"

Ashlyn's heart sunk like a stone in quicksand.

Kendra looked gobsmacked, but immediately backtracked and tried to change the subject. "So, I guess it will be you and me at the conference in January." She smiled weakly.

Ashlyn gazed at Kendra, processing this new information. Richard hadn't specifically reprimanded her for being a few days late with her final data reports, but to not even get an interview for the new position? She had been overlooked. Again.

Or worse. Outright ignored.

They're perfectly happy to have me stay in Lab #3.

Bottling up the hurt and disappointment, Ashlyn found her voice. "Did they say when they wanted to have the position filled by? And what about a lead scientist to replace Budhil?"

"Ash, I—I don't know," Kendra answered softly. "I *do* know that they're mad as hell to lose Budhil." She smirked.

"Thanks for letting me know. That the . . . hiring has started," Ashlyn stammered. "It's good. Now I won't be biting my nails wondering if they'll ever start. I'd better get back to it," she said, ending the conversation.

Ashlyn continued down the hall in wounded silence. *How is this possible? Can I do everything right and still never get out of Lab #3?*

And then the only question that seemed to matter: *Where do I go from here?*

52

Fire Away

The sadness welled up inside her, occupying every crevice and fissure in her broken heart and broken spirit. She clumsily wrestled her way out of her lab coat, dropped the tangled mess of it on her chair, and stormed out of Lab #3.

Most of the front offices were dark, many of the regular staff had left for the day. Outside, it was uncommonly dark as well. Dark storm clouds crowded the winter sky, hurling gusts of wind through the plaza. The twinkling Christmas lights clung precariously to the lampposts and twisted unmerrily around the decorated trees lining the sidewalks. The plaza and neighboring streets were nearly deserted. A few bodies, braced against the biting wind, pushed their way to waiting cars or bustled onto a cable car.

Ashlyn scurried home past a number of well-lit and inviting restaurants and bars, inside which lively merrymaking was well underway. Ashlyn shut it out, desperate to get to her dark and empty apartment.

She tossed her keys into the tin plate on the curio next to the front door. *Her* front door. She closed her eyes and relished the peace and tranquility of coming home, no longer dreading a confrontation with David. But as she flung open the front hall closet, her shoulders slumped. Even this favorite diversion gave her no comfort. Her closet muse was silent.

"Where do I go when I leave the lab?" she whispered to the naked hangers.

It was a vague question, but the little voice, hidden away and waiting to be invited to speak again, quaked. In the silence, she heard the question echoing in the abandoned corridors of her heart.

Where do I go from here? She probed deeper inside this time.

As she searched, her courage faltered when she neared the charred mark left on her soul the night her father died. The thumping of her heart masked any other impulse, silencing the voice yearning to be heard.

"I need a glass of wine," she announced, to break the deadlock.

Ten minutes later, Ashlyn popped open her laptop and settled in for a marathon job search. Without delay, she started browsing through the local and national job listings. Her heart, however, was not in it. The words scrolled by, but she wasn't really reading, only picking up every other word. A jumble of unintelligible black text.

Sigh.

Ashlyn leaned back from the screen and pictured all the people in her life whom she viewed as successful. Richard. Janine. Budhil. Even Kendra. *She makes up her mind and goes for it.*

As she lowered the delicate wine glass from her lips, it dawned on her that their success had little to do with the titles that adorned their name plates or business cards. It was the substance of their work, the milestones achieved, that marked forward progress in their journey. And each journey was unique and separate.

Marty said 'The journey cannot be shared.'

And they cannot be compared with one another.

Rory. Her dad. Janine. Budhil. Each one of them had an aura that projected a harmony of presence. Her dad, for instance . . . *His mild-mannered alter ego and his innermost superhero must have had an understanding.* They worked together, propelled forward by the fire in his belly, and confident in the wisdom of his inner light. *I'm starting to sound like Budhil or Sanjay.*

Staring into space, Ashlyn felt a gentle tug. Her sketchbook called to her. She'd been ignoring it. Ignoring it in favor of preserving a loveless relationship.

Ignoring it in favor of promoting herself relentlessly at FiberWorx. And then working overtime to cover up her mistakes.

Which had made no impression on Richard, one way or the other.

In favor of beating back the cruel taunting of the GOM,.

Who, in fact, I can't ignore, because we're somehow tied together . . .

"I admit, my 'logical' choices have not had the outcomes I've hoped for," she said, as though addressing a panel of all those successful people, a self-inflicted cruelty.

She made a silent accord with the voice inside. *OK, we'll try it your way. I'll release the steering wheel.*

Skeptical, but recognizing that she needed a different approach to solving her problem, she set aside her laptop and went to the settee in the corner by the window. She swung her *Cat in the Hat* blanket over her shoulders and pulled her legs up, hugging herself and her sketchbook.

Outside, the night sky was heavy with rain. The raindrops, illuminated by street lamps across the narrow street, fell gently, complementing the rhythm of her thoughts, slow, sinuous, and seemingly endless. But instead of the constant tug of war between head and heart, both moved in one direction.

"I accept," she replied to the sketchbook at last.

Curled up, content and at ease, Ashlyn lost herself in her drawings until her wrists couldn't bear the weight of the pencil in her hand.

"I'm really enjoying this," she announced proudly.

Joy. A feeling more exhilarating than a marathoner crossing the finish line.

Satisfaction. A taste sweeter than the dieter's first bite of cake after months of denial.

Freedom. A sensation more liberating than letting go of her relationship with David.

She could feel the fractured parts of herself coming together.

She stood to stretch her legs.

Glass in hand, weighty with a *full* pour, she walked up to the hallway mirror, searching her reflection, willing the intense stare of Old Rory to answer her. She still quivered at the thought of meeting his menacing gaze, but could think of no other way to understand his message than to face him head-on.

Peeling away the layers of his secret existence, unmasking his story, she'd learned that he was brilliant but arrogant, driven but stubborn, perceptive but impulsive, selfish but fearless. She understood that he had been a tortured soul in his own right. And, like it or not, they were connected. He had come for her. With questions? To demand something of her?

"OK. Fire away!"
Silence.
Or . . . she lowered her glass, *provide me with answers?*
Silence.
"Fine."

53

Fein Cretim

10 a.m. Thursday. She was still shell-shocked from, yet another, letdown at work.

"Is it Thursday?"

Shell-shocked and completely, all-over tired. Another restless sleep, for the third night in a row since she'd learned about the interviews.

She was back in Lab #3, preparing for a new set of experiments. *Like I hadn't busted my hump reviewing the R&D project reports. Or hadn't demonstrated "community involvement"—still ongoing! Like I hadn't even bothered to submit an application.*

Ashlyn's phone rang, jarring her out of her inner ranting.

No one ever calls anymore, unless it's urgent.

"Janine?" She read the caller ID. "Must be urgent."

"Hey, girlie!" she answered sweetly.

"Ash! What are you doing tonight?" Janine sounded pleasant, but you could hear that she was positively vibrating, ready to crawl right through the phone and grab Ashlyn by the collar.

Ashlyn dearly missed Janine. Since taking the leap of faith, she had become one of those busy people with a very full life. The type that get swept away for a time, but returns with a pocket full of amazing life experiences. *Bordering on stranger than fiction sometimes.*

"Ash. I need you," Janine said, finally admitting that a crisis loomed. "I've got a hot new artist to show. *Tonight* is opening night!"

Currently, Janine was the curator for a hip new gallery in the shopping district. "I foolishly tried using one of those online invitation sites. What a disaster!"

"Soooo, you want me to . . . be your IT support?" asked Ashlyn slowly, confused, but not yet convinced she needed to panic.

"No. NO! I can't tell if I'm going to have five people or five hundred! The RSVP options weren't very clear. A bunch of our best patrons complained that they had trouble with the site. So, what *that* means for everyone else is anyone's guess!"

"Well, five hundred people would be good, no?"

"Hell, yeah! But five people would be the end of me!" Janine was on the verge of a meltdown.

"So, you'd like me to make it six. Or five hundred and one, whichever the case may be?"

"Would you?" Janine pleaded, audibly relieved.

"You can count on me," Ashlyn said in a sing-songy voice, ecstatic to have a place to go after work. "Text me the location and time! Oh, and dress code?"

"Ah, whatever you like," Janine replied dismissively, "Business casual? We're trying to attract a younger audience. There'll be live entertainment and the first glass of wine is free."

"Perfect."

~

Ashlyn walked into the gallery and shyly looked around for Janine. Even with a personal invitation from the hostess and arriving early, she was uncomfortable.

As a first impression, the show appeared well-organized, professional, very elegant, and promised to be well attended. *No doubt Janine had considered and addressed every detail days before the opening night.* Overreacting in the hours before a big event was just her way of filling the void when there was nothing left to do but wait. It was part of who she was.

And, possibly, a charade for the gallery owners. Otherwise, they'll suspect she's not working nearly hard enough to justify the handsome salary she negotiated.

"Eeeek!" Janine let out a muted squeal of delight on seeing Ashlyn. Then, in her tight-fitting pencil skirt and Roger Vivier stilettos, she skittered over to give Ashlyn an excited hug and a light peck on both cheeks.

"Thank you for coming," she gushed, hardly able to contain her exuberance. "Looks like my ginger luck came through again!"

"Yeah, looks like it'll be closer to five hundred and one. You sure you need me here?" Ashlyn teased.

"Here you go!" Janine handed her a generously filled glass of sparkling wine from the tray that had followed her to the entry. "This is the good stuff," she whispered.

She turned to the young man holding the tray, a human canvas with splashes of vibrant colors to contrast with the black and white images of the art on display. "Brian, make sure Ashlyn here doesn't go to the bar," she instructed. And off she went.

Ashlyn took a sip and tipped her glass to Brian. "It's lovely, thank you." And he was off, trailing Janine like a rainbow-colored comet.

The art enthusiasts began straggling in minutes after the first bottle of house red was uncorked. She silently clapped her hands with delight as she noted the assortment of live mannequins entering the gallery in a wide spectrum of ensembles. In all the turmoil of the past few months, she had missed ogling the menagerie of morning commuters. Tonight, she could ogle away.

Oooo, this is *going to be fun!*

Ashlyn wandered through the exhibit, glancing occasionally at the door in the hopes of seeing at least one person she knew. *Huh. She seems familiar . . .* Ashlyn looked away to consult her mental rolodex. *Maybe from the pub?* The one she and David frequented.

Used to frequent . . .

David would never have agreed to come to an event like this. *Hmmm. No David. No pang.*

Brian waltzed by and paused to allow Ashlyn to help herself to another glass. *Yay, Brian.*

Ashlyn meandered through the gallery, sharing a few impressions of the paintings when asked, but mostly amusing herself admiring the cut of the hunter green corduroy sports coat paired with the chinos. And the elegant floral print on the flared skirt. *Is that a flamenco skirt?* And the hipster with the fedora . . .

"Is that . . . Ashlyn?" said a voice drawing near. "What a nice surprise to see you here." It was one of the PINQ ladies. "I met you last month at the card-making workshop."

"Yes, right, hello," Ashlyn replied. "You're the marketing agent."

"Yes. Marguerite," she volunteered and offered her hand to shake.

"I, uh, remember seeing you at the FiberWorx office. Where I work." And she stopped there. There was an energy and *joi de vivre* in the gallery and she could taste it. Smell it. But the very thought of the uninspired and sterile space inside Lab #3 deflected that feeling, like a force field against joy.

"So . . . marketing. Who's that with?" Ashlyn didn't want to talk about FiberWorx. "Any exciting clients that you can talk about?"

"Why, yes! Yes, I have worked with some . . . *peculiar* clients. Let me tell you . . . ," Marguerite said with relish. She had scads of juicy gossip and bizarre encounters to divulge. Ashlyn listened intently, relieved not to have to share.

Marguerite's partner gave Ashlyn a sideways glance, partly excusing himself and partly thanking her for the opportunity to wander off on his own. Marguerite waved him off and resumed her guilty pleasure.

"I once shredded a Versace original—oh, it broke my heart! And we had a plus-size model put it on. She rocked it! And the stunt worked. I convinced the clothing company that every *body* is different and we needed to make room for flattering fashion for everyone," she said, beaming. You have to remember, dear, I've worked with some of the craziest, most neurotic and narcissistic people. It's a balancing act, letting your passion run away with you, and then having to also keep it in check so you don't end up getting run over by it."

Marguerite was speaking from the heart, reliving the joy of her trade, savoring the highlights, and reaching out to connect with Ashlyn on a more intimate level. The energy in the gallery invited people to connect in this way.

Ashlyn recoiled slightly, feeling small. She was reluctant to say what she did; most people couldn't imagine what a chemist did outside of high school chemistry. Ashlyn smiled, but made no attempt to share her own stories.

"But, here I am, doing all the talking. Like I always do." Marguerite reigned herself in. "Tell me, what keeps you busy?"

"I—." Ashlyn paused. Maybe if she could muster some enthusiasm for the work, maybe if she could find the sexy in her daily routines that made a story worth telling, maybe she could accept Marguerite's invitation to connect.

"Well, FiberWorx is doing exciting research in e-textiles. Um, smart clothing, and other stuff."

"Oh, yes, dear, I remember that from the card night. But what about *you?* What keeps *you* busy? What do you do when no one's looking over your shoulder?" she asked, smiling encouragingly.

"Oh. I, uh, I try to get the most out of my day, you know. I go to yoga . . ."

Went to yoga.

"And I walk to work so I always get time outside," Ashlyn blathered as she strained to grab hold of Marguerite's meaning.

Marguerite laughed gently, shaking her head, so very matronly. "Oh, my dear girl. It's not our *purpose* to get the *most* out of every day. Goodness, that sounds exhausting!" She put a hand on Ashlyn's shoulder and gave her a gentle squeeze. "It's that we *enjoy* every day."

Then Marguerite got suddenly serious. "That was a big life lesson I learned, early in my career. Back in the '80s . . . no, it was the early '90s . . . ." She paused to take a sip of the sparkling white in her glass.

"Mmm. The hostess has excellent taste in bubbly. Where was I? Oh, yes, I landed a big client, with big headlines. I had taken on a particularly difficult client. Because I was ambitious. And he was wild." She shook her head, remembering. "Like so many talented artists of the day, either out of control or silently battling demons none of us could see.

"I had never lost a client before, not like that." She frowned, a sad frown. "There is a price to be paid for the things that we want, Ashlyn." She paused. "After seeing Rory's life cut short, so suddenly, so unexpectedly, I decided that I wouldn't just take *every* client. Only the ones that I enjoyed working with."

Ashlyn's jaw dropped. Marguerite had reached into Ashlyn's core and penetrated her protective barrier by speaking his name, like he was just some . . . person. Ashlyn nodded slowly but couldn't find any words.

"You know, I never saw my new assistant after that day. I sent Joel to call a cab for Rory." Marguerite tipped the last of her wine into her mouth, and smiled thoughtfully at Ashlyn. "For some reason, I still find Joel's disappearance more unsettling than Rory Mannix's . . . I guess *foreseeable* end. Something about it has never sat right with me."

She inhaled sharply, as though waking to find herself in an art gallery. "I see my husband has gotten himself another glass and hasn't bothered to get anything for me!"

Ashlyn snapped to attention. "Marguerite, before you go, can I ask you a question?"

"Of course," Marguerite replied.

"Are you familiar with—do you know what *fein cretim* means?" she blurted.

Marguerite's face lit up. "The Rory Mannix logo? Yes, I do. It's a good one: *To know oneself.*"

She looked at Ashlyn with renewed interest. "Many journalists and industry experts tried to dissect its true meaning, but they just didn't see what he saw. And Rory didn't have the patience to correct them. I don't know that I ever truly grasped his meaning, but it *is* largely what inspired my decision to hand-select my clients."

Ashlyn scrunched her face. "I heard someone else say it was a riddle, actually."

"Well, I suppose so." She looked past Ashlyn, her brow furrowed in thought. "You might say 'to know oneself' *is* a puzzle to solve. But it is a knowing here." With her whole hand, she gestured at her heart, tapping it the way Sanjay often did in his yoga class.

"From what I read, scholars are still arguing about the meaning of each of the three elements . . . ," Ashlyn prodded.

"Yes, there's the R and *M. Raido*, meaning 'journey' and *mannaz*, meaning 'self.' And then there is 'initiation,' *perth*." She drew a kind of zigzag shape in the air, the symbol from Lin's notes. Ashlyn's mouth went dry.

"All together, it's an invitation. To overcome the obstacles and cross the threshold. *Perth* is what ignites the heart."

"Ignite," Ashlyn repeated in a trance-like voice.

"Yes, exactly. You must walk through the fire, as it were. Rory said that, for him, *fein cretim* was a kind of summons. Something that he could not ignore."

Marguerite watched Ashlyn closely as the words sunk in.

After a moment, Marguerite gently touched Ashlyn's arm. "I hope to see you out again at another PINQ event, Ashlyn. It was nice talking with you." She turned, and in a swirl of tangerine chiffon, Marguerite disappeared into the crowded gallery.

Marguerite's words echoed in the dark, shuttered spaces in Ashlyn's heart. Finding herself standing alone, Ashlyn searched the crowd for Janine. *Or Brian would do.*

She had last seen Brian darting back to the kitchen with an empty tray. He had been excellent at anticipating her needs, so Ashlyn turned toward the kitchen, hoping to find him gliding up behind her.

A man stood before her. His face, inches from hers. It wasn't Brian. Their eyes locked. The penetrating stare was unmistakable. Ashlyn jumped back, letting out a shriek of terror. She covered her face with her hands, trembling. The band stopped playing.

She listened for it, but no one else was screaming. She was the only one paralyzed with fear. Slowly, Ashlyn uncovered her eyes.

"Sorry," she said hoarsely, looking around in embarrassment. "I'm—I'm OK."

A few sour faces continued to stare, but most of the guests started to murmur, and the low hum of many separate conversations in a crowded space resumed.

Across from her was the stunned face of Brian, still as a statue, holding a tray of freshly filled glasses of sparkling wine.

54

Perth

Embarrassed and frustrated and bewildered, Ashlyn threw her overnight bag on the bed and started randomly tossing in clothes without any thought of where she was going and what she would need. A winter storm raged outside, a perfect match for the turmoil she felt inside. She'd hardly noticed the weather coming home from the gallery, her tortured thoughts having filled every space in her consciousness.

She looked out the bedroom window. It was late. The roads were sure to be slick with freezing rain. And she had nowhere else to be but here, alone, with her misery. Finally, the levy broke. Her tears came, unrestrained, punctuated by soul-wrenching sobs. She collapsed on her bed and just let it gush. The hurt, and the feelings of being somehow *less*. The confusion, and feeling like there was no compass on the road map.

"Hell! There is no more road!"

Between the sobs, she spat out fragments of thoughts:

"It's burning you inside."

"You will die in that cage."

She lifted her head from the pillow. "Did you mean Lab #3, or that dungeon you keep me locked in?" she whimpered.

No reply came.

"The fate of the soul is on the line."

Was this the end of the line? Had she failed?

Despair.

At some point, the tears ran dry and the sobs gave way to yawns. She had been right when she told Budhil that her spirit was broken and that her mind was broken. And now, aching from exhaustion, she recognized that she had been burning the candle at both ends, her body was broken, too.

At last, she surrendered. Sleep took her swiftly.

~

Savage barking burst into her dream world. The white dog was back to usher in another nightmare. The barking gave way to low, savage growls that rattled in her rib cage.

She shook her head, resisting the temptation to cower. She'd been here before and now understood that she would need to see this nightmare through to the end. What else could she do? She had nowhere to go, nothing to hang on to.

She stood up, defiantly lifting her face toward the sound. It stopped abruptly and a mirror appeared. But there was no reflection. She held her breath, staring expectantly at the black hole. What did she hope to see? Old Rory, with step-by-step instructions, like the manual for the sequences she ran in the lab? Marty, who never lost faith in her?

"Faith. Light comes through faith."

Flames flashed to life inside the mirror. Suddenly, she was on the other side—the sirens, the shouts of the firefighters, the gasp of the crowd. Clips of scenes from the night of the accident replayed in rapid succession on invisible screens that surrounded her.

Finally, a brilliant light obliterated everything. The symbol, white-hot, sizzled and crackled from above and began to slowly descend.

"The *fein cretim*," she whispered.

The floor vanished, as it had before. This time, she didn't cower. This time she allowed herself to freefall into it, spiraling downward into a shrieking darkness that threatened to shatter her spirit, to hold her in its remorseless grip for all eternity.

Was this all part of the journey? Her fear again threatened to consume her, whole.

I don't think I can hold on!

Her heart began to race, feeling like the vortex would squeeze her mind, body, and soul into oblivion.

She had opened her mouth to scream, when Old Rory appeared. This version of the GOM had less menace in his eyes. He hung at the gateway of the vortex, ghostly and silent, like sheer curtains. His hand reached into the vortex and pulled her back. The delicate thread that connected them was strong like the silk spun by the spider for her web, but having a tensile strength greater than steel, ephemeral, and impossibly powerful. And unbreakable.

Hands clasped to forearms, their grasp seemed so real in that surreal space. The vortex was forced back, sucked away into a vacuum of nothingness.

55

Flashover

The vortex disappeared into the black space within the mirror. The mirror itself was now behind her, like she had, indeed, crossed some threshold.

She floated in the empty space, free of any restraints or tethers. The hand disappeared in a puff of smoke. She never locked eyes with Rory, unlike all the previous encounters. She never got to see him look at her with contempt or reassurance, impatience or encouragement.

"The soul's journey cannot be shared," said a voice.

A shadowy, but vaguely familiar, connection between the subconscious and the cosmic bubbled to the surface. That far-off voice that she had silenced long ago, that had been vying for her attention, became ever more persistent.

"I thought we had an accord?"

She sighed heavily. "Right. I need to stop forcing it. To let go of the steering wheel."

Instead of feeling fearful, she felt a surge of strength and confidence, long-forgotten but unmistakably hers.

"Fee-in. Cree-tim," the voice whispered. The words echoed in the empty space.

He knew. "Rory Mannix *knew* what the symbol represented," Ashlyn said to the voice. "What fein cretim *means* . . . Not just it's message, but living it."

The voice was closer now. So close. It would not be ignored.

"But you still haven't answered the question. Will you accept the invitation?"

From empty blackness, the thoughts she had been unwilling to face, to acknowledge, began to surface once again. *He had accepted it, the invitation.* It was painful to feel so much all at once, and to be on the edge of comprehension, but to have understanding just out of reach. It made her dizzy, grasping for what her spirit longed for.

When the dizziness abated, she opened her eyes again. She looked onto a scene that could have been a recording of any one of several days in the lab. An audience of one, she watched a moment in her life in which she held a graduated cylinder suspended above a flask. She was about to mix some chemicals, but the scene was frozen, like someone had pressed Pause. The person in the scene wasn't really there. Not in spirit, anyway.

"I've been chasing the wrong dream."

"*Even with an unlimited number of lifetimes, you will not find your way into the R&D lab,*" the voice confirmed.

That's not where she was meant to be. For all her work, all her effort, she was competent, capable, but she was never going to shine there.

"I will never be whole there."

CRACK!

Fractures began to appear in the cinderblock wall on either side of the prison door. She didn't flinch, though. An unseen barrier crumbled, the heavy pieces shaking the ethereal stage on which she stood as they tumbled down. The light surrounding her expanded outward and the vision of chemist-Ashlyn, holding the glassware, rushed at her and fused with her. She was back inside of herself, looking out.

But before she could despair, the entire room began to spin. It was as though she were inside a centrifuge, where the bright light was flung to the edges of her consciousness. Her safety glasses dissolved into smoke, her lab coat flapped wildly then it, too, ceased to exist. The glassware in her hands became soft fabric and fell flaccid, like a wilted flower.

The room was still. She was still. She was back in her prison cell holding Rory's scarf, gently caressing the luxurious fabric. As her eyes adjusted, the bulky cell door with the iron bars came into focus. A brilliant light stabbed through the newly formed fissures on either side of the door.

Ashlyn's heart thumped expectantly in her chest. The butterflies in her gut began flitting about, but this was not the aching tightness of fear, it was breathless anticipation. She positively vibrated inside, a fire in her belly had been ignited.

Fein Cretim. To know oneself. One's true self, at the core. An invitation to walk the path that leads to the heart. Where the mind, body, and spirit are unified.

"This was your message, Rory, wasn't it? But, in freeing yourself, you imprisoned me. That's what tied us together. That's why you couldn't leave yet. You came back to fix what you broke."

Her fingers, still absently plying the soft scarf in her hand, suddenly met resistance. She felt something solid hidden in the folds of the delicate fabric. Ashlyn looked down at her hands and groped feverishly for the object, sifting through the silky layers until she pulled it out.

"A key!"

Haltingly, she reached to touch the key with her other hand, lest the key be a mirage.

The silver-white object shimmered like asphalt in 100°F. She grasped it with her bare hand without hesitation. It was cool to the touch.

Ashlyn sucked in her breath. "It's real."

When she held it up to examine it, she knew immediately what it was. She stood, letting the scarf slip to the floor. Disbelief crept over her, threatening to hold her in place, but the key in her outstretched hand pulled her forward like a magnet. She moved slowly, as though in a trance, approaching the lock in the door.

"*Ashlyn O'Monahan,*" the voice called softly through the bars, the speaker remaining beyond the light. "*You were extended a great invitation. Fein cretim, the divine illumination of the creative. It appears only to those anointed.*"

Ashlyn lifted her head, tracking the sound of the voice, squinting against the brilliant light beyond the bars. The claustrophobic fear that had once filled the dungeon was absent. In its place, a yearning to know the truth, whatever it might be. She stood inches from the bars, holding them firm, watching, ready to confront her jailer.

Finally, a figure emerged from the outer from the shadows. The face, at last, came into view, bathed in soft, white light.

It was her own face, staring back at her, expressionless.

Utterly confounded, Ashlyn's legs buckled.

"You have been so focused on living up to external expectations and avoiding failure," the voice said, "refusing to acknowledge any other impulse, any deviation from the illusion of security."

"I wanted to save people," Ashlyn said defensively, but not convinced herself.

"That path, born of fear, would not—could not—lead you to the highest expression of yourself. To realize the meaning of *fein cretim.*" The voice was kind. Patient.

Visions of herself at FiberWorx—standing awkwardly at the coffee station, then looking out the small glass window of Lab #3, then chasing Richard down the hall—flashed in rapid succession and vanished again. Ashlyn relived the pain of those moments. Of feeling separate, and set apart, and the sense of rejection, of failure.

"Ashlyn, it is the nature of the creative to see from the edge, looking inward. The creative must stand apart to witness the revelations of the human spirit. Do not mistake independence for loneliness."

Images of Ashlyn sketching at the library and reveling at the Day of the Dead Festival, these moments of feeling energized and inspired, forced their way in, pushing aside memories from FiberWorx.

"You have resisted looking inside yourself to recognize the flowing spirit that lives within."

Not rejection. Not failure. It was the pain of her spirit reaching out to be heard and being shut out.

"I understand," Ashlyn whispered. "To accept the invitation was—is ever—the only choice."

And with that realization, all the empty spaces in Ashlyn's heart filled with light.

"Yes. You see the truth now." The voice continued, "Ashlyn, our name means 'born of the fire.' The fire of creation. Our fire cannot be contained."

To discover the mystery of herself, Ashlyn needed to reunite that part of herself that had been torn away that fateful night. To open the deep-set wounds, and welcome back the part she'd locked away so long ago.

The invitation: unifying the mind, body, and spirit.

For twenty years, her true self remained shut out. The nightmares had not been enough. What she had lacked was a source of ignition.

Rory.

Fein cretim . . .

Click—kuthunk.

The key slipped into the lock and turned easily. It was the most unassuming of sounds. The door swung open under its own massive bulk. Ashlyn stepped through, into the light, and the heavy wooden door thudded shut behind her. The sound had a finality to it that was immensely satisfying.

Then the door vanished.

A tear escaped, and even in this dream world, the sensation of it trickling down her cheek rippled through her. The two halves of Ashlyn's soul reached out to one another. The fractured pieces healing into a seamless whole. Ashlyn, mind, body and spirit, swelled as she filled with the light of the *fein cretim.*

56

Key in the Ignition

Six months later, Ashlyn found herself comfortably sitting on the griz—Rory's park bench. She'd brought Marty's serape, hoping she could finally return it, but the One-Shot had packed up and moved on to another location. *The playground crowd, I believe?*

She had agreed to meet Budhil in the FiberWorx plaza and go for coffee at one of their old haunts. She hadn't seen much of him since he'd moved on to his new position at Berkeley. She missed their coffee meetings.

With the morning rush over, the procession of sidewalk fashion models was sparser, but no less diverting.

I love the spring prints.

A woman, clearly pregnant, ambled by in a shape-hugging stretch cotton dress. *So simple. Fantastic. My god, she really does look radiant.* She smiled inwardly, her head and heart in synchronicity.

From the opposite direction, a set of three high-end suits strode by. Their gaits were confident and unhurried, but they covered a lot of ground with their powerful strides. Ashlyn scrambled to pull out her phone and jot down some notes for her DES201: Critical Practice & Interpretive Research course:

- No briefcases
- One attaché case - thin lines, sleek, black, tucked not carried
- Ties - bright hues, eye-catching
- Each has phone in hand —needed for discussion? or compulsive behavior?

When the three men approached, just steps away from her bench, Ashlyn realized that Richard was one of the them. He was deeply engrossed in their conversation and continued right past Ashlyn without a hint of recognition. Ashlyn continued her observations:

- *Only that which immediately surrounds him is present for him*
- *Everything else is invisible, unrelated to intended priorities*

She rolled the thought around in her mind. *That was more personal experience than critical observation . . .*

She stopped to search her feelings for some response. *That is his path. This is ours.*

Agreed. Ashlyn had moved on.

She finished her notes and swung her head away from the FiberWorx office tower. She went back to surveying the people on her private catwalk.

Another man, walking solo, stepped up onto the curb from the crosswalk. She noticed he was wearing the desperately handsome "Photographer Slim" moleskin jacket she'd seen before Christmas. Ashlyn smiled. And she didn't try to hide it.

The man was then joined by a smaller-framed, dark-skinned man wearing a tweed sports coat with suede elbow patches.

Really, Budhil? I should have gotten you a "Congratulations" coat to replace that tattered old thing. It looked truly hideous next to the moleskin jacket.

She couldn't hear his words, but his face was animated. Ashlyn watched with amusement as the excited Budhil talked wildly with his hands to the—*Young? Not young? Hard to say*—man who walked in step with Budhil, who was now approaching her.

"Ashlyn." Budhil stopped mid-sentence to greet her, pressing his hands together in a warm-hearted and genuine *namaste*, about as close to a bear hug as his religion and temperament allowed.

"Ashlyn, this is Jessie. He is a colleague at the university. Another professor in the chemistry department," Budhil began the introductions.

Still holding a slight bow, Budhil turned to his companion. "Jessie, this is my very good friend, whom I vorked with many years here." He motioned to the glass building behind them.

"Ashlyn has just started a new program at the Academy of Art University. You will tell us all about the design courses you are taking at the coffee house, yes?" He nodded, encouraging the group to move on to the coffee house.

As she stood up from the bench, Jessie extended his hand. She reached out to shake it, taking in his features: a smattering of auburn stubble surrounding full lips, reddish-brown wavy hair, tousled, but not messy . . .

A little rough around the edges . . .

And his muted green eyes held her gaze.

His hand was warm, his grip firm but not overpowering.

She sucked in her breath when her eye caught the logo on the breast pocket of that handsome jacket.

Of course. It's a Mannix.

She had to break away, averting her gaze so he couldn't see her roll her eyes.

Composing herself, she smiling warmly up at him. "Pleased to meet you, Jessie."

The logo shimmered, as if winking at her.

Then, a really odd thing happened. A song popped into Ashlyn's head, uninvited and completely bizarre: Bobby McFaren was happily crooning "Don't Worry, Be Happy" in her ear.

She unraveled herself from Marty's serape and studied the embroidered threads. They appeared to dance to the tune playing in her head.

Marty's song?
Seriously?
Probably.

You made it. Thank you for reading my debut novel:

IGNITION

I hope you enjoyed piecing together Ashlyn's puzzle, where the elements that led her to discover the truth about Rory Mannix had consequences for her own, unanswered questions. If you loved this book, one of the best things you can do is leave a review for it at Amazon.com. Or feel free to shout about it on your favorite social media platform.

On a personal note, I recently came across this piece of wisdom: When is the best time to plant a seed? Twenty years ago. When's the second best? Right now. I've been writing for nearly twenty years, though, the first fifteen years were exclusively scientific reports. I'm an environmental scientist turned fiction writer. This was no overnight transformation, of course. Twenty years ago, I had a summer job writing short stories for an interactive DVD about treasure hunting. Now, I hunt for nuggets of truth to spin into fiction. True story.

I hope you will seek out more of my stories in the future. Visit me at www.nicolestillwater.com